The POISON STREAM

Conor Cregan

POOLBEG

First published 1993 by
Poolbeg,
A Division of Poolbeg Enterprises Ltd,
Knocksedan House,
Swords, Co Dublin, Ireland.

ISBN 1 85371 278 7

Cover photograph by Gillian Buckley
Cover design by Poolbeg Press
Set by Mac Book Limited in Stone 9.5/13
Printed by The Guernsey Press Company Ltd,
Vale, Guernsey, Channel Islands.

The POISON STREAM

*For my mother and father,
to whom I owe everything*

1

They picked up their empty shells. Jack Clarke read the newspaper again and the thrill returned. He imagined the scene. Body stretched out on the sawdust floor, peppered with whatever calibre, an ironic companion to the animals on hooks around it. Maybe some screaming. No. No screaming. It was early morning. It was raining yesterday morning. Maybe one, maybe two, customers in the shop. He was probably still getting ready. His whites white. No screaming. Terror. Absolute terror. But silent. Real control.

The taxi driver swung the car around over Baggot Street Bridge and made the lights. Jack held on to the grip at his head. He felt the presence of the thrill again, the kind that peels your spine into strips. That was the way to do business. Direct. Calm. Clean.

Two each. Into the body. And then a *coup de grâce* to the head. Real pros. Then they picked up their spent shells and walked out.

On Pembroke Road, the girl from the nightclub the night before replaced the hitmen in his mind. But she had to compete with business. He was gearing up now for the meeting, reading the business pages, sifting through the company handout-based grey matter for the between-the-lines pointers. For those in the know. Ralph Martin got a good write-up. He would. It was his paper. All confident take-over talk. Nothing about the Gulf. Only the good stuff got out. The praise rubbed off on Jack. Spin-off praise. Employer to employee. He needed a morale booster after that girl.

He'd made it right up to her door before she turned and said no. It had been a perfect sting. To get him to bring her home. Killiney. All the way. She'd played it brilliantly. Hormone temptation at its best. All the right body language without saying anything.

He told himself it didn't matter. It did.

An emptiness invaded him for a moment, while they were turning into Jurys. Telling him none of it meant anything. Not the figures, not the deals, not the perks, not the money (he paused on the money for a while and debated with the emptiness about that; he could argue about money the best), not the power—the emptiness insisted on getting its say in. Ralph Martin would use economic four-letter words with him if he knew what he was thinking. It wasn't a very common experience, the emptiness, a hangover from earlier days. It all seemed so long ago and the kid in the jeans and woolly jumpers, and hair that came over his ears, didn't know what he knew.

Martin business took over—a purity of aim, spurred on by the sight of the hotel and the three Italian suits he could see in the lobby. These weren't just Italian suits. These billowed in the air-conditioning. They were charged by the centimetre. And if you were wearing one you felt like you were being massaged by six Swedish beauty queens.

They mattered, these Italians. Jack divided people simply: matters and don't matters. Ralph Martin groupings. The people that mattered wore the uniform. It was important. Because there were fakes and you had to be able to spot the fakes. You always paid lip-service to equality but you worked to division. It was expensive Italian suits, four-course lunches with wine, gold cards and executive suites versus sweat-shop bargains, pint and chaser snacks, betting shops and the Lotto.

He was deep in Martin territory now, relaxed like when something had gone well. Asked in for a drink. Put your feet up, Jackie. Martin always called him Jackie. He hated being called Jackie but he didn't say it to Martin. He figured maybe Martin thought he was being affectionate. No. Martin didn't make mistakes like that. Martin didn't make mistakes. Jack liked that. Ralph Martin got things done. Jack allowed himself the feeling of having contributed. Okay, Ralph Martin got things done but I'm the one that actually does them. His morale took another hike.

He let the taxi-driver open the door for him. At first the man wasn't going to do it. At first he was going to pinch his cratered skin and maybe pick some of the hairs from his cheeks—he had a clump of hair in one of his ears too—and read the smart guy in the back the riot act and tell him to stuff himself in parts of his anatomy that were impossible to reach, but then he saw the tip in Jack's hand, something Jack wanted him to see. Times were bad.

He cursed Jack Clarke and opened the door for him.

A long-legged woman came out of the hotel, holding an attaché case and looking at her watch. Aerobic figure, wore herself well, face well-formed, good structure. Like a good building, symmetric. Jack smiled and offered her his taxi. She took it and that recharged Jack's ego completely.

The coolness of those hitmen in Finglas came back to him as he stepped through the door into the hotel lobby. Machinelike calculation. Efficiency. He had an hour with these Italians; then he was flying to London, then Paris. Back by midnight. Not too bad. Decent night's sleep, maybe. He straightened his tie and caught a glance at himself in the glass of the door.

Four Americans passed him on their way out, in full dress tourist uniform.

He felt smart. Confident. Home player. Home turf. He could almost hear the crowd roar. Put 'em under pressure.

The three Italian suits were Milanese bankers. Shorter

than Jack by a couple of inches. That mattered. He went through the routine like Ralph Martin had said.

Jack had done his homework and knew Salvatore from Marcello and recognised Stefano's hair transplant. They looked the part. He had to admit. For middlemen. Because that was what they were. Middlemen. Lower end of the matter ladder. They weren't going to make any decisions. Just sound out the proposition. Make a report. Advise. Early days. This was a major play. They were just one move. Jack had done this with two Swiss a month before, five English three days earlier and representatives from Spanish, Middle-East and American banks during the past couple of years. Every time Ralph Martin made an advance.

Jack shook their hands in turn and said hello in Italian and made excuses for the weather and asked them if they'd had a nice trip. They all spoke English, so it wasn't necessary for him to put his crappy Italian on the line. Still, he threw in a couple of phrases for effect, as if he knew what he was about. That was the secret. The way that girl had lured him into the lift home. He ran through a couple of outcomes to that event but kept coming up against the sting.

The Italians were all happy faces and swivelling hips and hard macho handshakes. Jack decided to pull down a gear, emphasise the northern European coolness. Martin had told him to look for the possibility of playing it like that with them. Exude efficiency.

Like the hitmen in Finglas, Jack thought. He'd been that close to getting inside with the bird in the nightclub.

The hotel room was comfortable, functional, discreet. The way Ralph Martin had specified. There was hot coffee, some croissants, fruit and Belgian biscuits. And there were wet towels for those who might want them. Salvatore, who looked like he'd been fashioned by Michaelangelo, did most of the talking for the bankers. His skin was darker than the others, with stubble at the corners of the chin, and Jack felt maybe he came from the south. And maybe there was a divide. It was important to recognise divides as soon as you saw them, Martin said.

Bootstrap merchant with a brain, Jack thought. Ralph Albert Martin. It was a kneejerk reaction. It wasn't a big issue and it wasn't written in stone, but there was a class system and right at that moment, in the middle of conducting business deals in his name, when he felt he most needed some distance between himself and Ralph Martin, Jack Clarke wrapped himself up in his class, in old money, in a family name, in the right school, in Trinity, in the golf club.

"You have been to Italia?" Salvatore asked.

Jack was shaken out of his snobbery.

"Yes, lovely. Many years ago."

He was trying to sound older than his thirty-two years. He wore dark suits for that purpose and had his hair deliberately styled in an old-fashioned way. Paid more for it too. Maybe she thought he was too old for her. He couldn't get that girl out of his head.

"Milano?"

"Yes. The cathedral is beautiful."

Salvatore shrugged his shoulders, said something about Milan being very industrial and then added he was from Sicily himself. Jack congratulated himself. He threw in a few details about what he'd done in Milan. Most of them lies. But he'd taken the trouble to swot up on a few guide books before going out clubbing. Shit, he thought, that bloody girl.

They were sitting down around the table in the room, opening briefcases.

Dublin bootstrapper. Back to Martin again. Self-made. Completely bald, and proud of it, with a face like a preying weasel, and proud of that too, features that could cut diamond and a tongue that could pierce tank armour.

Worth?

You're worth what you want to be worth, Martin said. Never stop and count it. Use it, spend it, but never stop and count it. If you do that, you're dead. The little people always made that mistake.

"Mr Tallon?" Salvatore enquired after a short burst of Italian with his companions.

Jack couldn't understand what they were saying. He pretended he could. Anyway, the question said it all. He looked at his watch.

"Five minutes," he said. "Government business. You know."

"Of course."

All part of the plan. Delay the arrival of the government man. Larry Tallon was one of Martin's political hacks. He had about five of them directly on his payroll and another five indirectly. It was shadow-world stuff. Tallon was a horse man. Simple vice but damn difficult to service on a TD's salary. He'd have been better off being an S and M freak. Jack knew which ones were into that too. He knew about all of them. It was a small town, Dublin, and vice gossip travelled like an infection. Proof was only a picture or a tape away if you were willing. Martin had the best snoopers available. And Jack had access to it all. He knew the queers, he knew the womanisers, he knew the senator who liked clothes pegs attached to his nipples, he knew the minister who had a lover from each sex, and he knew the lovers' lovers. He knew more than the political dirt. He knew the dirt on everyone who mattered. Which newspaper editor was screwing which PR queen, which car dealer was up to his neck in subversive readies, which subversive was over-friendly with which Garda inspector. They meant nothing to him, except as leverage. Martin had taught him that. Use everything. And stay clean yourself. Martin stayed clean. Family man. Never catch him shooting anything more than a clay pigeon. But such weaknesses in others were useful.

It was a rough town now. Grown rough real quick. There was a lost innocence lying somewhere, victim of a hit-and-run. That thought brought back the picture Jack had of himself with the woolly jumpers and jeans. People got hit now. Got hit by people who picked up their shells and walked out.

As if on cue, Larry Tallon popped his flat-topped head around the door without knocking. He had a drink problem too, but so many people had that that it didn't rate as a vice any more. Jack had told him to squirt something in his mouth before turning up.

There was much handshaking and hellos and welcomes and pats on the back. Tallon was good at that. And the punters loved him for it. He topped the poll every time. The party loved him, too. Always making rallying speeches, Larry Tallon was, working them up.

"Jack, how are you?"

Tallon had moved into his elder statesman character. Jack watched and played his own part. Larry could make black white, fat thin, bad good, and he'd a neck like a rhino. No wonder Frank Costello put him on the box every time there was bad news to break. Paud Henry over at Justice said if Larry Tallon was ever arrested he'd have to try him in the Special Criminal Court because no jury would convict him, no matter what he'd done. Even if he'd admitted it.

No problem. Leave that to me. Tallon must have said it a dozen times during the discussion. Like he was agreeing to get someone more social welfare or have a bus stop moved. He was good at that, having bus stops moved. Twenty-five at the last count. All Jack could hear was fifty million. That was what Martin wanted from these guys. Anything else would have been failure. With cast-iron Government insurance as a guarantee. Martin had the Government's full support. Frank Costello would cover any export losses. And Larry Tallon was playing a blinder. He held himself in that experienced negotiating position, read slowly through the Martin expansion plan, very slowly, bifocals on the end of his lumpy beer nose. Going through every detail with the three Italians, pointing things out to them. Ralph Martin had given him a good going over, too. Ralph knew how to use Larry the way Frank Costello did, how to present him to the public.

Forecasts. Markets. Projected income. Returns. Jack Clarke felt the terrific thrill of control.

2

For a man whose personal wealth was estimated to be in the very high tens of millions and whose companies' turnovers rated nine zeros, Ralph Martin's offices were surprisingly spartan. But then Jack Clarke was measuring them against some vulgar norm he had accepted in the mid-eighties, having watched too many slick docu-dramas on the new rich—the boys who made money a fashion, gave it street cred among the young who'd once run from it with the panic speed of trend-conscious radicals. It had always been accepted that the radical, shackled by career and family and responsibility, would one day succumb to the lure of dreaded stuff. It was the postscript to idealism, the minor tragedy of that life played out in its logical sequence. But not Jack's lot. They'd gone straight out there in search of Mammon. As if they were on some huge value-system by-pass with all the lights stuck on green. One large act of communal cynicism. Led by the leaders, followed by the followers. Jack could not figure out which he was or where the pursuit of justice and equality had been dropped in the race for cash.

There were other levels of existence. Ladders again. Rungs below. Most of them well below, close to mere subsistence. Jack was aware of it only when he tossed a coin into a chocolate box or saw a solemn documentary backed by Christy Moore songs. A shot of Achill had stuck with him. It was of a farmer sitting on a wall, smoking a pipe. Jack could not remember the last time he had sat on a wall. He did not smoke a pipe. The colours had haunted him for maybe half an hour, which was an eternity in the hectic schedule he lived to. It had been a three-minute bite tacked on to the end of a current affairs slot, accessed while he grabbed some junk food while dressing while searching for a phone number and trying to scratch an itch deep in his crotch. People like Jack always accessed. There was an overriding dynamic in everything they did. The colours had changed as the clouds drifted, herd-like, across the face of the island and the sea was curtained in a delicate mist that told you you were at the edge of the world.

Ralph Martin always sat well back in his chair, a high-backed leather thing, designer-moulded to fit his frame. That frame was hard long-distance runner. He was on the first floor and his window had vertical blinds. They were open enough to let light in but nothing much else. Jack thought he recognised some of the light from the television programme on Achill. He had never been to Achill. He had been to Hong Kong and Taipei and Anchorage—he could not recall why—but never to Achill. The light played with his defensive eyes. Huddled eyes, deep set and protected by something more than skin and hair. Maybe a bit lost. Jack did not think so. Someone named Aisling who'd slept with him and sucked him off without wanting to know his name had said it.

The office had a bas-relief ceiling. Nothing special but enough to raise an eyebrow and get a conversation stopped. There were files all over the floor. Martin liked files. Liked to look through them. Sometimes for no reason other than to know he had them. The light was illuminating his bald scalp, reflecting the ceiling in it. Jack could see it. He stood to the side of Martin and behind him. A shaft of light shone across the desk, producing a fake religious effect. It passed through a coffee mug and a custard slice. Martin had a sweet tooth. The outline of an old Georgian fireplace was forcing itself through the wallpaper beside Jack Clarke. As if it was trying to tell him a secret. His eyes caught the outline of a pair of woman's legs out on the street. Stopped at the railings by the canal. He could not see enough to tell what she was doing. He found himself inventing a whole character for her and then imagining them in bed. It was automatic. It did not require any concentration. He could still pay complete attention to Barney Small.

Barney Small was one thin strand in the web of can-do-ism Ralph Martin had constructed around himself. Small was part of the outer ring, a distance apparatchik, always a step away, to put a buffer between Martin and the less savoury aspects of his business life. The food chain, he called it. Small was a Monaghan import-export trader who'd gone bust once too often and run foul of a Limerick loan shark. The creditor realised there was no way he was going to get anything out of Small, so he contented himself with dropping two concrete blocks on Barney's legs. The result was that one of his legs was shorter than the other. Barney wore seventies sideburns and jackets you could strike matches on even on wet days. He liked under-age girls, too, but that was his business so long as he did what he was told.

In the great scheme of things, Barney was a gofer. He ran the kind of errands Ralph Martin needed running. And he kept his mouth shut. Barney was border to his two-tone shoes. The family had a farm near Clones and were solid Frank Costello supporters. Loyal party members. Good soldiers. Barney'd fought his first election when he was ten. He knew how to get a man in and he knew how to keep a man in. Useful to Frank Costello. Though Frank was always quick to distance himself from Barney in public. Barney was a connection. He facilitated things. He was a lubricant. Apt description, Jack thought. A line. Unseen. Unproven. What intelligence calls plausibly deniable. That was how it worked. You saw it, you heard it, you knew it, but with links like Barney you could never prove it. And the band was so tight, you couldn't get at anything that would. Frankie bankrolled Barney for a pub in Finglas and Ralph Martin bankrolled Frankie Costello for a villa on the Algarve. And so it went on.

"Hoors!" Barney said when he had watched Ralph Martin for too long.

Martin was picking at the hairs on his hand. Jack wanted to intervene and pluck one out. Martin's hands were short and stubby and he had a large callus on the middle finger of the right hand from gripping pens too tight.

Small scratched his belly. Jack shoved his hands in his pockets and leaned back against the wall. This was Martin's play. He was there to observe. Say nothing unless spoken to. He was well used to it now. So used to it, he did it unconsciously.

"We're insured," Martin said, yawning. "We're insured. We have that."

There might have been the faintest hint of unease in his voice if Jack had been listening for it.

Martin thought some more. Then he looked at Jack.

"Larry Tallon might go out. What do you think? Larry's an old friend. He knows the desert sands well. And he knows your man. He'll pay. I know he'll pay. He needs our system. He's just flexing. It's the Arab way. Seeing what he can get away with. He's done it before. We've had this problem before."

"But not for this kind of wedge, Ralph."

Martin massaged his chin.

"Let's sit on it for a while and send Larry out there on his own. See what he can do. Keep it all low key."

"Fuckin hoors," Barney repeated. "I told 'em there'd be a better deal if they coughed up now. I told 'em. Fuckin hoors. I don't trust that bastard, Ralph. He thinks he's some kind of fuckin wonderboy. I don't trust him."

"We're insured," Martin said again.

He looked at Jack and indicated he should speak.

"Yeah, but the whole lot. Guts of two fifty. It's a lot. And there's the future of that market to consider. Big bucks, Ralph. Let's press for as much as we can get. Give them more time. Bit of a headache for Frank Costello if it gets out."

"Frank's problem."

"Bit of a headache though."

Jack knew he was understating. It was his job to understate. He could feel sweat at the back of his neck. It was a mild day, nothing to write home about, ordinary summer time, but the sweaty feeling was gathering. He recognised the billion-dollar stare on Ralph Martin's face. He'd seen it before. Usually on men with bankers crawling up their arses, looking for assets to liquidate. But his mind would not let him follow the logic of his thought in Ralph Martin's case. Keep your head when all about are losing theirs. A favourite phrase of Martin's.

The essential ingredients with borrowing for expansion are confidence and movement. You get the confidence of a major bank; that bank becomes the lead lender, and once you have the lead, other banks, the chasers, follow. It all rests on the bedrock principle that banks need to lend to survive and they prefer to lend big rather than small, especially if the loans look cast-iron guaranteed. And Ralph Martin had the best guarantee available. Frank Costello and a whole Government.

Once you have the loans, you just have to keep moving. All the banks want are repayments and if you can keep the repayments coming in no one asks questions. And you keep the repayments going by acquisition and expansion, then feeding off the expansion and borrowing for more expansion. It's a self-perpetuating circle. And it has its own mystique. That's the poker face the world sees. But the thing is to keep it all going. Don't blink. If it slows, then the revenues slow and the repayments can't be met and the bankers make phone calls and send bitchy letters. You have to keep it all going. Martin had hit the billion mark inside ten years doing this. There was no other way of doing it. Just keep moving. Jack was saying that to himself.

There were thirty banks involved. And none of them knew about all the others. That was how Ralph had always played it. He played money like he'd run races, with brains, speed and power. The secret to successful investing, he said to Jack one night when they were working late, was to use other people's money. Just don't let them all know who else is in on it. Don't use your own if you can help it. He bought a ten-million pound company for five million the next day, with borrowed money, stripped it bare and sold it on for a profit six months later. Corporate scalp hunter, they called him after. There was a legend and Ralph wasn't anxious to kill it. That was Ralph Martin. And Jack Clarke just sat back, watched and admired.

"Thanks, Barney," Martin said.

Small knew his time was up. He got up, nodded to Jack and turned. Before he got to the door, he turned his head again.

"I'll go again for you, Ralph," he said. "If you want."

"I know, Barney."

Small looked at Jack and Jack acknowledged him and Small left the room. Martin waited till he was sure that Small had finished trying to chat up his teenage secretary before he spoke again.

"Get someone to watch him," he said. "I don't want him getting depressed. He has a habit of getting—you know."

Jack nodded.

It was so easy to say yes to Ralph Martin. Do what he asked. He had a way of asking that made it feel you were doing something great. As if you were somebody. PR Martin they'd called him when he was a running star. Or the Machine. And when the Machine got working it was relentless. Charm offensives from the Martin house wore down even the most world-weary scribes. He had them eating out of his hand. That was when he was good-looking— when he had hair. He had gained weight but not too much.

He had lost some of his shoulder breadth but that wasn't so bad either. But his face was completely changed. Meaner. And you couldn't hide that. So he bought two newspapers to take care of it.

Money was the key. Opened everything. He enjoyed the speculation about his wealth. Sometimes fuelled it himself. Money was a tool, a weapon more powerful than a guided missile. Lots of people had it, the difference was how they used it. Most people defended with money. Ralph Martin attacked.

Being born poor had its advantages, he always said. Cut out all the crap. He had one basic talent: he knew how to use things, and he made the most of it. Running first. That opened local doors. He'd never really liked it but he put up with it for what it gave him. And when he'd made the most of his running, he moved on. Semi-states first. High-profile projects when there was Government money to back them. Then out before the Government money ran out and they hit the floor. Out and over to the States, to the big bucks. An MBA at the right college. When it wasn't fashionable. He got his name in the papers for that, too. He joined investment houses with impressive names and built-in inertia. Some people who hadn't much time for him and thought they knew better said it was a bad move. But they were way behind.

It was a good time to go into investment banking. While the rest of the world was out protesting. Those boys who weren't out protesting were having lunch in pinstripe suits and working out how to be millionaires really quick. But even then, Ralph Martin was ahead of the pack. He wanted more. More than the money. The others couldn't see past the money. That was their problem. He told them that. The money was a means to an end. But real power came with ownership, control. Companies, land, commodities, anything.

He had the avarice of the very poor. Though he was

never as poor as he made out. If his people had been that poor, he'd never have made it to university or run at the Olympics. But he enhanced that myth too, for the image. It was a carefully crafted image, connived at by people who were caught in his spell, no matter how much they tried not to be. He was a success in a country without too many successes. A success among mediocrity and failure. And they gave him all the attributes of a success, insight and sexual prowess. He let that go, too, but it was all rubbish. He was a faithful husband. But myth and legend were another weapon, like the money.

People used to ask him where it would stop. When he would be satisfied. He would always smile.

"You're still with me, Jackie?" he said.

Jack nodded.

"How's your dad?"

"Not good."

Jack's mind wandered for an instant. Along solid Victorian streets that spoke of permanence, through a wrought-iron gate to a door that spoke of confidence. His dad had inherited it from his dad and his dad had inherited it from his dad. The first had been a Port and Docks man, a part-time boxer who made a bit of ready as a bookie and in other ways that required a blind eye, the second became a lawyer for respectability and stayed a bookie for money, the third ignored his father's advice and stayed a bookie and lost his shirt. Jack remembered times when he'd looked up to his dad, when his dad was something else, when he could boast in school, give bogus information to those who would listen. The Clarkes owned eight shops once upon a time, up there with the best of them. And old Jack Clarke never missed a day on the track. Best of everything, Jack could remember.

They were good days. Two holidays a year to the Med when people weren't even sure where the Med was.

Then one day it all closed and they retreated back into

their Victorian inheritance in Rathgar and some cash his mother had from her father. It was enough to keep up an appearance. But the Clarkes weren't what they had been. And you could tell. Old Jack didn't get the respect any more. People didn't come up to him, looking for favours. And in Dublin, not having people coming up looking for favours was the best sign things were changed. It wasn't so bad. Jack was still a kid and kids cope better with bad fortune. But it had been better. And Jack had always said it would be again. Making promises to himself. When other kids were simply trying to figure out what to do with themselves, he was working out how the Clarkes were going to be top-dogs again.

That was the theory. Jack had a sneaking feeling it was pipe-dream stuff, a concession to the emptiness that sometimes tapped him on the shoulder for a talk, but it continued to fire him. It was a good excuse, anyway, for some of the things he'd allowed himself do. A good way to pass the buck. He even drifted into Martin territory, made things worse than they were, made up a whole history of pain and distress for his mother she had never had. Sure, times had been bad; they'd had to cut cloth different ways but the money she had and what was left from the shops and some of the lands old Jack had inherited all went to making sure that Jack number four got going.

His dad never recovered, though. Up top. He still smiled and told jokes in the bar and could shoot a two-under on his better days, but the spark had been killed off. His face had a grey tinge that greyed more and his hair lost its life and sometimes hung off the side of his head, making him look ridiculous. Jack hated that. And he held it against his father for failing. Now, sometimes, the old man couldn't climb the stairs on his own. Six, maybe ten months. No more. Death row. Waiting. And looking like he was waiting. And they called around and said bland things to him and talked about the old days and whispered on the way down the stairs about how pathetic he'd become and what a release it would be.

And Jack wanted to scream at them. That's my dad. That's my fucking dad in there. That withering frame. That's my dad. That's Jack Clarke. The third Jack Clarke. He was something once. He was really something. But whatever he had been was gone and so long gone Jack was not sure it had ever been more than a dream.

"We'll talk later, Jackie."

Martin pressed a button on his intercom and spoke to his secretary.

"Get hold of Dan Meehan, Sarah, will you."

Meehan ran Ralph Martin's papers. Unkind people called him Goebbels. Truth was, he wasn't on the same level as the good doctor. But he gave everything he had to Ralph Martin.

"Tell him to bring a business hack tonight. The lean guy with the beard. You know him. And get me a sandwich, too. Something with fish."

Martin turned to Jack.

"You go do what you have to. Be back by eight."

He went back to the intercom.

"Tell Dan, eight, Sarah. And make it tuna, will you."

Walking through the five-storey Georgian building from Martin's office, Jack Clarke put on a mask. It was one of several interchangeable complementary masks he wore and he put them on according to the situation he was in. Walking through the office he was the bright-eyed boy, brimming with confidence, full of energy, get-up-and-go. He knew what they said about him. He had a couple of them on tape saying it. But he had them on tape saying other things, too. And doing worse. He had learned quickly from Martin. What they said didn't matter, so long as he could look the part. So long as they said it, he was winning. When they stopped saying it, that was the time to look over his shoulder. Resentment was a barometer of achievement. Another Martin phrase. They came out unnoticed now. He slowed at Sarah and her wonderful breasts. She wasn't so pretty if he was honest but she had fabulous jugs. Jack and Sarah had had it off a couple of Christmases back. She'd been drunk. He'd been drunk. Quick poke. Office stuff. Cried in his arms after. He'd done the let's-be-friends bit and let her lean on his shoulder. She'd accepted. He had to endure the boyfriend troubles and the dreary aerobic trauma of the SINBAD phobia she sometimes lapsed into. In return, she kept him informed.

They talked when Martin wasn't around. And Sarah rubbed his back for him, too. Nothing more. Jack was half sincere about her. Playing big brother. It made him feel good.

She winked at him and he winked back and she went back to the more boring aspects of her work, feeling she had at least one friend.

It all followed a time-honoured pattern, same following same, the way he'd always played it, since joining. He wondered about that. Could have stayed in practice. The tedium of it forced that thought back into whatever subversive part of his brain it had come from. So he followed a well-worn path to his own office a couple of floors above. A friendly word with someone in accounts, a quip about sport with someone whose name he could never remember, and always the sure smile. He walked slowly. It was his choice. To join. He tried to remember the sequence of events. They did the audit; he came to Martin with some good ideas; Martin had come back to him with an envelope and a job offer and he'd said yes.

That was before all this. Before the big leaps. Ralph Martin had been home a year. His company, Martin Holdings, had been a small investment house operating from the bottom floor of a pension fund off Wall Street. Investment found property and property made a lot of money. And when Ralph Martin was sure Martin Holdings had enough liquid, he began buying businesses. When he could, he bought and stripped and sold. But he was ready to begin building now. He bought a brewery and a chain of local newspapers and a small radio station and didn't sell them. And then in Dublin, he changed Martin Holdings to MartinCorp.

When he came home, he came with a small computer firm he'd bought in California when it ran out of capital. They set up their first factory in Dublin. Frank Costello opened it. There were plenty of column inches about integrated systems and whole packages and total solutions. There were Government contracts, too. But the exports got the headlines. MartinCorp was everything politicians like Frank Costello wanted to see in the country. Advanced technology, young well-educated work force, go-ahead aggressive marketing strategy. Ralph Martin took what was offered and kept buying. Anything, anywhere. He moved into food processing. On a small scale at first. Taking stakes anywhere he could. It was his plan, he said; hi-tech was a good front image but he wanted to get into basics like food, retailing, too, for the control it gave him, for the cash it could provide, for persuading banks to lend him more money. And as he bought, he borrowed. And anyone who questioned the MartinCorp strategy was told they had no vision, that the future was big diverse-interest business, with a core to keep the whole thing ticking, the heart.

The first Gulf contract was announced by Frank Costello at a special press conference. The Martin Integrated Information System was a complete state administration package, hardware and software, perfect for a developing nation anxious to make the jump from paper to microchip. And downmarket enough not to run into the embargos that were tacked to some customers like health warnings. The Gulf contract led to a South American contract and more factories. Experts said the system was a substandard bootleg. Frank Costello hailed it as the beginning of an indigenous hi-tech revolution. And Ralph Martin kept expanding.

Jack stopped for a chat with two lean blokes from Carlow

who were new in marketing and couldn't stand him. All three of them were courteous but Jack was in command. Anyway, they weren't trouble. Trouble came from people at the high levels. People who resented him coming in and skyrocketing. People like Alan Kennedy, who had an office beside his but was never there. Fifty-five, pot-bellied and hard as they came. Face like a charging water buffalo. Kennedy was close in with Martin and had some grandiose title and a salary that was way out of line with what he did. Fact was, he didn't do very much. Except visit Martin for long talks. He hated seeing Jack there and usually made an excuse to leave if he found Jack when he got to Martin's office. Kennedy was supposed to keep order in the factories and he had some link with the unions that was never clear. But that was Martin all over. Showed you bits of people but never showed you everything. Jack Clarke was still trying to work out the puzzle for himself. F 51878 .

The building was bigger inside than it looked from the canal. There was an extension at the back which should never have received planning permission. It doubled the floor space and paralleled the Georgian house cubic foot for cubic foot. But the place was still too small for what they were running. Far too small. Jack always had the feeling that there was a huge staff somewhere else, doing the real work, maybe in another country, all the work he wasn't privy to, all the work Martin said he'd take care of himself. He swore and smiled, his eighteenth wide smile in the trip from Martin's office, at his secretary, Molly, a middle-aged woman with no womb and hair above her lip and a brain like a Samurai sword.

"For you," she said. "All for you."

She handed him a heap of loose sheets bound by string.

"What is it?"

"Signatures."

"What?"

"Mr Martin said you were dealing with it. It's a petition.

Environmental protestors. That thing in Offaly. Or wherever. Mr Martin said you were to handle it. Liaise with the legal and PR people. You want me to phone them?"

"I thought I'd done all that. Jesus, that's all I need. These bloody green-welly brigaders. I'm sure I took care of all that."

He could not remember it specifically. There was an echo of something in Offaly. Crosssomewhere. One of their plants, an assembly unit Martin had bought cheap from an Asian multinational. A small operation. But it had its uses. Jack didn't go further with that. He concentrated on the business in question. Some religious group complaining. About pesticides. Dead cows or something. But he'd taken care of it. Or Barney Small had. There was a court case threatening. But that would be years coming before the bench. And the opposition had no tangible case and even less money. He shook his head. There were bigger problems. This Arab business, for one. And the Britcop takeover. The British Imperial Foods Co-op takeover was Jack's baby. And a good delivery would mean Brownie points. A whole chain of processing plants and outlets. Three hundred and fifty million.

Molly saw his distress. He had a face gradually succumbing to distress these days, she thought. She raised her eyebrows and brought her chin up towards her mouth.

"Don't worry. We have the whole town on our side. Sure they all work for us. If we said it was bug-eyed monsters killed the cows, they'd go along with it. Try that."

Molly was a junior minister's mistress. It was a discreet arrangement, not discouraged by Ralph Martin. She had no problem with the by-products of her involvement. And she earned more money than other secretaries for her loyalty. Jack had been given her as his secretary and she was a damn good secretary but she was more. Molly and her junior minister lover made love once a month, in Jack's office, on the floor, after the rest of the staff had gone home. It was her

time, on that floor, for those two hours and it bought Ralph
Martin much more than any money could.

When he was inside his office, Jack Clarke could loosen
his tie and open his collar and rub his neck and pinch his
eyes. There was a washbasin in the corner and he went over
to it and ran a tap over a blue face-cloth and squeezed the
face-cloth and sat down in his leather swivel chair and put
the cloth on his forehead.

He undid the string on the petition without seeing it.
How many miles? he thought. He had lost count. Been on
the road now for four, no five, days, living out of a gold card.
Don't bother packing, Martin said. Just do what I say. Meeting
here, dinner there, lunch somewhere else. Back and forth
across time zones, jet lag tapping him on the shoulder and
asking him to slow down. Then pills. Uppers to keep going
then downers to come off the uppers and more uppers to get
back up from the downers, and so it went on. He didn't look
at himself any more. He was afraid of what he might see. Six
months now. The speed of gathering infinity, momentum
building. The girl in Killiney. The sting. How long ago? Last
time he'd even had a chance. He could still smell her. It was
dogging him. A week. Two weeks. More like three but
probably two. On the plane, off the plane. One plastic meal
after another. He'd jerked off in the toilet at Boston just to
get into some kind of shape. It had the desired effect. He
couldn't do it again. Wouldn't rise to the occasion.

The cold wet of the cloth seeped through his skin and
into his brain and eased the overload. It was a release in a
time of little release. Grand. After snobbery, it was all about
grand. How many k you earned. Hundred plus extras k. And
a German car. And the extras. The extras were worth as
much again. Made them dead jealous to hear. The ones in
the practices and merchant banks and the insurance
companies, panting for marks out of ten from their managers.
But they were the rules. It was all a matter of how many you
could get. That was your value. He was high up. All the right

clubs, all the right gear, all the right moves. And a BMW that could buy a house in the suburbs and still leave change for a cruise in the Caribbean.

His eyes relaxed. His body followed. He stretched out his legs and massaged himself between the legs. Ralph had it under control. Ralph Martin never let anything slip. He should never doubt Ralph. His little pep talk to himself worked itself in with the cold of the face-cloth and he let go his feelings of anxiety and suspicion and quoted the thing about keeping your head when all about were losing theirs. He didn't have to believe it but it helped him.

Two hundred and fifty million, though. He divided it into separate packages. Hardware, software, consultation, back-up. A hole big enough to drive a universe through. What was the big deal? It was insured. Frank Costello's personal mark on that. That made him think for a while. They were too exposed. This by itself they could deal with, but this and the Britcop takeover and other debt; it was costing more than they'd bargained for. They were becoming stretched. Steady, Jack, he said to himself. That's what you're here for. So the wog thinks he has us by the balls. Thinks he can squeeze a better deal. We'll just pull out. Leave them the pencils and shit they had before. There were better markets. The system worked. South America and Africa were screaming for it. Anyway, he needed them as much as they needed him. Maybe more. Jack censored his thought again. They were branching out. Past iffy third-world deals. Real big league stuff now. Britcop was the first of the big league targets Ralph Martin had his eyes on. And it was moving along nicely. Jack was back in line. He felt a surge of admiration for Ralph Martin. A thrill. It reminded him of some thrill he'd had a couple of weeks earlier but he could not put his finger on it.

When he had regained himself he threw the face-cloth into the washbasin and took a look at the petition.

3

The weather turned bad in the space of fifteen minutes. From clear evening sky to raging wind and blanket rain. The temperature dropped through the floor and Jack Clarke pulled the window shut and turned on an electric heater. The wind tore the blanket rain into ribbons and scattered them in every direction. It was as if some psychotic god had been let loose with a knife. The edge of chaos, Jack thought. He looked out at the evening rage and thought he saw someone watching him from a door across the street. He rubbed the fog on the window and reached back and turned off the lamp on his desk. Police and ambulance sirens chased each other through the streets. The odd car passed outside, sliding through the anger of the wind, pissed on by the rain. Jack watched the doorway. Nothing moved.

When he was sure there was no one there, or if there had been someone then that someone was gone, he came away from the window and turned on the lamp on his desk. He sat down and exhaled everything that had been building up in him. His room was warming up and the slight shiver he had been feeling had stopped and was developing into a pleasant blanket sensation. Jack loosened his tie.

What the hell was he at? he thought. Who the hell would be out there?

He swore at himself and opened a drawer containing a bottle, a glass and a tin. He took them out one by one. The bottle was in its last quarter. He poured enough to see the golden brown colour. He opened the tin. It was full of pills. Different colours, a pot-pourri of mood-swing, ecstasy to depression and back again. He took a couple out and looked at them. He took a sip of the liquid in the glass.

One. All he wanted was one. That would take care of things. Stop it getting on top of him. He rubbed his eyes and felt his fingers touch his brain. It was a burning feeling and it contrasted with the glowing feeling of the room and the sense of anxiety somewhere deeper. He popped a pill, not the first one, and downed the rest of the liquid. He could go now.

It was the first thing he'd noticed. That he was losing it in. Socialising. Something as pissy as socialising. Not going out on a belter down Leeson Street. Not head-banging at some acid rave in a penthouse in Mount Merrion. Where he blasted himself out of it with whatever came first and chased skirt like a heat seeker. Two, three, maybe more, in a bed, rolling over one another. Out of his brain all night, no sleep, throwing up, then shower, shit, shave and into work. He could deal with that. It was simple. It had a direction he could follow. Aims. Goals. It was the other stuff, the friendship stuff he found he was slipping with.

He had friends. Jack Clarke had friends. Not the barrow-boys he went hunting with, the aftershave arrogants who notched their pricks and pinned their condom packets to the notice board. He couldn't stand them. Like the two marketing blokes from Carlow. But that had to be done. Part of the power play. Test of strength. You had to win tests of strength.

His friends were a more reliable crew. From a before time, and he had never managed to make any others since. He'd read somewhere that there was a time after which you didn't make any more friends, only acquaintances. That there was so much you didn't have in common with people, nothing would make up for it. He hadn't believed it. He'd joined the practice in Mount Street, thinking he could make friends and they'd seemed like friends at the time. But as soon as he went to MartinCorp, they stopped being friends. Nothing in common any more. He gave up after that.

He looked at his watch and calculated how late he was going to be. He'd sent word he was going to be late, via Molly. She might be Martin's eye but she was bloody good at looking after him. He had that mother love thing that men have when they sense a surrogate mother around. You can never have enough mothers, Jack thought. He had a few. A few that fell for the charm. A few that needed to mother someone. Jack took what was going without questioning it. He could delay some more and arrive in the middle. Bring some flowers. He waited for the pill to take effect. He turned on his computer terminal and tapped into some files. Just figures. Enough to keep his mind off dinner.

It was getting to him. The gathering storm. The exposure was too big. He'd said that. Martin told him to shut it. He did. If Larry Tallon could just get part payment, smooth things over, that would hold it. Jack could feel his body shifting down a gear and time seemed to slow enough for him to collect all the thoughts he had been spilling all day. If Tallon could smooth things over. Get some cash. Then they'd have enough to keep the banks quiet for the Britcop take-over. Big bidding. Had to be played right. Greedy committee members. Lots of backhanders. Oil, Martin said. Lots of oil. Since the Guinness business there were jitters and talk of long stretches and big fines. So you had to oil some more. Make it worth while. And do it all without too much fuss. In a way it was easier now. The public had had their sacrifices. Boesky—Martin used to call him Bozo when he knew him in the seventies; Saunders. Keep your head down and play it cool. Frank Costello would come to the rescue. This was Frankie's play as much as Ralph Martin's. They were the cutting edge of Frankie's new order. Frankie's shock troops. Export-driven. Putting the country on the map.

MartinCorp. Undercutting the competition. For ten years they had made the running. Nothing got in their way. Now this. This, right when it wasn't needed.

He turned off his computer and went over to the door where his coat was hung.

The pill came to support him. Ralph Martin could handle it. They were blue chip. Cast-iron guarantees. Take more than some jumped-up little Hitler to derail them. Anyway, that wasn't Jack's concern at the moment. He was on the Britcop job. There were key committee members, proxy vote holders, to be targeted. About ten of them wanted scratching. There was a lot of travelling to do.

He pulled his coat on and wrapped it round himself, tight.

The kind of insurance Frankie Costello was going to have to pay out if the Arab in the beret didn't cough up would support whole countries in Africa for a year. There'd be shit to pay. And shit to pay they didn't need either. They needed a nice quiet business environment, the machine running smoothly.

More medicinal support. Ralph would sort it out. Ralph sorted everything out. He was relaxing now. Ralph would sort it out. With Costello and Tallon. Ralph sorted everything out, one way or another. Jack kept telling himself that.

It was time to go. Jack laughed to himself. Time to go and relax. He pulled up the collar of his cashmere coat and ran his hand through his wavy hair and pulled his car keys out of his pocket and tossed them and caught them. Then he left the office to itself and went down to the carpark.

The rain had eased off to an annoying drizzle and the wind had wasted itself on the city and was moving on out to sea with the clouds which weren't heavy and dark any more. The sun was a bump in the west and a lazy flicker of semi-light fought against the gathering night. There were some stars and a knife-like chill remained but things looked like they were were changing for the better and the faintest hint of pink on the horizon told of a better future.

The Hennigans were friends of Jack Clarke. Part of a small group of maybe half a dozen people, if that many, he could call friends. Stay-behinds. There were others who might have been friends. But they were gone. Vanished to the four corners. Some had come back and gone again. Two had done it four times. They had a refugee look when they came home. Lost in imaginary space, in-betweenness. The in-betweens. Their accents changed by the month and everywhere was better than everywhere else. You never saw their tears but you knew they cried.

Jack wasn't sure where he came in here. He didn't like to think of himself as a stay-behind. People who worked for the cutting edge of the new order were not stay-behinds. They were above the general order. They were the future. Storm-troopers of corporate expansion.

Carl Hennigan was a stay-behind. He had something to stay behind for. An accountant, too, he was still in practice, working for his father. Carl and Jack had been to school together and then Trinity. They belonged to the same golf club and their fathers knew each other. Carl's father had been the Clarkes' auditor in the days of the bookmaking business. He still looked after old Jack's affairs and didn't charge for it. Carl was a chip off the same block as his father. He was much taller than Jack and blond and had a head that seemed too small for his body. He had sharp blue eyes. Honest eyes, his wife said.

Angie Hennigan was about half his size. She was pretty in an indefinable way. It came from inside and you couldn't pin it down. Jack had gone out with her for a few months at college. It was stormy and it ended in tears. They made up when she started going out with Carl. Jack liked being around them. They didn't expect anything from him. They had a kid and Angie was talking about having another but it would mean maybe having to give up work and she wasn't too keen on that. She wore her hair very short and tight to the scalp and if you came up behind her you might think she was a boy. She had a will of pure iron. She proposed to Carl after two weeks. It took him four years to agree finally to a wedding date. He wanted to qualify. She wanted to move in with him. Carl was uneasy with that. Their parents knew each other. He gave in after two years.

Jack rang the bell of the small terraced house in Harold's Cross, holding a bunch of flowers and a cuddly toy he had brought for little Barry, the Hennigan baby, behind his back. He liked the kid because he was at an age that made him easy to like. Jack kept a store of presents in the back of his car for any visits he might make. He saw Angie's outline through the frosted glass.

"At last!" she said. "Thought you weren't coming."

It was a routine they were used to. He was always late. The high-powered kind of late. The later you were, the more high-powered you were. Ralph Martin never turned up at dinner parties he was invited to. But he was invited all the same by people who just liked to say they had invited him. That way they got the prestige of having him on their list and the chance of an invitation to the Martin house for one of his garden events. The Hennigan things were more genuine.

Angie kissed him on both cheeks and he caught sight of Carl coming from the kitchen, wearing an apron with Mickey Mouse on it. Jack whistled the Mickey Mouse tune and presented Angie with her flowers. She kissed him again and Carl threw his hand into Jack's.

"At last!" he said. "I'm serving. We waited."

"You shouldn't have."

It might have been rehearsed. But they all felt comfortable with it. Jack especially. They all needed that comfort. Faces had vanished with an unnerving regularity over the years. Old friends had a reassuring feeling. Jack showed his present for the baby and made some sarcastic comments about someone they only vaguely remembered, someone named

John who had dropped out of college years earlier and gone to Singapore and sold steel now. Angie Hennigan took Jack's hand and led him towards the dining-room. She knew he was on something. They all knew he took stuff. It was in his eyes. They were cartwheels in overdrive to anyone who cared to look. But she held his hand and took him with her and ignored what she knew about him. As she ignored what she heard about him. Even lying with her husband at night, pillow-talking, skirting around what had been said by this friend of that friend or that civil servant or that journalist. Jack had a bad name. There was no proof but he had a bad name. Carl said it was jealousy but Angie knew Carl and knew he was being loyal because that was what Carl did best. He was the most loyal man she had ever met and if she loved him for nothing else she loved him for that.

"Look what the cat dragged in," she said before they had come around the door.

"And have we got a surprise for him," Carl whispered into his ear.

Carl had a child's sense of fun, which made him a great dad but left Jack feeling he was a bit naïve, childish almost, needing to be protected. Typical bloke who goes into his dad's firm. Things mapped out. Nothing too big, nothing too small. Never a millionaire, never a pauper. Just bumping along. Jack thought he had his friend sussed pretty well. He thought he had everyone sussed.

Carl slapped him on the shoulder, winked and went into the kitchen.

The dining table was laid out with diplomatic-corps precision, the way Angie always had it. Carl would try and get it like that but it took some of Angie's iron to have it exactly right. Jack scanned the table for the familiar faces he expected. Jenny Myers on the right, where she always sat, and Andy Wright on the left. It was an old joke of Carl's that Mr Wright was always on the left. Andy had once been left-wing, too. It was a very in joke but they all laughed every time.

Andy was an anaesthetist who'd overqualified himself and couldn't get a job as a consultant. He was going to the States soon and he wasn't much happy about it. He talked a lot about making money over there for five years and coming back and going into forestry. He was very much into trees. He could tell you types, growing times, wood uses, all that kind of thing, if you let him go too much. He was Carl's cousin, too. It worked like that. Jenny was related to Angie in a distant way. She was a landscape architect and Angie was a commercial artist. Angie came from Churchtown and Jenny from Stillorgan. Andy and Carl were from Terenure. Except for the fact that Jack's family home was bigger than all the others, and the Clarkes had once been rich, they were all pretty even. Andy had gone out with Jenny for a year and a half. Jenny had ended it and gone out with two or three other guys before thinking she was better off going out with Andy. But by that stage Andy'd got a law student pregnant and wasn't interested. Andy's pregnant girl-friend had her baby and then dumped him and went to London. They'd heard she was married.

Jack had just left Jenny's wide eyes and was in mid-thought when he saw the extra face. He was still thinking about a very lustful night with Jenny one New Year's Eve at a party in this house. Top front bedroom. It was one of the reasons he liked being there. His mind left all that, left the lust-laden New Year's party and Jenny and her hungry lips and shoulder-length sandy hair, and the feel of her body beneath him and the shape of her breasts and the extra flesh at her sides and the hardened nipples and the moist eyes and the arching pelvis and the slow deliberation of their movements, desperately slow, achingly slow, hot, deep and slow—left all that and swung to the face beside her. His heart did a backflip in the direction of his mouth.

"Hello, Jack. How are you?"

He took the hand automatically.

"Surprised?" Angie said.

Surprised! If Jenny Myers brought on pleasant memories of well-satisfied lust, then Catherine Keyes unlocked a box of emotions he had packed away so tight he thought they could never be freed again. It caused him to shudder and sway but no one noticed. They were too full of their surprise. Jack still had her hand in his.

"Hello, Kate," he said.

He regained control of himself and affected a pleasant amusement that dampened the surprise. Maybe they were expecting him to drop his chin to the floor or jump back. They should have known Jack better than that. He held it against them. Not in any conscious way.

And Kate drilled him and didn't take her hand away.

She had a Mediterranean face and brown hair combed back behind her ears and a body that moved like it had a Formula 1 design team working on it round the clock. And she wore a cross at her neck. The cross, he knew. He'd given it to her. Six years ago. Maybe it wasn't the same cross. He couldn't really be sure. His mind was blank now, trying to conjure up images. As with Jenny. And there were plenty. But he couldn't. It was as if she'd paralysed him inside. Jack looked around at everyone. Their mouths were open, waiting. Angie had her tongue tight against her teeth. Angie's cousin was married to Kate's sister-in-law's sister. And Angie and Kate were best friends. Except that Kate hadn't been in the country for five years. Or if she had, no one had told Jack. He hadn't asked.

"How are you?" he said.

She swung her head and the brown hair fell away to one side. A shadow followed it across her face and Jack saw her eyes drift down his body for a second before she faced him off again. She had big lashes. That added to the sense of drift. He kept his mouth shut and concentrated a contrived stare at her. One of Ralph Martin's moves. They got everywhere.

"I'm fine," she said. "You?"

He looked around at everyone again.

"Terrific. I'm—"

He shook his head because it was all right now and it looked controlled, and he laughed, and they laughed too. The release was palpable.

"Shall we eat?" Carl said. He was standing at the door, smiling.

"Yes, let's," Kate said.

She had not taken her hand away yet.

What was there to say about Kate? PhD mind. She was lecturing when they were together. Then she was in Foreign Affairs. But she'd left that. He was trying to get it all straight and sit down beside her. Martin had warned him about surprises but he couldn't be ready for everything. She'd left Foreign Affairs. Angie said that. Moved to America. Then Europe. The EC. Environmental research. Big star in New York till she dumped it. You heard these things, second, third and fourth-hand. Theo White had worked with her in New York. White was a classic poacher-turned-gamekeeper. College radical who got auditor of the Hist in his last year through some neat crawling, and wangled his way into Foreign Affairs when there was supposed to be an embargo. He knew the right people. Right people on the right. He made a better conservative than he did a radical. He had a face like the back end of a tomahawk. They used to say that if you put him back to back with his brother you could make a pickaxe. Theo was still in New York so there was a silver lining to the cloud.

Kate was in Brussels now. He knew that. He knew more than he would admit. Could admit. That would mean it got to him. Ask her, to make it look good, Jack said to himself. Should have asked Angie. No. He'd closed that door. He was good at closing doors where necessary. And that had been necessary. No one knew how much. They were friends but not that close. Jack Clarke was as self-contained as they came. Except maybe when it came to Kate. He was wrestling with the jammed door.

"How long have you been back?" he asked.

"Oh, a week or two."

"For good? Where have you been? How long's it been?"

"Steady, give her a chance, Jack," Jenny said. "Always a rusher. Well, nearly always."

She gave him a knowing glance but he was paying too much attention to Kate to understand or care.

"For a while. I'm doing a report for the Commission."

"Right."

"And you're a high flyer, Jack. I even hear your name in Brussels and Strasbourg. Quite a meteoric ascent."

"Always good, I hope."

She shrugged.

"What do you think?"

Carl interrupted any embarrassment Jack was going to feel in replying by bringing in the food and changing the subject.

All Jack could come up with was sitting on a beach with her somewhere. There was wind and plenty of cloud, so it must have been an Irish beach. She was dressed in a polo-neck and jeans and he was reading from a book. Jack couldn't remember what it was or if it had ever happened. There'd been meals, too. But one restaurant seemed to blend into another. The beach was the most concrete memory for the moment.

They ate and talked, the six of them, and Jack's mind released more details for him. They drank wine and more details came out. She helped with some general background information, nothing specific, shared memories stretching back years. They'd known each other as kids, well, teenagers, but that counted as being a kid. Maybe that was the beach. She looked younger, much younger, on the beach. Angie eased the whole thing along, an anxious mediator, keeping the evening going.

It was when they were kids. Seventeen. Eighteen. The

beach was out west. Then they hadn't seen each other for years. Kate went to the States on a scholarship. Out of sight, out of mind.

"Kate's got a place in Dalkey. Near the sea," someone said.

Jack and Kate caught each other's eyes for a moment and smiled and looked away. He was relaxed except for his search. She went away and was gone and then she was back and working and they met at a bus stop of all places. Near the Dáil. She was waiting. He was passing. He'd just been down to Buswell's. To meet one of Martin's men. First time he'd done it. Simple procedure. Drink. Place the envelope down. Ignore it. Walk off. Let your man pick it up. No one noticed. Transaction complete. Big gobdaw from Industry. Couldn't pronounce his "th"s. Had a sharp accent. Never finished a sentence. Big ears. Why he picked Buswells was anyone's guess. Maybe it was his first time and he wanted to feel comfortable.

That was what she said. She wanted to feel comfortable. Their first time. It was flowing freely now. Their first time. That night. Her flat. Leeson Street. Pink door. Near the Burlington. They'd danced. But not there. Very humid night. They opened the windows.

He had to concentrate on what Carl was saying to him and he lost his train of thought.

"I should have it done up by next year. Then you can all use it."

Jack nodded.

Carl was talking about an old windmill he'd bought in France. Jack was watching two lovers love one another. It was a confused examination. The wine and the pills were taking over and confusing him. And he could not get sense out of it all.

"We don't see Jack very much now, do we, Jack?"

Jack swung his head to Angie.

"You know me."

"Megabucks," Jenny said. "I should have followed your lead, Jack. You should see where he lives, Kate."

"I can't wai—"

She cut herself off and smiled and they all smiled.

At one in the morning, the talking had slowed to a crawl. Everything new had been exhausted. They were back on the old stuff and the old stuff came out slowly. No one wanted to be accused of sentimentality but secretly it was the old stuff they all liked to hear. Kate sat away from Jack and Jenny sat beside him and threw her head back and told them all about her boy-friend who wasn't her boy-friend any more. She was about to cry when Angie put on a CD. Jack put his arm around Jenny and caught Kate throwing a second glance at them.

It was ending when the dog came in. The dog was a setter named Brian after a private joke between Angie and Carl. No one was much interested in the reason for the name but they always told people anyway. It was a ritual in the house if you came as a guest for the first time. There was another Brian, the butt of the joke, but he was far away and never came to the house as a guest. They all grabbed Brian, one after the other. Brian always meant it was ending.

Jack kept looking at his watch. It was ending and he hadn't had time to talk to her. Not properly. Not the way he wanted. And the seconds were becoming minutes faster than his thoughts could organise themselves. The dog did his usual round and then, like she was on cue, Jenny said she had a job early next morning. A year of her time in Scotland came out with the words. It made them laugh, then slag her off. Jack thought the lilt sounded good at one in the morning and if Kate hadn't been there, he might have offered Jenny a lift home and chanced something. He needed someone now. And the way her voice sounded, well, Jenny had been good once. But Kate was there. And most of what they had shared was now jammed up in his brain, desperate to be released. But he couldn't say anything, not there, not even with his friends. It was like some kind of eastern torture. He had to talk to her. He tried to slip it into the confusion of going.

"Can I give you a lift?" he said to her.

Kate looked at Jenny.

"We've a taxi booked," she said, without looking at Jack.

He felt like he was the butt of one of their jokes now. And that sucked. He heard himself say, shit. But no one else did.

Kate and Jenny were going to the door. Kate was still petting Brian. Carl had a glass in his hand and was saying something about share values to Jack. Jack wasn't listening. Angie came down with the coats. It was ending. It would be over and there would be no talk. Jack tried to come up with something. Anything.

"Listen, how long are you here?" he said to Kate.

She smiled and looked at Jenny. They were both drunk. Jack was embarrassed and he hated that more than anything. Fuck both of you, he said to himself.

"A while," she said.

"Maybe we could meet."

"Yes. Maybe."

The other three looked at them.

"Well!" Jenny said.

"I'll call you. I know where you are, Jack."

"Everyone knows where Jack is," Angie said.

She winked at Jenny and nudged her husband.

"Watch out for the formidable Molly, Kate."

She kissed Kate.

"So what is it you're home for?" Jack asked Kate.

It was a last question. Unthought. Something to keep links with this escaped past. Maybe to lure it back to where he'd had it penned up.

"You, Jack," she said. "In a way."

She looked at the other three. There was a shock on Carl's face. Kate held herself for a few seconds and then burst out laughing.

She was still laughing when the bell rang. And Jenny had begun to laugh, too. In a kind of feminine solidarity. Angie was going to laugh. Mostly because she liked to see Jack Clarke uneasy. But she had to answer the door to the taxi man.

"MartinCorp, Jack. We're looking into a complaint about one of your factories. Among other things."

Jack looked more confused than he was. It was an automatic facial reaction to criticism. Bought time. Martin ploy.

"Pollution, Jack. Community rules. I'm here to see what's going on. With the local people, of course. Always with the natives. Routine, Jack. A place called Crossfin. I can't say more. You understand. I think there's a court case. Am I right?"

She didn't wait for a reply.

"It'll look good on my CV and that's what it's all about, isn't it?"

She kissed Angie and Carl and walked off. Then she stopped and came back.

"I'll ring, Jack. I will. Nice seeing you again."

She kissed him on the cheek.

4

The Irish cabinet meets in a room on the right wing of Government Buildings, up a short flight of stairs, past a military police guard and in on the left from the main entrance on Merrion Street. The left wing of the building houses the Department of Finance. The rest is the haunt of the Taoiseach's department and assorted hangers-on.

The cabinet room has a single long table for business. The Taoiseach's chair has a harp on it. The walls are hung with pictures of Republican revolutionaries who made the transition to establishment icons. Otherwise, it is an innocuous enough room. On a good day, the view of the courtyard of Government Buildings, all sandblasted and fountained and looking very Continental, helps ease bad news and difficult decisions on their way.

That Monday, Frank Costello sat in the chair with the harp and stared across at his Finance minister and his Technology minister and dunked broken digestives in tea-bag tea in a china cup. The three of them comprised his cabinet's special Industrial Strategy Committee, one of a legion of cabinet sub-committees, permanent and *ad hoc*, which came and went throughout the life of any Government. Sometimes committees never met. Sometimes they met and did nothing. Most of the time they met and did things they didn't want anyone to know about. Their importance or not was defined by Frank Costello's membership of them, and his willingness, or not, to turn up at their meetings. The pissy ones he left to themselves, as they decided on the implementation of EC directives on vegetable sizes or the positioning of signposts.

This one was important. Costello had about five important ones. And Larry Tallon and Phil Cassidy were on all of them. Tallon because he was Costello's greatest supporter, Cassidy because he'd be a threat anywhere else. Costello practised the old adage of keeping your friends close and your enemies closer. It was no secret that Cassidy wanted his job. He'd even said it on television. That was a red rag to Frankie's bull and if Cassidy hadn't been such a power in the party, he'd have been out on his arse years ago. But he was a necessary evil and anyway he had similar economic views to his boss, whether he liked him or not. They were fast-trackers. Plan men. Full of strategies. Broad visions. Frankie's was the stronger now. But Phil never took his eye off the chair with the harp. An unfulfilled man. Dangerous, Frank Costello said. To be watched.

Not like Paud Henry. Paudie was as good a foot-soldier as you were likely to get for the price, but not completely up to it. That was why he was in Justice. Loyal gobshites always got Justice. Closet Nazis. Preferably those who liked bondage houses and lots of discipline. Paudie liked to be disciplined. Liked the smack of leather, Paudie did. He was obedient and zealous to a fault. But on something like this, on real decisions, on industrial strategy, Paudie was out.

The real business of Frank Costello's Government got done in his committees, away from the madding crowd. The rest, the party, the Dáil, the Senate, even the remainder of the cabinet, were merely for show. For the punters. To rubber-stamp. All he needed, Frankie used to say when he'd had a few, was a few loyal colleagues and a civil service with a nice javelin up its arse. And that he had.

"The point is, how do we fork out?" he said.

He looked at Phil Cassidy. Cassidy had a tight mercenary

haircut and the kind of threatening look on his face that tended to deflect even the most intense questions. He was a blunt man, which was why Frankie always preferred to let Larry Tallon do the television and radio. Cassidy had a scar which ran the length of his face, the result of going through a car window at speed. He also had a metal plate in his head. Enemies, of whom he had many, said the plate was an improvement on what was already there. It was untrue. Twenty-eight years of playing side-politics had sharpened the Kerryman into a lethal political blade.

"It'll knock the estimates right off the board, Frank," Cassidy said. "I don't know how we can massage it in."

"But it mightn't come to that," Tallon said. "I've been out there, Phil. I can swing it. I need more time."

"We haven't got much bloody time, Larry," Costello said.

He dropped a piece of biscuit in his tea.

"We could schedule payments. Slip them in slowly. Over a period. Get Ralph Martin to reschedule his repayments. Have a quiet word with the bankers. You know, let them know we're good for it."

"Come on, Larry," Cassidy said. "Once this gets out. Christ, it's a hell of an exposure to one company."

"I don't want it getting out," Costello said.

"How do we stop it?"

"We'll think of something. We always do, Phil. This is our baby, isn't it?"

A cold stare made it clear what he was saying. One in, all in. One out, all out. They'd thrown their weight in behind Martin. Key sector, computers. In the overall plan. They'd pinpointed key sectors and pushed everything into them. Cassidy threw his eyes down at the table. Frankie just pulled you in. He had that way. Cassidy allowed himself a brief moment of betrayal while his eyes were dipped to the table.

"I hate to think what's going to happen," he said. "Even if we keep it in house for a while. My people will go apeshit."

"Your people, Phil, will do as they're told. They work for us."

"How do you think the bloody banks are going to react, Frank? They'll be all over Martin. Looking for their money. We're talking big money, boys. Two hundred million plus."

"Banks follow money, Phil. If we rub them the right way, then they'll stick with Martin. They're children. Just need someone to reassure them. Tell them that things are going to be okay. That's up to you."

"I could borrow a little more. Revenue's exceeding targets so far. What we predicted. Another couple of hundred million borrowed wouldn't hurt too much."

Revenue exceeding expectation was a feature of Frank Costello's fiscal-rectitude Government. As opposed to Frank Costello's borrow-and-spend Government. But that was another incarnation. Borrow-and-spend was out. Cut-and-slash was in. And estimates always overplayed borrowing expectations and underplayed revenue expectations. Then when the figures came in at the end of the year and borrowing was lower than expected, it all looked good for a sound-bite on the television.

"It's possible. But I want the nature of the exposure hidden. Think of a plausible figure. That's the one we let out if we have to."

"Twenty—maybe thirty—million," Larry Tallon said. "We could get away with that. Temporary. Until this misunderstanding in the Gulf is sorted out. I think it's important we leave the possibility of payment open."

Costello slammed the table. His mouth tightened.

"I don't care what the fuck we do, gentlemen. I just don't want to have to stand up and tell that lot out there that we've thrown a minor departmental budget down some Arab shithole. And I don't want to have thousands of workers and their families outside my window, shouting for my balls. May I remind you that we have an election coming up within eighteen months. We must come up with something.

Worst case scenario?"

He looked at Cassidy.

"We have to pay. Without it, Martin's up the creek. We can't afford that."

Cassidy pulled at some of his tight hair. He had his elbows on the table and some of his mind was on a daughter with learning difficulties. Frank Costello sat back from him.

"No," he said.

"The polls are good," Tallon said.

"And how good do you think they'll stay if all this gets into general circulation?"

"If? I'm not sure we can keep it completely wrapped, Frank."

"I'm not asking for that. What we're talking about here is packaging. I have Alex Byrne working on a contingency. Come on, Phil, you trying to drop me in it? You're in this one, sunshine. Right there with me. You okayed the cover increase, son. You were up there beside Ralph Martin when we told everyone he was the future. Look, we have to put our spin on it. Cut the damage by spreading the impact."

He leaned across again.

"I want to sort this one out before the shit gets anywhere near the fan. We have other problems. We don't need this. There's telephone-number unemployment out there. The mob might be getting restless. We've a two-seat majority, Bell and his flycrappers to piss us off, a bloody huge hole in party finances and an election eighteen months off, coming at us like an out-of-control juggernaut."

"Well, I can't see why the hell he had to go for this Britcop takeover business at this time," Larry Tallon said. "When he was so bloody extended in the Gulf. I told him that. But you know Ralph, he wants to own everything. At least the other businesses are paying. At least there's some bread coming in."

Costello took his glasses off and pinched his hooked nose. He let his shoulders fall and sighed.

"I'm seeing Ralph Martin this morning. I want a decision."

"You're the boss, Frankie."

"Brilliant, Larry. I could get that sort of shit from Paudie. I want more from you, son. You'll have to fly out there. Use the jet. Take whoever you need. Fly out there and give it your best shot. Rearrange, spoof, do what you have to do, but get something out of him. Anything. Something we can hold up. Something Ralph Martin can show to his bankers. There's a time-scale here, you know. If we can hold this thing off for a month and sort it out some way, then maybe Martin will have the Britcop deal sewn up and then we'll be laughing. Every damn bank from here to Tokyo will be lining up to lend to him. Just, let's not panic here."

"Coalitions," Cassidy muttered.

"Would you rather we were in a minority?"

"I'd rather we had a good majority, Frank. I'd rather that."

"Think you could do better?"

"Come on, Frank; let's not get into that."

"No, you're right. This is something we're all in. Isn't it? Okay, leave it with me for a while. Larry, you go out there and get me something. And see if he'll see me. As a last resort. You know, former EC president. Good for his PR. Maybe I should have gone when we had the presidency. Though, Jesus, he's a fucking snake. Don't let him hang you, Larry. I don't want you on television on some kind of spying charge."

"Don't worry, Frank."

"Right, meeting adjourned."

Costello walked back to his office on the far side of the courtyard, pinching his nose-bridge twice more and feeling a surge of summer heat cushion his body. Fountain water splashed his arm and two junior civil servants from his department nodded nervously at him and muttered their respect. He liked to walk alone. Liked to cast his eyes up at the windows. See who was watching him. The frightened blue-suited file-carriers, his little pawns, he called them. Name of the game was moving the pawns.

It was a game he had always been good at. Knowing the right moves. Always a move ahead. He was sixty now. A young sixty. Bags under the eyes, skin losing its elasticity, maybe a little lethargy in his stride. But he could still mix it with the best of them. He had never lost that. There was fire in there. Enough to burn this lot, he thought. Frank Costello was one of those men who never have any doubt of their own destiny. And his destiny was the country's destiny. That was his justification for everything. And with himself, it worked. What effect it had on others didn't matter. The self-absorption was total. What was good for him was good for the country and vice versa. They were inseparable.

His office was over a small arch. There was a lift going up to it from the courtyard. The lift went on to a helipad. Costello had never used the helipad. Never had to yet, he used to joke.

Thirty years of service. He liked to call it service. He never made it clear who was serving whom. Thirty years. Youngest Finance minister in the history of the state. Youngest Foreign minister. Youngest this, biggest that, best whatever. The list was as long as his arm. Like Ralph Martin, he had achieved legendary status. Thirty years in the thick of it was more than enough for that. Gave him a feeling of untouchability. People liked that. It was pure escapism. From the imprisonment of the mundane. Ralph Martin and himself. And people wanted to believe the things they said about them. Especially about Frank Costello. They wanted him to be the one-time bad boy turned statesman. It made them feel good. He was a kind of surrogate champion for them. So he cultivated the image. He spread his own stories. The drinking, the women, hell-raising stuff. Most of it was rubbish. There were women. There was drink. There were other things. But it wouldn't hold the attention of a church congregation if you told the truth.

He had believed in it all once. But the sheer effort had pulled that skin off him years ago. Another him. Discarded. The lad who'd burned British flags at the right time and had his head knocked in at demos. There was something to believe in then. It was still possible, all of it. The fabulous dream the whole place was built on. All countries had their dream. Not many admitted it. But theirs had been a dream and a half. He looked behind him, going into his office, as if to check it was all gone.

His desk was modern, with a PC and a television screen. The room was small and prone to getting dark if the sun wasn't bright. Appropriate paintings hung on the walls. More cultured than the raw idealism of the revolutionary portraits in the cabinet room. But emptier for all that. Contrived. Interior-designed designer government. The image, the look. He felt hungry. It was mid-morning. The biscuits had done nothing for him.

The knock on his door was hesitant.

His private secretary came in. Younger and younger, Costello thought. Spotty. Self-assured. Full of Eurobull. Shitting themselves for a posting.

"The Minister for Industry, Taoiseach. He'd like a word," the young man said.

He had a Rolex watch. Frank Costello made a note of that. This scraper had a Rolex and his was a bloody oriental digital. Something was wrong there.

There were some ministers and TDs who had free run of Costello's office, could appear and walk in, but the Minister for Industry wasn't one of them. Those who were knew without having to be told, those who weren't were never told either, they just found it bloody difficult to see Frank Costello if he was intent on avoiding them.

Derek Bell was a fat man. Bursting out of his clothes. He wore a wig that everyone laughed at and false teeth that kept coming out of his mouth. He was carrying a huge file and the papers were beginning to slip out.

"Derek, you're back."

Bell was Costello's coalition partner. There were two of them from his—and these were Costello's words—flycrap little party, himself and a junior minister in health who spent all his time doing studies on different methods of contraception. Bell was a bit disorganised, a tough nut though, but seriously outgunned, completely outmanoeuvred and treated like shit when Costello could manage it without risking a premature general election. Neither of them wanted an election before they had to have one but Costello wanted one marginally less than Bell. Bell had Industry because that was the price of coalition, but Costello had Cassidy in Finance and that gave him the upper hand. Costello kept a tight rein on all decisions. Bell was supposed to be on the Industrial Strategy Committee but they never held meetings of any importance when he was in the country.

"You had a meeting without me, Frank. I just heard. You and Larry and Phil. I want a copy of the minutes."

Costello wanted to laugh. Those kind of meetings didn't have minutes. He could have some made up. He had a very junior homosexual in his department who did that kind of thing when asked. He was an ambitious homosexual. Ambition was a great incentive to co-operation. Costello kept his cool. Bell was a good minister, a good solid politician, but then it was all a matter of relativity, no great shakes really but as competent as anyone who was trained as a teacher, lost a farm, lost a pet-food business and found himself formulating industrial policy. Ralph Martin had bought the pet-food business. It left Bell with a sour taste in his mouth where Martin was concerned. Costello felt he could handle him. And so far he had.

Bell had written a book once, on Daniel O'Connell. It gave him a certain status with people who gave status to such things. He had an irritating manner. A kind of sanctimony that got up his partners' noses in cabinet. And he had a habit of pontificating. But that was fine as far as

Frank Costello was concerned. The man was useful in so far as he was useful. When they could get on without him, it would be adios. For his trouble and support, he had a whole department there to make him look good but Frankie Costello made sure the real decisions went all the way to cabinet committee. And that meant himself. Bell always got his say in, got listened to, but his minority position and the bad feeling between the parties made him vulnerable to Costello. And Costello could exploit vulnerability effortlessly.

"You'll have them, Derek. We would have waited if we'd known you were coming back. How was Brussels?"

"Lousy."

"Yes. All those bloody cogs. Jesus."

"There's a rumour circulating around out there that Ralph Martin is in heavy-duty dung out in the desert. Is this true?"

"Who told you that?"

"Is it true?"

"You're Industry, Derek, you tell me. You're supposed to watch these things."

Bell let his file slip onto Costello's desk. The papers fell out and some of them went onto the floor. Bell bent over and his jacket came up over his head and his shirt came out of his trousers, showing the cleft in his bottom. Costello nearly caved in and laughed.

"I'm making inquiries," Bell said.

"Good. Let me know what you hear. You have an interest there. But don't listen to those shaggers in that place, Derek. Overpaid spanners. How were they on the extra funding?"

Bell was still fiddling with his papers.

"Oh, thinking about it. Sitting on it. Debating. Deciding. Thank Christ, we're not sitting. Makes it so much easier to get things done. So that's not true, then?"

"What?"

"About Martin."

" Not that I know of. What are the papers saying?"

"His own are eulogising him as usual. Nothing in the others."

"There you go. He's a rough diamond. Probably just the competition trying to get back in the game. Times are tough. He's a winner."

"Right. Eh, those minutes, you'll send them to me?"

"Of course. Anything else?"

It looked as if Bell was trying to come up with something. Frank Costello broke the silence.

"Eh—Derek, I was thinking, better let me know immediately you find out what Martin's position is out there. We're exposed to him. Buck stops here and all. I think we'll have to have a meeting if it's true. So, give me a call with what you find."

He passed one last sheet of paper Bell had missed to the Industry minister.

"Ah, Paud!"

The piglet face of Paud Henry appeared at the door. Henry was a very pompous-looking man but his face gave him the air of someone who's either doing something wrong or considering doing something wrong. He was Frank Costello's lapdog. Had been for years. Always willing, never completely able. Which was why Costello kept him on a leash. He'd rung Justice and told Henry to get around from Stephen's Green pronto. Henry had dropped his midmorning snack. Some of it was on his double-breasted suit. The whole Government wore the same kind of double-breasted. The image consultants had insisted. Dark and serious and full of can-do.

Henry was there on the dot. Beaming smile, bouncing on his feet, big piggy cheeks red from the heat, thinning hair running with sweat. Costello figured he'd either run around or couldn't get out of his car. Paud always had difficulty getting out of cars. He was awkward and his size didn't help. Frank Costello had solved the same problem for himself by getting a bigger car.

"Hi, lads," Henry said.

His accent was midlands. You couldn't put your finger on it. Bell looked around and then back at Costello. He could see he was surrounded.

"I'll go then."

"Right."

"Brussels okay, Derek?" Henry asked.

As if he could have given a damn.

"Fine."

"Good."

All three looked at one another. The pressure was on Bell. There was nothing else for him to say. He had made his point. It was important to make his point. He was the conscience of the cabinet, he said. It made him feel good. Useful. Kept the supporters happy. Got him on the box for the right occasions. He was good on the box. Not as good as Larry Tallon. But good.

When he had gone, Costello signalled to Henry to close the door and then put his feet up on his desk.

"We'll have to watch him, Paud," he said.

Henry looked at the door and turned back to his boss.

"Sure, Frank. Being done already."

"I want to know who he puts on to Ralph Martin."

"Trouble?"

"Could be. Get me the name."

"Sure, Frank."

Costello smiled and folded his arms.

"So, Paud, any news?"

It was like pressing the button on a tape recorder. The Justice minister sat on Costello's desk and regurgitated the latest tapping information, slowing down at the salacious bits, taking it apart and showing each section to his master in great detail: journalists' love habits, radicals' cash problems, opposition in-fighting. At any one time the taps went into the hundreds. And Costello loved it. Not because he liked to hear stuff like that. Nothing like that did anything for him any more. But having Paudie there, giving it out, telling it like it was, all the grubby washing people wanted to keep hidden, all the rattling skeletons. Maybe it helped him feel clean. Reinforced that sense of right he felt.

And Henry moved awkwardly on his chair, gesticulating with his hands, grinning and giggling like a schoolboy at the ridiculous or the humiliating, particularly the humiliating, pulling one leg up and grabbing the knee in his hands, interlocking fingers tapping out a rhythm on the knuckles.

"I want you to put an ear on Phil Cassidy, Paud," Costello said.

Just like that. He was pulling a drawer open. To get an apple. He bit into it.

Paud smiled because he always smiled when Frank Costello asked him to do something. It took another while for the order to seep in.

"Phil?"

"Yes, Phil. Problem?"

Paud looked at Costello, and Costello's eyes shot out at him and bounced off his soul. It scared the shit out of him, that look.

"No."

"Make it special. You know. Separate, Paud. And everything straight to me."

"Of course. Department phones?"

"Yes. Everything. You know the drill. And we may need to go further. Would you do that for me, Paud?"

"Sure, Frank, you know me. Yeah, sure. Phil done something?"

"Let's say he could be losing direction again. It happens. You have no problems with direction, Paud?"

"No, Frank, no."

"Good. Like a drink?"

"Yeah, Frank, sure."

"I'll see you at about four. Call to the flat. We can talk some more. You know, we've done good in office, Paud.

Things are looking good. We were at the edge. We've pulled the country back."

Paud nodded. Paud always nodded when Frank Costello said something like that.

"There's more to do, much more, and it'll take tough decisions. Very tough. I can count on you, Paud, can't I?"

"Oh, yeah, Frank. Whatever you want. I'm always here. Always."

Henry stepped down from where he was sitting on the desk and almost came to attention. Costello looked his Justice minister up and down. There were welts on his back and Costello knew where and how they got there. But that was a trifling perversion. An indulgence which could easily be forgiven. God, you look old, Paudie, he thought. Is that young Paudie Henry, Moss Henry's son?

Moss Henry had ambushed policemen and shot up British soldiers for his first boss. Then he'd ambushed and shot up his first boss and his men for his second boss. The latter move proved better in the long term, though Moss and his second boss would never admit to being anywhere near the shooting the day his first boss was killed. Moss and his new boss took a day off to mourn Moss's old boss and then set out on the road to power.

In power, Moss went through eight different ministries and stayed long enough to see his son elected. Young Paudie inherited his father's eye for the main chance but very little else. If he hadn't tagged himself on to Frank Costello's rising star he might have remained just another nepotic hack who voted the way he was told and spoke a line a decade to keep himself in the papers.

Costello was going places. They all said it. Said it as if they knew where. It had a snowball effect. And once people had said it they didn't like to be proved wrong. So they made it happen even if it never should have. And at every stage, good and bad, Paud Henry was in the background. He almost ruined it for himself when he was starting out. Before the dad could get him elected. Got a girl pregnant. That was a hiccup. But she was paid off and her dad was appeased with a small council job and the whole thing kept out of the papers by a system that was so discreet you could not see it happen. They were good days. So much to do. And it looked as if it was going to get done. The world was right for doing it in. They wore flash suits, their own choice though, and they talked like men on the move, on the make, and everything was possible.

"What would you think of a snap election, Paud?" Costello asked.

Henry relaxed and stared hard at his boss. "Polls are good. Get rid of the flycrap."

Paudie smiled. Piglety. Teeth showed. Gaps in teeth showed. Tongue tipped teeth.

"How soon?"

"Few weeks."

"Are we ready?"

"We might have to be. We'll need funds. We'll need a lot of funds, Paud. And we'll need intelligence. That's where you come in, boy. Put the wind up them. I want to win the biggest overall majority ever. So solid we can stay in for a decade. Do what we have to do. It's us, Paud. We're the right party for the job. It's always been down to us. The others, they just make up the numbers. You know it's true. Your dad, the rest of them, they handed it on to us. We owe it to them, Paud. We owe it to the country. And I think they'll give us the mandate this time. No shit. No compromises. We play to win."

"All right, Frank. Yeah!"

"By the way, let's keep this to ourselves, Paud. I want you to prepare a plan. Action plan. How to make sure we get what we deserve."

Paud searched for more information. But Costello wasn't going to commit himself.

"Be imaginative, Paud. Remember, those who aren't with

us are against us."

This kind of talk had Henry almost wetting his pants. Just what Costello wanted. He brought his feet down from his desk and stood up. Henry went over to the window and looked out at the courtyard. Costello followed him. He stood behind him.

"Play to win, Paud," he said. "Play to win."

5

Kate Keyes sat reading a magazine, trying to watch the world around her. The problem page had a young girl complaining about difficulty in penetration. The agony aunt was recommending surgery. Kate felt a surge of sorrow for the girl. She stopped reading and glanced at the people around her, on other benches, sitting on the grass, messing with a cricket ball. She tried to figure out how many of them had things like that making their lives a misery. Or worse. But the shields were too strong. Whole universes of disappointment and frustration were held tight behind those shields. There was a screech of car tyres and some uncontrolled horn-blowing on Nassau Street. A tourist bus pulled away from the line on the far side of the wall. Kate cast an eye higher, towards the skyline, to the top-floor windows, wondering.

The girl in the magazine had a boy-friend she loved but couldn't love. Kate felt a pang stab her in the guts. They did everything they could to get close but they could not get as close as they wanted. He was understanding. She was distraught. Surgery was the best thing.

Beside Kate, a couple of young girls, who might have been students, except that most of the students would be somewhere else trying to earn a buck so they could be students for another year, burst into laughter.

She read some more problems and then tried to earwig

their conversation.

They were Spanish. Kate could speak tourist Spanish. Enough to get around, order drinks, ask questions of policemen and waiters. She could speak French too, much better, and German better still. Her Italian was worse than her Spanish but then she didn't much like Italy. Bad for the bum. She sighed. She wasn't having much luck with the earwigging. She told herself it served her right for trying.

All morning she'd been asking herself why she'd agreed to meet Jack. She'd promised herself she would not. Before she was certain she was coming home. In Brussels. On the plane. At the airport. In the taxi. At the flat. Then came the meal at Carl and Angie's and something unseen, something way beyond her, took over. A kind of release. And all the plans and resolutions vanished as if they had never really been there.

Two of the Spanish girls were calling the other a *cobarde*. The victim was reddening, if you could call it that on such an olive complexion. She had a weepy left eye and a set of teeth which did not look like they had ever made it from baby to adult. Kate had noticed this with Spanish women. She noticed a lot of characteristics of people around Europe while working with the Commission. All the things you weren't supposed to admit existed. Racial stereotyping. But all the political correctness in the world couldn't stop Italian men being pains in the arse or German women acting like surrealist girl guides. The Germans went around with a giant imperative rammed somewhere uncomfortable, she felt, that made them the way they were: dynamic, progressive. It didn't mind stepping on toes. But it always apologised afterwards. The friction was incredible. She could never understand what held it all together. In the end, all she could come up with was the money and the fact that it would be too difficult to tear it all down. So it ploughed along, pursuing ideals with a certain Stalinistic lunacy, employing policies that were so weird and indefensible no one dared query them. The emperor in his new clothes dancing to Beethoven.

There were good points. And she was in one of them. Environmental vanguard. Fighting to keep the green from turning brown too early—and the brown turning black and blue. Preserve something for the future. Not have her grandchildren asking what a fox or a salmon was. And on the fringe, at the rear lights, where the worst excesses she'd seen on the Continent had not yet happened, they could get in on the ground and do something good.

She went back to the magazine. To sort out problems. That girl should get some surgery.

The Spanish girls were picking up their shopping bags and the two who were calling the girl with bad teeth a *cobarde* were now pushing her forward. They were not as pretty as she was. Maybe that was a reason for their actions. Kate considered her own.

She should go. Go now and say she couldn't make it. Pressures of work. The work was deadlined. There'd be no lie in saying she had to shift down the country. And anyway, there was a problem. Possible interest conflict was the jargon. The Martin factory part of her investigation wasn't so cut and dry any more. One of the bits and pieces the great man had picked up on his way to the top. You could eat your dinner off the floor. And there wasn't a thing in it you could link to the dead animals. Pesticide had done that. Stuff so old it had been banned years ago. It was supposed to be just a report. But she was being sucked in. There were people hurting. There were claims and counter-claims. It needed more time. More time and more print. Eurospeak of Community realism. They were probably in breach of some Community directive or other. As far as Kate was concerned, being alive and breathing broke some EC directive somewhere. The thing was, no one was quite sure which one or where it was in the great book of directives. The built-in safety mechanism. It was just too big to move itself. Got other people to do its work. It just sat and contemplated itself.

She did a one-eighty with her head and saw no sign of him. She checked her heart and felt nothing special. But then there had been nothing special the other night. She'd known he was coming. Angie had told her, warned her she was going to say. But told her was enough. Given her a pep talk. No, okay, it's okay, Angie, I'll be fine. Water under the bridge. Then he was there and the gentle return of lost feelings happened during the main course and could be noticed during dessert. She had stopped drinking alcohol to slow it down but it was a holding action and there was nothing she could do. What do you do when that happens? When all the plans you have go down the tubes and you're left feeling what you don't want to feel? Story of her life. She could easily go.

When she'd told them she was going to meet him, Angie and Jenny had pinned her to the couch, surrounded her, coffee mugs and chocolate chip cookies, Roy Orbison playing on the CD, tell us, years of catching up, filling in. All that time seemed to shrink and she was so pleased to be able to play the part they had for her that she went through everything with them. Everything meant men. What man? Which men? Lots of screaming and excitement. Lots of looks which said more than any words could. Where are you going to meet him? When? It was accepted that Jack and Kate were an item. There was no logical reason for this. They had not seen each other for five years and if she had not been sent to do this report, another five years might have gone by and there would never have been any hint that they had once been together. But she was back and she had met Jack and Jack and she were linked, no matter how many other men she had seen or liked or fallen for, no matter how many other women Jack had felt the same for. She steered off discussion of Jack's love life because it made her feel too uncomfortable. But Jack had been out with Angie. Kate didn't know about the night with Jenny. Angie knew but didn't want to tell Kate, and Jenny couldn't bring herself to do it either. But they had a notion that a Jack-and-Kate connection was what should be and that was the way things were played.

Kate straightened her skirt and flicked through her magazine again. Rubbish. Glossy rubbish. But she loved it. She loved loads of things she shouldn't. Political correctness had worked its way into her consciousness more than she realised. She'd had a hint of it the other night, talking to a UN refugee bore at a cocktail do run by the Commission. Every line she spoke she vetted before it came from her mouth. As if a little censor were working overtime, editing and re-editing her speech. It was automatic now. Sometimes she sat back and asked herself what she was, what she had become: one of the PC clones devoid of any individual thought, spouting lines and spewing viewpoints, making sure the whole thing just kept moving, not for any noble motive any more, just for its own sake and for the sake of those dependent on it. Living the life of the endless papers and reports and seminars and studies, an academic thesis with no conclusion, cocktail parties and dinners with the right settings, no tempers, no flare-ups, containment, continuity, routine, a wonderful traditional dance that never seemed to end.

Kate flicked the magazine open again, at an article on women in power. As if women in power were any different from men in power. As if they brought some kind of gentleness to ruthlessness. Sure, they cut your legs off at the knees but they're very nice when they do it. And if they could succeed in squaring that circle, fulfilling the paradox? Magazine writers didn't go beyond the superficial. The glossy paper and the expert layout helped pass the time though.

She was seriously considering going now. Angie was telling her to stay. To meet him. Falling back into the couch beside her, they had just returned from a tour of the west and they were climbing the walls on sisterhood. Angie was the rock. Married and happy. In love. They used to scream about it. She was in love and married and happy. Like some kind of mining discovery. Eureka! Jenny was toying with moving in with this guy, Stephen, from Belfast, who was going to London if he could get the job he was going for. Stephen was dry and interesting but neither of the other two wanted her to get too close with him. They had their idea of where Jenny should be going. They had a few possibilities lined up. For her own sake and for theirs. And for Kate?

Jack was coming, hands in his pockets, strolling down the path from the Arts block. There was a tour behind him, with a loud guide who sounded as if he had been at a good English public school and dressed like someone in a Merchant-Ivory picture. Jack was not paying the slightest bit of attention. That kind of history and tradition thing bored him senseless. It was only for people who couldn't deal with here and now, he used to say. In museums and galleries he'd tap his feet and she'd have to elbow him and tell him to go have a drink or something and meet her later.

He was more relaxed than he had been at Carl and Angie's. Hennigans was a set-up for Jack, something to put him off keel, a clever way of bringing the smooth bastard back down to earth. People like the Hennigans never came out and said things like that, barely discussed it with one another and then only used guarded phrases. But they understood body language and always had an agenda.

He was better groomed than she remembered. His hair was styled now instead of just being cut, old-fashioned, but styled. She'd always been on at him to get it styled and he'd argued that only poofs got their hair styled. Secretly, she suspected, he'd always wanted to have it styled but his brash bigotry, or his image of himself, had stopped him while they were together. His suit was up a notch, from being very good quality to the very best; the jewellery too: Cartier watch, gold tie-pin. Subtle marks of quality. He had a well-balanced stride; it looked good when he was moving with his hands in his pockets. She examined his face and saw more hidden tension there than she remembered, even under the smile. It was well defined, his face, though you could see build-ups threatening where they usually did with men of his age, promises of deterioration to come. And his hair had the odd strand of grey, though she couldn't see that now; she was just remembering it from Hennigans.

The prospect of their being together got to her and forced her to swallow. She looked for another word to describe what they had been. Lovers came quickly but she was not comfortable with that. This was a reunion of old friends. They had been friends. She said that to herself and then looked around quickly to see if anyone had been listening. She wasn't sure it was true. If they had ever been friends. She went back through a list of things that denoted friends and came up with lovers again and dumped the discussion and watched him for the last twenty yards of his approach. His smile was broader but the hidden tension was still there. And something was missing in his eyes. But Kate was forced to ignore that and speak now.

"I thought you weren't coming," she said.

He leaned over her and kissed her on the cheek. It caught her a bit off guard and she was almost pulling away when his lips touched her. The touch of his lips coincided with a breath of wind. It felt good. She stopped retreating. He sat down on the bench.

"I got delayed."

"Big deal."

Jack didn't know how to interpret that. She had intended it to be ambiguous. She was a bureaucratic functionary. Ambiguity was her stock in trade. She did a quick, close examination. He did look good. For a guy who wasn't gorgeous, he looked fine.

"So, where'll we go?"

She shrugged, dipped her head and smiled. His answer to

her lack of decision would be important. There were about four places he could suggest which would tell her what he was thinking. Places they had always gone to, places where things had been said, places where promises had been made, places where another world with the two of them in it had once existed. If he suggested one of them, then she would have to take action. As it was, there was a nice familiar calm between them. Jack was leaning forward, his hands hanging between his knees, kicking some stones.

"We'll grab something in a pub," he said. "There's enough time before the lunch crowd get here. Unless you'd like to go have a full slap-up."

"On Martin?"

"Of course."

"Professionally not on, Jack. I'm not even sure I should be seeing you at all."

"Come on, Kate, you're looking us over for pollution, so what? We get that kind of thing all the time. This agency, that body, this pressure group. Wide-eyed and sprouting leaves. Clear up, don't chop, fungus rules, okay! We manage. We have a forward policy on the environment. Last year we gave at least—"

He held himself short.

"Well, we gave a lot of support to environmental groups and projects. You won't find us lacking."

"Right, Jack. Let's leave business behind. We'll have a bite and a drink and just talk. We haven't seen each other for five years, Jack; we must have something to talk about. Unless you'd rather we didn't."

"No. I want to talk."

"All right."

They talked. They spent about half an hour wandering around the Grafton Street area, trying to find a place to eat, but neither could agree where to sit down. It became a kind of power-play game with them after a while. Each of them doing down the other's suggestion. At one stage, they bought apples and stood watching buskers dressed in monks' habits play skiffle. There was no animosity in their struggle: it was just that neither was going to give in and the more they disagreed, the more they felt they had to disagree; and so the game took on a momentum all of its own, distinct from what was actually happening.

What was actually happening was they were enjoying each other's company. They kept their distance and their dislike of suggestions for places to eat was based on logic rather than pure feeling, each one coming up with several good reasons why the suggestion should be shot down. Food, price, crowd, hygiene.

"How about we skip town?" Jack said.

They were running out of steam. Kate could see that. It had reached the stage where the next place, even if it had served cold pigswill, would have been fine. Her legs were hurting. High heels made you look good. But there was a price.

"Johnny Fox's."

Kate felt her heart beat again. Inspired, she said inside. She held back approval outside but capitulated after some thought. Jack took it as a sign of victory. She didn't care.

They talked outside Johnny Fox's, over smoked salmon and brown bread and glasses of Guinness, with a good afternoon sun and surrounded by open space that stretched on out into the mountains, bog-skinned and heathered, pine-treed and ferned, green turning different green, so many you could not count. They had hiked here before, once, as kids, so long ago it was hard to believe they had ever done it. That day had ended in tears but they didn't go into that now. They talked about about Bolivia instead and the farm.

Jack had found a company selling land at next to nothing. He'd it all worked out. Kate had sat there, eating her sandwiches, listening to him spell it out: what they'd grow, what they'd husband, how much they'd need to put in at first, how much they'd make in their first year, all the bits and pieces of going into business, two kids planning a kind of empire. She'd wanted to watch the birds. And the clouds. And maybe they had kissed. Neither could remember. Depending on the way they were feeling, they had kissed or not. It was negotiable.

Over their glasses of Guinness, they retraced steps carefully, as if they were treading on some delicate surface that might break up at any moment. It was becoming one of those not-meant-to-happen meetings which turn out to be very pleasant in the end. It could have been a quick drink. Jack had asked her to meet him for lunch, not knowing what it meant. More out of curiosity than anything else. Residual affection had not managed to assert itself and pieces of the jigsaw that had been their life were still missing. That was not a problem with him. He was unsure of how he felt. He liked the idea of there being some distance between them. Something to keep it safe. The sense of fresh start gave him something to aim at. As if they were on a first date. And it had the difficulty of a first date. There were various misunderstandings and awkward pauses and a lot of underlying tension.

He wanted to ask her so much. Questions were queuing up to get their tuppence-worth. But he held back. He was in uncharted waters and he held back and let the couple of hours they were supposed to spend together grow into a whole afternoon and when it came time for dinner they just ordered more fish and coffee and more beer and kept talking. Neither of them wanted to stop.

"Is there anyone special?" she asked him.

That should have been a simple thing to answer, only Jack wasn't ready. And he looked at her as if she'd broken some agreed rule of engagement. Fragments of what they had been presented themselves to him in a jumbled mess and he sucked slowly on as much air as he could inhale. The answer was straightforward. There was no one. There had been no one for some time. Except the odd randy wife. He'd had three of the company wives. But none of them had meant anything more than a pleasant release from tension. He could have told her there had been no one that had come near to her. But he wasn't in the mood for truth; he was just having a good time, not in the mood for admitting distasteful things. She should have known not to bring all that up.

"Not that I know of," he said.

In an instant, the whole thing had taken on a new urgency, and Jack was not sure if it was the realisation of what he was looking back at—like the light of some great star which takes years to reach the eye—or whether he had had too much to drink and the way she looked and moved and let her hair fall and the way her lips touched one another and the lines of her body and all the thousand and one things that go together to make attraction had stirred him. But he was stirred.

"Would you know?"

"It depends."

"On what?"

"On who it was."

"On who it was?"

"I'm slow on the uptake."

"Yeah, Jack, sure."

Slow. Jack Clarke slow. He had her in bed the same night they met. She reconsidered that version of events. It was a stupid way to phrase it. The wolf versus Red Riding-Hood version. They went to bed the first time they met. But that wasn't true either. They had met when they were kids. They went to bed the first time they met after she had gone away and come back. It got more confusing every time. That night was clear to her. She would have liked to have said she was drunk but they had drunk nothing. She would have liked something to protect herself from the raw emotion that it revealed. The power of it had overwhelmed both of them.

She suffered still from symptoms of the view that women didn't really, or weren't supposed to, like or want sex. That it was something to be put up with, something men needed, something unclean they had to have and part of a woman's duty to her man was to give him that. At least it was in some sense under control that way. And despite everything she had tried, that way of looking at things was always there with her. She left them in bed and drank some more Guinness.

"It's a stream, Jack," she said after a long silence.

"What is?"

"Down there. Crossfin. The Martin factory we're looking into. You can see the Slieve Blooms. Runs into a tributary of the Shannon. The water they say you polluted. Killed all their livestock. Ten cows."

"I thought we weren't going to talk business. Professional etiquette."

"Right."

Jack couldn't resist hitting back.

"We've had our own people down there and they say there's no proof of any pollution by us. Some kind of pesticide, was it? There's a dozen farms around there. Ask. We run a tight ship there. They're weirdos anyway. Some kind of cult. Jesus knows what the hell they're giving their animals. Come on, Kate."

"They're Hare Krishnas."

"Weirdos."

"Terrific, Jack. Always the tolerant one. Tell me one thing. When you get it all, what then?"

He opened his mouth to speak. Rolled his tongue. This was what he'd loved about her. This kind of conversation. He couldn't get it with anyone else. He stopped himself making the reply he wanted.

"Who said I wanted it all? So I'm ambitious. Is that wrong? I want the good things of life. Is that wrong? I want to be able to say 'fuck you' to people, Kate. To do what I like.

You tell me you're not ambitious. Look at me and tell me you're not ambitious. You may not earn as much in a year as I do in a couple of months, but you're still out for the same thing. To be the best. To be heard. I know what I am, Kate. Do you know what you are? You cover yourself in degrees and nice Community titles and you go around making yourself feel good, feeding from the gravy train, doing what you're told, saying the right things, using the right knife and fork. When have you ever had to make a decision which would cost you your future, your job? Come on. I do what I do and I take the heat."

"I think maybe we should get back to small-talk. How's your father?"

"That's it, Kate, patronise me. Look down on me."

"I don't."

"You do. It's easy to look down on people from an ivory tower. Academia does that to you, Kate: gets you nice and insulated so you can make objective analyses. Well, that's a luxury I don't have. Sure, we fight hard. Ralph Martin fights hard. We're in to win. There are no runner-up medals here. And we have people depending on us. Thousands of them. You know. It's dog-pack country out there, Kate. We're up against it. Against people who have subsidies and kickbacks and favours and we're expected to play it all above board."

He stopped himself short and reached out with his hand for hers. The alcohol had more of a hold on him than he had thought.

"Don't, Jack."

She pulled her hand away.

"Never to meet," he said.

"Doesn't look like it, Jack."

On the Vico Road, the BMW parked half into someone's gateway, with a clear view of the Sugar Loaf and Bray Head (one hundred thousand quid's worth of view, Jack said; he liked to express everything in cash terms) Kate picked wild flowers and stood beneath a For Sale sign on a Victorian cliff dwelling with turreting around its roof and a price tag running towards half a million. Period piece, the brochure said. Then there was a bedroom count and a list of rooms which had become extinct in Edwardian times. Finally, the view. And that was done to death by the copywriter.

She was going to have it. She told him. He stood beside her and watched her assemble the flowers and make them into something you might sell. Small insects hovered around the edge of the trees to their right and they could feel the heat rising from the road. There was a lawnmower going somewhere and a motorbike was heading back into town.

"I'll buy it for you," he said.

She did not reply. She walked on, further down the road. He waited. He wanted to follow her but he waited. She did not look back at him.

I don't know what you're doing here, he thought. I used to dream about you calling me or knocking on my door. I used to hope Jenny or Angie would talk about you when I was there. But they didn't much. And you never called or turned up at my door and I let you slide. And now here you are. Walking thirty feet ahead of me and I'm not sure you're real.

"Will I see you again?" he asked.

She was leaning on a wall. She tossed her hair and looked up to the sky. A couple of gulls were circling out at sea and there were swallows returning to their nests in the trees behind her.

"I don't know, Jack. I have work to finish. We shouldn't really. I'll be working hard. Maybe after."

"It's a nice house."

"Yes, it is."

6

The answering machine clicked on again with a sharp tone and Jack Clarke put down his phone. He would have sworn except he was under his duvet and the unearthliness of it and the sweaty smell of his body made it seem like too much of an effort. He didn't want to come up for air. He figured he might last maybe an hour before a build-up of carbon dioxide and methane would get him. Maybe he'd get some sleep then. It'd be too late. He'd had his chance and blown it. Daylight was breaking through all around him, forcing the room to show itself. He listened to himself breathe and tried to work out how long it would take. It was a fruitless exercise.

Half a bottle of spirits and some heavy-duty sleeping pills had given him about two good hours' sleep. He could feel his body in overdrive, heart pounding against the wall of his chest. God only knew what his eyes looked like. His hair was sticky. Bad night sticky. His mind was racing around, particle physics style, thoughts appearing, disappearing, reappearing, bouncing off one another, smashing each other to bits, fusing, all out of control. His mouth was a combination of a sandpaper and glue, in equal proportions.

Where the hell was she?

Three days he'd been ringing. She'd said, yes, they could meet again. Right at the end. As she stepped from his car. A quiet unconcerned yes. His mind raced from trying to figure out how many times he'd rung to wondering whether she'd actually meant it. Meeting like that. Beer and food made you say things. Maybe she was just saying it to humour him. She should have been back by now. He'd thought about ringing Roy Doherty in Crossfin. See if she was down there. Doherty managed the operation there. He knew very little about computers but he did some useful jobs with packaging that Jack didn't want to go into. But Doherty was Alan Kennedy's man and he'd spill to Alan Kennedy and Kennedy would spill to Ralph Martin and Jack didn't want Ralph knowing he was connected to anyone investigating Martin companies. Ralph had a built-in paranoia about investigators. Customs, Department of Industry, European Community—they'd had them all in at one time or another, complaining, warning about fines. Ralph Martin dealt with all of it the same way: arguments, legal threats and Frank Costello.

Jack had rung Angie. He'd rung Carl really but Carl wasn't there. Angie said he should hang on, not to rush it. Not to rush it! Five bloody years and she turns up with the roast beef and strawberry soufflé and he's supposed to play it cool. Jack tried to get his mind off her, on to something else. Business. Out of the frying pan into the fire. Larry Tallon was going back out to the desert. Frankie Costello's decision. He was sure Larry could get something. And something was better than nothing. For image. Image mattered a lot to Frankie. Maybe Larry'd twist arms. Get the lot. Jack didn't think so. It was something he'd seen, in Larry, in himself, even a hint of it in Ralph. He wouldn't admit to it in Ralph, though. But he had to face up to it in himself. His confidence was buckling. Maybe he was just too tired. Before this, he would have been perfectly confident that Ralph, Larry and Frankie could have pulled off anything, but now things were tightening. Again, nothing you could put your finger on, just a trend.

The Britcop thing should have gone through by now. But people were unwilling to commit. Committee members bought and paid for changing their minds. Talking about taking a poison pill. The greedy bastards wanted more. He'd seen the poison pill thing tried before. An American drinks company they tried to take over. They just swallowed debt till Ralph backed off. It was crazy. They were a good company. But they got it into their minds that Ralph Martin wasn't having them. No matter what the price. They never recovered. Folded a year later. But this lot were different. Just talking about it. Greedy bastards. There were five of them. The damn value of the co-op had been falling for a year before Ralph made his bid. They were fat and lazy. But they had outlets, scores of them, and you couldn't get that kind of outlet space for anything near what Martin was offering from scratch.

He left the British and went back to the Gulf. He hadn't had much to do with the Arab end of things for a while. Ralph Martin handled most of it himself. It was sensitive. It was dangerous, too. Jack had said it to him before. That it was dangerous. Megalomaniacs made bad customers. Everyone else had pulled out. The British and the French had only ever sold for cash up-front. Give them credit and they give you a load of promises. And not a cent. Wogs, Jack thought. He launched into a full frontal attack on Arabs, a reserve of racist vitriol, hidden beneath his liberal southside veneer. Then, when he'd worn himself out, he just said it was Costello's problem. They'd have to cough up if the desert boy welshed. Simple as can be. And there was no way Frankie could do anything else. Martin was his golden boy. The Martin plan was Frankie's personal project. His name was stamped all over every PC they sold. He laughed and the laugh got squashed by the duvet. He couldn't wait to see how they explained this one to the punters. Not his problem though.

His problem was Kate. It was busting his guts. It shouldn't have been. It should have been so easy to have lunch with her, talk, discuss mutual interests, say goodbye, maybe arrange for a drink, fit each other into busy schedules, avoid discussing contentious issues, but that wasn't the way it had gone. She'd buggered off on this bloody green crusade and left him having one-way conversations with her answering machine. With computer music and a cartoon character inviting you to leave your name and message.

Jack decided that he hadn't time to wait around for the carbon dioxide and methane. And he didn't want to. Too strong a desire to live.

He pulled the duvet off and fresh air replaced the gathering carbon dioxide and methane. He reached over for his watch. Six. An hour to get into some kind of shape. He was usually up at five. Bed at one, up at five. Four hours' kip if he could persuade his mind to stay still long enough. That always involved pharmaceutical help. He sat up and examined the room.

The bed was low and latticed, for his back. He had a gammy back from when he'd fallen from a horse near Enniskerry. Something had popped out or been squashed or maybe cracked and knitted badly. He couldn't remember. It wasn't a big thing then. But it was giving trouble now. There were clothes lying across a one-piece chair. More in a plastic washing basket in the corner. Underwear on top. The dressing table was crammed with after-shaves and powders and lotions and a million-and-one other new-man essentials. He wasn't much of a new man, but he took what appealed to him and threw away the carrot juice and emasculated babysitter image. A couple of weights lay on the floor near the washing basket. Bars and dumbbells. Exercises. To strengthen his back. He was fit. Could do fifty press-ups without feeling too bothered. Looked good for it. The right muscles showed the right way. Nothing too ostentatious. But when he stripped off, women looked again. He touched his stomach and felt the solid mass of muscle.

Carl shouldn't have done that, he thought. Shouldn't have just brought Kate along and said nothing. He blamed

Carl because Carl was someone he could blame. He felt superior to Carl. Carl was fine as a friend but the pecking order dictated by their relative salaries and position said that friendship was fine but Jack was doing better. And doing well sold tickets. Made you a star. Got you enemies. The number of enemies you had gave you weight, clout. Like notches on a gun. Particularly if you got one over on them. Jack allowed himself to feel good. The sandpaper and glue receded for a moment.

Everyone liked Carl. Liked Carl and Angie. Everyone's grand couple. Do anything for you. Salt of the earth. Jack felt the sandpaper and glue returning. He couldn't stand that term. The reason everyone liked Carl was that Carl never did anything to anyone. The Hennigan practice was one of those nice little family firms that dealt with other little family firms and never really had to go out there and mix it with the best of them. They settled for a quiet second best and were content and derived a certain prestige among their peers for being old and reliable and respectable. Solid as a rock. No threat. Jack was considered a shark. People nudged one another about him. One or two threw punches at him in Baggot Street pubs. He took that in his stride. Envy. That was all it was. Healthy envy. From people who couldn't expect to live up to their expectations. The whole country was full of people like that. And they got their rocks off slating the few who lived up to and went way beyond their expectations.

But Carl knew his place and was respected for it. So Jack could respect Carl like all the rest of them, for what he was, and he could be angry with him too, for what he was not. Maybe that was why they were friends. Carl was his only male friend. He juggled with that and tried to contradict it. But it was true. Andy Wright was Carl's friend. Anyway, he was going. Any other friends Jack had were women. And they had a common thread. He'd been to bed with all of them. He wondered what Carl thought about that. Probably discussed it with Angie. Probably agreed that it was before the two of them got together. Probably said it was in the past. He resented that in his friend. His ability to let bygones be just that. Jack used to kick up shit with Kate over her other lovers. The jealousy just got into him and wrapped around his emotions like a weed. That was what all the fights were about. He'd wanted to possess her totally, own her completely, there was nothing else he would accept. And the fights. Enough crockery thrown and broken to stock a department store. As if she'd had dozens of lovers. Maybe three if you counted someone named Richard in Chicago one summer. Carl would have dealt with it. Taken it in his stride. Carl didn't want to own the world. Jack wanted everything.

But Kate was supposed to accept him. That was different. He was a bloke and blokes could do it without it meaning anything. Angie was an infatuation. Young stuff. Experimenting. So were the others. Kate had been willing. To overlook the times he'd gone off when they were together. For the conquest. It was always for the conquest. Like a precious stone. You have to have it. It didn't take away from his love. He'd loved her just as much. But he had to have the ones he wanted. You only lived once. And Jack always found willing partners. Girls he could sweet-talk. He had that skill. To play them where they were weakest. It was savage to watch. Uncaring. Though he never had a complaint.

He was back massaging his ego. He pulled the curtains and the birdsong got louder. His flat was on the third floor. He could see Howth. It was so clear he even thought he could see people on Howth Head. There was a boat heading out to sea and another coming into port. The out-to-sea boat was lower down and had more gulls around it. The into-port boat had rust stains on its side and Cyrillic lettering on its stern. Traffic and train noises competed with the birdsong. The sunshine swept through the whole landscape of neat gardens and solid Edwardian real estate and gave it all a golden tan. He could see birds digging in the sand about two hundred yards away and a jogger bent double by a Martello Tower, blowing out the excesses of the night before. He opened his window and the bay breeze, a kind of saline after-shave, touched his face and cleared what needed to be cleared in his head.

It was coming to him now, what hadn't come to him before, what he'd been searching for. The sick feeling of knowing someone else had touched her. It should have been easy to accept. To reverse. She'd touched them. She'd had her fun. But Jack didn't look at things like that. The way Carl would have. For Jack it was an attack on him. Those bastards. They'd touched her and had her and it all ate into him and he was back throwing things across a room in temper, Kate in her dressing gown, sitting on the bed, crying, pleading with him to stop. He slammed the window shut.

Laughable really, he said to himself. He kicked a towel which lay on the ground up into his hands and headed for the shower.

He was in a shirt and trousers, squeezing an orange for juice when the phone rang. A jet of citrus hit him in the eye. He dropped the half of orange he had in his hand and reached for a tea-towel. Then he rushed into the bedroom to the phone even though there was a phone in the kitchen. He fell on the bed, still rubbing his eye with the towel.

"Where the hell have you been?"

He recognised Martin's voice immediately. The bloody thing came out of the phone and grabbed his ear and nearly pulled it off.

"I've been trying to get a hold of you since five. Since five, Jackie."

"Sorry, Ralph, I was using the phone."

"What the hell were you on the phone for at that hour of the morning?"

Martin wasn't in the humour to see the irony in his words.

"Personal."

"What do you mean, personal? You don't have a personal life unless I say so, Jackie boy. I pay you to be there when I want you. I pay you to be at the other end of my phone. I pay you to do what you're told."

"Yes, Ralph."

"It would be a bloody miracle if you'd heard it."

"What?"

"The news, Jackie. Don't you switch on the satellite channels? Even put a radio on. The news."

"No."

"Marvellous. Well, for your information, our friend in the Gulf has just been toppled in a coup."

"What?"

"Yeah. Him. Several thousand well-armed fundamentalist gougers woke him up last night and shot him. I'm listening to it now. You should try it, son. Jesus, Jackie, I put a lot of effort into you. I saw potential, Don't let me down."

"No, Ralph."

"Right, get in here."

Kate Keyes left his mind in an instant. It was a general clear-out. She was just another excess load he could not afford to carry. It brought him down from wherever he had drifted during the night and locked his feet to the ground. A kind of objective silence surrounded him. As Kate left, his first thoughts of them in bed together followed with her. The first time he had managed to bring them to the surface and now he had to drop them. But importance had a realignment. Kate was suddenly devalued. Bottom had dropped out of love and love-making, and even thoughts of love-making, suppressed, re-emerging, had to go.

Coups were difficult to deal with at six in the morning. Jack had a neighbour who claimed he'd been overthrown in some ancient kingdom by extraterrestrials. Said he spoke to them at the travel guide section in Eason's. Out of his head. But loaded. So he could afford to be out of his head. Poor and out of your head, you're crazy and pathetic and probably better off incarcerated or dead; rich and out of your head, you're eccentric.

He was rushing around his bedroom trying to find a tie. Coups card-indexed their way through his consciousness. He turned on a bedside radio and messed with the dial. Martin was exaggerating. This bastard killed people just for looking at him the wrong way. It was a few raging soldiers firing a couple of shots at each other, exchanging words. Your mother is the product of a cow and a pig. Your father sucks camels for a living. He left the radio and grabbed a tie and tried to get it round his neck while he plugged the television in and found the right channel. The knot came out wrong and he had to do it again. Shifting sands, he thought.

Jack had seen the shifting sands routine himself, years ago. When he'd been to Iran for Martin. When he was still climbing. In the middle of a war. Selling to all sides. They were the new kids on the block. Ralph Martin just wanted export sales. Business was business. Except there were hidden charges. Jack's mind was straying where it shouldn't. He held back.

Young kids holding AK47s too heavy for them and carrying the keys to Heaven. Jihad smiles and death in their eyes.

Yes, always yes. We can. We will. The best system you can get for the price. All the usual lines. And the usual cast-iron Government guarantees with Frank Costello's thumbprint on them. Ministers queueing up to put their tuppence-worth in. They didn't mind acknowledging Bobby Sands then. For the sake of a good contract. First thing they said to you in Tehran. Bobby Sands. Thumbs up and Bobby Sands. Tallon had sung rebel songs at a get-together. Very Iranian get-together. Minerals. Respect. Very solemn and spiritual. Rebel ballads allowed, though. Tallon was good at that.

Then they produced a picture of Larry doing his thing with the opposition. Faces changed. Jack thought his bowels would empty on the spot. Larry had to backpeddle like crazy. All Jack could think of was those kids with Jihad smiles and death in their eyes. He had changed money on the black market. He couldn't explain why. He couldn't have spent the money in a million years. They got out with a review of present contracts and a favour owed for any future ones. And Jack gave his black market stash to a beggar. Ralph Martin hit the roof and then smiled and said the Iranians would be back. Favours was the key word, he said.

It was true. The television had said it, and now the two-piece slip in your pocket digital tracker car radio was saying it. The new men were accusing the old man of treason. Something to do with an oil well and a strip of desert he'd given up at the end of his last war. They wanted it back. Commentators were talking in solemn tones about shifts of power and the spread of fundamentalism and war. Women dressed in black and young men firing automatic weapons would be filling the television screens.

Jack drove into Dublin way above the speed limit and told himself he was in the right because there was an emergency on at MartinCorp and an emergency at MartinCorp was a national emergency. They should have provided a motorcycle escort, he felt. But there was nothing much on the road anyway. Only a few late-shifters going home and maybe a few other people with emergencies of their own.

Jack's mind was going through all the possible plays. The bad side didn't stay long with him. He couldn't allow it to. Not without Martin around. So he went further. Maybe it would mean a bloody good war again. With the Emirates and Saudi thrown in for good measure. And after the mess, MartinCorp could supply everyone. There was that chance. Long-term good. And if these new boys were planning a war, they'd be out shopping. Shopping needs trolleys. Jack's heart pounded, You did what you had to. The fellow in the beret had always been on the look-out for hi-tech trolleys. Always had a special shopping list. Smart war. Television had made smart war sexy. Computer-guided missiles that knocked on your door to check if you were the intended target. Jihad smiles and keys to Heaven had nothing on integrated information systems and total solutions. That was MartinCorp's strength. Always willing to adapt to the particular circumstances. Neutral in the best possible sense. Jack's spirits rose when he was passing the RDS. There was a couple holding one another at the railings, maybe kissing, he could not tell, but holding one another in an embrace. One they meant. You could tell the ones who didn't much care for each other from the ones that did. It was the way they held each other. As if they were the only two people in the world. That train of thought jammed something in his exit chute, something that had been ditched as soon as the order had come in from Martin to report for action. Jack kicked at it to try and dislodge it but it was caught. By the simple sight of two lovers holding each other in the early morning sunshine.

Jack switched channels to a rock station, wall-to-wall oldies and plenty of feel-good factor. That was what it was all about. Maximising feel-good factors. Feel-good to feel-bad ratios. Jack fiddled with the dial again and moved from one feel-good offering to another. They sounded the same.

He had turned into the MartinCorp underground car-park when the realisation hit him like a punch after a dozen jabs. He'd been their biggest customer. By a long shot. And everyone knew about the Martin contract there. No matter what happened, no matter what bloody cash Frank Costello supplied, there'd be jumpy bankers on the phone, asking questions about their readies. Bankers were just like that. First sniff of trouble and they were jumping ship. Had to be calmed. Frankie Costello'd have to calm things. Insurance first. More guarantees to bankers. Then wait and see if another deal could be done. And it would screw up Britcop. Bound to make them think twice about being taken over. The sweeteners would have to be bigger. More money. It all cost. The knock-on effect. Jack felt his heart trying to push its way out of his body. The sinking-ship feeling he rarely let in paid him a quick visit. It lasted until he got up to Martin's office.

"I've had four banks on to me already," Martin said.

Alan Kennedy sat across from Ralph Martin with his head back against the wall. There was a bookshelf at his shoulder. He was holding a blue file.

"Frankie Costello will pay up," he said. "All we have to do is calm things. Don't let it get out of hand. We're going to have the press on to us in an hour or so, Ralph. I'll handle that. Dan Meehan's getting something ready. We have stuff to go in our papers. Play down the exposure."

"I'll see Frank Costello this morning. We're going to need immediate payment. Maybe you should have a few selected hacks out to lunch. Dan's place. It's nice and cosy. Play it cool. I'll make sure nothing comes from Merrion Street. Thank Christ for summer holidays. It's a holding action till I can sort out the insurance cheque. Otherwise Chairman Flanagan and his popular-front loony lefties will be sucking blood from us. But it's only a matter of time. Jackie?"

"Yeah?"

"Well, what's your pitch? Our main export customer has been murdered without paying us. I thought you might be able to enlighten us. You know, give a where-we're-at statement. That big gap we have. Borrowings against commitments. Frankly, I don't think we're going to see a red cent now. And we've not just lost the cash; we've probably lost the market. So we need money. Jackie?"

"Eh, right, I think that's right. Best thing. Get the insurance quickly. Get someone to rub the banks up the right way. What about Britcop?"

"Indeed."

Kennedy knocked the wall with his knuckles. His shirt sleeves were rolled up. There was a tattoo on his forearm. Some kind of dagger and lightning bolt.

"It could come back at us. Drop us in it, Ralph. And we're wide open if this gets out of hand. If we don't shore up very quick then I think we should quietly withdraw, to lick our wounds. The thing now is to get the banks on our side and get the insurance cash out of Frankie. Then we can decide what we're going to do."

"No bloody way. I want them. We're going all the way. You hear that, Jackie. You keep on them. Right to the end."

Jack nodded.

"Ralph!" Kennedy said.

"The press'll go for us, Ralph; they'll run with this," Jack said.

He did not know why he'd said it, except that he felt he was shrinking. Right in that room, with both of them, under their gaze, he was shrinking, and inside he could only think of his own stake in Britcop—his reputation was tied up in the deal—and of what would happen if they had to withdraw their offer, of what would happen to him. It was blocking his moves and Jack Clarke was a mover. What else had Ralph Martin seen in him?

"Getting the jellies, Jack?" Kennedy asked.

He showed his yellow teeth to Jack, as if to demonstrate something. Like a made man signalling his superiority to someone who hasn't made his bones yet.

"We get this kind of shite all the time, Jack, all the time. We'll handle it. We handle everything. Thing is to keep business moving, keep money coming and sort everything out with minimum fuss."

Jack was going to ask what he should do but he thought he'd better wait for Martin to issue orders. Martin was cutting a piece of cake with a penknife. Into slices. He broke the slices in two and then placed three of the pieces in his mouth and chewed. Jack watched the action of Ralph Martin's mouth while he chewed.

"I want you here," he said to Jack. "I want everyone on call. You do your business from here. We play it nice and slow. Till we see which way it all bounces. I'm having a party next week and that's going ahead. This should not be a major problem if Frank Costello lives up to his end of things."

He picked his phone up and stood up.

"Right, I'll see you two in an hour. I'm going to see Frank Costello. Alan, get Dan to prepare a press pack on our friend Flanagan in case he joins the battle. Where is he sunning himself?"

"Italy, I think."

"Should be bloody Siberia. Jack, you get hold of our people. I don't care where they are. If they're in Marbella, get them on the next flight. If they're doing constituency work, I want them chauffeured up. I want bodies and I want voices. Alan, ring the computer plants. Tell them it's business as usual. Tell them to prepare units for shipment and then get back to Jackie when they're ready. Don't say where they're going; just make it look like we're shifting a million of them. Tell Dan to mention South America. Barney Small will know what to do when that's done. You get in touch with him once the plants have contacted you, Jackie. And I want you here, son. You're to stay here all day. All night if I need you. Clear?"

"Yeah."

"Right, off you go. I'll see you before I go, Alan. And, remember, get those bastards up here, Jackie. I don't pay them to sit on their backsides."

Jack Clarke limped back to his office ahead of Alan Kennedy, like a convoy ship returning to base badly damaged, his confidence deflated, his mind desperately trying to clear the decks for action. He made coffee and took some pills and poured water over his neck and began ringing and thinking.

It had been a rug on a floor with furniture pushed to the walls. A large rug on a carpet with Chinese designs. And they had lain there, apart, touching, hands first, fingers. He wanted to keep the memory with him but it was already slipping away. Fingers found one another and bodies mirrored movement and lips touched and kiss sought kiss and hardness excited wet and wet made hard harder. Then closer, together, words of love and urging spoken, tenderness in slow syllables, scent mingling with scent, oneness. And in, wide open, accepting, willing, in, come in, a sudden shudder, words again, of love and comfort, of gentleness and caring, up and in and tongue found tongue and teased, touch to touch, all body now in motion, faster, slower, rippling pleasure pushing, pleading, short of breath, hunger digging, flesh in flesh, now faster, faster, going out, out further, out of control, love words mixed with short breaths mixed with moans and urgent pleads and all dizzy, loving dizzy, dancing, twisting, spinning, drifting...

He let go before the climax. He could not have stood to remember the climax. The sheer ecstasy of their climaxes, the incredible togetherness it brought to him, the being in love. He was alone now. He needed to defend that. The memory vanished.

7

He liked the house because it never changed. It was solid. Something he could anchor himself to. He did not tell anyone this. Men in his position never told anyone they were scared, no matter how scared they got. But once he was inside, he could pull down a few screens and come down through the gears and be our Jack or young Jack and have his mother tell him to do things in the kitchen and his father complain about the state of the greens at the golf club. The house was a reflection of a soul, such as it had been, caught somewhere, in a time warp, fixed, almost waiting for him to return. But Jack Clarke never had.

So it served as no more than a reminder. A gentle palliative. A conscience panacea. A mausoleum to lost dreams. Maybe that was what houses were. Or became. Because they didn't ever start out like that. But the years and the disappointments gave them a museum atmosphere. Mausoleums to wannabeeism. Stocked with wannabee relics. Jack Clarke didn't stray too far down that road. He reserved deep thought for short bursts of anger and then ditched it for something more gratifying and less demanding. He had never been seduced by thought. A mistress with the power to turn you to stone. Jack went into his classics for a reference but could not remember one. Classics had been forced on him. Business, he chose.

His father was in a chair in a room with a huge sideboard

made of mahogany. It was full of cut glass and silver, inside, behind the doors. Most of it still in the boxes. Sometimes his mother would pull out a piece and tell Jack it was for him when they were gone. As if to prove something. She had pictures on the sideboard. Of her. Of her husband. Of Jack. Of the three of them. Some of them were fading, the colour already vanishing. Twenty-year-old photographs of some casual happening. But his mother could get an hour out of it. She had reached that point in her life when all there was was past. The future held nothing more. It was not a sad thing. She delighted in the past. And despite their ups and downs, it had been a fine past when you weighed it up. It took some creative memory-accounting to come up with that conclusion but with a dying husband and a son she saw maybe once a month, it was possible for her to commit heavy-duty memory fraud and not get caught.

Old Jack had a smell about him. And his son could not figure out where it came from. It was a staleness. It was only noticeable in that house. His breathing was like the sound of a squadron of tanks passing over gravel. He was frail in the worst possible sense. A kind of grey had wormed its way into his skin, and each time Jack saw him, he seemed greyer. Maybe his father was being turned to stone by his thoughts. Maybe that was what they meant by stone-faced.

It was okay. The line was secure. Ralph Martin was holding it. Doing what he did best. Using contacts. Meeting people who owed him or wanted to meet him or wanted to owe him. He had Frankie Costello's style in that. Or was it the other way round? They'd hit the banks first, with reassuring noises and Government voices, more forging to cast the guarantees they already had. Frank Costello, Larry Tallon, even Paud Henry at one stage. Then they got the drop on the press opposition. It was silly season and the coup had everyone jumping around so much they didn't give much time to what was happening over at MartinCorp. Dan Meehan and his "selecteds"—that was his pet name for his own private press corps, payola jocks who'd write anything for a down payment on a time-share—got the boot in first.

Jack had worked his grid. The Britcop deal was still on the rails, maybe slowed down, but the takeover ground was laid. He'd slept in the office a couple of nights. On a camp-bed. Thought of Kate, too. Thought of Kate more than he slept. Tried phoning her again and came up against her damn answering machine and its cartoon put-down.

It was good it was happening in August, Martin said. Sitting in his high-backed chair, feet up on his desk. Good because the boys who could really make trouble were off on the Med, working on whatever you worked on on the Med. Jack admired Martin's calm in the face of the storm. It was the calm of a man who expected to win. Expected to fight but expected to win. Jack Clarke just followed orders. Insurance, Martin kept saying. We're covered. All the time. Kept repeating it during conversations, like some kind of trip-wire in him sparked it off. The insurance was their trump. And Frankie Costello was going to cough up, the lads had made that clear to the banks. Jack just wondered. Two hundred and fifty million. Martin talked as if it was a simple cheque away. And no one questioned his reasoning. If it had been two hundred and fifty billion, they'd have acted the same. All eyes on Martin. Just thinking about it all made Jack Clarke draw breath. Thinking about it and Kate made him want to get away. For the first time. He could not explain it except that he had to get out of there, get off that phone. Time to lick his wounds. Time to think.

His father was reading a paper and chewing on some grapes, spitting the pips into a bowl on a small glass coffee table beside him. His father still had all those habits which used to drive Jack up the walls as a kid. The embarrassing ones. To someone like Jack, who liked to be perfect in everything, the slightest infringement into bad habit grated like chalk on a new blackboard and set his teeth on edge. It was always the small things he got caught up on. Never the whole picture. He was constantly blaming his parents. Never outright. But underneath. Passing responsibility on to them. It was a subtle shift. It helped him survive with Martin. It had helped him survive Kate.

Kate had been on his mind all week. And when he couldn't get hold of her, he drifted into a study of what had gone wrong between them earlier. It wasn't an impartial objective study. Jack still wasn't at a stage in his life where he could contemplate an equally shared blame, if blame was the right word. He looked for what she had done. Twisted the whole play into her court. His dad had liked her. His mother had thought her a bit stand-offish. Cold. But then mothers had a secondary motive when dealing with sons' girl-friends. There was always a subtle fight going on. Oedipus, move over.

He should not have been troubled like this. It was not in the plan. It was eating away at him. Jack had always been a self-confident man, fixed in his views and with a reinforced determination, a complete careerist, lacking any doubt, who believed that if he played it right he would get what he wanted. The result of a sheltered existence if he examined it. Despite the graft he had been involved with. He'd always been protected. At school, they told him exams were the way forward, so he'd worked his arse off and got the points. Then he had to get good results at college to get into one of the big city practices. The course was always laid out. He'd gone from school to university, done the business there, gone from there to a big practice, done the business there, and from practice to MartinCorp where he was doing the business, just following the rules. Whatever rules were laid before him, he followed. If Jack Clarke was honest with himself, which was asking a bit much, he'd never made a difficult choice for himself in his life. There was always a cushion of insulation around him.

"I see your man's dead," his father said.

Jack was sitting on the couch beside him. Wondering how all this trouble was building around him. He fell back on his economic circumstances for reassurance. Money. He was doing well. People said he was doing well. Sole determining factor now, money. Didn't matter how you got it, once you did you were doing well and to be doing well was the thing. Times when discussing money was vulgar had disappeared with the dodo. It was too scarce a commodity to have any hang-ups about. Camels were queuing up to jam themselves in the eyes of needles.

"Who?" Jack asked.

"Him."

His father pointed to the business section of the paper. MartinCorp were mentioned. It was good press. It was one of Martin's papers again. They always referred to him as Dr Ralph Albert Martin, his full name with some honorary doctorate he'd picked up in America tacked on. Martin insisted on that. Jack searched for the supposed dead man. His father had a fixation with the dead and the dying. He would spend hours on the deaths column, learning off the details, and then recite them back over dinner. Made for quick meals and silence from his wife. Jack gave up looking.

He wondered if his parents were married in the traditional sense any more. Or of they were just together out of habit or duty. Maybe both. He desperately wanted to ask his mother if she still loved his father. But he could never have dealt with the answer if it wasn't the one he wanted. That was Jack. Avoid what you can't deal with. Deal with what you can't avoid. He had avoided dealing with his bust-up with Kate. She had walked out on him in his mind. Simple physical function. People left him all the time. Jack never left people; they left him.

He watched his father turn the pages of the newspaper and read on. There was so much he wanted to talk to him about. So many intimate things he wanted to know. But there was a barrier and they would never cross into each other's territory: it was not possible for either of them; it was against their nature. So they would continue to sit with each other and talk about things that did not matter and old Jack would refer to things that his son could not understand and the comedy would go on, both of them trapped by it, orbiting each other, until the old man finally gave out.

If he and Kate didn't really love each other, it was not a case of them falling out of love. It was probably a case of the reason for their love having gone. All love had a reason. Sex. Mutual need. Money. Loneliness. Maybe all of them. Jack was convinced of this. It was a pure economics view of life. Based on the laws of supply and demand. There was no room for the irrational. What seemed irrational on the surface always had a rational motive. All actions were essentially egocentric. There was nothing bad in this, he thought. Most egocentricity had a mutual benefit spin-off. It was in the interests of egocentric individuals to keep an eye out for what went on around them. But the base motive for that too was egocentricity.

His mother never opened the presents he gave her. Just left them in their boxes alongside the vegetables in the annex to the kitchen. I don't know how to use that, Jack, she'd say, or, we get on fine with this, you shouldn't have bought it, there was no need. There was always an excuse. Like she just would not be beholden to him. He was determined to get them back up and they seemed determined to stay down. Their wants never really bothered Jack. He knew what he had to do and he was going to do it whether they liked it or not. He was going to restore his family to where it had been. He was doing everything for his family. Except that his mother and father did not acknowledge his help. That made him want to scream more than his father's dying.

"Peel those, Jack," his mother said.

She passed him a bowl of spuds and a peeler. She was a handsome woman, his mother, maybe five years younger-looking than her age. But with good posture and a gentle manner. That gentleness was a superficial thing, Jack thought. He made sure to peel the spuds the way she liked. She had a way for everything and that was the only way in that house. She had the air of a woman who'd spent most of her life as an unwilling spectator. As if she'd have have preferred to have been somewhere else. Jack felt her thoughts drift out the back window to a bird on an apple-tree which hadn't born fruit that year. She could talk about apple-trees and fruit and birds and a hundred and one things. But what she said had no impact. Nothing she did ever seemed to have an impact. She had a master's degree but never used it. The house was littered with holiday brochures but they were never going to go anywhere. It wasn't because they had no money, and anyway, Jack could have helped, but you just knew anything she did would have no conclusion.

"He's well, today," Jack said.

"Yes, he's very well. Maybe he can get a game in on Saturday. If he's better. I think he'd like to get a game in. Ask him."

Jack was digging deeper into the spuds than he should. He saw his mother's eyes watching him, locking on to his movements like radar. He expected some kind of reaction soon. Was that what their lives had reduced to? The possibility of a game of golf? Jack hadn't the insight to realise the arrogance of his thoughts. He went on. Did they talk? He tried to think back to the last time he had visited. He could not remember them talking. Maybe they had not talked for years. He didn't know. And not knowing made Jack more scared. The slippery self-assuredness was always gone at home—he always called the house home though he hadn't lived there for seven years.

"Kate's back in town, Mum."

"Who?"

Jack stopped himself explaining. Five years, he thought. How was she supposed to remember? Like most people, Jack had an idea that the rest of the world followed his life like a saga. Kept notes of all the characters in it, well, the important ones anyway, and Kate was about the most important he'd ever had. The only one he'd ever said, I love you, to. Including the woman standing next to him and the man in the room with the pictures. They knew Kate. They knew Kate's family. But his mother still said, who?

"Well, she's back," he said.

"You look tired, Jack. You should take some time off. Go somewhere. Get away from it."

Get away from what? Jack felt like a paint stripper who every time he strips away a layer of paint discovers another underneath. And there seems no end to the stripping and the discovery except that every layer is the exact same colour.

They had a set-up here, he said to himself. He was at the gate. They had eaten lunch, he and his father, and his mother had eaten in the kitchen, watching a daytime soap. You eat with your father, I like my soap, she said. It was persuasive stuff. She sat there and he obeyed and carried a tray in to his father who was asleep in his chair, his head to one side, dribbling from the side of his mouth. He had missed the hairs at the side of his mouth when he shaved. Said he couldn't see them any more in the mirror. Bits of him disappearing before his own eyes, he said. Jack nodded but did not get the meaning. He was on Kate again. It seemed as if every time one of them wanted the other, the other wanted something else.

One of whom?

Jack looked at his watch as he ate his soup, folded a buttered roll and shoved it into his mouth. His father watched him and broke his own into small pieces.

"Can't manage that, son," he said.

It was like watching the last breeding pair of some kind of endangered species. Shy and timid, not really too interested in surviving, maybe gone beyond that, maybe already dead, just waiting for some expert or government department to confirm it. He wanted to scream at them, tell them to wake up and get out there and do something but he was not able. The best he could come up with was to ask his father if he was going to play golf on Saturday. His father nodded. Said he would if he could. There was no more interplay.

He had been beaten up once, outside the gate. He persuaded himself there was still some kind of stain there. The shades of the concrete helped him create the illusion. Warmth and wind brought back the day. An exhaust day. He could smell the car fumes. They hung on the air, thick like dollops of sour cream, and he had just stepped outside the gate. They were waiting for him. They'd come from somewhere else. Knackers like them always did. Knackeraguans. From the inner-city terraces or the sixties flats or the carbuncle concrete toytowns on the west side of the city. They had short hair when no one wore short hair and they looked like they never washed. Their accents could cut razor wire and they moved like fighting was all they ever did.

Straight across the road at him, five, maybe six, of them, right into him with the boot, no messing about. Into the stomach and down he went. Into the stomach again when he was down. Then into the mouth. Two teeth immediately. He was talking five or ten seconds. They made no attempt to take anything. They just kicked the shit out of him and went off down the road, laughing, looking back at his heap on the path, cursing at him. And Jack had just lain there, not feeling anything, not the broken teeth or the eye which looked like an overripe plum or the lip which was swelling up to his nose. He was afraid.

He stared back at the patch and had a couple of thoughts about it, nothing substantial.

His father had come out. Come out to the gate to see what had happened. But he did not come through the gate. He spoke to Jack from behind the gate. Are you all right, son? Who did it, son? Get up, son. The first two gave way to endless repetitions of the third. Get up, son, what will the neighbours say? You're making a show of us. And Jack could not get up. Eventually his father reached out and grabbed his leg and pulled him into the garden and along the little path to the porch. The two teeth remained for three days out on the road. Jack could not pick them up. On the fourth day, a dog ate them.

Jack strolled along the road with his hands in his pockets. It was a road of well-kept gardens and painted railings. There was a cancer hospital and the noise of a car alarm and a barking dog. All under a crescent moon in the late afternoon sky. He wandered on and bought cocktail sausages and chips in a chipper and ate them in his car, licking the salt and vinegar from his fingers when he had finished everything else. He picked up his car phone three or four times to ring Kate's number again but he could not bring himself to do it. He did not want any more disappointment. Instead, he went for a drink and had three or four and watched some sport on a big screen from a satellite channel and listened to other people talk about their troubles. Back in his car, he rang Molly and said he was held up and told her to hold everything for tomorrow. She didn't believe him, he could tell, but he did not care.

The evening paper, another one of Martin's, had a piece on the takeover of Britcop. It was all proceeding well, it said. Things should be finalised within a couple of weeks. The MartinCorp offer had been more than generous, pundits said. They had good pundits. Economists. High priests of the free market. Martin paid well for their blessings. He had big plans for Britcop, they said. The Britcop committee were anxious to have the thing done with one way or another. They were still studying. It didn't mention trips to Birmingham and Manchester by Jack Clarke. It didn't mention numbered accounts in sun-soaked islands. It didn't mention the leaning. It didn't mention the acquisition of confidential information. It didn't mention the electronics in the Britcop committee room. Ralph Martin played to win.

The right people in the right places and the wheels began to move with their own momentum. Probe the weak links on the board: there were always weak links, men in debt, men with ambition, men whose sexual habits were considered abnormal. Ralph had it all. It needed one more push and the whole rotten mess would fall over. And the minute he got it he was going to fire half the staff. The place was hugely overstaffed. Jack had seen it before. The press statement that all jobs were safe, the follow-up visit by Jack or Alan Kennedy. Hi, we're from head office and we're here to help. Then wham, the redundancy notices. On a Friday. Out now. Slick as a striking rattler.

He felt arrogant in a good sort of way, thinking about it. All the sycophancy that would follow. The first fellow to come up and shake your hand without a good reason was the first out. That was a Martin rule. Then look at their waists and the stupidity of their titles and their expense accounts. It was fun. Like passing death sentences. Call them in for a talk individually. Watch them sweat. Some of them could sweat a reservoir. You knew everything. But you made out like they should tell you. And you made notes. Some of the stories Jack had heard from bastards trying to hold on. About what they did. Always smile.

Jack sat in his car for a long time before starting up. He went through all the petty added extras: the anti-lock brakes, the power steering, the suspension features, the fuel injection, the whole one-up feeling it brought to him. They'd done it. They'd held off the challenge. The cavalry was on its way. Costello and his lads. Prompt payment of the insurance and a quick takeover of Britcop to follow. He was writing the statements himself now. The Britcop business would help cash flow. Good supermarkets, and supermarkets made cash and cash was king. Jack opened his top button and undid his tie.

"Kate," his mother had said.

He was going out the front door after saying all the things you were supposed to say.

"She's a nice girl, Jack."

He looked back at his mother. She had a potted plant in her hand. She was caressing the leaves. Her cheekbones caught the reflection of afternoon light in the frosted glass beside them. It was a complicated geometrical route for the light, but it did something to her and made her son feel a glow inside.

"Yes, Mum," he said.

"Is your dad going to play on Saturday?"

"I expect so. Ask him."

He looked at his watch and told a lie.

"Listen, I've got to get back. Up to my neck."

"You always are, Jack. I'll put some water on this."

She took a look at some other plants around the porch.

"You know what you're doing, Jack."

He thought for a moment it was a statement but then he wasn't sure. He turned to go and she said something else which he didn't pick up. He waved from the gate.

Back in his office, Jack studied a file on a British politician he had to grease down. It was an easy job. The man had debts some countries would be ashamed of. He had two wives and a mistress. It was for the move into Britcop again. Another push. A way of making sure that things got done quickly. Without fuss. Martin wanted all the ground prepared. The Britcop business was only the beginning and he wasn't keen on having anything like bureaucracy getting in the way. So it was Jack's job to iron out current creases and anticipate future creases. A little more subtle in Community countries than in Africa. In Africa it was all very open. You just paid the top man what he wanted and a cut of everything else and everything happened. No problems. Whole towns got moved if you wanted that. Just so long as you paid.

The move for Britcop was the first step in a series of

megamoves, into Europe, into the States. The targets had been lined up, the torpedoes were being armed, the battle orders were being circulated. The disturbance in the Gulf would be sorted out. If necessary, a new market could be found. There were always other markets. Other countries needed good systems at good cost and on time. Martin could guarantee it all. And he had men like Jack Clarke to see it got done.

Jack read through the man's details with a degree of superiority he did not deserve to have. But then Jack Clarke had a way of containing unpalatable things and reinforcing prejudices. It was his armour and he didn't intend to give it up. He even had Kate waiting for a call from him now, but he was too busy, he would call later, when he had the time. He took something that made his head relax and brought a lake-like calm to his body and he laughed to himself and read the file through.

8

Ralph Martin never said anything of consequence over the phone. He had seen too many transcripts in his career to put any trust in the phone, even with the most sophisticated sweepers available. Anyway, he had men like Alan Kennedy and Jack Clarke to take care of most of what needed taking care of. Ralph Martin was a master of the three Ds: discretion, disinformation and distance. Jack Clarke said he was so careful that he didn't even tell himself what he was up to, that instead he used codes and euphemisms, words that could get the meaning across and satisfy his belief in himself, that got what had to be done done and helped him carry on with the day-to-day detail of keeping MartinCorp afloat. It was a war footing he adopted, which allowed any residual morality to be suspended, for the greater good. This was the Martin vision. It had appeal. To Frank Costello. To others. Martin was no cheap grafter. The vision had a plan and the plan used the vision and its associated mythology, a parallel support system, something to take the strain. And it enabled him to make decisions outside the normal framework of business practice.

There was a school of thought expounded by Martin in lighter moments of his career, in off-the-record briefings with hacks whose loyalty he could depend on, that all business was essentially immoral. Charging more for a product than it was intrinsically worth. After that transgression, everything else was just an extension. Once you accepted the first premise, it was simply a matter of how far you were prepared to go. And only the very strong could go the whole way. Martin liked to think of himself up there with the very strong. He got a kind of self-satisfied kick out of being out ahead, fresh air, he called it himself, away from the stale odours of mediocrity.

He was good for the quotable quote, Ralph Martin; good too for the funny anecdote. Martin could hold an audience of a thousand spellbound. And yet he had a contempt for all around him, for the system he worked in, for his competitors, for the people beneath him, the little men, he called them, the ones who fed like fleas off his back. He hated them the most.

A young reporter asked him once what his political philosophy was. He said pessimistic communist. The young reporter laughed and looked around to see if the joke had worked. No one else was laughing. Martin went on to explain that anyone with any kind of brain would see that sharing and co-operation were far more productive activities than competition, that any rational being preferred harmony to discord. The reporter was busy scribbling by this stage, pushing his shorthand to the limit of its endurance. Then Martin ended the lesson by saying that he was pessimistic about the rationality of mankind and that so long as the law of the jungle was the one preferred by the majority out there, he would play along and eat as many of them as he could. He patted the young reporter on the shoulder and told him to print it like he'd heard it. The young man tore up his notes.

It was a lie to say Martin was a bootstrap merchant. Jack Clarke and everyone else said it but that was their way of getting something on Martin. An attempt at getting even for his ruling most of their lives. That rule was one of the things leaning heavily on Jack Clarke now. One of them. He could not place it in a list of importance.

Martin's family were never anywhere near rich. There weren't many rich Catholics in Dublin before the Sixties. There weren't many rich anybodies. But young Ralph went to college when it was not a normal progression. There was money from an uncle somewhere along the line too but no one knew much about it. It didn't matter. Once he'd started, it was Ralph Martin who made things possible for himself. Took the opportunities. He got on with the right people. Got them to do things for him. And essentially that was what he'd been doing one way or another all his life. Some he had to pay, others he had only to ask. Martin made a point of boasting that he never used his own money to start anything. Not quite true, but it had an element of truth. Like everything with Ralph Martin. It was the element that won the point.

He made a lot of money in the States although not as much as people said, but more important, he made contacts there. Ralph Martin had learned the importance of contacts from his father, Todd. Todd was a small-time tradesman who managed to become a union official with a lot of work, a lot of graft and a hell of a lot of contacts. And Todd passed his expertise and quite a few of his contacts on to his son. It was helpful that young Ralph could run well. Running at the Olympics got him international exposure and it was concentrated the way it never could have been if he'd been a team player. He was charming, too, though now, in his fifties, you might be forgiven for asking what all the fuss was about. But Ralph Martin could pull women and favourable headlines in equal numbers, and he knew how to manipulate.

It was the beginning of times when a sportsman with a brain could do things for himself if he played his cards right. Even a sportsman without a brain. Runners had to because they were going to get shag-all from the sport. And Martin moved as well off the track as he did on. Plenty of high-profile positions, plenty of photo opportunities, plenty of drinks and plenty of brave-new-world statements, all the new dawn...let the word go forth...stuff that went down so well in those days. The country needed faces. Ralph Martin was one. And Frank Costello was another. Fresh faces, out of hibernation.

But Ralph Martin never stayed anywhere for the sake of it. When he had sucked all he could suck from the state sector in Ireland, he left. There was a blaze of publicity there, too. He said there was no freedom for the visionary. Across the Atlantic, his kind of self-salesmanship fitted in beautifully to the hyped mentality of corporate America. The investment houses liked the headlines he brought them. Good-quality copy, in the right journals. They got him more though. Bank confidence and stakes in companies that made everything from chocolate to dishwashers. America lasted only long enough for him to make his pile and get some high-profile banks on his side. He never liked the place, he said. But it was useful.

Those who said he was just a money-grabbing son of a bitch misunderstood Ralph Martin. If it was just money he was after he could have stayed Stateside. But there was more. He was just another blow-in over there. And things achieved didn't have the same meaning. In order to satisfy himself, he had to go home, to make it among his own, not just big but mega, be the best at home and then branch out. But it had to be started from home.

There was one part of Ralph Martin's success that he never admitted to. His ego would not allow it. He probably knew deep down that it was a major factor but the myth he had created squashed it out of existence.

Luck had a bad taste.

But Ralph Martin had been lucky. In the right places at the right times. Things had gone his way. And in the way of luck and success, more luck and more success followed. There was a self-perpetuation about it. But he liked to think it was all down to him. Any luck was made. Deserved. And there was no shortage of people to believe him, to conspire to keep luck out of the equation. Those who looked up to him, needed him as an example, many the very mediocrity he despised, did not talk of luck when they spoke of Ralph Martin. Instead they talked of strokes and good business sense and ability. But there was always luck there, and luck is that wonderful invisible substance which keeps the universe in a state of balance. If it goes against you nine times out of ten, it finally has to go with you. The reverse is also true. Now Ralph Martin was finding that if luck hadn't left him, it wasn't as good a friend as it had been before. Problems were beginning to multiply faster than he could meet them.

He had stopped the rot setting in over the Gulf mess for the moment. But the mad ass in the beret hadn't paid and his successors weren't going to pay either. So Martin was still massively exposed. He needed insurance quickly to shore things up. The banks were calm again, staying with him. Frank Costello had personally guaranteed that insurance would go through by the end of the month. The ship was stable. So all he was left with was closing the Britcop takeover and finding new business for his computer operations. And who knew what would happen in the Gulf? Threats, counter-threats, troop movements, it had a definite momentum. And new wars brought new possibilities and changes of mind. The thing was to be afloat and moving when things happened and Ralph Martin was both, he felt.

He was reading some projected figures ahead of a meeting with Britcop committee members when the door of his office burst open. The force of the opening nearly took the door off its hinges. Martin swore and pushed his seat back to the wall behind him.

"Ralph!" Dan Meehan said.

Meehan, a pencil-thin man with skeletal features and the most sunken eyes Martin had ever seen, was at his desk, panting for breath. Sarah was at the open door, a look of disordered distress on her face. She had had no time to stop Meehan entering. He had stormed past her and gone straight through, nearly smashing his aquiline nose into the door. Martin was already standing up, as if to counter Meehan's forward move. Sarah was wondering what he would say to her. It was a thing of his, no one got into the office unless he asked for them. That meant everyone from Alan Kennedy down. Meehan's lower lip was quivering and he was contorting his thin frame as if he had a severe pain in the gut. He waved a sheet of paper at Martin.

"We're finished, we're finished," he said.

Martin took a look at him and then drilled Sarah.

"Shut the door. No one in."

He grabbed Meehan and shook him.

"What the bloody hell is this about?"

Meehan was still waving the paper in his face.

"This, this. I just got it this morning."

"What?"

Meehan was in no state to be coherent. Martin got him by the jacket and shoved him against the wall. Martin always prided himself on being a calm logical calculating man, but he had a temper that could kill if it was let loose on the wrong person. And at that moment Dan Meehan looked like he might be the wrong person. And what he told Martin made it even worse.

"He's not going to give it."

"Who? What?"

"Derek Bell. He's going to withhold it. I have it here. It came in to my office. One of our people in his department. First he's going to suspend it, then he's going to investigate us. They're saying we've been in breach of EC and UN embargoes. Smuggling. Fraudulent exports. A rake of charges like that. That it invalidates the insurance. The bastard. The bastard's been looking for a way to do us, Ralph, and now he has. Finished us right off. Right off the pitch."

Martin let Meehan drop and Meehan almost fell over but he managed to right himself and hold on to the piece of paper he had been waving under his boss's nose. Martin grabbed it and read it.

"Is this reliable? Can he do that?"

"Yes, he's the minister in charge. We'll be getting official notice of the investigation in the next couple of days. That bastard's had it in for us, Ralph. You know that. I said it. I said it before. I said to Larry Tallon and Frankie Costello that he'd try something. They would have to give him that bloody portfolio. Why the fuck couldn't they give him something else? Why the fuck...? Why the fuck...?"

"Is it out?"

Meehan walked away from him, to the window.

"Is it out?"

"Out? What do you mean, Ralph? We're fucked."

Martin went after him and threw his hand out in a full swing. It caught Meehan across the face from behind and knocked him against the bookcase between the windows.

"Look at me, Dan. Look at me. Get a hold of yourself. Is it out? Has he released it to the papers?"

Meehan was holding his face, feeling the glowing sensation in his face pass to the plan of his hand.

"I don't know. I don't know."

"Shit. They just keep coming; they just keep coming."

He walked over to his desk and scribbled something.

"Right, you'd better get yourself into some order, boy," he said to Meehan. "You're going to earn some overtime. I want a meeting with the lawyers. You schedule that and get back to me. I'll get hold of Frankie Costello and sort this out. With any luck it won't get by him. Frankie won't let this go by. Not with Bell. He can't stand Bell. I'll bet Frankie doesn't know. Do you know if this is due to be announced publicly?"

"I can find out."

"Good. I'll sue the bastard clean."

Martin sat down at his desk and pressed his intercom.

"Sarah, get me Frank Costello. Ring his home. Get his wife. She'll get him. You got that? And get Jack Clarke back. Molly'll organise it."

The whole morning Martin's mind was in overdrive, calculating, counting, working out projections. He had a meeting lined up with Frank Costello for lunchtime. Costello had been down the country, opening a factory. The factory was a Japanese job, assembling pieces for machines that would in turn be assembled into bigger pieces in some other country that would in turn be made into whole units somewhere else. But no one knew where that was going to be. Not that it mattered, what mattered was the news of the few jobs and the publicity and the couple of minutes on the "Six One News." Costello only did the good stories now. Anything distasteful and he sent reliable Larry Tallon out to battle with the opposition.

Costello nearly fell over when he heard the news. He'd had no idea it was coming. His first inclination was to kill Paud Henry on the spot for that. Henry's taps on Bell and his department should have picked it up. What the hell was the point in having people on a job like that if they didn't pick shit like that up? It was essential. To steer his coalition partner in the right direction. But this. Without him knowing it. Costello swore he'd have Paud Henry suspended by his balls from the GPO.

Jack Clarke was in New York, arranging for two members of the Britcop committee to cast their proxy votes in favour of a Martin takeover. Martin had a ceiling offer he wanted accepted at a certain time. It had to be timed and the right people had to be persuaded to go for the deal. The whole thing was complicated: any grease payments had to be hidden, so a series of front companies, nameplates and offshore holdings, had to be set up to throw any official who might get a scent of what was on. So long as the deal was kept tight, there should be no problem. So long as it was kept tight and people were generously reimbursed for their work. Small members, little people who trusted Britcop committee members with their votes, well, they were so much chaff and the wind was blowing strong.

Jack was eating a slice of pizza near Times Square when his pager sounded off. Two cops beside him made a move for their weapons. Jack grinned a boyish grin and wiped his mouth with a napkin and went to find a phone.

The problem built up its own head of steam while Frank Costello and Ralph Martin met in Costello's Wicklow home. Built in the 1850s, it had about three acres of gardens, all designed by Costello. It was made from Wicklow granite and had the hardness of the stone in its façade. Nothing ornate or decorative on the front of the house, except creeper which tended to cause damp. But Frank's wife loved it so they put up with the damp. It was an impossible thing to heat in winter and a beautiful rainbow of colour in summer. The Costellos had a flat in Dublin 4 for the season, which included most of the winter. The house had belonged to Rita Costello's family. Frankie was a city boy. The house had been in her family for two generations before her, her family being well-to-do grocers before the supermarkets came along and made well-to-do grocers redundant. It didn't much matter to Mrs Costello; her family already had the money they needed and she had her eye on Frankie Costello. Naturally, her family disapproved. He was a gutty. Inner-city. They were genteel folk. Naturally, she married Frankie.

Martin drove himself to the meeting. He always drove himself to meetings with Costello. He liked to keep their relationship as private as possible. Meetings never lasted more than an hour. And they were never seen together. When Ralph Martin's father died, Frank made a phone call instead of appearing. They were not friends in the traditional sense. Martin hated politics and Frankie Costello thought Martin spent too much time behind his desk. Costello had grown to like good things and wealth but he considered them tools of patronage rather than anything purely economic. He had a greater view of himself, chieftain-like, surrounded by splendour, dishing out favours. The only problem with this was the country he was attempting to do it in. Pissarse, he used to say. People like Ralph Martin were supposed to change all that. He found himself cursing Ralph Martin. But only for a moment. He needed Martin, he needed Martin's money. The party were desperate for the kind of cash Martin could provide and the economy needed him thriving. It was as simple as that. Martin was too big to let fall. Not without giving up power. And Frankie Costello wasn't about to do that. Over dead bodies, he used to say.

They sat in a period drawing-room with French furniture and a marble fireplace. The piano was Japanese, though. Frank Costello sat upright. He had a weak back which had a habit of slipping out of place. Ralph Martin leaned into him and they talked in low tones. Each of them had a small glass of sherry and Costello was smoking.

"It's in his hands, Ralph," Costello said. "He is the minister in charge. I wish to hell you'd told me all the facts before."

"You're the bloody Taoiseach, Frank. You going to let some little nothing tell you how to run this country?"

"He has someone. Someone who's making allegations."

"Who?"

"I don't know. I thought you would."

"I'll find out."

"Is it true?"

"What?"

"You were sanctions-busting. These are serious charges, Ralph. Guidance systems, chemicals, surface-to-air missiles. Is it true, Ralph? No bullshit."

"We had contracts. We won them against tough competition. You do what you have to, Frank. You didn't ask me this when I gave you jobs to announce and factories to open. Everyone does it, Frank. We made no extra money out of it, I can tell you that. What the hell does it matter to us? We're a neutral country. We have no strategic interests. So why the hell should we toe the line just because the big boys decide someone is a bad guy? Someone they were selling every sophisticated piece of machinery they could to when he was on the good guy list. Look at Iran, Frank. When we went out there, we had to do it in secret. Everybody hated them. Then the Yanks come and ask us for help in shipping a few spare aeroplane parts. The same guys who told us it'd come down hard on us if we did business in Tehran a couple of years earlier. It's true what they say, Frank, there's no morality only interests. We did what we had to. I won't say any more. You don't want to know any more, Frank."

"Shit, Ralph. Shit. I just wish you'd told me. We signed agreements. It's bad enough the Americans know we've done business over there before. The way this new regime is mouthing off, they're likely to push for a whole string of sanctions. We won't even be able to sell them bottled water. Jesus, the way Washington is spinning you'd think your friend was a fucking saint. It's a bugger."

"You think I don't know, Frank?"

"Yeah, but chemicals, Ralph."

"German chemicals, Frank. I didn't ask what he'd do with them."

"It is a bugger though. A bloody nuisance."

"We live in an international market, Frank. It's difficult enough doing business without having bastards like Bell screwing us up. If he goes through with it. If the banks see this, well, you can kiss goodbye to MartinCorp, Frank, you understand. They'll take us to pieces. You want to see someone kick people when they're down, you just look at your average bank. They're the best in the business. They'll have us up to our eyes in flash-suited accountants, Frank. And then they'll start asking questions. And the questions will come back to you, Frank. Shut him up, Frank. Do what has to be done."

"He has me over a barrel, Ralph. The bollocks has me by the short and curlies. And it's not just him. I've problems in the ranks. Phil Cassidy's been sounding out the troops again. There was a meeting. I know who was at it. He's saying it's time I was on my way."

"You've had that before, Frank, and you've seen it off. You'll see him off. Anyway, Phil's in on this. He won't try anything now."

"I'm sick of his disloyalty, Ralph. It's no good having people in the team always pulling against us. We'll have to do something about it. Him and Derek Bell."

·· "And I can help, Frank. Listen, I know Phil. I know what he does, I know what he likes. I know his problems. And he owes me. So we can shut him up quickly. And we can make sure you win the next election and get this bastard, Bell, off your back. All high and mighty. I'm telling you what I told you then, Frank, you should have told him to fuck himself. Him and that shower of liberal wankers he calls a party. Jesus, they fuck me off."

Martin leaned back. He rarely used language like that.

"Look, Frank, you and I know each other. We can do something together. Something good. We're this close to the Britcop deal."

He demonstrated with his hands.

"Jack Clarke's over arranging last-minute details. Just that bloody close. Then it's into the really big league. Up there with the best in Europe. Us. Food, drink, media, hi-tech. The future, Frank. And inside ten years, Frank. We did all that. And now this bastard wants to hang us out to dry."

He waved his hands about.

"You'll go on this one, Frank, and believe me, maybe not now but later, they'll get you. We're too tightly linked."

Costello shifted his body to ease the pressure on the side of his back which was hurting him.

"What do you suggest?"

Martin rubbed his bald scalp. He took a deep breath. His eyes were wide open.

"What have you got on him?"

"Derek Bell?"

"Who else?"

"I'm ahead of you, Ralph. I have Paud Henry coming over in half an hour."

Martin tightened his expression. He had never met Frank Costello with anyone before. It wasn't that he didn't know the Justice minister, even though he didn't like him, it was just it was a break with tradition and at that moment in time breaking with tradition gave Ralph Martin a bad feeling.

"You should have told me, Frank."

"Paud's loyal."

"I know but—"

"We have to use what we can get, Ralph. And Paud's my eyes and ears. You realise this can only come under national security."

"Of course. I won't say any more. How long before Bell makes this known?"

"He says, a week or so, maybe. I've had to play along with him. Make him feel I'm with him."

"Jesus!"

"He could walk out. That'd mean an election."

"Good, I'll pay for it. I'd put a bloody contract out on him if I thought it could be done in time."

"I didn't hear that. And I don't need an election now. And I definitely don't need one on his terms. That would kill us."

"Just get him off my back and get me my money, Frank."

"I'm going to. He may not have any weaknesses, Ralph."

"We all have weaknesses, Frank."

"And what are yours?"

Martin smiled.

Paud Henry had run from his car to Costello's door. Rita Costello had answered. Paudie'd had the hots for Rita and her red hair and blue eyes for years but he barely kissed her this time. It surprised her. She usually had to fight Paud off. He left her lipstick intact and raced on into the house in his shirt sleeves, his underarms soaked and a long trail of damp down his spinal column.

"Worst case scenario?" Costello asked him.

He looked at Martin and brought some saliva to his mouth and cleared his throat before answering.

"You'd have to sack him, Frank. Then we'd have an election. It would sure up-end Phil Cassidy if nothing else. He's talking about having you gone by Christmas and having the poll maybe spring next year."

He passed Costello a transcript of two of Cassidy's phone conversations with what Costello termed the unsound wing of the party. Costello read the first and passed it on to Martin.

"Forget Phil," Costello said.

"Worst case scenario would be an election," Henry repeated. "Then we could—assuming we get the majority— then we could give insurance. Or work out some other deal. It'd be messy, Ralph. We'd come under fire. Lots of it."

"I'll go down the Swannee if we don't stop him. I'm open to any suggestions. I'll back you all the way in a campaign. Whole bill down to me. Name the price."

Costello was reading the second transcript from Cassidy's phone. He looked up and moved his back again.

"Tempting offer, Ralph. I'm thinking about the jobs. If you go, what the hell happens to the jobs? Jesus, that's a hell of a lot of votes."

"I'm not going to go, Frank. I'm bloody well going to sue that bastard. Let him prove what he's saying. If he has any proof."

"He says he has," Henry said. "Someone from one of your factories in Offaly. Place called Crossfin. Back of nowhere. Know it?"

Martin shook his head.

"Some little nobody. Kelly, I think his name is. You sacked him. There's a cult or something involved. I can get more. This Kelly says you polluted a river. Says you killed cattle. I thought that was a bit of a laugh."

"Jesus."

Martin was wrestling with a threatened court case he could barely remember the details of. Some bunch complaining about a chemical spill. He couldn't remember much more about it.

"And we sacked him?"

"Yeah."

"Well, then he's unreliable. I'll sue Bell, I swear it, Frank. He's doing this for spite. He says I put him out of business. Years ago. A bloody pet-food factory he couldn't keep going. Jesus. What was this bastard's name again?"

"Kelly. He sounds good. He's spilling everything. They've had him for a week now. I have three men on the taps, Frank. He says you were shipping weapons and chemicals in computer boxes. And he has pictures and copies of false export certificates. The Yanks'll hit the roof. Some of the stuff he says you were sending is very sensitive. Is it true?"

"Shut up, Paudie." Costello said.

"How many of Bell's people know about this?" Martin said.

"Three or four. I'll get you the transcript, Ralph."

"Jesus," Martin burst out, "it's that bloody cult lot. I remember them, hatters; I think some of them are foreigners, they said we killed their cows with pesticide. They've been going on for months. I think we're going to court. What the hell would we be doing using pesticide down there? Jesus!"

"Okay, okay, Ralph. It's a matter of stalling, isn't it?" Costello said. "Muddy the waters."

"That's okay for you, Frank, I've this Britcop thing in one week. If he lets fly, that's finished. And once that slips and it's known we're not covered, you watch my bankers gather for the kill."

"Kelly says he's been thinking of contacting a television reporter, Ralph," Paud Henry said. "There's some EC bitch involved. Derek told him to hang on before going public. Until the department can investigate more. They want concrete proof. They haven't even brought Customs in yet.

And none of my lads have been approached."

Costello stood up.

"Why didn't you say that, Paud? You sit there and calmly announce doomsdays for MartinCorp and maybe for us and you have the fucking solution standing up like an elephant's dick, man. Muddy the waters. Thank Christ for Derek Bell's honesty. Jesus, I never thought I'd be so pleased to have an honest man in my cabinet. The bastard is going to miss the boat. Okay, Ralph, you go ahead with Britcop. I'll give you a personal letter, saying we back you and you have full cover for the Gulf mess. I'll also hint that we're getting business from the Libyans."

He looked at the two of them.

"Well, we are, just about. I've had people from my department out there five times already. Maybe, I'll announce a deal."

"That's all I need, Frank. Just your support."

"You have it. And we get the election cash when we need it?"

"All you want. Paud can pick it up himself. Can't you, Paud? No one has to know where it's coming from. And we start to take out these shites, Frank, all of them, now."

"Agreed. Paud?"

"Right, Frank."

9

The flat was a ground-floor post-modernist job in a development near Dalkey, down towards the sea, full of sharp angles, seeming to have been designed to look like just another jut of rock along that coastline. The sea, oily going on undercoat grey, lapped at the pebbled shoreline below the development with a sucking sound. There were stone steps leading down to the shore and the smell was of seaweed and redundant industry.

Jack Clarke parked his car near the gate, facing out. Travel fatigue was written all over his face when he stepped out of the car. In a small twitch between his nose and cheek. In a pimple at his chin. In a sty forming on the lid of his left eye. And his brain in constant lag. He should have been back at MartinCorp but this had become more important. He did not go into why. He wasn't interested anyway. It just had. As if he was a kid again and it was something he just had to have. The obsession had grown all through the business in New York. None of the excitement involved in setting up the grease deals had anything on the thought of seeing Kate again. Of just casting an eye on her. Jack could do nothing about it. And he swore at himself for being so weak, for not going straight to the office. But as soon as he'd stepped off the plane, he'd driven straight to Dalkey.

It had begun with a call to Carl from JFK. Kate was back in town. She'd been down the country, over in Brussels, in

London, was back for a couple of weeks, might be going back to Brussels for some of that time, would he like to come to dinner again?

Jack felt his heart double-somersaulting in his chest and had a sense of incredible happiness he could not remember ever having before. He came to the conclusion he must have had it before, with her, it was just so long ago he couldn't remember it. Never mind the pressure on Martin, never mind that he had done enough in New York to get himself a ten-stretch, never mind he was playing for stakes higher than he'd ever imagined, he wanted Kate. Carl had been his usual understanding self, full of good advice, full of concern and interest in Jack's dad's condition. The old man had played golf with his old man and had to give up after fourteen. Jack made another call to check on his father and found him out, playing snooker. His mother was drunk, maybe, but Jack didn't mind that. She should take a lover, he thought. He didn't say it. If she had, he didn't want to know, if she hadn't, he didn't want to be the one to encourage her.

Why the hell did Carl have to be so bloody nice? Jack said to himself at the door. The intercom crackled and he thought he heard a voice but his announcement of his name brought nothing in reply. He stepped back and tried to peer in through the closed curtains. Maybe she wasn't there. Drizzle had begun to fall. The kind that can fall all day and get through the toughest rainwear. A very subtle rain. Barely announces itself. He could feel the change in temperature from Manhattan. Manhattan had had near one hundred per cent humidity. A bloody glasshouse. Maybe that had played some kind of trick with his libido. It all raced through his mind on rails. Reasons. Jack Clarke always liked to have reasons for everything, and he was good at coming up with good reasons, but this was different.

On the Vico Road with her. And that house she wanted. The offer to buy it for her. He could have touched her. He was in her space. She'd allowed him in. But he didn't. Then all the way back to town, wanting. Sitting beside her, telling himself it was just the beer, the good food, the view, nothing more; it would be gone by the morning; she was history. She should have been history. Five bloody years without a word, not even a hint. That was history. How much more did it take for it to become history? To get it out of his system. Stop phoning her. He cursed her answering machine. Only battle he'd ever lost. He didn't go chasing Jenny or Angie any more. He didn't have to call around to them like some oversexed teenager. He was angry with himself now, for making such a fool of himself. The door opened before he could act.

"God, Jack, what time is it?"

For one awful moment he expected to see someone in another dressing gown come behind her and ask who was there. It had happened to him once before. With this girl he'd fancied a couple of years back. In Amsterdam. He'd decided to call around with flowers early in the morning, while he had time. She wasn't anything really special, though he'd gone through all the imaginings, all the possibilities, but it had finished miserably. This tattooed body-builder followed her out and had a go at Jack. On an Amsterdam street in the morning. Jack was more embarrassed than anything. The fellow caught him with a punch to the side of the face and left a yellow and brown stain there all week. Jack broke the sod's toe with his heel and left him screaming and cursing on the ground.

"Always wear shoes," Jack said, running off down the street.

There were pieces of daffodil all over the cobbles.

Kate's hair was forward over one side of her face and her dressing gown was riding up at the back. She had not fully opened her eyes. She signalled to him to follow her in. What time was it? she kept asking. He told her three times and she did not hear him once.

"I'm back," Jack said.

"From where?"

"I've been trying to get in touch with you."

"I told you I'd be away."

Was there something in women that made them deliberately miss the obvious? Jack thought. Here he was, up with the birds, earlier really, and all she could do was ask him what he was doing there so early. What did you have to do? She was giving him the tumble-dryer treatment. The feeling of humiliation in him was growing fast and he was considering turning around and walking out. Except that he was watching her move around the flat on a kind of slow-motion autopilot.

It had temporary written all over it, the flat. There were boxes in the corner of the living-room. There were two suitcases on the floor of her bedroom. The blankets of her bed were on the floor by the bed. Jack found himself fine-tooth combing the place for any hint of somebody else. Files were stacked high on the dining table in the kitchen. The table was small and it gave the kitchen a feeling of being bigger than the rest of the flat put together.

"Put on coffee, Jack," she said. "Decaf."

She left him alone in the kitchen. Looking for the coffee and hanging on to all the words he had stocked up since New York. He heard the door of her bedroom close and he put the kettle on and sat down.

That was another stupid thing, he thought. Going in to get changed. To maybe look better. It didn't matter. Didn't she see that? They'd lived together for a year. He knew her back to front. In all shapes and sizes. And she had to go on with this kind of pretence. The whole modesty bit. Jack was having arguments with himself he thought had vanished for ever. Carl Hennigan said he should try to be friends with her again. Try. He was friends. But there was more. There would always be more between them. Surely Carl could see that. But Carl was part of that group of human beings who make compromise their daily bread, for the sake of harmony. Jack was way off from that. Jack Clarke went for things wholeheartedly or not at all. When he hated he hated so much he could kill and when he loved it was worse.

He poured a bowl of bran for himself and smothered it in milk. There were photographs of old Dublin on the walls, and Jack walked around spooning bran into his mouth, staring at them, as if he could find something in them, something missing now, a kind idyll captured and framed, a time to be envied. It all looked so understood, so studied, so apparent. He was running up against real fear for the first time in his life. He used to love shooting close to the chaos, testing himself, pressing the pick-up-and-carry-through to the edge. But there was always the Martin net. The net was tearing, the chaos was out and unfettered, and the odds were widening. It was all ruled by probability, and the odds changed according to how much he moved outside things he had immediate control of. Even in the safest environment, there was an element of catastrophe probability which meant that the whole thing could just flip on its head. Look at Kate. She was supposed to be gone. He had packed her away. Consigned her to the files of history. He had a feeling he was carrying a set of dice in his hand.

"Did you make my coffee?"

Kate was rubbing her hair with a towel. She had a comb in her other hand. She wore a pair of cotton slacks and a sweatshirt. Her lips were pale and unpronounced. He could see the tips of her top front teeth at her lips.

"The kettle's boiled," he said.

"Thanks, Jack."

She walked over and made her own coffee. Jack was trying to finish his bran. He felt a bit caught out, eating her cereal. It was getting to him. His personal ideology was being chipped away. Personal and group ideologies, the shields all humans need, they were falling apart everywhere. No one had much faith in ideologies any more, of any kind.

They were enslaving. High ideals. Attempts to set life in stone when life itself depended on the flexibility of possibility. Fix life like a picture in a frame. Jack Clarke's personal philosophy wouldn't be remembered as one of the great ideals of history. It was, maybe, the most long lasting, but even its longevity was wearing thin.

Kate switched on the radio. She played with the dial. It occurred to Jack that he had not explained himself and she had not asked him to explain himself. Maybe she was more in tune than he thought. He placed the bowl on the table and came towards her. Kate was leaning back against a press with her red mug cupped in her hands. She was looking into her decaf.

"So?" she said.

"I've been in New York. I tried to get in touch. You weren't in."

"You know where I was, Jack."

"Look, I—I had to come over here. I know it sounds weird, but I just had to. I'm right off the plane. Can I have one of them?"

She gestured to him to help himself.

She had been expecting an explosion and it hadn't happened. What the hell was he playing at? That was why he was there. To ball her out. She followed his body language for a sign. Then she let herself make a judgement. She had been holding back. Professional distance and personal loyalty. She did not know which was the stronger. Christ, Jack. What have you been doing? She thought. He had a mug in his hand. Professional lost out to personal.

He looked a bit lost to her. His shirt was creased. His hair didn't have its usual symmetry. His tie was loosened at his neck. Jack had a good neck. Well-proportioned. Kate turned and put the kettle back on. She knew that was what he wanted. She knew more than she was letting on. That was her way. She had played it the other way with him before and had her insides torn out. She wasn't doing that in a hurry again. She'd somehow expected this. The way he'd been with her at that lunch. And after. She had allowed him into her space. He was in her space now. God, it was getting complicated.

In a way, work had given her a breathing space. A place to ease off. Get herself together. Consider everything at a safe distance. She stared at Jack and began to catch up with the morning. She had a small hankering to go over and hug him. She resisted. She allowed a hidden smile. Jack was propped against a chair.

"Sugar?" she asked.

She knew his preference. But she asked it all the same. That was her protection. Allowed her keep a distance. And she did need a distance. The sudden arrival of the past in all its gory detail was not easy to cope with, and only she was up to her neck in this pollution investigation, she might have had difficulty.

Jesus, she thought, maybe he didn't know. They'd had someone from Martin on to Brussels, threatening bloody murder. And a barrister. It had mushroomed. It had begun as a simple item in a general report. Now she did not know where it would end up. But she was in too deep to leave. And they needed her. Those people. They hadn't anyone else. She looked for any sign he knew in his eyes. There was nothing but tiredness. She decided he didn't know. He'd have said if he knew by now. But he shouldn't be there with her. Not the way things were turning. Her stomach tightened at the thought of all those allegations. She couldn't tell him to leave, though.

The old attraction had not gone. She was that bit further from it at the moment, but it wasn't gone. She could study it more, be detached, examine the minutiae. But it wasn't gone.

"I couldn't get you..."

He stopped himself because he knew he was sounding stupid and Jack Clarke hated sounding stupid.

"Don't come on like that, Jack. Stop and think. I know things are difficult. I know MartinCorp's having its problems."

She kept it like that. Vague. Not giving herself away. It was the professional thing again. In control. Personal problems couldn't be allowed cloud the issue. She wanted to talk to him about it. She'd been thinking about ringing him. She felt she had to. But not now. Not here. This was another them. Deep-rooted.

"We can handle problems," Jack said. "The best."

The old arrogance reasserted itself and she found herself turned right off again.

"I'll bet. You should have a holiday, Jack. When was the last time you had one?"

"I didn't come here to be patronised."

"Sorry. Force of habit. I can be a patronising bitch sometimes. You never stopped telling me that, did you?"

He stopped himself replying. If he had hit back it would have gone on, maybe ended up like before, with one of them, or both of them, firing something at the other. Jack made himself a coffee. He stood right beside her, touching her with his shoulder, enjoying that, and that was enough for the moment. He had changed. Before that would not have been enough. Nothing less than bed would have been enough. He criticised himself for his haste and then criticised himself for his lack of decision. It was difficult.

"Let's have breakfast, Jack. I'll make toast. Set the table. Maybe we can talk. Would you like to shower?"

He didn't know how to answer that. The old certainties with her were no good. She was five years on. More in control. Less sensitive to him, he felt. If he accepted would it signify some kind of unmeant sexual overture? Was the offer a subliminal offer? Did it matter! He was sticky. Most of New York seemed to have hitched a ride on him.

"You look wrecked, Jack. Go on, I'll get breakfast. Better than bran. Bacon and eggs, okay?"

They didn't talk about anything deep or meaningful over

breakfast. She was glad he'd called around, glad to have his company. The Hare Krishnas in Crossfin were fine for a while but the rigours of their life-style made it difficult to let go with them. They were full of good humour but too pessimistic by half. She hadn't their faith in the virtues of self-denial. No meat, no booze, no gambling, no sex. The footpath syndrome. Humanity got lost somewhere. Kate Keyes needed open interplay, no matter how she tried to protect herself, which was why she got hurt so much. It never put her off but it did slow her down each time. Her last involvement had been nine months before with a Dutch journalist. He had been serious about her but not serious enough. She could never get over the lack of enchantment. He did not enchant her. Not like Jack had. She cut herself off and concentrated on Peter's fabulous looks. He had the kind of face she thought only existed in high-class fashion ads, where the model invariably turned out to be gay. But Peter was straight and full of humour for a Dutch man. Kate still had the notion that the Dutch were humourless. Not Peter. He had a good black sense of humour. Necessary for a guy who'd seen enough war for a million of his kind. He had a scar on his shoulderblade. The bullet had gone in and down, taking a piece of lung, a kidney, two inches of intestine and exiting at his thigh a millimetre from an artery. That was why he was in Brussels. Nice safe job.

"How was the flight?" She asked.

His answer was predictable. But they were each playing a part now. A role mapped out for them by therapists and people for whom life was a scientific experiment. Where analysis was the basis of a mutually beneficial relationship. And respect was its policeman. What exactly respect was, apart from something which achieved very little of any consequence, was difficult to find out. Usually it was a feeling that people had when they got around to doing what they'd wanted to do all along but were so scared they'd lost interest or were so retarded that they never got anywhere.

But for the moment, it suited them both to follow the analytical path, the step-by-step approach. They didn't need the suddenness of a first embrace, the incredible energy of kissing on first glance, the sheer magnetism of making love the same night they met. Nevertheless, they felt sorry for anyone who went through this when they first met. It must have destroyed much more than it ever encouraged.

"I brought you a bottle of whiskey," he said.

"I don't drink whiskey."

"I know. I do."

"Do you want a drink?"

"Love one. Thanks for asking."

"Where's the bottle?"

"The car."

"Do you want me to get it?"

He held up the car keys.

She took them and ran her hand through his hair. The first contact they had had all morning and they had been sitting there two hours, talking. He followed her out and let some more thoughts of before out of where they were kept, thoughts so personal they came with a health warning and stung on contact. They had been coming all week, in clusters, at night, during the day, at work, over dinner, making love to a girl he knew in Portmarnock. She was his reliable playmate when things were lean among his regular women. And they had been. Since that Killiney girl had given him the shove, he'd had nothing. So Sandra put out on demand and allowed him ease his frustrations and told him he was good. It meant less than nothing to him and if Sandra had disappeared before his eyes he probably would have carried on screwing. But Kate was reappearing for him in excerpts, five-year-old excerpts, and they were difficult to handle.

She poured him a drink and mixed a ridiculous cocktail for herself, saying it was her day off and she could do what she liked. She hadn't had a midday cocktail since Jenny and Angie had come to Brussels and they'd all gone out and bought bottles of booze. They brought them back to her apartment and mixed the lot and got pissed out of their brains. It was always a quick way to break the ice if ice needed breaking and it usually did in a life that relied on intense meetings over a few days. You never knew when you were going to see people again so you did your best to be open and free when you did see them. They didn't discuss Jack Clarke much that day, except as an object of puzzlement. Jenny thought Jack was lonely. Angie said he hadn't any feelings outside work. That being the best at what he did was his fulfilment. Nothing else mattered. Jenny'd wanted to confess to her fling with the subject but she held off for Kate's sake and for her own, if she was honest. The night had ignited a flame she did not need and she had doused it with a hell of a lot of effort and did not want it to reignite.

Jack was on his fourth drink, starting to feel drunk as opposed to slightly tight. Kate was somewhere around there, too. They were leaning over the table. The radio was playing opera music. The sun had replaced the rain outside and they could hear cars coming and going in the car park of the development. Jack was running his finger round and round in a small pool of whiskey Kate had spilled pouring him a drink.

"I think you're in trouble over this pollution thing, Jack," she said, trying not to say it because she had promised herself she would not say anything about her work or compromise herself.

"Leave it, Kate."

He made an effort to lift his head towards her but the fatigue and his state of inebriation prevented him. Who the hell cared about anything? he thought. She was beautiful. He drifted from indulging in her beauty to indulging in his father's illness. Nothing could save him. Not a million, not a billion. There was nothing Jack could do. That was too distressing. He went back to Kate's beauty.

"You're beautiful," he said.

"So are you, Jack. Are you sure you should be here? We're concentrating on Crossfin, you know. The thing's escalating, Jack. I don't know what you know. We did what we had to do."

Jack didn't know what she was getting at. He didn't much care.

"Doesn't matter," he said. "You do your job. Nice neat report. Ralph will sort any problems out."

He looked around.

"I could make your hair stand on end, Kate. I could—"

"Don't tell me, Jack."

He wasn't going to. He wanted to tell her things, things on his mind, that were bothering him, but he was not drunk enough for that, and he did not think he would ever be drunk enough for that. She was still a stranger that way.

"You don't like me, do you, Kate?" he said.

Oh, Jack, chemicals. You saw what they did with chemicals, she thought.

"Why do you say that?" She said.

"You're all matter of fact. You wouldn't care if I walked out that door now, would you?"

"Stop feeling sorry for yourself, Jack."

She remembered telling Angie Hennigan that she hated him, right after they broke up, that she hated him and if he came and asked her she'd drop everything and go immediately she loved him so much. Did he know that? Did he have any idea of the turmoil he had caused her? And now he wanted to do it again, it seemed.

"You want to get into my knickers, Jack."

He pulled his head up from the pool of whiskey he was drawing in. His eyes were drawn and drooping, his top lip came over his bottom lip in a missed bite.

"Yeah," he said.

His words were slurred.

"At least you're honest."

"I love you, Kate."

"Come off it, Jack. That might work with some bimbo on the Strip but not me. I know you, Jack. I know what you think and how you think it. I know what you're going to do and when you're going to do it. So don't try that on me. It insults me."

"I mean it. I do. I can't get you out of my mind, Kate."

"You managed for five years."

"That's unfair."

He knew it wasn't. Up until he had put his head around Hennigan's dining-room door he had managed to keep his memories of Kate Keyes down to once a week, maybe a bit more often if he was feeling low, but even then they were brief mentions of her name and a sharp intake of breath, nothing more. He looked at his watch. He should be at work. They'd be looking for him. Ralph Martin would be screaming his name all over the place. Where's Jackie Clarke? Get him up to my office. Yes, Mr Martin, no, Mr Martin. Jack was experiencing a shift of loyalty he had not envisaged. It was moving him into territory he was not familiar with. It had happened before New York and even in New York he found himself questioning what he was doing—something he would never have done before. He was coming to a crossroads; he could see them up ahead and the lights were in danger of going against him. Thing was, he didn't have any breaks.

"I have a hundred grand on deposit," he said.

Kate stuck a finger at him. She was not sure what he was getting at. If he was telling the truth. Little red lines crisscrossed his eyes when she looked closely at him.

"What for?"

"I don't know. I need it there. I started saving it the day you left."

"I left?"

"We split. I started then. Why did you come back? I—"

He drank the rest of his whiskey and soda and held out his glass.

"You're not going to sleep with me, then," he said.

"No, Jack."

If it had been the full truth it would have been difficult to say, but as it was, with the warmth she was feeling in her stomach and the light head she had and the numb and tingle which danced through her body she knew it was too close to call. Right and wrong meant nothing in this case and if she was sober she might have come up with a million good arguments for both sides, but she was defenceless, shields down, relying on raw emotion, and the emotions were contradictory, pulling her in different directions, tearing at her heart and and knotting her guts. It had happened the way she thought it might but hoped it would not. That wasn't true either. Nothing she thought or told herself was exactly true. There were pieces of truth fighting for a place in her consciousness, playing games with her, and the rain had begun again outside.

Jack Clarke finished two more whiskeys and fell asleep on her kitchen table.

10

The radio played something from the sixties, three chords and a large amount of hope, and some deer watched from the safety of the trees. A couple of men walking dogs passed. Detached step-over-body faces. The sun was dropping below the tree-line, a melting nugget streaming across the sky and along the horizon, hardened by a sharp cold and capped by a huge slab of cloud on the mountains to the south.

Barney Small smoked his third cigarette without counting, threw the butt to the ground and stood on it. He pulled the collar of his polysomething coat up and shoved his hands in his pockets. The car was a leased early-eighties Ford, and like everything else in Barney's life, it had the appearance of what it wasn't. Barney had been sitting in for an hour before he got out. The short leg, varicose veins, cramp and haemorrhoids queuing up to give him grief.

The bastard was late. Dead late.

Barney took his mobile from his pocket and started to dial. Third time. Both other times he'd thought about waiting longer, now he thought about being earwigged. He put the thing away.

The papal cross grabbed white light from the evening sky and threw it around in javelins. Tracking deer eyes made Barney look around him again. He was tired. Maybe too tired. Out on the piss the night before. With a gang from

Hamburg. Showing them a good time, buttering them up. One of the things he had going; one of the many: the introductions, the go-betweening—what Barney did. He pulled at his sideburns and lit another cigarette. Another fifteen minutes, that was it.

It was a simple job. Dead drop. On the picnic-table across the road. In the trees. Perfect. Your man puts his down and collects and then Barney moves in for the pick-up. Dead straight. No words. Into your own car and piss off. He'd done a thousand of these before, for Ralph Martin. And there was a nice wedge in it for himself and a smile and a pat on the back from Ralph. He wasn't supposed to know what he was picking up, not his concern. Just do it. He'd learned that early on. Minnows can't afford to hang around, ask too many questions. What you don't know, you can't say. Still, Barney had his ways.

Barney stubbed out his cigarette and clapped his hands together.

The news wasn't good. It was all hands to the pumps. Word was about that Ralph was heading up a creek without a paddle, that Derek Bell had a dozen machine-like investigators going through his company with an electron microscope. Rumours, mind. There were others, and they got printed in Ralph's papers, that Britcop was in the bag and that MartinCorp was looking for bigger prey in the States. Jack Clarke had been over there for a week. Barney was trying to figure out who to believe. Ralph had an injunction against a Sunday paper that wanted to suggest his business wasn't in order and there was talk of a television station chasing him with cameras all over Dublin. Barney tried to weigh it up. He'd had a chat with Larry Tallon—Tallon and Barney went back years, almost to the flood. It was a common joke that the two of them had arranged it to win an election.

His shorter leg was hurting more now. The gathering cold. It had hurt more in the car. He reached in and switched off the radio and fiddled in the glove compartment for something to read. He settled on a racing page. It was old but it had some form and you could always study form and see how it matched up on the day. Barney had many weaknesses in life but betting on the horses was up there with the best. He'd taken part in a couple of coups in his time, was something of a legend in racing circles, but in the end he was just another mug punter and the balance sheet showed a massive loss over the years. Barney had the reputation of being one of those men who would bet on two drops of water running down a window. He'd done it once, as he'd done most things once, but only to prove a point. The point being that he would bet on two drops of water running down a window. Barney's was a small legend but it *was* a legend and legends had to be protected.

The new lot, the Jack Clarkes, they had no class, he thought, not interested in legends, only money. Cash freaks. Boring as hell. Educated. Greedy. Sure, he was greedy, but not for himself. Barney spread what he had about. Soft touch with one whiskey on him, bloody charity with any more. Barney had fallen for every sad story imaginable. And a few that weren't. He didn't care. Money was there to be spread about. Barney was going in style. He had the look of a second-hand car salesman who was convinced people took him seriously. He'd spent so much time lying to himself, he believed the lies himself now. His wife had left him, his kids had all buggered off around the world with everyone else's kids, and all he had left was the legend. So everything went into the legend. And if he was lucky, he got his picture taken with Frank Costello at party functions and got a chance to speak when things were quiet.

Barney was taking a leak behind the Ford when the Japanese car made its appearance from the Islandbridge side of the Park. It moved slowly. As if whoever was in it was making sure. Barney watched it approach, marking its rate of progress, trying to make out who it was. He had a fair idea who it was going to be. He knew all the faces, and this or that one's name, though he never said that to Ralph Martin. Barney had his sources, he wasn't completely in the dark.

Clarke got up his hole. With his Trinity accent. Barney Small had no problem with prejudice. He belonged to an era where it was fine to say what you felt, and hate was a prized commodity. When anything worthwhile was owned by Protestants and you were brought up to believe you had a place and that was where you were going to stay. It seemed like a million years ago. But they'd overturned all that, the old oligarchy, men like him and Frank Costello. Given people like Ralph Martin the chance. They had nothing to be ashamed of. All Clarke's kind had were Jap businessmen breaking the speed limit to factories in Longford just to prove they were only an hour from Dublin. They applied formulas to everything and couldn't understand when they didn't work. They spoke right, joined the right clubs, cleaned themselves so much they probably had no skins and squirmed in a kind of retroshame when a slapper like him opened his mouth in public. He returned the contempt with venom.

The Japanese car pulled up on the road across from the car park. A small dark man, who looked Mediterranean, got out. He wore a long coat. He stood for a while beside his car and smoked a cigarette. He stared across at Barney Small. Neither man acknowledged the other. Small checked around. The dog-walkers were far away. A couple of joggers were coming. Barney watched them pass in front of the dark man in the long coat.

Joe Conroy was technically a private investigator. He specialised in tracing missing persons and insurance fraud. At least, that was what his business card said. Conroy had another side to his expertise. He was what was known as a plausibly deniable agent. Agent of what depended on how much folding was on offer. Conroy had very few ethical problems that couldn't be overcome by a heap of cash in an envelope. He fitted every stereotype of the sleazy gumshoe.

His eyes were sharp and probing; his dark face was lined, as if someone had taken a plough to it and his hair was greasy and combed back sharpish, almost a hat. His fingers were dyed with nicotine and his teeth had a multi-coloured look. He walked with a stoop, as if he was trying to avoid looking at people. But he was the best at what he did and he always came up with the goods.

He worked for Ralph Martin by proxy. They never met. They never talked. First contact was by small ad in an evening paper. All meetings were by intermediaries. That was where plausible deniability came in. Conroy was a digger. Boring, methodical, he kept digging and digging until he came up with something. He charged a flat fee. If he found what you were looking for in a day then it was worth while; if it took a month then he'd covered himself.

Conroy was unfailingly discreet. He had one bad habit but he always went abroad to satisfy it. He had been a cop in England but had resigned when his habit had been found out. One of the boys was found beaten in an alley and identified Conroy as the man who'd done it. There were no charges. But he was watched and it was easier to resign. Then there was the Far East for a few years: Singapore, Hong Kong. He slipped back into Dublin almost unnoticed and set himself up as a private detective. There were stories about links with British Intelligence but nothing was proved. A splinter group of a splinter group that had links with a minor left-wing party with special activities in the counterfeiting business took him for a ride one night and he spent two ugly hours hooded and questioned. But that had more to do with a newspaper article about sex habits than British Intelligence. They released him without saying anything.

Barney Small knew him well. A couple of Barney's more nationalist contacts in the border area suggested him for polite inquiries. Apparently, one senior Provo had hired Conroy to find out if his wife was having it away with a

Castleblayney councillor. Conroy produced the photographs, tapes, videos, and statements from a credit card account the councillor had set up for his mistress. The councillor had to cancel the account a couple of days later and transfer the money into a new account. The Provo chief made a point of breaking his index fingers. The videos, they said.

Conroy waited till the time agreed and then walked over to the picnic-table nearest to him and placed a manila envelope at one of the legs. He did it with the discretion for which he was famous. Ralph Martin said Conroy was so discreet that if he was dying in the middle of the street he would make sure no one would notice. He bent down and made like he was doing his shoelaces.

Barney Small was already walking in his direction. Conroy reached under the table. Taped to it was his fee. It was a simple job to remove it and put it in his pocket. Conroy watched a young kid playing soccer with a friend in a field behind him. He allowed himself a long look. Then he began walking back to the car.

He was in his car and pulling away when Barney Small crossed the road. The Japanese car was twenty yards away, heading for the main road, when Barney reached the other side. He stopped to look around. Now there were only the two kids. It was clear. He strolled over to the picnic-bench and sat down and smoked a cigarette, watching the solitariness around him. His pulse rate had increased. The chill he had been feeling was gone. His feet were digging into the hard ground. His shorter leg wasn't hurting any more. He smoked and then stubbed out his cigarette in the grass, leaned down further and picked up the envelope at the leg of the table. It was inside his coat before he straighted up again.

Thin Lizzy played "Whiskey in the Jar" while Barney Small drove through the assembling darkness. Lights were already on. Some reflected in the river and came back at him in odd angles. A couple of Garda cars passed him, lights turning, sirens announcing to the whole world that they were off to catch someone. Barney could never figure out whey they did that if they didn't need to clear the roads of people. And they didn't need to this time. Maybe they were on the way home for dinner. He drove down the quays to the East Link Bridge and on to Jack Clarke's flat. That was the way. Ralph Martin gave orders and people like Barney and Jack carried them out. Ralph was briefed only when necessary. The plausible deniability worked up further than Conroy.

Small parked away from Clarke's flat complex and phoned him from a box. The call consisted of three rings and then a hang-up. That was it. Clarke would know he was coming. He walked along the sea front and tried to count the lights on Howth Head. There were men fishing not far from him and a DART train went by without causing him to look around.

Jack Clarke watched from his front window while Barney Small let himself in. He stayed, watching while Small took off his coat and poured himself a drink. It seemed clear. Just in case, Jack had a man watching the gate. Barney Small didn't know anything about that. Barney knew only what Barney was supposed to know. Barney thought he knew more. They all thought they knew more. Jack found it hard to carry that on to his own position.

"It's a cold hoor," Small said. "For the time of year. It was bloody boiling yesterday."

"Fall of the wall," Jack said.

"What?"

"Fall of the Berlin Wall," Jack said. "Changed everything. You watch, Barney. It'll all unravel. All the old certainties. Like pulling a loose thread. Wait and see. That it?"

"Yeah."

Jack sat down. Small was already commenting to himself silently on his young colleague's cardigan, making derisive remarks about yuppies and the shitty designer crap they tried to use for image. Nothing behind it. Legends lasted for ever. They had no concept of an hour from now, he thought. The rest was all hot air, no substance, would buckle at the first sign of trouble. He was always expecting Jack Clarke to break up. Alan Kennedy used to press that. Said he was sure Clarke would fall apart when things got really bad. He'd only seen the good. They'd all seen the bad before. Part of making you, the bad was, when it got really rough. When the raiders smelled pickings. That was when the fun really began. And they could.

Jack Clarke read what was in the envelope in silence, unnerving his older companion. Small hated when he did that. Clarke knew Small hated it. But it was his way of stamping his authority. This was Jack's show. It was his speciality. A fixing job. So used to it now, he didn't even bother wondering who it was any more.

He had Kate on his mind again. When he found out she was behind the insurance mess, Jack nearly broke his hand on his desk. What the fuck was she doing? She was a bloody environmental researcher. For a bloody report that would probably get filed anyway. He tried to phone her but she was gone again. It was ridiculous, Jack thought, one bloody witness and he turns out to be weirder than the weirdos. Claiming compo. Did Kate have any idea what she had done? He swore and then held back any more thoughts about her. Ralph should have signed a cheque on the spot. Months ago. But he was bloody-minded when people attacked his factory standards. Very high, he used to say. And he wouldn't have anyone saying different. Kate reappeared in his mind. Going to her place, ending up drunk over her table—it had all been a shagging mess. And then he'd had Martin shouting him into tomorrow for not being where he was supposed to be. Well, fuck them all, he thought, he could decide what he was going to do. It wasn't true. He was missing Kate. He swore again. Ralph would go ape if he found out about them.

"Have you had a look?" he asked Small.

"No."

"It's interesting."

Small looked from where he was sitting, trying to see what was the big deal. But his eyesight let his ego down. He sat back and poured himself another drink.

"I made a pile on a London futures option," he said. "I have a contact."

"Good for you," Jack Clarke said, without looking up.

"I could let you have it."

"No need, Barney. Look, maybe you should go home, get some rest, leave this with me. I'll be in touch."

Barney downed his whiskey and grunted. Jack said nothing more.

Jack was reading through the stuff he didn't really need to know. The family details. Bell was squeaky-clean. Married his first girl-friend. Two kids. Both doctors. Two properties. One in the constituency, the other in Dublin. Son of a butcher. Farmer for a while. Busted. Ran his own pet-food business for ten years till it was forced into liquidation. Workers blamed him for being away too much. Ralph Martin bought the pieces cheap. Maybe he knew Ralph too well.

There were details of people who had grudges against him. The CV was bland, just as Conroy said it would be. The documents told a fuller story. Bank statements. You could tell a man's whole life story just by reading his statements. A kind of shorthand summary of all he had done. There was more. Dud investments. The mortgages on the properties. Both were double-mortgaged. Bell had gone guarantor for a brother's hotel—another dud—with his own property. He placed that bit to one side and read on. Letters to creditors. They had a pleading tone. Letters to benefactors, supporters who liked to remain anonymous. They all had them. Some were only shopkeepers, others were Ralph Martins. But they were there for the same reasons.

Then there was his party. He'd been an independent for years until someone suggested he should try expanding. It worked for a while. Eight seats at one stage. Down to two now. And up to its eyelids in debt. Ralph Martin had given money once. At the beginning. Ralph saved his best intentions for Frank Costello but he greased other palms too, just in case. There'd been a request for more and Ralph had turned it down. There was a copy of the letter. Basically, Ralph had referred to Bell's party's chances of seeing out another election in unflattering terms. Said it would be a better investment to put his money on a dog. Bad move, Ralph. Jack stopped himself when he said that. He'd never said that before. But he was reading further. At the next election Bell's twosome held the balance of power and the honourable Derek became a minister for the first time in his life at the age of fifty-eight.

"Always short of cash," Jack said.

He was running through a short-list of approaches. How they might do it. Cash was the key. Perennial problem in Leinster House. This would be simple. He was on a limb, Bell. One good push. Paud Henry could help. And Larry. Larry would make it sound good. Larry could make being evicted feel good. Maybe Larry should do it on his own. Ask for a meeting. Explain things. Suggest ways out.

"He owes a builder we own," Barney said.

"I thought you said you hadn't read this."

"I haven't. But it can only be Bell. And I know he owes a builder we own. That hotel thing he got into with his brother. It was like pouring money down into a pot-hole. The fuckin road leading up to it was full of the fuckin things. He's had threats. He asked Paud Henry to look into it. Put an extra guard on the house. It won't help. The threats can be switched on or off according to Ralph's say-so."

"Who is this guy?"

"You don't know him. Ernie Wilson. In London now. Fixing something for Ralph."

"I do, Barney."

"I shoulda known. Know what colour my jocks are?"

"They're Y-fronts. And they were white."

"Fuckin bloody…"

"Hey, Barney, I'm here to get some work done. Keep your feelings to yourself. I told you you should go home. I'll get in touch."

"How old are you, son, just how old are you? Let me tell you…"

"Barney, lay off the drink: it doesn't become you. Concentrate on the work if you're going to stay."

"Jesus, you lads piss me off. Fine fuckers you are. Hoors. Let me see that."

He made a swipe for the papers. Jack let him have them. There was no point having a row. They were working against a deadline. The approach to Bell had to begin in the next few days. A story had to be ready. To brief whoever had to know. Something airtight and friendly. Judging by the phone calls, Derek Bell was on for an ulcer soon. They had him; all they had to do was handle him with care. Make it sound plausible. Get information about the weaknesses, Jackie, Ralph Martin said. Find it and keep it and let it out very slowly. Pace was everything. Let it out and draw your man in, so he thinks you're on his side.

It hadn't always worked like that. They'd had to use strong-arm tactics with some people. But that was Barney's end of things. He could whistle up the requisite fellows and have them put on the pressure. Ralph didn't like it too much, but the end always justified the means in his mind.

With Bell, they'd go softly softly, Jack said. Get someone to discuss his problems with him. Larry, maybe. Tell him they were behind him. There was a possible heave against Frank Costello. That Phil Cassidy was thinking of throwing his hat in the ring. That Phil had backers. Wouldn't it be better to have Phil in the harp seat? Larry knew people who had access to the kind of money that would sort things out for Bell. Put him in a better position. Because Frank was thinking of going to the country now and his little party couldn't afford their deposits let alone an election. And if he lost this one, he was gone for ever.

Move it like that. Then slip Ralph Martin in. His difficulties. So maybe laws had been broken. But there were pressures. Jobs at stake. How about a quiet rebuke and a small fine? Then forgive and forget. Depending on how he reacted to the first move, they could decide whether to throw Ralph in. Ralph Martin could make it good for him. Could sort out problems if he laid off for this one. Otherwise it would come down on him like shit from a hippo with dysentery. There was only one smart move. It had to be pointed out. Better in office, working with Phil Cassidy than out, signing on.

"He has this thing about being past it," Jack said.

He picked up a sheet from a recording transcript.

"There, he says it twice. Pillow talk. Scared shitless that he might lose it all. Fucking stupid name his bloody wife calls him. Imagine being screwed by him. Makes you laugh, doesn't it?"

Another weakness.

"You can smile," Small said. "I could feel sorry for him."

"Getting soft, Barney?"

Barney sat back and threw down the papers he was reading. He pulled off his glasses to give himself more cred.

"Look at you. Still have acne. You want it all now, don't you? You can't wait. Everything quick. The ladder only goes up for you. Well, remember the snakes, lad. I'm sixty-three years old. I smoke and I drink and I worry myself into contortions sometimes. But I'm still here and I don't owe anyone. See this..."

He touched his shorter leg.

"A snake did that to me years ago. I was in a hurry. Now I want to live a long life and keep my name good. Anything I can do to ensure that I fuckin do. There's nothing more to it. I'm not trying to outdo anyone, I'm not calculating a score. It's all for me and mine. You see, I'm scared, son, scared of being old. Of being useless. I've watched friends die and become invalids, and I'm scared."

He stopped himself there. He recalled what Jack had said about weaknesses. He cursed himself for having too much of the bottle.

"Right," Jack said. "You want in. You're in, Barney. So listen. We can't be seen anywhere near this for now. It has to be at a distance. We send Larry in to Bell. He tells Bell he's been talking to Phil Cassidy. They're getting *muy* fucked-off waiting for Frankie to vacate the senior job, that Phil's fit for duty, the heart trouble is well past him now—it wasn't much more than indigestion really, Phil was looking for sympathy after trying to do Frankie— and Frankie's getting paranoid and things are slipping from him. He invites Derek Bell to consider his position if Frankie goes to the country. We can have a couple of our other boys go to Bell in secret. People he thinks are Persil white. From his neck of the woods. People he can trust. You can handle that. They tell Derek there's disquiet in the ranks, about the future, finances, stuff like that. It doesn't matter. What matters is we make Bell think he's being approached genuinely. Then if he goes for that, we hit him with this and whamo! And what better Judas-goat than Larry Tallon."

Tallon had done a similar job on Garret Nolan, Frank Costello's predecessor. When Frank wanted the job, Larry told Garret he might as well do battle, that the party was solidly behind him. In fact Garret didn't need to go. There was no cry for his departure, but once he did the lads on the benches became jumpy; loyalty, always a difficult commodity to quantify, became fluid; bargaining unsettled the *status quo*, the rumours spread and Larry and Frank worked their sting to its conclusion. Exit Garret Nolan; enter Frank Costello. Barney forgot his previous sympathy for Bell.

"So it's money then," he said. "Why can't it be sex? I'd prefer if we could show him photographs, you know—see the bastard's face. Fuckin squeaky-clean cunt. Maybe we could do a job on Paudie. I hear Frank has photographs there. Of Paudie in a compromising position. In a lot of compromising positions. Now that would be a laugh."

Jack Clarke underlined the sections he wanted. He had moved himself into a monodirectional setting and was not aware he had done it. Even Barney Small's crudities were irrelevant. Paud Henry could do what he liked so long as MartinCorp got what it wanted. There was no other scale to work from.

His father had collapsed. Tried walking up the stairs when he wasn't able. Jack didn't want to think about it. Not now. Not when he was doing this. His mother just sat there, looking at her husband, not saying anything—hoping, she said. Jack asked what she was hoping. She didn't answer. She told him to peel something and then turned on a soap opera. His father rang a bell upstairs. I want you to be married, Mum, Jack said. Or words like that. He could not remember. His father was yelling from his room. His mother wasn't paying any attention. She turned and told him to go and see what his father wanted.

Barney Small turned to him before leaving. "You're this thin, lad," he said. "Transparent."

"Go home, Barney."

"I don't think you have it. I think you'll fuck up."

"Like you, Barney?"

"Takes one to know one, Jack."

"You have a problem with me?"

"Yes."

Jack hadn't expected that.

"You go see Ralph Martin, then."

He placed Conroy's report down on a coffee table. They had him. It would work like a fine Swiss watch mechanism. And no one would ever know. It had an excitement all of its own, this kind of job, way outside the normal shoot he got from his work. But there was something else too. Almost hidden. And he could not figure it out. It had something to do with Kate and his father and it had been with him now for weeks, there, watching, saying nothing, another self. He could not ignore it.

11

Aengus Ignatius Kelly had two things in common with the Minister for Industry. He had once been a farmer and he was out to get Ralph Martin. He had the hard face of a farmer even though he had not farmed for six years. His hands were scarred and warted and yellow around the nails and his body smelled like the product of a sewage treatment plant. He was not a likeable man. He had bought his farm when it seemed that farming was a good idea and subsidies were sprouting from the ground like grass shoots. This was after a long time at sea in the engine room of a cargo ship operating between Southampton and Rio. If you examined his skin closely, you could still see traces of oil beneath the surface. He had the stare of a man who'd spent years in an engine room and it complemented the predictability of his factory floor movements.

Kelly had gone from the busted farm to work at Ralph Martin's computer factory in the space of a week and spent the next six years doing exactly the same eight-step task, surrounded by a dozen other men, doing similar eight-step tasks.

Kate Keyes stopped reading the report in front of her and picked up a chocolate biscuit and sucked the chocolate off it. She recalled Jack Clarke telling her about a summer he'd spent making blinds. That led her down a dark track she did not want to follow. It wasn't her business, she told herself.

The pollution was her business. She moved back to the safety of Jack's summer job. He used to say it was one of the reasons he was going for gold, the memory of that. His was a seven-step job. Seven movements, four of them repeats, that was his life for four months. Soul-destroying was not the word for it. Dehumanising maybe. But it was worse than that. Because it didn't take away your humanity. It just locked it away. It was like being a prisoner, he said. Jack talked a lot about being a prisoner. He carried a certain claustrophobia around with him all the time. She should have rung him. Had it out with him.

She had met Kelly twice. And much as she'd tried, she couldn't find anything in him to like. He was rude and his table manners defied belief. She left the first meeting, wondering if all her Brussels cocktail parties had turned her into a snob. It might have but at that stage she didn't care. She looked at the clock across from where she was sitting. She had half an hour. She read on.

Obnoxious and all as he was, Kelly was their star witness. Kate had lost any impartiality in this case. It was too much to maintain. A billion-pound multinational against a bunch of celibate, peace-loving vegetarians. There was no contest. And if she needed back-up, she only had to remember the hostility of everyone in Crossfin.

Freaks, fucking troublemaking freaks, they said.

It was ridiculous, she thought, this ape whose presence made your flesh crawl, this Aengus Ignatius Kelly, was a bloody environmental zealot. Animals, to be precise: dolphins and whales in particular. But he was into everything that didn't walk upright and have a facility for deceit. And this whistle-blower admitted to six years of routine illegality without blinking an eyelid. Obeying any orders given. No matter how questionable. When she'd asked him about it, he'd just shrugged. The money was good. There was a certain amount of shame on his face. Maybe that was the reason for his action. Part of her wanted him to be lying about the illegal shipments to the Gulf. But that would hurt her own case. Heads you lose, tails you lose.

Everyone down there said he was odd. Kelly. A case of kettles and pots, she thought. Then when the Hare Krishnas moved into Crossfin House, he started visiting them. For a Sunday meal. They'd put stickers up in town, inviting anyone who wanted to. Kelly was the only taker. Crossfin wasn't what you might call a pluralist town. One meal led to another and then he was turning up to help with their cows. Late milking was his favourite. They accepted him, without question. At the Martin plant, his career prospects were nose-diving. He argued with everyone. And then he broke the foreman's nose. That was when they sacked him.

Why the hell did you have to go and do that? Kate heard herself say. Really trips the case up. A good lawyer will go straight for that.

She read on. Doing devil's advocate.

His testimony was too accurate, too detailed, for him to be lying. So what if he was a misfit. He was there the day of the spill. And he could tell exactly what pesticide was used and how much.

It was a pity nothing else was killed, she said to herself. Then she scolded herself. Then she wished someone else's livestock had died. Just one other victim. The vet's autopsy corresponded with his testimony. Except that was months ago. But it was all good circumstantial evidence. She was going to fight this one all the way. With whatever she could get.

Kelly was devastated when the cattle died. Kurt, the Krishna leader, said Kelly fell on one dead animal and cried. Kurt was a gentle Berliner in his thirties, very tall, six six, very thin, very Germanic, suffering with arthritis. His joints were red and he slept by a bar heater. He was trying to control his suffering with diet. He got up at four every morning to prepare the community altar. Kate had tried to keep to the schedule when she'd stayed there but had collapsed back to sleep at her second attempt. They were all gentle people. They didn't deserve the grief they got. She shook her head when she thought of all the cardboard in the broken widows of Crossfin House.

"They don't understand us," Kurt's wife said.

She was short and Irish. Sinéad. Her head was shaved. She joked that she'd done it first and that she had a lousy singing voice. She wore an old woollen pullover that stretched to her knees.

The airport had filled up since she had arrived. She was keeping an eye out for Jenny Myers. Jenny was in turmoil again. Jenny rang on average once every two months with her life in turmoil. Usually at shit hours of the night. Usually with too much to drink. In Brussels, that was fine. Kate could listen, provide a few words of encouragement and then get back to sleep and forget about it. Now she was home, Jenny was a flesh-and-blood problem. There was a consistency about Jenny's problems. She had to admit that. There was always a man. It didn't matter what the problem was, there was always a man involved. Even if her flat was leaking or a ten-tonne JCB had smashed into her car and pulped it, there was a man somewhere as the root cause of distress. It made Kate despair for her sex sometimes. Then she thought of herself and Jack and held back passing judgement on Jenny.

Jenny was a girl who had everything except someone to live with. And being at that time of life when she was running out of childbearing time faster than she wanted made it all the worse for her. She had men, good men, loads of them, but she just could not find a partner.

"Someone whose breath I like," she once said.

The ones she tried out invariably turned out to be shits. All men are pigs, they used to cheer together at the bitching sessions on her couch. Angie used to forget she was happily married and come up with some obscure problem with Carl so she could join in. Then Jenny would lead the session.

Jenny was just a type, Kate told herself. The world was made up of types. And individuals were variations on a theme.

Types passed her in the self-service. Air hostesses with their catwalk figures and a superiority that had once been based on something solid but had long since lost its gloss. She listened to two girls planning a trip to Portugal. It embarrassed her. They were building up to fever pitch. Voices switching from controlled executivedom to high-pitch dolly-bird, crudity levels reaching the top of the scale. Escaped prisoners, she told herself. They were bitching about work. Did anyone like work? she wondered. If you asked people whether they would like to give up work, how many would? If you offered to pay their salary still. How many people went through life disappointed?

Aengus Kelly was a disappointed man. That was something to watch, too. The feisty cripple. Say anything to get at people. But that wasn't his style. He'd only hit the foreman over the dead cattle, he said. He could have ignored it. Taken the factory line. It was someone else's fault. Cattle died. Farmers used pesticides. All the time.

She weighed it up. Important to weigh it up. Her report had to be detailed. There was more than his say-so. The vet was sympathetic but he was scared of losing goodwill. And eight farms in the area had that stream running though their properties. And none of their animals had died. But they were well downstream of the Martin plant and Crossfin House. It was still a fragile case.

He took under-the-counter, he said. Bad move, Kelly. Jack Clarke's name had come up there. She dismissed that. Not her concern. Maybe he was a feisty cripple. Just wanting to have a go at Martin. And this spill was the catalyst. If the Krishnas weren't so bloody nice, she might have accepted that. Packed her bags and gone back to Brussels. But they were so genuine. So bloody harmless. And everyone down there was out to get them. Now she questioned her own motives.

She kept asking herself if he was kosher. What if he was just a troublemaker? It was convenient they should get a guy who was there on the day of the spill to talk to them. Saw it all, remembered everything. When everyone else was staying mum. The whole damn town was staying mum. She couldn't blame them. They were scared. The factory was the town. Any threat and they closed ranks. Close the factory and you close the town.

She didn't know what they were scared of. Martin's briefs would hold it up for years. Have them chasing their tails. That led her to ask herself if there was any point going on. She had to, she told herself. She was in the process of telling herself a lot of things, trying to sort her life in the space of a coffee and chocolate biscuit.

I won't see him again, she heard herself say. It crept in and hijacked another argument about Kelly's bona fides. She had not known it would come but it must have been there, waiting. Jack Clarke. The hormones were pumping inside her at the sound of his name. She had done so much to rid herself of him. Completely. But that was all destroyed now. He was slowly getting back at her. Coming around, calling. I don't need you, Jack. It isn't there any more. I'm beginning to feel sorry for you. And I don't want that.

Back to Kelly again.

How would he be on the stand? She thought of those seedy eyes, seeming to molest everything female they found. Maybe he was into animals. It was possible. Jesus, if that came out it would blow them out of the water. It would mean serious problems back in Brussels. Nights of heavy-duty Eurospeak. With Emile Hoffmann. Emile Hoffmann was God's representative on earth as far as Kate Keyes was concerned. He could make or break careers with the movement of a muscle and he had done more of the latter than the former in his time. He was a short man who looked French, sounded German but was in fact Belgian. His feet were too big and his shoulders were rounded and gave the impression that he was in some way handicapped. But he could kill with a look at one hundred yards and obliterate with a phrase at any distance. When he was not in action, he held himself with the air of a mouth full of solid blocks of butter.

The breaths reached Kate's ears before the words and the words were well ahead of the running body.

"I'm sorry, Kate, sorry, I couldn't find a damn parking-spot. God, it's crowded. I hate airports. So much sadness. I'm so bloody sad. What would you like?"

All this was out before Kate could reply or think to reply. She was still working out her position *vis-à-vis* the savage M. Hoffmann, the butcher of Brussels.

When she was upset or just supercharged, Jenny spoke like a Gatling gun being fired. If Kate was somewhat reserved, Jenny Myers found it difficult to hold even her subconscious in. And it all came out in a kind of tripping fashion, thoughts falling over one another. She loved often and desperately and she lived in dread of her mother finding out she wasn't a virgin any more. Her mother had fixed views on everything but she had a special thing about virginity. She had a particular devotion to the Virgin Mary which led to a hell of a lot of screaming and roaring when her children visited. Jenny was convinced the whole thing stemmed from a Freudian fear of sex in her mother. She used to say her father looked as if he'd never really enjoyed himself in bed. Kate pointed out that he might have been the problem. But for some reason Jenny couldn't accept that. It was her mother was the problem there.

It had been fine when she lived in Scotland. She could live with anyone she liked, and she did, and it felt like a thousand feet of burial dirt had been lifted from her, but at home, the spectre of her mother hung over her, haunting her.

"Why don't you marry him, Jenny?" her mother used to say about whoever she was seeing. No matter who. No matter how long she'd been seeing him.

Then the arguments would begin: biological clocks, settling down, freedom, fulfilment, careers, the whole kit and caboodle. Funny thing was they both had the same aim, except that Jenny could not accept that.

"I don't know, Kate," Jenny said.

Kate had heard this before. When Jenny was like this she was totally caught up in herself. Nothing else mattered. It was an annoying side to her and none of them could bear it too much. Angie had had to bear most of it over the years but then Angie was a bit of a saint. All groups of friends have their saints and Angie was theirs. Jenny was the neurotic and Kate—she didn't fit easily into any pigeonhole.

"I thought you said he wanted to marry you."

"I did. I thought he did. I thought I did. He thought I did. I thought he thought I did. He thought I thought he did. We went up and back and forth and over it all. They end, Kate. They end too damn often. I can't."

"You can't?"

"Well, he can't."

"Which of you can't?"

"It's mutual."

"Now it's mutual. Come on, Jen. Mutual or what?"

"You're so bloody together, Kate. I hate you when you're like that. Why can't you just weaken a bit? Just once. When was the last time you screwed a guy for the fun of it?"

"Jesus, will you keep your voice down, Jen. Jesus."

"There you are. God!"

She pulled at her hair. She pulled out a packet of cigarettes.

"I hate them but I have to have one."

There was a mark on her lip which became highlighted when she was distressed. Kate had noticed that.

"Just calm down."

"Calm down. Calm down. My entire life is going up in smoke faster than this bloody fag and you tell me to calm down. Where are you when I need you, Kate? Off to—to—to bloody Brussels."

"I'll be back."

"I need you now."

Need me. There were times when friendship was strained to breaking point, when old wounds opened again to remind you that people you considered friends had their limits. Where were you when I needed you? When Jean-Paul died. Just a few cards, saying how sorry you all were. No one came over. Maybe you felt I didn't need anyone. With him for only four months. Then he wraps himself round a lamppost. How much could he mean in four months? Well, he meant a lot. Kate could feel the anger in her surging. She wasn't sure what Jean-Paul had meant. He had been fun. She could say that about him. In a social scene where most of the men made Belgians look exciting. But Jean-Paul had an excitement about him and a passionate dedication to the Third World. That was their common ground. Kate had her ambitions. But you had to put your time in to get what you wanted. The Jean-Paul thing and the Third World brought her right back to Jack Clarke and she had to put the brakes on the whole train of thought.

"Look, I'm sorry, Jen," she said.

She put her hand on her friend's and could feel the shaking.

"I'll be back in a couple of days. You have my number. Give me a ring. You have to ask yourself if you love him. And if you do, do you want to live with him for the remainder? And then does he want you?"

"You make it all sound so easy, Kate. I adore him. I hate him. Sort that one out."

She drew long and hard on her cigarette and then stubbed the rest of it into her saucer. Kate saw lines under her eyes and a mistiness about them. As if she was hiding from something. It had always been there. Maybe it showed an unwillingness to face up to things; maybe of having to do it too much. She'd never had any problems herself. Except maybe lack of interest when she'd wanted interest. Then her father was dead and her mother moved and years and distance buffered thought. She left her own circumstances the way she'd left thinking about Jack.

Poor Jenny. She either had to go abroad for good or face up to constant interference for as long as her mother stayed alive. Kate had herself putting bets on that.

"I have this friend in Brussels, Éamonn, on secondment. He's gay. He says he begged for the secondment. It's up in a year. He's going to resign and stay. He's not going back. He drinks a lot now just thinking about it."

Jenny looked at her as if she was supposed to take something from that. She tried to figure out the message.

"You think I should go away again?"

"No, no: it's just that there's other problems out there, Jen. You know."

Jenny scrunched her face. She felt as much embarrassment as it was possible for her to feel and a lot of resentment at her friend for pointing out the obvious. Kate grabbed her hand again and squeezed it.

"Maybe when I've finished here, you can come back with me for a while and sort yourself out. How about that?"

Jenny caught hold of Kate's hands and pulled her towards her and kissed her on the cheek, a big wet kiss with plenty of noise.

"I love you, Kate, I just fucking love you. I'll do that. I'll come now. I told them I wasn't feeling well. I can get time off. I can follow you over. You don't mind. Jesus, why didn't I think of that? You're a pet. Let me ring the office. Three—four days..."

She was already running for a phone.

"How long did you say you'd be away?"

Kate tried to shake her head. It wouldn't obey her. This was not what she'd meant. Not at all! She kept saying that to herself. The Aengus Kelly stuff kept interrupting her when she was trying to make sense of what had happened. What *had* happened? She had set out to try and ease Jenny's neurosis and ended up inviting her to Brussels. It was crazy. Nothing worked out as you wanted it. Nothing.

It's not insensitivity, Jenny, Kate said to herself. It's just that I'm past all this, way past it, darling. Sure, I get worried about it, about being over thirty, about how much time I have left, but I have other things, things that are worth while. Why the hell didn't you marry Andy when he wanted to marry you? At least stay with him. You should have stayed with him. But that was Jenny all over: once she had something she had to have what was next. She was a fabulous landscape architect but she couldn't settle on a layout for herself. And now Andy was going to America without his girl-friend or his kid and he was unhappy, and Jenny was running around like a headless chicken because of a bloke none of them really liked, a bloke with an Italian surname who came from Belfast and talked in an accent that was a cross between Dublin 9 and mid-Atlantic, who drove a Renault 5, who wore dungarees when he was lazing about, who read parenting guides and talked home-made wine. You could have married Andy. Andy's a good bloke and you loved him or came as close to really loving him as you're ever likely to get. Kate had to stop herself there for three reasons. One was Aengus Kelly, the other was Jenny returning from the phone and the third was Jack Clarke making a hobo ride on the train of her thoughts.

"Bugger you, Jack."

"What?" Jenny said.

She was beaming. Her lips had come out in a colour that made them look like fresh spring blossoms. She had shaken off the withering foliage look she had come with. Fresh life had been injected into her and Kate could not bring herself to question her friend or her motives.

"You're crazy," she said.

"I'm not the worst."

Somewhere between Dublin and Brussels, at about thirty-three thousand feet, while drinking a plastic cup of coffee and staring out at the bed of clouds they were resting on, Kate met Jack Clarke again. A memory sparked by a memory sparked by another memory brought him to her, wanted and unwanted in the same instant. Jenny Myers was not the only one with a paradox of a personal life to cart around with her. They had been to—she could not recall where, maybe it was Brussels, but no one went there except when they had to or found themselves there by accident—they had been somewhere hot. Jack looked good with a tan. It got into him. It took ages to fade. He didn't look healthy now. He looked bad now. As if he was going to tip over. Maybe that was why she was being so tolerant. Or maybe she hadn't ejected him the way she thought she had. The memory got drowned for a while in a sea of side-orders and arguments. Most of them old stuff, none of them solvable in that moment.

They had joined the mile-high club. In the toilet. It had been tacky as hell and they'd laughed about it being tacky as hell but Jack wanted to do it and she was pissed and in love. That was the first time since seeing him again she had admitted to herself she had ever been in love with him. It had snuck in, another uninvited guest. She ignored it and concentrated on the tackiness of the mile-high experience. It took her mind off everything else. And right there, with Jenny, at thirty-odd thousand feet, on a bed of white cloud, condensation on the windows, a subtle movement in the wings, she needed to have her mind on something ridiculous. For the relief. The escape.

She hadn't told anyone and it felt like the kind of thing they told at quiz nights in the city-centre bars. The kind of thing you should be ashamed of if you had any idea of the things you should be ashamed of. She was stepping back from it now. It didn't fit in with her view of herself. Up and coming senior whateverocrats in the Commission should not have mile-high status. Though the sexual acrobatics of the Community and its honourable members of parliament would make the average tabloid reader's hair stand on end.

There was a shop that sold oranges and she could not figure out where it came into the story. But Jack had two oranges and he had peeled them and was slipping the segments into her mouth in that stainless steel cubicle. She kept thinking the whole plane would have its eyes fixed on the engaged sign.

Trying to move in that stainless steel cubicle, a kind of compromise of motions, a telepathy of want. She let it pass her by in all its frenzied ecstasy, the first touches: his belt— she couldn't get it undone; her skirt above her thighs; her hands still trying to get his belt undone; he was forcing himself out; she almost ripped his trousers off, he banged his head and she had to stop to check if he was all right. He was, he was all right, he said, he couldn't even feel it, and his belt came undone and his trousers went down with the speed of the silk at her waist and in a second the whole frenzy reappeared and multiplied infinitely and he was moving up into her and she had wrapped her legs around him and she was pushing down on to him. They had to keep quiet and that made it better and when it was coming, she could feel it coming in her and his body was moving in a way she knew it was coming in him; and outside the noise of the engines on full, thousands of pounds of thrust, driven, head swelling, brain dizzy. Push more, harder, slow, slow and hard. It came against the stainless steel, cold and her hands held it and felt the cold of the steel and the warmth of him and she threw her head back and opened her mouth as if to suck the whole world in and the world came in and went out and time and space stood still and exploded in an instant of everything and nothing and they sank against the stainless steel, laughing and kissing and loving.

"I'll have work to do," she said.

Jenny looked at her.

"I know. I wish Angie was here. The three of us. We don't

do things like this any more."

"No."

Kate was already back at work. Examining what they had on paper. What she could tell the venerable M. Hoffman. The man who brought a whole new meaning to the words chemical spill. And Jack was there. In there with this lousy mess. They would fight it to the end, and Jack was one of them. Those poor people were losing their livelihood and he and Martin would employ everything in their power to make it worse for them. Her Jack. She ceased to use that phrase again. Her Jack was someone else. Her Jack had never been her Jack. That had gone on somewhere far away, a distant land, where lovers could exist outside reality and knowledge was as dangerous as poison.

They had both eaten the fruit since then and they knew too much, about themselves, about each other and the way it was could never be recaptured. She tried to tell herself she was telling it like it was, that Jack was a nice blast from the past, nothing more, a reminder of a time that had been good and was now gone. Never go back. She kept repeating that when they were coming in to land. As much to put off the fear of landing as anything else. She had a terrible fear of flying. Take-off and landing turned her into stone: she became so stiff. So she repeated it to herself. Get on with the work. Get the report finished and get out of there.

12

F rank Costello leaned over his desk, tipped his head to one side and looked the young man standing in front of him straight in the eyes.

"I don't think shouting is going to get us anywhere, Denis. I am aware of the difficulties. I assure you."

Costello opened his arms in a friendly gesture he had learned at a PR agency, then he followed it with some more practised routines devised to deal with the public. He had a look of concerned determination he had been practising for an hour before the delegation arrived. It was one of ten or maybe more he had in stock for such occasions. There were three more delegations to be met that day and he would greet each with its own unique designer facial expression and body language. He pushed his steel-rimmed glasses back up to the bridge of his nose. He had been going over a submission and had deliberately let them fall down, another routine advised by the handlers.

The young man looked around at his female colleague and, noting the blank expression of the civil servant to Costello's right, sat down in the chair provided.

"Maybe some tea," Costello said.

He looked at the civil servant, who did not change his expression. He got up from his seat, stepped outside the room for a couple of seconds and came back.

"You see, Denis, and I hope I don't sound uncaring, you

see, the fundamentals of the economy are sound, Denis. You do see that. This Government has brought inflation down, we have low interest rates, the climate for growth is good. You do see that. We—and maybe I should emphasise this more—we found the books in a hell of a mess when we got in. It was a terrible shock. A hell of a mess. The precipice was this close."

He showed with his thumb and forefinger. The young man wanted to point out that Frank and his lads had helped to cause most of the mess in the first place but he was caught up in Costello's routine and it didn't seem as if his remark would get through.

"It's not just us. There's a general downturn. We're victims of forces outside our control. And, of course, with things bad across the water, we're getting emigrants coming home."

He shook his head.

"Is that a bad thing, Taoiseach?" the young woman on Denis's left said.

Costello paused. He looked at his assistant, who had come back in almost unnoticed. With the same blank expression he handed Costello a couple of sheets of paper.

"You see, we've managed to hold on to employment levels. You see the figures. We've been solid there. Employment is falling everywhere else. But we're solid. It's just..."

"You'd rather more people left."

"Ah, now Denis, that's not fair. I agreed to meet you because I'm concerned as much as you are. It's our top priority, jobs, our top priority. The fundamentals are good. And you young people, you're the future. Our biggest resource."

The handlers had insisted he use that. Frank Costello wasn't so sure. He could tell now which clichés worked, which platitudes would make it.

"Then why are there no jobs?" the young woman said. "Why are our unemployment rates twice everyone else's? Why, Taoiseach? You know—you know—they scream in places like Australia and Britain that they have ten or twelve per cent out of work. Jesus, we're twice that, Taoiseach. Fucking depression levels."

"Now calm down—eh, Gráinne, is it? We'll get nowhere losing tempers. This requires steady nerves. I admit, the figures look bad, but as I say there's more to this, other elements. If you knew the whole—"

"Bollocks!"

"Please—eh, Gráinne, I can't allow that. I know we have our differences, but please respect the office. Now, please, I do understand. And there were mistakes made in the past. But they were mistakes we had no power over. The last Government…"

He went on to list the failings of his predecessor.

"How long?" the Gráinne interrupted. "How long are we supposed to wait? There isn't one survey says you'll get the figures down by the end of the century. You expect people like me to hang around, sitting on our fannies, waiting for you to give us hand-outs. Because we won't. I'm not in some kind of dress-rehearsal, Mr Costello. I want to have a life. And I want it now. And if you and your lot don't do something about that, I won't hang around any longer."

"It's always your prerogative to emigrate, Gráinne. Lord knows we hate to see our young people go. But if they choose that, we do help. We're in Europe now. We should be thinking in a Community way. I think that's where we should be looking for the future."

"While you grease your favourites, your Martins and that lot."

"Now that's not fair. We have to encourage entrepreneurs, you know. They create wealth. They create jobs. And that's what we want."

"How many?"

"What?"

"How many? So far?"

"Oh, come on, I can't give you a figure. But I told you

we're holding employment levels."

Gráinne sighed.

"What kind of country encourages its people to leave?" Denis said. "Tell me that?"

Costello sat back and let his mouth open wide enough to show he was shocked and stunned at the suggestion, even insulted. It worked. The young man's lower lip quivered.

"I hope you're not implying..."

The Taoiseach's assistant broke in.

"You have a meeting in ten minutes, Taoiseach."

Costello smiled. He gathered himself, then he stood up and put his hand out. The two young people facing him did not know whether to reciprocate. They were angry and they had promised one another they would not lose their tempers and give him the chance to patronise them. But it had happened and they were angry at one another and feeling it was best to get out now before they really looked like schoolchildren arguing over chocolate.

"I will give this submission my total consideration, I promise you," Costello said, when they had decided to shake his hand. "It is our top priority. Jobs. And we're thinking of a forum. You know, to get input from as many sides as possible. I feel it is a national issue and above party political issues. Maybe you two would like to sit on a steering committee. Naturally, it would be salaried. There you are, jobs already."

That completely up-ended them. They winced at each other and nodded their heads. Better inside than out and a job was a job.

"Ah, Paud," Costello said.

Henry had been told to make his appearance at this time.

"Government business, I'm afraid."

He introduced the two unemployment action representatives and Paud Henry showed he fancied Gráinne, who, except for a certain amount of acne at her chin, was fanciable.

As they were leaving, Gráinne turned and said: "I meant what I said, Taoiseach. I won't hang around, blowing off. I'll take what I want. And there's more like me. So don't take us for granted."

Henry made some patronising remarks and the civil servant escorted the delegation from the Taoiseach's office.

"Put a watch on that one, Paud," Costello said. "The usual routine. See who she's screwing. Complete job."

"Wouldn't mind getting a leg over meself, Frank. Wouldn't mind at all."

He slapped his hands together. Costello gestured to him to sit down. The real business of the day could begin. Costello had left orders that once Derek Bell arrived, they were not to be disturbed. It was his first time to talk to Derek Bell face to face since Bell had launched his investigation into MartinCorp. It was a chance to try and stop the thing going any further, before it ran on ahead of him, out of his control. If it got to that then who knew what would happen. Frank Costello didn't much like who-knew-what-would-happen land. It was prone to storms of flying excrement. Too prone.

He was going over some old ground with his Justice minister when the knock on the door came. Henry opened it and turned to his boss, looking puzzled.

"Tea, Frank?"

Costello turned from the painting behind his desk. He had been looking at something, a woman, trying to figure out what she was doing. He told Paud to let the man in. The tea. They hadn't had their tea. That was what they would say to the press. He offered us tea and then didn't give it to us. Frank heard his curses rebound around his head. He should have remembered to give them the tea. First rule of politics, try not to offer certainties, and if you have to, make sure they're simple and make sure you deliver. He took a digestive from the tray and bit on it. Bell would be along soon. He was always on time.

"Pour us a cup, there, Paud," Costello said. "And help yourself. Anything on him?"

Henry shook his piglet head and fumbled with the silver tea pot. Some tea spilled. He should have more to report to his boss. Henry hated coming to Costello with nothing. He liked to have something. To please. His worst nightmare was Frank Costello displeased. Henry gave Costello a cup and took a biscuit for himself and slurped his tea.

"Ralph Martin has done a bit of digging," Costello said. "I want you to meet that snot-nose he uses, Clarke, and find out where we can co-operate. Larry'll be with you on this, Paud. How are the party finances, by the way?"

"Real or imagined, Frank?"

"Well, I think we can have these funds we were promised. Almost unlimited," Costello said.

Henry's eyes lit up. He watched his boss dunk a digestive and tried the same himself. Half the biscuit fell in his tea. Costello watched his Justice minister fumble with a spoon to try and extract the sodden half of digestive. He shook his head.

He'd have preferred Phil Cassidy to be the party bagman, if he'd had the choice. But he didn't have a choice. Amazing, he thought, the way people always looked in on things and saw unity. Once they were inside all they saw was division. If only the bullshit about unity and solidarity were fractionally true, instead of the actual situation of constantly having to battle with people supposed to be on your side. Frank Costello had beaten off five challenges to his leadership, all but the first with good margins, but it took so much energy that he felt it diverted him from his main mission. It never weakened the bedrock of his determination to hang on, though.

It was that very determination to hang on which was unsettling the troops. Already there were half a dozen senior ministers who, the press were saying, had no chance of succession now. The cracks were visible. Give people no hope and they lash out. He had that young woman's last words on his mind. Phil Cassidy wanted his job, still thought he was young enough for it, said it to anyone who would listen. But Cassidy hadn't the support. And Paud was keeping an eye on the Cassidy camp, so that Frankie knew what they were thinking before they did. Bell could screw it all up; he was a different kind of threat. Kept denying he had any interests outside serving the nation, and, he was good on television. Believable. It was his credibility that Frankie Costello hated. Cassidy was believable, too, but television didn't help him. He was an old street fighter and it showed. Sometimes Costello was forced to think maybe he would be better off getting the hell out of it all and leaving them to it. That line of thought never got very far. The game had him. It had long ceased to exist separate from his life. It was his life.

Frank Costello thought of himself as an idealist. He still considered himself a torch-holder. It was just he was more realistic now, knew what could and could not be achieved. Everything he did was for the good of the country. And the good of the country was intricately tied up with his own good, so much so now that he could not see any difference. It was an easy defence. The paranoia of self-righteousness. The benevolent *una voce, uno duce* refusal to see any other viewpoint. A belief in a determined right to power. And power was the drug which kept it all going. Without the power, Frank Costello would have given it up years ago and gone back to being a barrister. He had been a good advocate. In the early days. Especially when he defended people he believed in. Then, as an orator in a Dáil that was devoid of orators, he shot to notice, with words that came dipped in gold. The power: that was the bottom line. And he was not prepared to give it up.

"You could sack him," Henry said. "Bell."

"Terrific, Paud. That would go down a treat. An immediate bloody election. No, I want him turned or neutralised. I'll call an election on *my* terms. I've stood by too long with him around. I want to have it out with him now. I want him fixed, squashed and silent, Paud, and I want this Martin thing cleared up. Jesus, doesn't he know the whole fucking future of industry here is at stake? And he wants to send it down the river because of some fucking principle. Who's going to replace all the jobs that could go? Who's going to invest here if we're blacklisted in the States? This is trying to get me, you know. Me. He's been out to get me. He thinks I don't know. But I know. I see it in him. It's naked. He's had it in for Ralph for years. Since Ralph bought the remains of his business. And me because I'm—because I'm what he'll never be. Fucking envy, that's what it is, Paud. And he'd sell his fucking country down the fucking drain for it. What the hell did we ever see in him?"

"Definitely not money. I can't believe he's in such a mess. Offer him Europe, Frank. He'll jump at it. Loads of tax-free there. How the hell did he get himself in this bloody mess? This is all true, I hope?"

Henry was reading a summary of Bell's financial position.

"Course it's true. A good man who gets the job done did it. A good soldier, Paud, like you."

Henry liked compliments. They raised his self-esteem which was usually rock bottom. He nodded thanks to his boss.

"Sit over there when he comes in, Paud. I want him to feel comfortable. And for crying out loud, don't say anything till I've finished what I have to say."

They sat in silence, waiting. Frank Costello was already way ahead of Henry, planning what he would do in the event that Bell still refused to call the dogs off Martin and give the insurance. It was a tight one, he told himself, but then he'd been in tight ones before. It was a matter of being able to distance himself enough from the mess. Larry Tallon was Technology. Technically, all that business was his lookout. He should have known Martin was shifting illegal hardware. As if they'd cared at the time. The stuff could have been Mars bars for all they cared. What they wanted was business, contracts, export orders, sales, money coming in— for the balance of payments, to make the economy look good. Give it the air of a fast-growing, dynamic economy. A can-do place. You had to support the boys who were going out there to win. Put your weight in behind them. If you tried to look after everyone, nothing would get done. The press would have a field day. All he needed was some prick in Industry leaking that they were investigating Martin, holding back insurance. It made him shake. At least Paud had everyone involved on tap. If they so much as gave the shagging carpet colour in the department away he'd have the Branch around and lift them. I'm going to survive this, he told himself; I'm going to survive this.

Bell sat staring at Costello.

"His name is Kelly, Frank, Aengus Kelly, and he says they've been sending embargoed technology to the Gulf. Most of it not even Irish. It's a whole network of underground deals. The Americans will have to be informed. I don't see an alternative. He says a lot of other things too, Frank. Precursor chemicals, weapons. You want the list?"

Costello put his glasses on and read what Bell shoved in front of him.

"I never liked the man, Frank," Bell said. "Martin. I always had a bad feeling about him. It stinks, Frank. They've been playing us like cheap musical instruments. We've written a blank cheque and they just have to fill in the amount. I seriously think Paud should have a look into all this. And I'll have to ask Customs to investigate. When it's completed I'm sending the file to the DPP. Paud, your people will have to check it. I'm sure the whole damn thing is rotten. If they've been doing this, what the hell else have they been up to? Think about it!"

Henry had backed away and was sitting in the seat the stone-faced civil servant had occupied.

"I'll have the Commissioner put someone on to it, Derek.

We're pretty stretched at the moment. But if there's evidence of wrongdoing then rest assured I'll see it gets investigated. I could do with more cash, Frank, more equipment. And the barracks are in a shit condition around the country. They keep coming to me, complaining. Maybe we could get a few extra million for my lot. You know, if we're to have a modern police force, it costs money."

"Sure, Paud," Costello said.

He was glad that the wind had been taken out of Bell's sails. That was what Henry was doing . Frank had told him to. First chance he got. Do anything, Paud, to divert. Get him moving. Off the point.

"Bar this—this Kelly fellow—do we have any evidence of what you're saying, Derek? I mean, how reliable is he? Do you have documents? Photos? Evidence, Derek. It says here he's some kind of animal lover. What kind of an animal lover? Paud's had a look at him, haven't you, Paud?"

Paud nodded.

"They fired him for hitting a foreman. What kind of animal lover hits a foreman? I mean, is this the sum total of your information? His word. I understand he was a bloody troublemaker, hanging around a bunch of foreign loonies. What are they?—Hare Krishnas. Some kind of cult. I mean, come on, Derek, distance yourself a bit. I know you and Ralph Martin go back a while."

"That's nothing to do with it, Frank. We have documentary evidence to back up his claims. I can say no more at this point. Except this is serious. I have my investigators going through it all. A special team. They're ready to work with Paud's people. I'd like help from Larry, too."

"Sure, I'll ask if he can spare anyone. But get a case first. Prepare a proper file. I'll want to see it. Lazy, inefficient, incompetent, these are strong charges against Kelly."

He passed the report from the local gardaí.

"What if you're wrong and they sue? It could cost us a

fortune. The AG says it's possible. Phil would flip. And these charges against him don't come from his bosses. These are his workmates. You know. You'd want to have a better case than this if you're going to pull insurance. Jesus, have you thought what a successful legal case would do for our estimates? For our credibility? I mean there's more here than just right and wrong, Derek. Do you get me? Do you see what I'm saying?"

"There's the national interest to consider," Paud Henry said on cue.

It was a slow, methodical play they worked on Bell. Praising his work, sounding astounded at some of the allegations he was raising but not completely surprised, suggesting further inquiries, repeating the national interest angle. Time was the thing here, Ralph Martin had said to Costello. Costello had agreed. At least get the Britcop deal through before any shit, no matter how much, hit the fan. Then they could cope more, plug the gaps. But Martin needed time and he was calling in a lifetime of friendships in the party.

Costello stood at the window, looking out at the courtyard. Another grey day. He hated Dublin when it was grey. It sucked the character out of the city. As if someone had frozen it in a kind of hibernation. Life seemed to slow down and things that you wouldn't normally notice took an age. A van came in and stopped at the steps of the main entrance to Government Buildings. There was a television crew at the gate, hanging around. The van driver got out and stood by his vehicle and the television crew chatted with a couple of gardaí. Frank Costello wanted to open his window and yell at them all: get up, get off your arses and get moving. He had spent all his life wanting to get that into his people—because he considered them his people, a kind of bequest from the generation before him, the ones that had done all the work, the ones he felt he had to live up to, the ones he was envious of. He wanted to get it into their heads that they had it in them, that all the timidity, the insecurity, the gombeenism could be overcome. But now he was touching on a secret store of idealism that he did not need. He concentrated on the business at hand. He looked at his watch. He didn't have much time with his Industry minister.

"Cabinet will want to hear this," he said.

"Of course, Frank," Bell said.

"They're not going to like it," Henry said. "Not one bit."

"Stakes?" Costello asked.

"Us," Henry said.

They were acting as if Bell weren't there. He looked from one to the other, feeling fascinated and humiliated at the same time.

"We're not talking party politics here, gentlemen," he announced. "This is above parties. Above us all. We're talking fraud. Deception. Criminality. And it runs deep. Do you hear? I will investigate it and I will bring it to the attention of the house and the people. It is my duty. My duty. I can do nothing else."

Costello stretched over his desk at Bell.

"What the hell are you saying, man? Where the hell do you live? I'm the fucking Taoiseach. You talk to me about duty. I know all about duty. What the hell are you going to do about your duty to this nation's economy? When one of our biggest crashes into the dust. Look really good in an *FT* front page article. Do us the world of good. And what about your duty to the people? You were a businessman once. Well, you know. All those bloody jobs that Martin will have to shed. You think the French or the Germans give a shit what their people deal in? No, they want business, markets and money. That's all. Duty! Jesus!"

Costello was standing with his hands in his pockets.

"You think you'll have one seat left if you do this? You'll be lucky to get elected to a parent-teacher association. And let me tell you, Mr Minister for Industry, I don't like what I'm hearing. If you're looking for an election then I'll go for it. I won't like it but I'll go for it. Jesus, where the hell did we get you?"

Henry saw that Costello had lost his rag, something they had said he should not do. So he came in to help, a bit scared because Frank Costello in a rage always put the wind up Paud Henry.

"Taoiseach, I don't think Derek was trying to destabilise the Government. Were you, Derek?"

Bell was still recovering from the attack. He'd heard of Frank Costello's menace before but never experienced it. He had his handkerchief out. He rubbed his lips, cleaning away the residue which had gathered on them.

"Certainly not. No. Never. I—eh—listen, Frank, this is happening and we're involved. I have to follow it through. I have to. My department's involved. The country's reputation is at stake."

"I don't think the Taoiseach's suggesting you don't, Derek."

Bell was becoming irritated with Henry's conciliation. The two men were further apart than stars in different galaxies. It was common knowledge they couldn't stand each other. Bell, who was not known for his vitriol, had in a moment of weakness during one of the heaves against Costello a decade earlier referred to Henry as a spineless parasite. Henry had never forgotten it and although the hatchet was nominally buried it was easily accessible. Derek Bell wanted it now. He was well aware of the consequences for the whole export drive the Government had been encouraging. He was well aware of the consequences of a general election for his political prospects. He was well aware of Martin's support for his partners. You couldn't but be aware. But he wasn't the only one. There were others. Frank Costello played it as if Martin was the cornerstone of the economy. That was bullshit. No. Bell was sticking to his guns. The investigation continued and until it was through, insurance was suspended.

"I don't know what your relationship to Ralph Martin is, Frank, and to tell the truth, I don't want to. But if you feel you might be compromised by an investigation I seriously suggest you consider your position. For the Government's sake. For the national interest."

The tone of his voice bit hard into Costello.

"Jesus, Derek. I don't shagging believe this. Are you threatening me? A minister in my cabinet threatening me. Don't you ever fucking dare threaten me, son. I know what you're at. You made speeches against me ten years ago; you made speeches against me every time someone made a move for my head. You've always wanted me out. Flawed pedigree. I'll fucking give you flawed pedigree. I'll shove it up your arse. By Christ, if you go against me again, I'll see you chairing council meetings on the Skelligs. Consider my position. Don't you fucking tell me to consider my position. I'll tell you to—I'll fucking give you positions..."

"Frank, Frank, please, Frank." Henry didn't know how many times he repeated the Taoiseach's name. "Please, we're on the same side."

Bell was out of his seat at this stage and pointing his finger at Costello.

"Don't bullyboy me, Frank Costello. I know—I know—you think—you think—you—we could have it working well, we could, but you, you and your damn—him and the rest..."

He pointed to Henry.

"Look at them. Look around you, Frank. Look what's happened. So you think you can yell and I'll jump. Well, I won't. This is going the whole bloody way. I'll go by the book. Every damn step. But I'm doing what I said I would. And if I find I'm meeting dead ends, Frank, or if Paud's lads aren't following it up, I'll go public faster than you can fart, Taoiseach. Now, excuse me, I've work to do."

He slammed the door behind him.

"Oh, shite, fucking shite," Paud Henry said.

13

The day after the Britcop deal was sealed, Jack Clarke was buying a small redbrick two-up-two-down in the Liberties. Right behind the Cornmarket. The whole Britcop takeover went like clockwork, and Ralph Martin's daily ran a full-page colour piece on its proprietor, praising him as the way forward for the country's business. Words like tough, shrewd, intelligent, were thrown around like the autumn leaves in the early winter winds. Even the banks rang up to congratulate. There were few dissenters. One business magazine had planned a five-page spread on Martin's debt exposure, but Ralph Martin had obtained an injunction the day before publication. It cost the magazine a fortune. Ralph had waited for the entire edition to go to press. The article wasn't particularly damning in any case. Ralph Martin rang the publisher the next morning to make an offer for the magazine.

Jack Clarke said the two-up-two-down was an investment. He had no intention of living there. Despite the influx of yuppies into the area, Jack had a feeling his hubcaps would be safer where he was. And he said he preferred waking up to the smell of the sea rather than the smell of fish. The fish market smell from around the corner had a habit of lingering longer than it should. Anyway, Jack already had a taker for the property, a spotty southsider who worked for some amorphous financial institution and said things like, get your people to contact my people, and played squash and chased past-pupils of Mount Anville and Alex. The broad vowels coming out of his mouth defied description and Jack only put up with him as a good source of money info and a nice patsy for a sting like this. The rent more than paid the mortgage and your man was doloighted to be gutting bock to the reel Dooblon. Jack kept watching the street through the laced curtains, checking his BMW was still in one piece.

There should have been more elation after the Britcop thing went through. But all Jack could recall was a sense of hurdle cleared. It produced more sighs than smiles and everyone cleared off early rather then celebrate. Ralph Martin was in London with Dan Meehan, doing the PR bit. Jack had been left behind to work on the insurance problem full-time. It was euphemistically referred to as that now. And Jack was to be the chief operator with Larry Tallon and Barney Small. No more discussions on the subject with Ralph Martin till it was done.

Jack should have liked that. It was the usual way with a job like this, but there were doubts in him and the Britcop success hadn't quelled them. He had considered going to Martin to talk about it, maybe ask for some time off, only he knew what Martin would say. Martin men were supposed to run until they dropped and then some more. They didn't have doubts and they didn't have problems they brought into work. And most of all, they didn't have ex-girl-friends they still wanted who were ready to stitch the company right up. Jack felt disloyal. But to whom he could not say.

There was something about this Bell business, too, which had alarms ringing all around it. This wasn't some Third World nobody who'd sell his country out for a fiver and a gold watch. Bell was about as big as they'd ever hit. If it went right, no one would know; if it went wrong, he would get it right in the teeth. And Ralph Martin would disavow any knowledge of his actions. That was the way. All the way up, he had known this was the way Martin worked. He'd seen it for himself: people disavowed. But they were usually wasters, third-hand heavies, and they got good pay for their trouble. He'd always trusted his ability. Felt safe. Well, now he didn't feel so safe. Kate and his father had something to do with it, but it was bigger than that. He kept remembering a jibe he'd once heard about reaching the level of your own incompetence. And too many people in the building smiled at him too often. People who wouldn't ordinarily smile unless he did it first.

Molly was replaced by a small matchstick teenager one day. Molly was supposed to be going on extended leave. He never heard where she did go. It wasn't unusual for secretaries to be moved and for people to disappear on extended leave for long periods, but Jack was in a mood where extra sugar in his coffee would have made him suspicious.

He was suddenly playing for higher stakes than he had ever dreamed of. And he could feel himself blinking. It had happened almost without his noticing it. He rested his brain on the first dodgy bits of work he'd ever done for Martin. The first backhanders, the first lean-jobs.

They'd leaned on a government minister in an African banana republic: nothing much, just a few compromising photographs from a Soho massage parlour. But it had been so easy and it was necessary so the end justified the means. And one lean-job led to a backhander and another backhander led on and soon he did that kind of fit and set like it was second nature. Everyone does it, was the usual excuse. And he was right. When you were operating near the stratosphere, trying to reach escape velocity, it was a knife-edge game. Once you broke free whole governments got overturned. Small countries got shifted and changed as if they were counters in a board game. He knew the players and the movers. Which CEOs did cocaine, which had people rubbed out, which had organised a coup here, a revolt there. It was going on all the time. If you didn't get in first, you got stood on. He used to argue it with Kate when they were living together. When she took bits of expensive pottery he had brought back with him from different corners of the world and threw them at him. It was a different world, he tried to explain. Where the ordinary rules did not apply. People like her, with their nice research grants and their white wine-drinking vegetarian friends didn't have a clue. They accepted the fruits of the battle. But they wouldn't get their hands dirty. How the hell did she think she got her cheap commodities, her cheap clothes? Because we, the west, we're winning the war. We set prices, we control flows. You think it would be this way for one moment if they had it their way? They have the oil and look what that's done to us. Think about it, love.

That was when she threw two jars at him and sobbed in the bedroom all night. He slept on the couch. She moved out a week later. Then moved back in for another month, then moved out again when he was away for a week. There was a small note and a flower. The flower was meant as a symbol but it didn't work on Jack. He drank heavily after that.

Bell was a bloody hostile mark. Bloody dangerous. Even Barney Small, who'd bribed and blackmailed half the oligarchies south of the equator, had a drier expression than usual. Barney was drinking more, too. Jack wanted to shift him out but Martin insisted he was in. And Barney would have kicked up shit if he'd been squeezed out. For the first time, Jack felt scared that he wasn't seeing everything. Running blind. Or half blind. Small kept saying it wouldn't come to the heavy stuff. Larry Tallon would work his magic and Bell would be eating out of their hands in a second. See what was good for him, good for the country, good for everything. If he wasn't such a stuck-up, self-righteous git the whole thing could have been handled by Frank Costello over a drink and no one would have been the wiser. But Bell had to be a crusader. And he'd send MartinCorp down the plug-hole to prove a point.

Jack had a drink with his new tenant, far away from the redbrick two-up-two-down, and went for a walk to clear what was left to clear of his head. He'd increased the pills again. More of more of the same. The colours were mixing in his mind. He didn't know which ones he was taking now; just taking whatever came to hand whenever he needed it. He was edgy. A kind of giddiness dogged him. Made his hands shake. If he walked he could calm it down. Stop the shakes. A couple of drinks did it too. He kept telling himself he was up to it, as he'd told Martin. But he wasn't sure any more.

There'd been a call from Kate. On his desk. A note from the new matchstick secretary they'd given him. He had tried to have lustful thoughts about her but his libido level was well down. He could hear the alarms there, too. His mind went back to the call. She'd left a number. It wasn't her number in Dalkey. He didn't want to phone it. No reason he could explain. He thought maybe he should go out to her flat and wait. He wanted to see her but he didn't want to answer her call. Love her and kill her at the same time. The kind of paradox he was experiencing all the time now.

He had a hamburger in a fast-food restaurant and then some chips in a chipper. It was a junk-food jaunt, nowhere special. Up O'Connell Street, down a side street, he saw a pickpocket caught by an American tourist; he saw a woman after she was mugged near Moore Street; he saw a girl arrested for selling fireworks. He bought some apples and a grapefruit and put the grapefruit in a dustbin. Then he went into a bookies and put a hundred on four horses. He tried to watch and be interested. A kind of tribute to his dad.

His dad was much worse. A lot of shaking heads from doctors who referred rather than diagnosed. Poor doctors referred to richer doctors. Only rich doctors could tell you you were going to live or die. Jack said it had to do with insurance and litigation. It seemed the whole world could be boiled down to that now. He wandered back across Capel

Street and stopped for a pint and then moved up a couple of dilapidated narrows to Smithfield and the cobbles. They'd had a shop around there, the Clarkes. Very popular with the markets lot. He could still feel a tremor in his right hand.

The Britcop deal had shown he still had it. He could be proud of that. Even Alan Kennedy admitted that Jack had oiled it well. Needed a lot of fieldwork. Linelaying. Keeping the thing secret. Dan Meehan spinning the right stories to the right hacks. Their people. And not just in Martin's rags. All over. It was another buffer. For every story circulating that Martin was having problems with debt exposure and nonpayment, there were two or more coming back saying it was all in hand, the exposure was small, it was covered with insurance, cast-iron guarantees, Government-backed expansion plans. Martin had the name. And if there was one important thing, it was having the name. And the name came with Frank Costello's imprimatur.

Behind the scenes, Jack Clarke had organised the key votes, kickbacks to the right people, the right kind of intimidation, subtle, nothing identifiable, done at second or third hand, against weak links. It was a long process. Money channelled through holding companies, offshore shells, that would take a hundred lifetimes to trace, a system so complicated that if you used it the right way they could never get you.

It was always some little shit somewhere way down, someone so bloody obscure no one even knew he existed, that presented the problems.

Jack sat in the Four Courts, watching some three-time losers go through what seemed like a regular routine. He was fascinated by the kind of fellow who came before the bench in the lower courts. Not the big stuff. He had a kind of sneaking regard for bigger criminals. But the weekend brigade and the petty losers with brains not much bigger than a walnut, they made Jack Clarke feel good. Made him feel he was in the top rank, scared him, too. This was what was waiting for those who got left behind. This or worse.

Aengus Kelly. It took two days to get someone who could tell him anything about the whistle-blower. Dan Meehan was jumping up and down like he'd just shit himself. Cursing Kelly to the hell. It was a real display. Jack didn't know if Meehan was playing a part or if he really meant it. Meehan didn't know either. They got everything they could on him. If Bell went public with this kind of stuff, if the bloody television people got hold of it...and they were still sniffing. Meehan was apoplectic. Jack had to grab him by the shoulders.

Jack shook his head. The judge ahead of him was whispering to a defence lawyer. They were smiling. Jack thought it strange. When it came down to it, they were on the same side. Lawyer and judge. They had more in common than either of them had with the poor sod they were dealing with. He was a long-haired man in his mid-forties. He had dried blood in his hair. There was a fresh cut on his forehead and one eye was closing. Jack concentrated on the pockmarks in his sunken cheeks. There were big blackheads in them, the kind you feel sorry for. They brought Jack Clarke back to his teen years. When some joker gave him mountains of the stuff. Right when his hormones were in total offensive mode, his face became a scene of plague. He could never explain that to people. The ones who thought he was a brash arrogant git. That he'd been afraid to go out the door. Afraid of looking someone in the face. Who gave shit about that? He was still trying to defend himself in the Winding Stair.

The Winding Stair was one of a couple of places Jack Clarke went to switch off completely. On the top floor, sitting at a table by the window, drinking a cup of tea, watching the muddy flow of the river, trying to see if the odd shopping trolley or racing bike showed through the water, up high above everything, surrounded by old books on subjects he had not given the time of day to for years, he could drift back to that jeans and woolly-jumpered individual who'd spouted philosophies he barely understood to other spotty youths who understood them even less. It had a quality, mainly because it was in the past. The past had a togetherness about it. Wrapped in string. You could examine it.

They would have to get to Bell soon. His men were getting close. Customs were in on it, too. Despite delaying tactics. Ralph wanted the button pushed. It was a matter of a couple of weeks. Already there was a hell of a lot of movement going on. And hacks who should have known better were knocking at the door. He kept thinking of his father. In flashes. Edited highlights from a life nearing its end. He was a brave man, his father. Braver than Jack. Jack didn't admit this to himself. It was important he believe himself better than his father. But he knew. And on the top floor of the Winding Stair, he could admire.

He needed a boost. For his ego. So he concentrated on all the favours he had done. His dad was getting the best because of him. He gave his mother a cheque every month. She should be grateful, he thought. It was as if he was competing with some unknown force of indeterminate wealth. He had to prove himself. Kate said it was a childish side to him and one she didn't like. Was there a side she'd ever liked? She wanted someone like Carl. Safe and correct. Said all the right things, Carl. Good father, good husband. Never find old Carl cheating on his missus. Not on little Angie. She was too cute to cheat on. Jack had cheated on her. But then Jack and Angie was so far away it was another life and it didn't matter. It hadn't even the power to embarrass any more. Carl didn't mind taking favours. Never came looking but he took them. Jack put business his way. Business firms like Hennigan's wouldn't get in a million years if they were out on their own. Pub practices they were known as. But the stuff Jack threw their way paid for extras, gave them the middle-class assurance they had, provided another layer of insulation from what was really going on around them. Contentment personified. Carl and Angie. He tried to be angry with them for their naïveté but all he could manage was a bit of sarcasm. Even that was tired and automatic and lacked conviction. Jack Clarke had seen too much to risk sarcasm. Real sarcasm was for beginners. A defence mechanism.

He looked at his watch. He was in the habit of looking at his watch every five minutes now. It was a thing he could not control. Years earlier, in bed with someone, it might have been Kate, it might have been Angie, it might have been someone else (he hoped it was Kate). Whoever she was she had asked him to think about what the world would be like if all the timepieces in it were suddenly destroyed. Jack looked at her, laughed and then felt a shiver down his spine.

The aspiration closed in. Nuclear household, dog, four-bedroomed semi, holiday in the sun, saloon car, joint account, fistful of credit cards, mortgage, insurance, overdraft, golf club, tennis club, private schools. The contentment culture. It walled itself into its contentment and let the world get on with the ugly stuff. It could be condescending to everything because it was part of nothing. It was self-sufficient in everything. It met itself, loved itself, married itself and—in Jack's own words—fucked itself.

It was something he was free of. Something the Clarkes had retreated into when they had hit the rocks. It was a nice shelter in a storm. But it required a degree of shutdown that Jack could never have taken. He was on the way out of it. He psyched himself into gear again. A heavy pep talk. Full of the kind of achieving bullshit American football teams thrived on. Necessary to get the job done. Go the extra mile. There was light. And there was reason. What more did man need?

He was thinking about ringing his mother when he saw her legs. Kate's legs were identifiable in a crowd of a thousand. She was sitting on the comfortable sofa in his new matchstick secretary's office. The sofa was comfortable, but not as expensive as it seemed. But you would have to be a good judge of furniture to know that. His first instinct was to roar at her but he held back.

"Hello, Kate! What a lovely surprise!" he said.

Inside he was thinking what a fucking bitch she was to turn up there. In his office. In Ralph Martin's building. He swore again.

But outside he played it cool. He threw his hand at her.

"I hope you haven't been here long."

All his morning's feelings concertinaed. He almost walked into her. She stood up and straighted herself. He went to kiss her and she backed off and he got the hint and didn't pursue it. His matchstick secretary never saw it. Jack Clarke was too polished to let it show.

"I'm here on business, Jack," Kate said.

All Jack could could think of was getting her behind a closed door and then getting her out unseen.

"Business? Yes, come inside, come inside. Would you like something?"

She could smell the whiff of booze from his breath, even under the tea and the wholewheat biscuit.

"No, thanks."

He led her through to his office.

"Bring us some coffee…"

Jack could not remember his new secretary's name. She blushed and her big bovine eyes went weepy. Come-hither eyes, Alan Kennedy said in one of his cruder moments.

In his office, Jack sat on the corner of his desk and picked up some stuff to make it look as if her visit didn't mean as much as it did. He was desperately trying not to show his discomfort. Outside, he could see flocks of birds circling. And a smoky haze hung over Dublin 2. He counted the yellowing leaves on the tree beside his window and saw two of the furthest gone give up the fight to stay stuck to branches and float to the ground. A neat circle of fallen leaves lay at the base of the tree.

"I was thinking of you," he said.

He did not know why. Maybe because he was.

"No, Jack, none of that," she cut in.

"I just said—"

"Stop. I'm here officially."

He looked uneasy. He couldn't quite take it seriously. He knew he should. But he couldn't. He put down what he had in his hands and stepped forward.

"Yes, I hear you've been active, more active than your brief. I've…"

He was going to say he'd had Larry Tallon ring Emile Hoffman in Brussels to complain but he thought she probably already knew and he didn't want her knowing he had anything to do with it.

"Okay, shoot."

"I want you to tell me what you know about this pollution spill."

Jack shook his head.

"Crossfin. I should have done this earlier, Jack. You know the place, Jack. Everyone there knows about you, I'm told. Your messengers come down there all the time. They call you Santa Claus. Your men bring presents, Jack, in nice brown envelopes."

"What are you getting at?"

"I'm asking you what you know about the Crossfin spillage. There's a whole load of other stuff. But it's not my concern. Jesus, Jack! Did you buy people off? Did you have a Mr Roy Doherty—he's the manager there—did you have him get a gang together to intimidate the Hare Krishna community at Crossfin House?"

It wasn't that Jack wasn't keen to answer: he just couldn't remember if he'd been the voice that had sent the muscle. It could have been him. But it would have gone through Barney Small. He could not remember. So he countered her charges.

"Come on, Kate, it's me, Jack. We used to live together."

She almost stood at attention and leaned her head to one side. Her eyes fixed on him. Locked on, maybe. It was a look he knew. It had usually preceded a blazing row in the past. Or the throwing of a glass at him.

"This is going to go to court, Jack," she said.

"You've no proof that it had anything to do with us," he said. "It was pesticide. We're a computer plant, Kate. Pure as the driven snow. What the hell would we be doing with pesticide? I suggest you look elsewhere. For the record, we're denying any liability there. They're a bunch of weirdos, Kate. They don't get on with the locals. So some of the local boys got drunk one night or something. Don't blame that on us. And please don't let any feelings you might have towards me interfere with your professional judgement."

"Bollocks, Jack. And I didn't say what they did."

"Look, this is very serious stuff you're saying, Kate. I can't believe what you've done already. Do you realise what you've done?"

"You bet. Christ, Jack, if half what this Aengus Kelly says is true, you lot have been complete bastards, Jack."

"Look, Kelly—yeah, I know about him—he's a trouble-maker. A no-hoper who got fired because he couldn't do the job without clocking people. Now he's bad-mouthing us. You got anyone else down there on his side? Besides that bunch of nuts who say we killed all their animals. We don't accept it was our factory. And that's what we'll say in court. If it ever gets there. Jesus, Kate, you have Industry and Customs crawling all over us. You brought him to Derek Bell. Why?"

"He had evidence. I felt it was the right thing to do."

"The right thing to do. We're..."

He held himself back.

"What, Jack? Going to lose money? You've lost sight of it all, haven't you, Jack? What the hell have you become? You mean something to me, Jack, but when I look at you now and I see what's in your face, the hate. You have hate in your eyes, Jack, towards me. Do I have to watch myself on dark nights from now on? Christ, Jack, take a look at yourself."

He reached out to her and then pulled his hand back and stuck it in his pocket.

"Look somewhere else, Kate. Frankly, I'm surprised at you, Kate. You sure you're not letting your personal feelings get the better of you here? I know we didn't part in the best of circumstances. But it's past. And I've still got a lot of affection for you, too."

Now he extended his hand.

"I've been thinking about you all morning, love. I only realised it when I saw you. Look, we can sit down and talk about all this. But not here. How about dinner, love?"

"Please don't call me love, Jack. I've been talking to some television people. A couple of guys I know."

"You've what?"

"I'm thinking of putting them on to Kelly."

He dropped her hand.

"Jesus, that's bloody irresponsible, Kate. What the fuck are you going to do that for?"

Kate was having trouble holding her temper. But she gripped her fists tight and stuck to her prepared pitch. She had gone over how it might go. She had rehearsed it down to the last letter of her accusations but she couldn't have prepared herself for the mixture of personal and professional that confronting Jack Clarke would bring. All the old wounds tore themselves open in one move. As someone had pulled out stitching or ripped off bandages. Years fast-forwarded and caught her from behind and she had to use everything she had to stay and stand her ground.

"We have his statement and the other photographic evidence."

"What? Some bits and pieces for automatic rifles in our boxes? We make computers. Not automatic weapons. Come on, we have competitors who'd like to see us in the shit."

"It's been enough for Derek Bell to order an investigation.

Enough for that. So why not television?"

"This some kind of career kick with you, Kate? Win at all costs. Or is it really what I said? You really have it in for us."

"Embargoed technology, chemicals, guided missiles, rifles, ammunition, false end-user certificates, false stamps, circuitous routes, come on, Jack. And then claiming for stuff you never sent. Sure, there's a bit of personal. But it goes beyond that. It's rotten, Jack. And I've met the people whose lives you've hurt. They're peaceful people. They wouldn't hurt a fly. I tell you, Jack, when they told me what had happened to them, I felt ashamed. Everyone had it in for them. No one wanted to help them. And for what? All you'd have got was a fine and slap on the wrist. But you lot were so high and mighty, even that was too much to take. I was ashamed, Jack. And so should you be."

"What is this, Kate? Some kind of get Jack thing? You find this pisshead in some bar or something, buy him some more suds and he tells you what you want to hear. You're a pollution head. Some kind of Eurogreen. Now you're fucking Eliot Ness and you think you can spread any old shit around you like. We'll sue. We'll take you and your man Kelly and any fucking television station that broadcasts this shit and screw you all. Chemicals! You think I'd get anywhere near that shit?"

Jack saw his anger was only producing more determination. He had put aside his feelings towards her. Without noticing it. This was business survival and Jack Clarke had a built-in business survival skill that kicked into action on autopilot.

"Kate, Kate, it's me, Jack. Look, we've just done our biggest takeover deal ever."

He realised the angle was a bad one but he carried on.

"You know, we're on a high here. Any problems we were having we've managed to overcome. And it's been difficult. The Gulf was a difficult market. This coup thing there might have ruined us. But we put our heads together with the

Government and sorted it out. This is a good company. We're bringing this country into the big league. And, hell, we're as green as the next corporation. We said we were willing to let any investigator into our plant down there to see for themselves. Did we block you? You said it yourself: you got full co-operation from us. Kate."

He took a couple of steps towards her.

"Jack."

He raised his hands.

"Look, no hands."

He winked.

She did not reply.

"This is dangerous stuff you're saying. There are jobs at stake here. Income. You know? Don't act without seeing all the facts. That's the thing with the green people, they never see the whole picture. Their efforts are commendable but they have a habit of running roughshod. You have muscle on your side. But you have us guilty before you have fully investigated the problem. We've had Government inspectors down there before. Health people. Environment people. Environment gave us a clean bill of health."

He reached back and swung his computer terminal around.

"Look what he said."

He tapped in to the terminal.

"Look here, see for yourself. There was no evidence that the death of the animals had anything to do with MartinCorp. The stream you keep shouting about had been polluted before. We have a report. Farmers dump effluent in it. God knows what other shit gets thrown in. But because we're big and successful and you find this Kelly fellow you put it down to us. Is that fair? Answer me that. You're supposed to be guilty till proved innocent."

The way he said that, the way he always said things like that to her, with a kind of a pleading smile and eyes that drew her into him, made her drop her stance. She leaned in by him and read from the screen.

"At least give us a chance," he said. "And for God's sake don't go spreading wild collateral allegations. There's a whole community down there depending on that factory. Please, Kate, for their sake if not for mine."

Kate struggled with his arguments for a few moments before nodding. But when he asked her if she would have dinner again, she said no.

14

J ack Clarke threw up in the toilet before he went in to the meeting with Ralph Martin. It had been coming all morning. He had been awake since two. Staring at the ceiling. Watching patterns from passing lights. Maybe his UFO-freak neighbour was making contact. Maybe they'd take him with them, he thought. Feeling his guts contract. Till nothing could stay down. Not even a slice of toast and a cup of black coffee. He'd tried running. Put on a tracksuit and run along the strand. But it didn't last. A knife-edge feeling chased and caught him. The sun trying to break through the haze which shrouded the meeting of sky and sea mugged his eyes and kicked shit out of his brain. It was cold. And everything seemed distant. And he puked.

"This Keyes bird," Martin said.

He sat rigid at the end of the table, surrounded by the hardest rays of that mugger sun Jack had had a run in with before. It gave Martin a kind of god-like aura. His bald head helped. He had a pencil in his hand. He broke it once, then he broke it again.

"Are you telling me she's something to you, Jackie?"

Martin leaned forward without shifting. He turned his eyes to Jack Clarke, who was on his right. Alan Kennedy followed Martin. And Dan Meehan was only too happy to make up the third. Six eyes focused on Jack Clarke in a moment, as if they were all under a central control. Martin's were the most dangerous. They had a gunsight quality, fixed, black with a hint of red that only made them more dangerous-looking. Meehan and Kennedy were incidental except that they were there with Martin's. Kennedy's had a watery film that was ready to spill out and Meehan's seemed to split and go in all directions. Jack kept coming back to Martin's.

It had followed a regular pattern. Could he get his arse up to the board room. Now. It was Sarah. And she was upset. He tried to get her to calm and tell him what was the matter. He knew already but maybe he felt if she said it, it would prepare him more. He could have cut himself off from Kate. But he'd asked her out to dinner again, and she'd said no again, and then they'd kissed on her doorstep and she hadn't asked him in and he'd asked her out again and she'd said no again. There was nothing he could do. He lied to Martin.

"She was."

"And?"

"She isn't."

He found himself praying Martin couldn't see through his lie. Inside, he knew Martin would know, one way or another. It was only a matter of time.

"That's it, is it? This Miss Catherine Keyes PhD, pollution consultant, comes over here on some stupid European Commission pollution junket. Some bloody cult down there—where the hell is it?"

"Crossfin. Offaly, Ralph," Dan Meehan said, anxious to please.

"Yeah. So she comes down because there's enough noise and suddenly I've got people accusing me of fraud and environmental vandalism, I've got Industry investigators, Customs people and God knows what in my factories, and now I have television cameras outside my house."

He broke his pencil again. Jack wondered how many times he could manage it.

"Correct me if I'm wrong but there seems to be a fucking huge leap between a small Euro-junket and a major shagging mess, Jackie."

Jack did not say anything. There was nothing he could say. He waited for Kennedy or Meehan to add their views. Then maybe he'd have something to play with.

"This Kelly fellow, he's the cause," Meehan said.

"Yes. Aengus Ignatius Kelly."

Martin read through a report he'd had done. Then he pulled out another file. He tossed it at Jack. Jack read it.

It was a report about him. It was stamped confidential. About Kate and him. Times, dates, places. Even things he had forgotten. Some very personal. There were references to phone conversations. His gut tightened some more. Not because he was in a spot with Martin but because he was slowly realising what a hold she had on him. It had never happened to him before, not even when they'd lived together, but now, all he could do was watch what was happening to him. Unable to do anything. Anyone else and he would have swatted them like a fly. He'd have gone to Martin. Then to Barney Small. The job would have taken a day. But Kate was inside him.

"You had me watched?" he said to Martin.

"It doesn't look good, Jackie. You got the hots for her again, lad? It's been a long time, hasn't it? All those years and she suddenly turns up. Turns up and happens to be going to investigate us. Odd, isn't it?"

Jack was behind Martin and the reasoning was dragging him to an unpleasant conclusion. But he could not accept it. Not him. Not Jack Clarke. And not Kate. Not her style. No, he knew her better than that. He'd stake—he was going to say his life but he thought that a bit dramatic—he'd stake his career on it. But Martin had the idea. Kennedy pressed it. His tone was patronising, as if he knew he had Jack and there was no way out. He could take his time.

"Jesus, Jack, do you not see?" Kennedy said. "You've

been had, boy. Now what have you told her?"

"What?"

"What have you told her?"

"Nothing. I swear. Jesus, what are you saying?"

"Honey trap, Jackie, lad, honey trap. God knows, you've set up a few in your time. You had her here, what did you say?"

Martin was upright again. Jack was in danger of spilling his guts. Either end, it didn't matter. A honey trap. No way. He'd done a few of them himself. He could spot one. There was no reason for her to honey trap him. Anyway, he'd told her nothing. He'd been trying to hold her back. He swore this to Martin and Martin nodded. Martin was very calm, very deliberate in his gestures. Jack went through everything, explained every meeting, every word he had spoken and had the feeling Martin knew most of it already. The others just nodded at everything Martin said.

"This spill," he said, scratching his stubble.

He hadn't shaved well. His stubble jutted out in small growths, uneven. Jack saw small beads of perspiration on some of the hairs. They glistened in the cold mugger sunlight.

"This spill, what's our position, Alan?"

Kennedy was doodling on a small sheet of paper. Drawing circles, interlocking circles.

"There was a small spillage. Last year, Ralph. They had a rat problem. They were using an old pesticide. They shouldn't have been. But there you go. One of the lads dropped a can. Anyway, some of it got into the water. That lot were using the water in their trough. They got a concentrated dose. No one else complained. Ironic, really. Considering."

"Yes," Martin said.

"We couldn't admit anything," Meehan said. "That stream runs into a tributary of the Shannon, Ralph. Christ knows what kind of claims we'd have against us. There's been no complaints, like Alan says. It was a small spill. People are always dropping things into it. So who says it was us? We did it. Then this Kelly creep comes along and says, yeah, he saw everything."

"Are you saying we did spill?" Jack asked.

"Shut up, Jackie," Martin said. "It should have been handled better, Alan. Well, there's nothing that can be done now except to fight them. Stupid bastards. See, Jackie, trouble-makers find one another."

"And the other stuff? The chemicals your man says we were shipping to the Gulf, Ralph?" Jack asked.

Martin looked at Kennedy. Kennedy looked at Jack and said nothing.

"High-tech stuff, a few rifles, some other gear," Jack said. "When his back was to the wall. Okay, fine by me. What use he made of them was his business. But chemicals, Ralph—I saw what he did with chemicals."

"She say what Kelly was saying about that?" Kennedy asked.

"He says we helped ship chemicals in our boxes. Is it true, Ralph?"

"If you're asking whether we made and sold chemicals to him, then I can say no."

"Arrangements, Jack." Kennedy said. "We had to facilitate things. There was a lot of money at stake. You knew. You knew the other stuff. I didn't hear complaints then."

Jack wanted to say something; he felt he should say something but he could not think of anything. Everything she said was true. In a way, he was glad, it killed the honey-trap idea. He wanted to say something, but he knew it would make no difference: there was nothing more he could say to Ralph Martin and Martin had probably had it with him. You didn't get a second chance at Martin, and Jack had been proved a liability. Martin would never say as much but Jack could almost predict how it would go.

"I'm disappointed, Jackie," Martin said. "I'm very disappointed you didn't tell me. Why? I put trust in you, Jackie. I had plans for you. You know. I'm disappointed. Are you still with me, Jackie?"

There was no other reply Jack could give.

"Of course, Ralph. I told her nothing."

Jack did not want to say it but he apologised. It was an instinctive reaction.

After the apology, Martin asked for the file on Jack. Then he stood up. Jack was almost relieved when Martin came over to him. Martin placed his hands on Jack's shoulders. He leaned over him and whispered, loud enough for the other two to hear.

"It's Okay, it's okay," he said. "You're still able for what you're doing?"

"Yes, Ralph."

"Good."

Then he moved back to his seat at the top of the table and Jack felt a weight had been lifted from him. Except he could not figure out which weight. He noticed, too, how empty that room was, spartan, as if thought was the only valuable commodity allowed in.

"We'll say no more about it, Jackie," Martin said. "But I want her watched. And I want you to arrange it. And stay away from her. She's done us enough damage. Right?"

Jack nodded.

"Right, business," Martin said. "What's the news on our money situation, Alan?"

Kennedy replied with information Martin already knew. This was a set-piece discussion. Its underlying meaning hidden in a simple code.

Martin's speech was a vintage affair. All those present could read between the lines. Nothing particular was said about anything, agreement was asked for on everything. When it came to Derek Bell, Martin made a point of telling Jack that they were out to ask the minister to see reason, to wait until a broader picture could be obtained. Lawyers were being briefed. He was being far too rash for such an important subject. There were hidden orders. Jack understood them.

Jack Clarke sat there, listening, in two minds. Both equally confused. And he was up against something he had not faced before. It had just appeared right in front of him, like someone stepping out in front of a car. He was angry at Kate for dropping him in it. It kept eating him all through the meeting that maybe she was using him, that maybe she had been suckering him along, but his affection for her and his ego would not let him believe that. That and the admission of what had happened in Crossfin pushed him right up against Ralph Martin, an act of rebellious intent that scared the shit out of him. Jack had never before understood the power Martin had. He tried desperately not to let his growing mental treachery betray itself on his face.

And all the time he was thinking about Kate, not the Kate they called a honey trap, the Kate he'd denied to Martin's face, the Kate of the meeting in his office, the Eurocrat with the impeccable table manners and conversation so diplomatic a paranoiac could find nothing insulting in it: the other Kate, the one he had lived with, shouted at, hugged, kissed, loved, fought, it all came back to him in an instant and it was all he could do to hold himself back from crying at one stage, something he felt extremely foolish about, something he was even more scared of showing to Martin than his mental betrayal.

His father was sitting on the patio in the back garden, on a folding beach chair, wrapped in a chequered rug, with Indian leg-warmers over his shoes. Jack had bought the leg-warmers as a present years earlier, as a student, in the States, when he'd taken a car across from New York to LA. Carl had been there. They met Angie in LA. He got all sentimental for a moment when he saw the leg-warmers.

His father was drinking red wine from a bottle on a table beside him. He had a book on golf, lying face down across his legs, the plastic cover marked with fingernails at the spine. The older man had his eyes closed and Jack watched his thin chest move as he drew breath. There was a lack of harmony in the breaths, an engine not firing on all cylinders, Jack thought. The sky was ice-blue and a breeze blew leaves from the base of an apple tree along a path leading from the patio to the garden shed. The garden was shedding its skin.

He could not think why he had come to his father. Except that after the Martin meeting he had to come home. To escape. His mother was in watching a daytime soap, eating soup. His father's soup bowl lay on a tray beside his folding beach chair. There was a leaf in it. The leaf was red. His mother had asked him to see if his father wanted anything.

"Why don't you, Mum?" Jack replied.

"I don't like to," she said.

He wanted to ask her if she was scared of him. Or if she just didn't care. He did not.

He shook his father. Old Jack's skin was loose and pale and it was thin at his neck and around his jaw. It was cold. For a second, he thought his father was dead. It was so brief he did not get a chance to see what his reaction would be. Then his father opened his eyes and Jack told himself that doctors could be wrong. They gave you six months, and you died six months later to the day. But that was only because they'd programmed it into you. If you said, no, fought it, you could beat it. He heard himself urging his father to fight it.

"You're here," his father said.

Then the old man farted.

"Clearing myself," he said.

Jack smiled and rubbed his father's hair. The hair was dead and Jack took his hand away.

"I came to see how you were, Dad."

"I'm farting more."

Jack didn't know whether that was good or bad. He did not know whether he should ask. All the old screens were still there. Jack pulled up a plastic chair from the table with the wine bottle on it. He poured himself a glass and handed his father the glass he had been drinking from. There were faint prints on the glass and a piece of dried soup. The doctors were saying any day now. Confusing, Jack thought, if you were intent on hitting the right time for them. But they were probably deliberately confusing, so whatever day you died, they could say they were right. Good for their cred. Didn't help you fight. Confusion doesn't help a fighter. Every time you think you've beaten a deadline, they tell you it might not be quite yet. Finally, you just give up.

"How are you, Dad?"

His father was drinking from his glass.

"Nearly dead."

"No, you're not. You've plenty of life in you. Look at you. You'll be here this time next year, believe me."

His father shook his head slightly.

"I can't play golf, Jack."

"There's other things, Dad."

"What?"

Jack couldn't think of anything else. He was going to say his mother but he was not prepared for the possible reply. It was following a familiar pattern, this conversation. He had come to his father, hoping they might be able to talk, maybe discuss things, and nothing was being said. The circling was continuing.

I want to talk to you, Dad, Jack said to himself. I don't want you to go. Do you see that? I—it'll be so lonely without you, Dad. Everything, Dad, you'll take it all with you. Please talk to me.

"They give me pills for my farting," his father said.

He reached out and gestured to his son to come closer. Jack leaned into his father's mouth. His father pointed to the house, emphasising the movement.

"She wants me gone," he said.

He winked. Then he drank some more wine.

"No, Dad, she loves you. We want you alive, Dad, we do."

He had seen them once. Years ago. In bed. He knew what was happening. He'd found out at the back of the Irish dancing class. He wasn't sure of the technicalities but he knew what it was. His mother had been on top. There was music. He could not remember where the music came from. There was no other noise. Only movement. His mother had breasts that fell too far, he thought. They were too wide apart. His father had his tongue out. His hands were on her shoulders. Hers were on her hair. She had a plaster on her foot. It ended quickly and his mother fell back to his father's feet and pulled some bedclothes over her. The music was Strauss.

"I'm in trouble, Dad."

Jack was not sure he had even said it. It was such a shock. He had never said anything like it to his father before. He thought maybe he was imagining it. His father did not respond. Jack looked away. There was some relief in his mind. Saying it, if he had said it, opened too much for him. He concentrated on his mother and father. He had never seen any other sign of affection between them, and now he did not even see them speak. But she did love his father. She had to. She had left his flowers on the kitchen table.

"No," his father said.

He held up his glass for more wine. Jack gave him a refill.

"I drink too much, Jack. But I like it. What's wrong?"

Jack was pouring himself more wine. He spilled it over his hand and it ran down his hand and onto the white plastic table and into a groove on the table and onto the patio. It gathered in a small pool on a piece of brown stone with a clump of moss on it. Jack looked at his father.

"You're in trouble. What's wrong?"

The older man's voice had a strength about it Jack had not heard for years. It frightened Jack. He tried to speak. He could not. He poured some wine and drank it all. The wine burned the back of his throat and warmed him inside. He wanted to touch his father. Just to hold him. So he could speak.

"Is it a woman?"

"No, Dad—well, not directly."

"But there's one there."

"I suppose there is."

"All the best problems have a woman."

He whispered.

"Look at me. She'll kill me."

"No, she won't. She loves you. I love you. We love you."

The "Soldiers' Chorus" from *Faust* had been playing when the business went. Jack was upstairs. He could hear the music. He could hear the shouts. Words said. Words that should not have been said between lovers. He shook them off.

"It's work, Dad. I'm..."

His father was staring at the far wall of the garden. It had pieces of glass embedded into the top of it. Jack reached out and touched his father's shoulder. He could feel the bones. They felt like they might break through the skin.

"I've done things, Dad. Things I used to think were fine because I was doing them for a reason. For us. For the family. For you, for Mum. I wanted—well, you know, you must have done it yourself. Or maybe I'm imagining that. Kate thinks I'm some kind of gangster. Did I tell you about Kate? She came back, Dad. There I had her packed away and she came back and God, I can't—Jesus, this is difficult, Dad—I did a lot of stuff. Well, you do, don't you? You say yes to one thing, and you're really shiting yourself, but you say yes, and then you get away with it. After that it's easy. And you don't notice it pass because it's all for the right reason. We were doing what everyone else was doing."

He squeezed his father's shoulder.

"They played just as dirty. Ralph didn't invent the rules; he just played with them, played better."

Jack laughed.

"We found we could get the boot in first and we did. You see? Oh, Jesus, I don't know, Dad, maybe I'm just getting soft. Maybe I should give myself a good kick and get on with it. But it's been getting to me. I've been doing it but it's been getting to me. And now Kate coming back—I know I've never—but, Dad—"

A helicopter went overhead. It had Air Corps roundels. The whole garden vibrated to the sound of the engine.

"And now…"

He looked down at his father. The older man's eyes were shut. Jack exhaled and took a drink. He touched his father's brow. It was colder. There was a wet breathing coming from old Jack's mouth. His son squeezed his hand.

"I was going to tell you I'm in too deep now, Dad, that I can't stop myself. I was going to say I'm doing it for you. I hope you'll understand. I want you to. I'm tired, Dad, very tired."

He dipped his head.

His father had the weight of a child and Jack carried him from the patio through the house up the stairs to his bed. His mother looked up from a crossword she was doing and watched when they passed. She had marks around her eyes that made it look as if she might have been crying. Jack did not ask. He tucked his father into bed and propped him up on two hard pillows and gave him his glass of wine. His father's face was expressionless and when Jack asked him if he wanted his face to be rubbed with a cloth, he did not answer. Jack went into the bathroom and rinsed a face-cloth and came into his father and stroked his face with the cloth.

"I need some wood for the fire, Jack," his mother said.

Jack was chopping a carrot.

"He looks okay, Mum."

His mother did not reply.

Jack put on a pair of wellington boots and went into the garden to chop wood. The house was centrally heated. There was no need for the fire except that his mother liked a fire; said it was the best kind of heat. She liked to fall asleep by the fire, watching the "Late Late". He said it was dangerous; she did not reply to that.

While he was chopping, a neighbour put his head over the fence. He asked Jack about his father. Jack said he should go in and say hello. The neighbour shook his head and became agitated. He didn't want to upset him, didn't want to disturb him. He should get some rest, maybe some other day. It was the usual ritual. None of them meant any harm. It was just something they couldn't cope with. A point in time and space where all the ordinary rules of life broke down. Indeterminate. They were pulling away from old Jack as if he were some kind of black hole and they were all scared of falling into him.

"I want it now," his father had said to him.

When he was rubbing his face with the cloth.

"Want what, Dad?"

Jack thought his father was talking about wine or food or something like that.

"I'm not afraid. I'm glad."

"No, Dad, don't."

"Would you be glad? Would you be able? Now, here?"

Jack didn't answer. They were back to where they had begun.

When he had cut the wood and chopped more vegetables, Jack left and got drunk.

15

Larry Tallon's driver picked Jack up at a wine bar off Baggot Street. It had been prearranged. The driver appeared to be one solid piece of granite. His hair was curly red, his face chiselled and his eyes looked capable of disarming a man at ten paces. He didn't speak.

They drove to a small house in Clontarf and picked up the minister. Tallon had a selection of small houses he liked to visit around the town. Jack was aware of what went on in them but it wasn't as much fun looking at the pictures of Larry Tallon as those of Paud Henry. Larry had once been caught with his pants down at a house in Streatham and was saved from a very difficult situation only by a timely arms find in Louth and the extradition of an escaped subversive to Belfast. The Met dropped any charges but kept the file.

Jack steered his thoughts away from that subject now. It had lost any of its appeal. He watched the granite driver walk to the front door of the house and press the bell. There was a metaphor there, Jack thought. The granite driver kept scanning almost three hundred and sixty degrees. Maybe Martin had someone on them. Jack found himself scanning, too. Unless the old woman pulling her shopping trolley behind her was one of Martin's people, they were free.

Martin had been on his mind all morning. He was going through with it. Though he did not want to any more. But there was no real choice for him. And he was scared. Of

Martin. Jack could not remember being scared as much as that before. Even when he was being beaten up outside his house all those years ago. This was a fear that got into your nerves and closed them down. Where every step was almost impossible without help. He'd covered up the wine with a mouth spray. No sense in being at a disadvantage, he thought, even if he didn't want to do it. There was a degree of professional pride he felt he had to maintain. But this—he was going to say this was it but he was not sure; so he settled for telling himself he needed a break after this.

There were sound reasons for doing it, he told himself. He needed to keep telling himself. It wasn't as if every other avenue hadn't been exhausted. They were fighting for their survival. There were careers, jobs, families at stake. The psych-up was working, combined with the wine and whatever coloured pill he'd chosen that morning. He was working himself around. Tallon appeared at the door. He was combing his hair. He looked left and right and his granite driver walked out ahead of him, doing more scanning. Tallon was adjusting his double-breasted suit. The handler look. Larry looked well handled. He walked towards the car. Jack saw a lace curtain move in one of the upstairs windows. Larry did not look back.

"We're going flying," Tallon said.

He had a look of satisfaction on his face. There was a solitary hair at the corner of his mouth when he got into the car. He looked in the mirror and wiped it off without saying anything. The granite driver was already pulling around a corner. Jack sat in the back, silent. He'd heard of moves like this before though he'd never been on one. Larry's flights of fancy, they called them. Tallon kept a small Cessna at Dublin Airport. He used it for everything from seduction to taking his mates to Cheltenham. Known as one of the big betters at the festival, Larry was. It was on a Cheltenham weekend that he had been caught in Streatham with one luncheon voucher too many. He used the plane for getting himself around the country during elections, too. Tallon always had the busiest schedule during elections. The man the party liked to see on every soap-box in the country. There were always requests for Larry to come and speak to the local troops in the backwaters. And Larry Tallon would do it. Because Larry still believed in what he was doing. He believed in the party, in what it stood for. He believed in Frank Costello, in a way Jack Clarke could never understand because they came from different times. Jack's kind had seen too much of the mess left behind by belief to have much faith in anything that wasn't practical. Tangible stuff if anything. Things aimed at contentment. The house had been bought and paid for, they were just out to make sure the garden looked good for barbecues. Tallon and his mates were still paying off an old mortgage.

The set-up was simple enough. Larry Tallon had invited Derek Bell up for an afternoon's flying. Bell had once said he was interested in taking up the sport. Months earlier, at a cocktail party. Tallon had a computer memory for facts like that. It was just right for their purpose.

Tallon had another plus as well as his computer-like recall. He was trusted across party lines. It was a superb act of balancing he'd worked hard at all his political life and it meant that Bell would be off his guard. Bell and Tallon got on well socially. Tallon had done most of the negotiating for the coalition closeted with Bell. Their wives were friends. Each had agreed to respect the other's politics. They rarely discussed the subject in each other's company in private and in cabinet—with Frank Costello's approval—Larry Tallon always went out of his way to see Bell's point of view.

He'd found Bell nervous and jumpy in his office. Scratching the back of his neck. Where his wig looked worst. Tallon offered his shoulder. It was accepted. Bell's insides had a permanent ulcerous feeling. The Martin investigation. He was anxious. The last thing he wanted to have was an election. The coalition was working well. What was the point? Maybe Larry could try and sort things out with Frank Costello.

"It's Frank, Larry," Bell said. "You know, without him...now I don't mean to interfere in the affairs of another party."

Larry nodded his head and showed his teeth.

"I see. Well, you know I couldn't comment on anything like that, Derek; it wouldn't be right."

"Oh, no, Larry, but maybe there's talk. You'd know."

Tallon had always been the party shoulder, where TDs in trouble would go to be comforted and have it sorted out. Where ministers went to sound out ideas. Where men not moving as fast as they thought they should went to find out what had to be done. A fixer. It was a brokerage he was more than willing to run and more than able to cope with. He was past the age now when he would ever be Taoiseach. There was a time when he would have gone for the job, if Frank Costello had been ousted. But Frankie was king and pretenders went the way of all losers, so Larry stayed on the sidelines, remaining loyal to Frank and maintaining his image as an honest broker.

"This Martin business," Bell said. "It's wasting good departmental time, you know, but I feel it's my duty. For the country's good name. Frank was bloody rude to me. I can't allow that to go on. You do see?"

"Sure. Let's have that flight. It's relaxing. Get you away from this. If only they knew. How much trouble all this is."

He cast his hand around.

"You should have run last time, Larry," Bell said. "You'd have got it."

"Thanks for your vote, Derek."

He was a supreme realist, Larry Tallon. A man who knew his limitations. His strengths and weaknesses. He knew he might have become the top dog but that the price would have been too much. He knew too that it would have been a short-lived affair. He never had the wad of grass roots that

Frankie Costello could call on nor the junior backbenchers who thought the sun shone out of Frankie's arse. Now even Frankie couldn't be sure he had it any more. The young sun-worshippers were getting restless. Larry figured he'd made the smart move. This way he could go on until the vultures got him. Frankie could take the heat. And he could do his bit and maintain his prestige.

He'd managed to follow Frank Costello from the earliest days, without being seen as a Costello sycophant, like Paud Henry. Everyone knew where Henry sucked. But Tallon had played the game right. Costello had respected him for it. And together they had convinced one another that they were the right ones to lead the country and that their interests and the country's interests were one and the same. Once that had been done, it was easy to use influence to secure personal gain Because it was for the country it was easy to nobble opposition; because it was for the country, it was easy to rub the backs of friends, because it was for the country.

Tallon was to give his best shot to persuading Bell to change his mind for the good of the country. He was to hit Bell with all he had about the seriousness for the economy of a collapse of the Martin organisation. What it would do for overseas confidence. Tallon had done a lot of talking with Bell already. Under Frank Costello's orders. Frank wanted Larry to press the disenchanted party-elder bit. Tallon and Bell held two meetings in Bell's flat in Ballsbridge. Transcripts of both were on Costello's desk both nights.

Tallon worked it well. He was a grand master of doublespeak. Hinting to Bell that discontent with Frank Costello was gathering pace, that the party might be ready to elect a new leader, maybe Phil Cassidy—better than going to the country for an election no one wanted. And Bell had taken it all. Bollocks, Frankie Costello said when he read the transcripts. The bollocks was trying to do him. Frankie was torn between laughter and anger. He threw an apple across his office.

Bell kept asking if Frankie might not prove a liability in another election. He was blocking so many people. New leadership would give the coalition new life. They could get things done. Larry listened and didn't comment much except to agree with enough of what Bell said to make the Industry minister think he was making an impact.

"His popularity's steady but unemployment is sky-rocketing and he has no new ideas to beat it—none!" Bell said. "And he won't listen. Now I was talking to Phil and—"

"I understand what you're saying, Derek, believe me. I understand."

It had been so simple that Tallon thought Bell was on to him at first. Just playing him along. Tallon let Bell know that Phil Cassidy was already canvassing support. Bell smiled and poured another drink and showed a picture of his son in graduation garb. Tallon let his coalition colleague speak on.

Tallon had a way of mentioning things, by the way. He had a way of hinting too, without saying. Costello couldn't but marvel when he read the transcripts. It was all roundabout talk. Nothing definite, yet when he had seen Derek Bell twice, Frankie Costello felt Larry Tallon had come away with Bell in his back pocket.

Jack Clarke waited for Larry Tallon to bring Derek Bell over from his Mercedes to Tallon's Mercedes. Two men, talking beside a landcruiser, stopped and watched the ministers greet each other. Tallon took Bell's hand with both his own and reassured him about the weather conditions and the flight. Neither of the onlookers wanted to say to the other that they knew who the ministers were, they were both of a type that considered it naff to acknowledge personalities. It was very unstreet. Better to let the well-knowns pass without a word. They got as far as saying nothing but their very silence left them looking on like mesmerised groupies behind the stage at a rock concert. Jack thought he recognised one of them. If he was right, the guy was a barrister, the worst kind of win-friends-and-influence-people shape, oozing false charm, the original tapeworm. Jack held back until the two onlookers had gone before getting out of Tallon's Merc. He stood with his hands behind his back, watching Bell's eyes.

"This is Jack, Derek," Larry Tallon said. "He's a beginner, too."

He made like Jack Clarke was just another friend among the legion of friends he had. Derek Bell shook Jack's hand and stared at him longer than he should. Jack held his expression. There was no reason Bell should know him. Maybe his surname. He thought about that, what would happen if Bell asked his surname, but Bell never asked. The minister had a nervous look on his face, it was pale and his lips were dry except for a thin line of sweat right across the top one. The airport wind blew all their hair around and the flaps of their jackets flew up, causing them to hold them down. It was a handy distraction.

At the gate, two Branch men sat in a car, watching. Larry Tallon put his thumb up to them. He gave his driver some money and whispered to him. Jack kept his eyes fixed on the ground. An empty crisp packet flew into and then out of his view.

A couple of jets were lining up for take-off.

Jack showed his teeth to Bell in an effort to establish a rapport, a common experience. It worked. Bell thought he looked nervous and inoffensive. Jack smiled to himself. It had worked before and it would work now. You bastard, Ralph, he thought, you knew it would work. He allowed himself a brief moment of rebellion and thought about pulling out. But it was going well and he could not pull out while it was going well. If Bell was thick enough to buy it, then *caveat emptor*. A RyanAir jet screamed into the sky.

They climbed up over Dublin, circled the airport and flew along the coast. There was a toytownishness about it all, Jack felt. He sat in the back. He watched Bell. The Industry minister was quiet, his movements jerky. Below them, a couple of windsurfers raced along the bay. Jack's stomach let him down in the first sudden movement. He swore and kept it to himself. Larry Tallon pointed things out to Derek Bell. Jack tried to keep his eyes on Bell and hold his stomach down, wondering if he'd have to throw his head out the window at any moment.

Right hand on the control column, left on the throttle, Larry Tallon flew them down as far as Bray, talking the casual talk of the experienced, pointing out more landmarks, explaining functions and instruments. Derek Bell sat hunched in the right passenger seat, another tiny line of sweat running from his temple to his neck.

Good, he's nervous, Jack thought.

He had just about managed to catch his stomach before it jumped out. He reached into his jacket and felt the long envelope in his inside pocket. Wait, he thought, Larry's play for the moment.

They had levelled out at a few thousand feet above Bray when Bell turned to Jack.

"Good, isn't it?" he said.

He was fighting to overcome his discomfort. Jack recognised the symptoms. Jack smiled and took in more oxygen and rode three big bumps. The bumps made Bell turn colour again and he had to face forward.

"A little airsick, Derek?" Tallon asked.

Bell shrugged.

"Don't worry, you'll get over it. Go with the aircraft. Learn to anticipate. Here, you want to take her?"

He let go the controls and showed Bell what to do with his set. Then he guided his cabinet colleague in a slow banking turn to the right.

"We'll head inland," Tallon said. There's this place in Kildare. Farmer friend of mine. Owns his own forest."

He turned to Jack, raising his voice over the noise of the engine.

"There's fierce money in forestry, you know, Jack. Huge

grants from the EC. He brews his own. We can land and have a drink. What do you think? Make an afternoon of it. Derek?"

Bell was rigid at the controls.

"Yeah, sure. Are we allowed do that, Larry? Land there?"

"We're the Government, Derek; we can do anything we like."

He slapped Bell on the back and burst out laughing.

They flew around for an hour. Bell got more confident and Tallon let him have control for most of the flight. Behind them, Jack Clarke kept his mouth shut unless asked a question and watched the landscape spread like a carpet till it fell below the horizon. Your whole perspective changed in an aeroplane. It was the first time he had ever noticed it and Jack could count his flying hours in the thousands. But up there, in the ice-blue, with nothing but beauty for a backdrop, the need for things he had once been certain of vanished and reasons he had been wrestling with gave up their fight and he wondered. It was a precious feeling.

Bell asked Jack about himself when Tallon was bringing the small aircraft in to land. Both of them had lost some of their nervousness, though Bell was uncomfortable with Tallon's approach and Jack's stomach was still dodgy. Jack said he was an accountant. Bell didn't go any further.

Tallon had a reception arranged. The donor of the farm was up in Dublin for the day, hoteled courtesy of MartinCorp though he didn't know it. He was a good soldier and he knew enough not to question Larry Tallon's request for his house. To make sure no one disturbed them, Larry had Paud Henry put three of his finest at the gate. Home-made beer and smoked salmon sandwiches lay on a table in the living-room. There was a small coal fire, too. The three men sat in armchairs by the fire.

The home-made was a Czech recipe and had a proof reading that could have categorised it as an explosive substance. And Larry made sure Bell had more than he needed. It was easier than it should have been. Bell was enjoying himself as he hadn't done for years. And all the ulcerous troubles which had kept him awake at nights, all the shit that made him wonder if maybe he shouldn't just quit, seemed to vanish in the magical evening light. It was Tallon who steered the conversation on to the subject of Frank Costello. It was in a friendly style. Even Jack was impressed.

Bell looked at Jack before saying what he wanted to say. Then at Tallon. Then at Jack again.

"Don't worry about Jack here. He's discreet, Derek. You can say what you like with him."

Bell inhaled through his nose, ate a sandwich and slugged some beer.

"Right. Frankie's had it, Larry. Frankie's had it and he's going to pull the rest of you down with him if you don't watch out. I'm saying that and I'm not saying anything else. You lot had better sort yourselves out. I like you, Larry. You're not a journalist, Jack?"

Jack shook his head.

"Accountant," he said again.

"Yes. Well, I like Larry, here. We're—we're—and it does happen—we're friends. Cross-party. And I like to think we can co-operate for the good of the country. Don't you, Larry?"

He ate another sandwich.

"What do you think, Jack?" Tallon asked.

"Maybe it is time for a change. Maybe Phil Cassidy should be given a chance."

"There, you see, you see," Bell said. "A supporter of yours and he agrees with me. We'd get rid of our problems at a stroke, Larry."

"Not all of them, Derek."

Tallon smiled. He drank some beer and took the poker from its rack and moved some coals. They were getting close now. Jack wanted to speak but he held back. Tallon watched him and they both watched Bell. Bell moved in close to them, shoving his head in between them.

"It'll get him, Larry," he said. "I think it's very serious. I'm telling you. It'll get him."

"It'll get all of us, Derek. Then where will we be?"

"I..."

Bell threw his hands up and looked at Jack.

"Actually, I thought we might be able to talk about that, Derek," Tallon said.

There was a silence for a whiie. Then Tallon continued.

"Down here, away from it all, so to speak. Neutral ground. Jack here is one of Ralph Martin's bright-eyed boys. Aren't you, Jack?"

Jack said nothing. This was Tallon's play. They were right at the edge of the critical zone, a point of no return. Bell looked confused. His features contorted for a moment. He looked at Tallon. Tallon smiled.

"I said I'd see if you might be amenable to dialogue, Derek. As an honest broker. You can walk out now if you like, but I'd like you to listen. At least that. You know. Now if you want to go, we can fly off. Jack's here at my request. He'll shut up if you want him to."

He turned to Jack and laughed. Bell sank back in his seat and drank some more.

"I'm—I'm not sure about this," he said. "Is this some kind of official approach, Larry? Because..."

Tallon put his hands up in a surrender gesture.

"Unofficial, Derek. Just you, me and him. Look, I'll put my cards on the table. And you know what they are. I don't like what I'm hearing about Martin any more than you do, Derek. Shit, I'm the Minister for Technology and they've been making me look stupid. No, ideally, you're right—now I think you'll have to agree with me there, Jack. There's no other way of putting it. But we're not in an ideal situation, Derek. We have Irish industry about to lose one of it biggest companies. Can we afford that? For the sake of principle?

Principle is terrific but is it worth the mess it will bring? Because it will bring a mess and we'll all get sucked in. Now, what I'm about to say could sink me with Frankie Costello. So I'm putting myself in your hands, Derek. What if Frankie were to go? We could come to some arrangement with Martin. Fine him by all means, quietly, for any export illegalities, but stop short of going public and pulling insurance. Think about it. Frankie gone; Phil, Taoiseach; things on a more even keel. Ralph Martin is even willing to support Phil. Now that's completely unattributable. You see, I'm putting my arse on the line here. Think about it, just think about it. What good would it be if this Government fell apart? And that's what's going to happen if you and Frankie keep going for one another. People can see it. I can. I want this Government to survive and I'm willing to do what's necessary. But if we're going to go against Frankie, we'll need help and help doesn't come much better than Ralph Martin, Derek."

"Martin's in bed with Frankie already," Bell said.

"People change lovers," Jack said.

He was going to add to it. He did not.

Bell kept looking into their eyes, searching for something. He was sobering up faster than he had ever done in his life. His gut had a wrenching cramp in it.

"I'll be plain," Larry Tallon said.

Bell should have moved if he was going to at all, Tallon felt. He was between holding back and pushing harder. He had decided on the latter.

"Because I'm a plain man. You know that, Derek. No horseshit from me. Mr Clarke's company is one of the biggest in this country and one of the bloody best. It's climbing up there with the biggest and best in Europe. It could be a world player if it got the chance. And all because of some short-term difficulty, they run the risk of being walled. Now, is that justice? Which country hasn't had blockade runners in its time? I ask you. Personal feelings aside. Because I know you haven't much time for Ralph Martin. And if you want my personal opinion, I don't either. Arrogant son of a bitch—eh, Jack?"

Jack thought, then nodded.

"But personal feelings have to be put aside, Derek. Have got to be. For the country. We're in a cruel world. No one knows that more than you. Where business can go well for years and then suddenly fall foul of circumstances."

He slowed his conversation down and made references to the Dublin Mountains and the colour of the sea and climbing Bray Head as a kid.

"I'm Minister for Technology, Derek, and I'll lay my cards on the table. Maybe Ralph Martin has been a bad boy, maybe. Maybe they were in breach of the law. Maybe they helped shift some iffy stuff they shouldn't have. Maybe they pulled a few fast ones. But let's face it, they're doing it everywhere. I know it. I've seen evidence. So we're more moral than they are. That's good. But we've thousands of workers dependent on men like Martin. Where the hell do they go if we allow men like him to go down? You see."

"But they're claiming insurance under false pretences. They broke a UN embargo. They broke an EC embargo. Hi-tech American gear. Not to mention what else they were helping to export. Chemicals. Arms. It's illegal. And we're not talking about penny claims here, Larry. Two hundred and fifty million."

"Look, no one knows that more than me, Derek. But look at the wider picture. Think ahead. The country. Your party."

"What's this got to do with my party?"

Larry Tallon knew he was losing it. He raised his voice.

"Come on, Derek, come on: don't say you couldn't do with some extra spending. What the hell are you going to fight the next election on? Going to take out another mortgage? And if you go through with this and Frankie goes to the country. Jesus, will you see sense, man."

Bell was seeing. But not what Tallon wanted. And Jack Clarke could only watch as the great fixer lost control of the situation. Bell put his glass down and stood up. His face was calm and he did not say anything at that moment. Instead he asked where the toilet was.

"Fuck him," Tallon said when he'd gone.

When he came back he sat down and turned to Tallon.

"I can only assume your motives were honourable, Larry. I appreciate that. But I cannot, I repeat, I cannot, in all conscience, let this one go."

Then he faced Jack. He rubbed his mouth. Jack tensed himself.

"I think we should go," Bell said. "Why spoil a good day?"

They flew back in the dark. The lights below looked like jewellery on a black velvet background. Tallon turned the focus of things back to flying, as if he was trying to erase everything he had said back at the farmhouse. Bell looked happy enough to go along and when Tallon offered him another go at flying, he took his control column.

"Feels good, doesn't it?" Tallon said.

They were over the coast again. Jack could see boats, little flickers of light at the furthest extent of visibility. His stomach was under control this time. Maybe it had something to do with what was going to happen. He touched the long envelope in his inside pocket. He could leave it. Just let it go. No, there was no way. He had no control any more. He pulled the long envelope from his inside pocket. Bell was smiling again. He seemed to have almost forgotten the tone of the earlier conversation. Jack opened the envelope. Tallon turned to him and signalled with his eyes. He was on. Tallon pulled on a set of headphones and took the controls from Bell. Jack's cue.

"We would be willing to help you out, Minister," Jack Clarke said.

Bell turned to him.

"Sorry?"

Jack raised his voice. Tallon was looking straight ahead. Bell shifted his big bulk in the small cockpit.

"Well," Jack said, "you are facing certain financial difficulties, minister. Two projects you have a lot of capital in have gone into receivership. And of course—and I think this has been mentioned—your properties are mortgaged to the hilt. It will be a potentially very embarrassing affair for you if it is allowed run its course. There's other sundry debts."

"How the hell do you know all this?"

Bell tried to get close to Jack but his size and the small space prevented him. He looked foolish. Jack was taking papers from the long envelope and assembling them.

"We have our sources. We are also aware that a business venture in New York has turned sour and left you exposed. And, of course, you have been heavily involved in offshore exploration. And we all know what the market thinks of Irish exploration stocks. Frankly, Mr Bell, for a Minister for Industry, your investment savvy sucks. You're in trouble. Here's a list of your immediate business creditors. You'll find several of them are MartinCorp companies. There's a conflict of interest there, I think you'll agree, minister."

He handed the relevant papers to Bell.

"Jesus!" Bell said.

He turned to Tallon. Tallon kept looking straight ahead. Bell shook his head.

"You bastards," Bell said. "Both of you, bastards. You did—"

"We haven't much time, minister," Jack said. "Here's your bank statements. You'll see they verify my assessment of your position."

Tallon looked at Bell and raised an eyebrow. He turned to look frontwards. Bell took on the look of a cornered animal. As if every terror he had ever had but didn't want to believe because it would completely paralyse him was coming true.

"What do you want?" he said.

"It's clear, I'd say," Jack said.

"I call off the dogs or you screw me, is that it?"

"Your words. I think you should consider your position."

"You're a smooth bastard, Jack Clarke, a smooth bloody bastard. You just come along like this, all smiles and good manners and promptly blackmail a Government minister. And you..."

He looked at Tallon and closed his eyes for a second.

"What I said, stands," Tallon said. "You just wouldn't see, Derek. I'm sorry, but you just had to have your way. It can all be wiped out, all your problems, at a stroke. Just reconsider. Nothing else."

"I was a bloody eejit."

"You're up to your eyes in it, old boy," Tallon said. "And there's no way out. You're a good minister, Derek, but, Jesus, you live on another planet. You must see that!"

Jack handed the minister a piece of paper with a figure scribbled on it.

"Enough to take care of everything," he said. "And some more. And then you're back to fighting strength. Then we can examine what's best for the country. Going towards the end of the century maybe there is a need for new blood."

Bell was shaking his head. Little movements. His eyes were wide open. Jack could see the pupils dilating.

"My God," Bell said. "I thought this only happened in cheap thrillers."

"Only the cheapest," Tallon said.

"Here's some more documentary proof," Jack said. "Better keep it. We have copies. We'll give you time. Say a day. Otherwise we shall be forced to take action."

"Jesus, Ralph Martin trained a little pit-bull like you well. Bet you enjoy human flesh. You get some kind of kick out of this? Get your rocks off, lad. You bollocks."

He tried to swing at Jack but he hit the cockpit wall and he only ended up scraping his knuckles. He struggled to get another swing at Jack but Larry Tallon reached over and held his arm. Tallon's eyes went right through him.

"Hey, hey," Tallon shouted. "You want to cause an accident, Derek? Cop on, man. Listen to what's being said. Just fucking listen. Now calm down."

Jack Clarke found himself studying Bell, the various changes of colour in his face, the quivering hands. He passed the minister some more documents, bank statements, mortgage agreements, loan statements, letters of credit, copies of other letters, all private. Bell looked at each one in turn.

Tallon banked the aircraft round again. Jack could not keep his eyes off Bell's Adam's apple. And it had a choking motion. He half expected the minister to cry. He wanted to say something consoling but it would have been fruitless and hollow. Better to stick to the script. If he went further out he could not be sure he would get through it.

"You have commitments," Jack said.

Derek Bell kept shaking his head. His hand was bleeding but he did not bother doing anything about it. Was this it? All there was? He had seen dirt in politics, used some himself, nothing much, couple of unfounded allegations against opponents. He had turned a blind eye to activity that went beyond that: secret committees that got their money in shopping bags and opened bank accounts in the name of Smith. He had connived in the ousting of opponents, for his own benefit, something he felt bad about later, but that was politics. He had heard of other things, phone calls that left men white, photographs that made you grey prematurely, but he was up against the real thing here. This young man who could have been his son—well, maybe— was calmly blackmailing him. There was no threat, there was no definite pressure. But they were there, like the long streaks which shadow objects in the sun. And beside him, piloting the three of them, as if he didn't even know what was going on, Larry Tallon, kingmaker, Dáil favourite, the fixer, the matteradamn man, the one who'd suckered him, suckered him with his biggest weakness besides his inability to do a decent business deal, his own ambition. Bell felt small and weak and terribly stupid and if he had had the courage he would have opened the door and jumped at that moment.

16

He had a single tin of beans on his mind. Jack Clarke sat in a chair, staring out through the flaws in the condensation on his living-room window. The tin lay before him in the middle of the floor. It was unopened. Drizzle tapped on the red balcony tiles beyond the window. He could hear overflow rushing through the drainpipes running down the block. He had eaten a pizza and downed three cans of lager and was starting on a bottle of Australian wine. There was a small saucer with some pills on it beside his dinner-plate on the glass coffee-table. He felt weak. As if all the power he had ever had was drained from him, sucked out in one go. When he considered it, he should have seen that it had been coming. There were signs. But when it did come, it exploded on him like a no-warning bomb. He was close to collapsing or falling apart. They were the same. He kept drinking and breathing heavily. The drink numbed him and the heavy breaths were an attempt to control what was becoming uncontrollable.

The news that his father was dead had come at seven in the morning. He thought it was Ralph Martin. Calls like that were usually from Ralph Martin. The first day had passed and they had heard nothing from Derek Bell. No one even knew where he was. Kennedy wanted to put the screws on tight. Martin said, wait. Jack did not give a fuck. He would have said it only he was not asked his opinion. He had done his bit. There was other work. He tried to square it, put it behind him like any other job, but it would not fit and he found himself thinking about it all the time and feeling a degree of disgust he had never known before. He was losing the faith and no matter how he tried, he could not stop it slipping away.

Bell did not appear on day three. Frank Costello had Paud Henry tearing the country apart, looking for him. One of Bell's assistant secretaries said his master was taking a couple of days off to spend more time with his family. Frank Costello nearly put his fist through the bloke. And Ralph Martin broke a mirror when he heard it. Almost took Alan Kennedy's head off with it. It got Kennedy going. Not that it took much to get Kennedy going. They were going to stitch Mr Bell up so tight he'd stop breathing, Kennedy said. Truth was, they were worried at MartinCorp. They had expected something, one way or another, but complete silence and a disappearance were not on the battle plan. Jack Clarke felt a growing regard for Bell as he watched all this take place. Detached. His mind was on Kate when it wasn't mud-wrestling itself on the ethics of what he had done during his years with Martin. And even then, one of the sides always had Kate's voice in the argument.

The phone had rung at seven and there had been a pause. Then his mother's gentle voice.

"Jack, Daddy's died. Could you come over?"

No more. She put the phone down when she had given the message. There were a few seconds when Jack thought it was a dream. He lay back and let it penetrate. Someone had walked over his grave.

The funeral had been in the rain. He had seen graveside scenes in the rain before, been at a couple, but the sound of the raindrops on the mud, beating out taps for his father brought something more than sadness to Jack. He kept looking around at the faces of the mourners, the immediate family crying with heads lowered, holding one another; the extended family, just heads lowered; the friends of the immediate family, straight and solemn; the acquaintances of the immediate family, whispering to one another, another step removed. The shock wave had run out of steam by the time it reached the ones at the back who were probably only there because they felt there was some gain to be made or wanted to be seen.

If they did want to be seen or make some gain, it was futile effort. This was a yesterday's crowd. Existing on dignity, nothing else. Men and women who talked like they had money but knew they could barely raise the price of a hatchback if they had to. Still, they owned the golf clubs and kept the churches running and they had a quality about them, a reliability that had probably worked against them. But they were a million light years away from Ralph Martin.

Jack had not expected Ralph Martin to turn up. And he had not been disappointed. None of them turned up. All of them shook his hand in the office, even the two lads from Carlow in marketing, shook it hard and with meaning, all the meaning they could muster, but not one of them turned up. Business, workload, deadlines, all the usual excuses were rerun over the phone. Molly sent a personal wreath. There was a wreath from the company and a Mass card. But they were standard, kept in a small room for such events. Jack had used the room himself.

The death of his father tore Jack Clarke apart. He had never really respected his father; he had spent most of his life angry with the old man for losing what the family had had, but he found out, looking at the box being lowered into the ground, that he did love him. Jack was not strong on emotion, on discussing it, on admitting it. He had always rather liked things to remain noncommittal, to let it be assumed that he had feelings, because he had a thing about the link between emotion and weakness and a contempt for weakness. It was childish and Kate Keyes had told him when they were living together that it was childish but that was how it was with him.

Kate was not at the graveside. He rang her flat and got the machine and cursed her and cursed himself. Angie said Kate was coming. Carl said she'd have been there immediately if she'd known. Jack wanted her there more than anything. He stood with his mother at the graveside, among a group of aunts he knew but didn't give enough time to because he thought that somehow they were above and beyond time, as he had once thought his father was above and beyond time. Only when his father was sick did he see the man and discard the image. Well, now the image was smashed and the man was dead and Jack Clarke wanted to cry but could not. He held his mother's hand and it felt cold as he watched the faces around the graveside while a man his father always called a druid read a selection of prayers for someone he did not know and who did not believe in the religion he proclaimed.

The reason for existence seemed to disappear completely with his father into that muddy hole. The need to prove something was no longer there. It was as if a whole canvas he had been painting had simply been whipped away and he was left with a great empty space. He drank more than anyone else at the wake and laughed harder and talked to everyone he could find and went around again for a second time. Kate was at the wake. But she had to leave again. She'd be back, she said. She had good words to say about old Jack. They all had good words to say about old Jack but young Jack didn't recognise the man they were talking about. His mother sat surrounded by women who looked like her and she never stopped smiling.

There'd been an argument with Kate but he had hardly been aware of it. With Carl and Angie looking on, trying to play guidance counsellors. It was over the pollution thing again. Jack arguing something he did not believe any more. If he ever had. Kate, arguing with all the passion she could find. She kept saying he should come down to Crossfin and see for himself. Tugging at him. Neither of them had wanted to argue but it seemed the only way for them to work out their feelings. Jack would have gone anywhere with her then.

Water running silver over rocks, tree-lined, branches dipping, bubbles breathing, smooth flow, small fish, she said. The kind of poetic sucker description she was good at. Then the spill. Then the life was gone. It just died. And fish floated on the surface, belly up. Anything else drinking that water died. She kept saying it. She had belief.

Another time, another place, he could have taken that argument and given back as good as he got. But the death of his father and his retreat from Ralph Martin made him throw back whatever he could get his hands on and they had a stand-up until Angie pulled Kate away and Carl brought Jack out to the kitchen for a drink. When they came back, Kate was gone and Jack was cursing himself again.

His father's death had taken away a layer of protection Jack had hardly noticed. It was like losing a layer of skin. It was a raw feeling. Nerve endings exposed. And it compounded the fear he was feeling. He took more pills, just to keep going now. Neither up nor down.

The news about Derek Bell came in a radio flash when he was sitting in his father's study, looking through the old man's pictures and papers.

Blood pressure trouble. The minister was going to be in hospital for a while. There was talk of a heart attack. Jack nearly shit himself. The feeling was indeterminate. Then Dan Meehan rang.

The first minute of the conversation was taken up with a string of abuse against Derek Bell. Then Meehan broke his abuse to say Jack could have some time off if he wanted but they needed him. It was an emergency. Jack didn't say very much. Something inside him was cheering for Bell. He let Meehan parrot on. If Ralph Martin wanted him, then he could ring himself. Jack knew he would not ring. Meehan kept switching direction. It was all linked to Derek Bell. They just couldn't believe he hadn't cracked. He was ruined. Did he not know it? Jack told him to shut his damn mouth. Meehan apologised and asked how Jack was. Jack didn't answer that.

"Ralph'll sort things out, Dan," Jack said in the end. "He always does."

It was just to get Meehan off the phone.

It had been a shit week all round and sitting there before his pizza crumbs and that single tin of beans in the middle of the floor, Jack couldn't even convince himself that being drunk was any good.

He put on some music.

The music just highlighted everything. A confusion of angers surrounded Jack Clarke in his living-room. He wanted to lash out in all directions but he could not figure where was best to start. The paralysis had set in immediately he had come back from his father's wake. He had offered to stay with his mother but she was being cared for by her sisters and they could do more for her than he ever could. That got to him, too. The fact that he was no good to her when he wanted to be of some use. His father dying was difficult enough—he had believed right up to the end that his father would not die, that it wasn't possible—but his mother not needing him was just another kick in the balls.

When the bell rang, Jack was in two minds as to whether he should open the door. There was a part of him that just wanted to remain sealed in. Keep the world out. He had a suitcase packed in his bedroom. It had been packed since he'd had the news of his father's death and he could not remember why he'd packed it. But it was the first thing he did. As soon as he had realised that the words his mother had spoken were real, he had just gone to his wardrobe and presses and packed a suitcase. Then he went into the bathroom, locked the door, turned on the shower and tried to cry.

He left the chain on the door when he opened it. He could only see the side of her face. There was a flicker of golden brown in the pupil of her eye he had never noticed before. She wore a raincoat and a pale lipstick that softened her mouth and made it more attractive. He hair was wet.

"Hi, Jack," Kate said.

She was reluctant to say any more.

His hair was tossed and he was wearing red braces. There was a stain down the front of his white shirt. Tomato sauce, she thought. It might have been blood but there was no evidence of his having cut himself anywhere near the stain. She still didn't know why she had come. Maybe the sight of him trying to defend himself and knowing he was defending the indefensible. Maybe the fact that his dead father had dragged the stuffing from Jack. Maybe she just loved him more than she let on and she couldn't stand to see the pain on his face. There was pain on his face at the wake she had never seen before.

"Let me in?" she said.

"I didn't think I'd see you."

"I said I'd be back. I had to go. I'm here now. I probably shouldn't be. But there you go, Jack."

His hand shook trying to get the chain unhooked. He made a quip about letting strangers into your home.

"Please!" he said when he had done the job.

He motioned to her to come in. She stepped just inside the door and tried to take him in.

"You look awful, Jack," she said.

"I try."

He turned his back on her and walked into the living-room. Kate closed the door behind her and put the chain on. The flat smelled of staleness. She was going to make a remark about single men living alone when she remembered one of their sore points, his neatness and her sloppiness. She loved being sloppy at home. He'd always chase her around their flat, telling her it was important they kept up appearances for whoever might drop in. She never knew who he was talking about. Anyone who did come was a friend and it didn't matter to them. But it seemed to matter to Jack. Like a lot of other irrelevant things.

She stood at the living-room door. He motioned to her to take a seat without saying anything. She came forward to the couch and then headed for a chair. His gaze disturbed her. The beer cans and the empty wine bottle disturbed her more.

"I just had a call from Jenny," she said. "She's engaged. To a guy she met with me in Brussels. François. From Strasbourg. He's fluent in Chinese, and he's been married before. Could be a bit of trouble with her folks. Your dad's death did it to her. Some good news. You're not interested, are you, Jack?"

He made a face.

"Are you going to talk to me?"

"Sure."

She took off her coat and stood up. She was going to go and search for a cloakroom but she settled on placing it over the back of a chair.

"Still sore about my report?" she asked.

"What?"

"My report. Crossfin and all that. You're in trouble, aren't you? We had to fight with what we had. I don't regret it."

"Oh, that, no. That's gone. Or will be. Ralph Martin will sort that out. Ralph always does things like that. He'll get himself out of whatever you try and trap him with. That's Ralph. I've seen—sorry, can't tell you, confidential. I never shipped chemicals, Kate. Do you believe me? Dad's dead," he said.

She looked at his eyes, thought, then nodded. "Okay," she said.

"How much of that stuff have you had?" Kate asked.

"Loads and not enough."

"Come on, Jack, don't do that."

"Showing some concern, are we? I don't need it. I can't understand why he didn't say something about me. He was alive for an hour. Conscious. They were trying to stabilise him. But he never said anything about me. I thought he'd call me. He relied on me. I gave them money, you know. No one knows that. But I did. I'll still give Mum money. I'll look after her like I took care of him. But he never asked for me. Why do you think that was? When Ralph Martin wants something, he asks for me. He's already looking for me. There's a bunch of others do, too. You know. I've helped Carl, too. I've helped people. But he never asked me. When I asked Mum if he did, she just said no."

Kate came over to him and picked up the mess on the coffee table and brought it into the kitchen. There was a bigger mess in the kitchen. More unwashed plates with dried-on food, the kind of thing he used to go apeshit with her over when they lived together. There was one mug, stained so deep with coffee she thought it would be better off thrown out with the rubbish. She was doing this because she could not think of anything to say to him. This man on his couch, drinking wine. She opened a couple of windows and poured herself a glass of water. When she went to pick up the beans tin, he told her to leave it.

"Okay, okay, Jack, I'll leave it, I'll leave it all. I'll leave you here to stew in whatever you're stewing in. Look, I know what you're going through. I went through it. And you were there for me. I remember that."

"I was, wasn't I?"

"Yeah, and I appreciated that. But..."

"What?"

"I don't know. I don't even know why I'm here. It's as if I don't know you any more. I mean I know your face, I know the sound of your voice but what's inside has moved on. Five years, Jack. And I've moved on too. There's a whole chunk of my life you don't know about."

"I thought it was best. That we didn't contact each other. You know."

"I know. I know. Who knows?"

She shrugged.

"Please stop drinking," she said.

"I do a lot of this. Have you loved anyone since me?"

She did not answer.

"Please. I'm asking. I have to know."

"Yes. I lived with a man, Jack. Only for a few months. He was killed."

"Oh!"

"Is that all you can manage?"

"You never told anyone. I never heard."

"There was no need to tell you. You know me. I come and go. I'm here now."

"I didn't."

She was kneeling at his feet now, holding the tin of beans.

"Didn't what?"

"Fall in love again. Silly me. I couldn't even come on time the last two times I did it. Too early. Messy lad. I think it's getting around. Last girl I tried it on with just took me for a ride. To get home. Then she dumped me at the door. That's the way it's been since you. One failure after another. God, I don't know why I'm talking like this. I feel sleepy. I think I'll sleep."

He fell asleep right in front of her. She watched his eyes turn, the lids come down and his body loosen. The long-stemmed glass in his hand slipped out and onto the carpet and the leftover wine in it dribbled out. Kate picked it up. She went around the flat again, picking things up, cursing him for having to pick things up, cursing herself for doing the little-woman bit and picking things up. But she had never seen him like this before. She had seen him upset. When they were living together, he was upset every day, about something, usually about things she wasn't interested in. His ambition ran roughshod over everything they shared. That kind of upset she could do without. He was an obsessive bastard when they lived together, and she had allowed herself to be pulled along by his obsession. Allowed herself? She was being too harsh. She cursed herself for being too harsh. Jack dragged her. Where he wanted to go. Always where he wanted to go. And because she loved him—she paused at that thought and considered how much it had been re-entering her mind in recent weeks—and because she loved him she did everything he asked and more. Well, that was what you did when you were in love, you did what your lover asked because that was what love was about. She listened to her explanation with contempt. It was as if she was reading from some teenage magazine, a kind of push-button happiness.

"You were a bastard to me, Jack," she said.

She was standing over him.

Played around, too. Jack chased skirt like it was going out of season. None of them ever mattered, she knew that. But it wasn't easy to convince yourself underneath all the hurt of knowing he had come from another bed. She could usually smell them on him.

"Come on, let's get you into bed, you poor man."

She lifted him in a kind of fireman's lift, his feet touching the ground. He came back into the world of the conscious somewhere between the living-room and the bedroom and made a comment about a soccer match and drifted off again.

She's gone, Jack, she thought. That girl. The one who worshipped the ground you stood on when she first met you. You could make me come by smiling at me, you know. I can't understand why now. Had something to do with dreams. It all has. Well, she's gone now, Jack. I'm here in her stead and I'm content being me. There's none of the—and she paused again to consider the right words—none of the fire really now, there wasn't even much with Jean-Paul, but

I'm more together now, and I don't lie awake, crying, because you're not there. I did that and more when I left. I did leave or did you throw me out or what happened? All of the above, I suppose. It's always all of the above. The whole damn thing just collapsed. Couldn't take the strain any more. Or couldn't sustain itself.

She dumped him on the bed and tossed the duvet over him. Then she pulled the curtains and walked to the door.

"You sleep it off, Jack. We'll talk then. I'm not going away. I think you'd like that. For me to go and then you could say I went. Well, tough, I'm staying and I'm going to clean this bloody place."

She brought him tea and toast when he woke. He drank and ate in silence. It was midnight.

"You stayed," he said.

She sat on the bed beside him. He let his eyes run up and down her body. She saw what he was doing and she thought about getting up and going into the television again. But there did not seem to be any point. It was fine for him to do that. Flattering. She had a good body. A fine body. She liked it to be noticed. You put a bit of effort into something, you like it to be noticed.

"Did I say stupid things?" he asked.

He wasn't sure. His feelings were out of gear. But she had stayed.

"No," she said.

He thought for a while and then put out his hand and took hers. She did not take hers away. They remained there, holding hands, talking.

"It's not wrong to grieve, Jack," she said. "I think you despise yourself for feeling sad. You should feel. You should cry. Have you cried, Jack?"

He had wanted to ask Derek Bell that same question in Larry Tallon's Cessna when they were coming in to land. He had seen Bell's face wither in an instant and he wanted to ask him that question.

"I tried. I couldn't. I haven't. Not since you and me..."

He squeezed her hand.

"Not since you and me ended. There you are, I can cry. Not for my father, for you. I cried because I could not keep you. That's really Jenny Myers, isn't it? I'd expect it from her. Not from me. But I don't know now."

"I thought I'd—I don't know—I thought I'd find you changed. Angie said you hadn't changed. But friends always say that about one another. When they see each other regularly. But you hadn't when I saw you and I remember thinking, God, he's exactly the same and it nearly made me jump up and leave the table. But I was wrong. I only saw the outside. I think I'm seeing something different now, Jack."

"They'll fight you."

"I know."

"They'll win."

"Maybe."

He did not know why he had said that. There was no reason. There was nothing to prove to her. He was always trying to prove something to someone. Was that what he was doing now his father was dead? Looking for someone else to prove things to. He had always wanted to show his father he was better, that was the basis of everything between them, a thirty-two-year humiliation game he had not even realised he was playing. It filled him with disgust. At his father for accepting it, for praising him, for thanking him. At himself for being such a shit. He kept returning to Derek Bell's face. He had never seen a mark with such an expression. With such doom written into his face. They had him but he had escaped. He had escaped in a way they could not have realised. The escape of the man with nothing to lose. And Bell had nothing to lose. The realisations came at him in squadrons.

"Lie beside me," he said.

They had been there an hour, talking trivia.

"I don't...it wouldn't be a good idea, Jack."

"I'm not asking you for anything, Kate. Anyway, I'm the no-can-do kid now. Perhaps you've read a poem about me on some toilet door in one of the Leeson Street clubs. Only way is down. Just lie there, please."

She struggled with the wrong answers until she lay down beside him. Nothing happened. His breath still stank of booze. But she could cope with that. There was another smell, his smell, and it was still there the way she remembered it, the way it had always been there, especially in the morning when they woke. They had always slept in each other's arms. That had been a rule. No matter what had happened between them the day before, they always slept in each other's arms. She was convinced that was what kept them together so long because there was nothing so lovely as sleeping in someone else's arms. She had never met another man who did that.

"It's nice to have you here," he said.

"Yes."

"You don't have to be anywhere?"

"No."

"It's nice."

They said it was nice to each other for another thirty minutes. Then they fell asleep.

17

"That son of a fucking bitch!"

Ralph Martin picked up a complimentary corporate silver digital clock and threw it at the wall of his office. Bits of complimentary corporate silver digital clock rebounded in all directions around the office.

Alan Kennedy sat motionless in front of him. Dan Meehan just shook. Meehan was a nervous man at the best of times, useless when things got rough. Kennedy called him King Brownnose and said he could smell Meehan coming a mile off. Meehan had similar feelings about Kennedy, whom he called a rabid Rottweiler, but only when he was sure he was in friendly territory, usually in bed with his wife. He didn't know Martin knew those cosy pillow chats by heart. But then Martin never told Kennedy he had him during moments with his wife, too.

Kennedy had been in the office before Meehan. Meehan hated that. When he arrived second. And this was a press-relations nightmare. The headlines were big enough to blind you. A far cry from Meehan's appointment as head of Martin's newspapers a year earlier. He'd been going for the job for years, licking up to whomever it was necessary to lick up to, knifing where he had to, playing the corporate game. What choice had he? It was the only game in town. You could either stay as some petty copywriter, trying to put the best gloss on washing-powder, or you could play the game and move on. And Dan Meehan had opted for the latter. Moved out from his position as a permanently parked vehicle to one that was back in the race. Attitudes changed to him then. Once they saw he was competition. It was all about competition. Your so-called colleagues became competitors in the pronouncing of a few words, men and women who had smiled at you and joked with you were now trying to get the low-down on you. Everything was fair game. Nothing after that was what it seemed. Even a friendly word had a hidden meaning. The calculations were endless. You smiled at those you wanted to influence; you ignored the fodder. There was nothing personal, it was just the way it was. Everything done was the right step. Nothing was done for its own sake. They said he was pure slime but that was only because he was moving faster than they were. You had to have your shields up the whole way.

"How the hell did this happen?" Martin barked at him.

Meehan could feel the blood draining from his head. The whole exquisite public relations spin he had been nursing since he had arrived at MartinCorp, destroyed in a single press run. Meehan tried to wipe the perspiration from his brow and took a sip from the Ballygowan he had in front of him.

"Eh, we're running a damage limitation exercise now, Ralph. It's to secure things."

"This is Bell. I know it. I thought we were going to choke this bastard off. This, this—"

"Kelly," Alan Kennedy said.

"Yeah. I want our lawyers on this. This bastard has fuck all to back him up. He goes around making allegations— shag it, I bet Derek Bell is behind this. Official sources. Bastard."

He slammed his fist down on the board table.

"There's no detail of the allegations, Ralph," Kennedy said. "Only the suspension of insurance. No specifics."

Martin's face turned to stone.

"No, they've just announced to the world that we're

broke. Serious irregularities. Shit!"

He hit the table again.

"I want this thing cut off before it gets any further. You're about to earn your money, Mr Meehan. You get everything we have on this little snot, health, medical, financial, personal: I want to know what condoms he uses; and you get our people to print it. I don't want questions, I don't want ifs and buts, I want him choked off. I thought this little shit was being kept under wraps by Bell's people. I bet Bell's behind this. I'm going to make that shit wish he'd never been born."

He looked at Kennedy.

"Right, Alan?"

"Right, Ralph."

"Where the hell is Jackie Clarke?"

Meehan shrugged his shoulders. He wanted to put the worst slant on Jack Clarke's absence. To take the heat off himself. This was a cock-up of gigantic proportions. Hostiles, as they were called, were usually choked at birth by disinformation. Meehan had people in all the opposition papers; he knew every story going out before it went to press. But this made it out without getting to him. He was already going through his payroll book, striking out names, preparing anonymous calls. There was a routine.

"He's not been in since his father died."

"This is a bloody emergency. I don't give a shit if his whole family's just gone off a cliff. I want him here. This is his damn mess. His bloody bird and her friends. He's finished. Useless bastard. This has Bell written all over it. I know it. Get what Jackie has. Get it, Dan! Call in Bell's money and see it all gets published. I don't care what Frankie Costello says; I'm taking the gloves off. I've given that bastard every chance. He's out to get me. Well, I'm not letting that happen."

Martin pushed his intercom.

"Sarah, I want Jack Clarke. I don't care how; just get him."

Sarah sat back from the phone. She could hear the

aggression through the walls. She didn't need another warning that orders were to be obeyed without question. When he had gone, she told her boss to fuck himself and then set about doing what he wanted.

"Okay, Dan," Martin said.

He came around to Meehan and put his hand on his shoulder.

"Top priority. Fuck whoever needs fucking. No limit. Cash only. Use Barney Small. Alan will take care of the legals. I want to go at these people. I'll get Frank Costello and we'll see where we stand with Derek Bell. That shit. I knew he rolled over too easy. Larry Tallon said it: he said he didn't like the way Bell had taken it. He wanted to see a row. He wanted something more. But Jackie says, no; we have him over a barrel. We have him and there's nothing the bastard can do if he wants to stay a player. Well, the fucking player's just walked off the pitch. He must know that. Unless he has someone else. Jesus, what do you think?"

He looked at his two lieutenants.

"It's possible," Alan Kennedy said.

Dan Meehan, suddenly reinvigorated when he realised he wasn't going to be fired, found a new courage.

"No. Not possible without us knowing. Anyway, who? Everything's been swept clean and shut tight."

"You're supposed to know. He's going to do us. I can feel it; I can feel it. And we're going to be facing a two hundred and fifty million hole and Christ knows what else. Jesus!"

Martin was still calculating as he spoke. It was one of the ways he had of calming himself. He loved to calculate; he had a mind like an abacus where figures were concerned. He was taking figures from his interests around the world: cash flows, capital investments, stocks, trying to square them up with the huge debts his company now had. All those banks, all those scared banks. They'd be at him like flies around shit. He had a special contempt for bankers, Ralph Martin. He called them manure: a stinking necessary evil if you're to grow, he said, but that was all. He continued to calculate. Bell wasn't going for it. Jackie Clarke had failed. Larry had failed. And Bell was hitting back. He'd let it all out. And added Kelly like some kind of dressing. The calculations multiplied. The bankers were his main problem. But he had one up on them. He was into them for so much, the problem had reversed itself: they were into him. They couldn't let him go under, not without heavy risks to themselves. Especially the lead banks. Careers were at stake there. There were still moves he could make, cards he could play; whatever happened, he would stay in the game.

"I'll sort it out, Ralph, I will," Meehan said.

"Cut their balls off," Kennedy said. "I mean really go for those bastards. And rubbish this Kelly, Dan. So his own mother wouldn't trust him. I think we should take legal action immediately, Ralph. Get it into the courts. Slow it down."

"Yeah. Do that."

Meehan was glad to get out of the room. When he got back to his own office the first thing he did was pour himself a couple of large drinks. Just to steady his nerves. The thing was to keep his head, he kept telling himself, to keep his head. He could feel the blood turbo-charging around his body. The excitement was forcing an overload on his brain and he could feel a headache beginning at the back of his neck and working its way forward to his forehead. He just had to hang on; he just had to, he thought. He picked up the phone and set to work.

Ralph Martin met Frank Costello in Paris. Ireland had suddenly become too crowded to risk a meeting which might be seen. The allegations being thrown around kept dragging up Martin's political connections. And there was a television programme on the cards. Martin had his lawyers trying to get an injunction against the programme but it was proving difficult.

In London, the Department of Trade and Industry were

hinting that they weren't happy with the Britcop deal. More allegations. There were rumours everywhere. It was fair game on anything to do with Martin. And Martin couldn't believe how inaccurate everything being said about him was. It was fine, he felt, if people were going to have a go at him. He could deal with that like swatting flies, but with this kind of petty jealous rumour-mongering, he was just as likely to go down for something he hadn't done as for something he had.

The hotel was a small one near the Pompidou Centre. Martin had arranged to take a room. The room was small with a single double bed and a dresser. It had an attached bathroom. The wallpaper was old and had flowers motifs. There was nothing to recommend the place except the price if you were a budget traveller and the location and discretion if you wanted to have a secret meeting.

"What's your maximum damage, Ralph?" Costello asked.

"Maximum? My banks take me over. There's a sell-off. There's maybe thirty. The big ones will be the first. I think the Americans will lead it. If they do, then we're in serious trouble. There's no way we can meet current repayments. No way. Even if we hived off Britcop. But that would leave us in even more trouble. The market would laugh at us. You couldn't get tuppence for the company if that happened. We'd never get near what we paid. There's trouble, too, with the DTI in London over the takeover. I don't think it's so big we can't handle it. But it's another small headache. There's fuckers out there, Frank; there's real fuckers out there, Frank, and they don't care what they do to the country. Lousy jealous nobodies who can't leave well enough alone. I'd have them done if I could."

"All right, all right. I saw Derek Bell. It is heart trouble. He's confined to bed. Timely, I know. Says he wants to resign. That's annoying right now. With all this. A few weeks ago, maybe. But not now. He wants you first, Ralph. I didn't think he'd go this far. He could sink us both. He wants MartinCorp, Ralph. Nothing else matters to him. And with all this, I can't protect you much longer, Ralph. The party's under strain. I'm doing my best. Larry Tallon has done his best. There's talk. Usual stuff. I've made my reputation on that kind of talk but it's getting louder. Sure if I'd done all the things attributed to me I'd be dead by now. But we're talking damage limitation here, Ralph. What's this damn documentary going to say?"

"What Bell's saying, I suppose. I'm getting legal advice. What's the chance of getting the cash now?"

"Two chances, Ralph. I'm trying to hang on to my Government. If I could find a word better than fuck for what I want to say, I'd use it."

Martin could feel a gap being wedged between himself and Costello. It was nothing he could put his finger on and it was being done so slowly he could not be sure except that his gut feeling told him it was happening and he always believed his gut feelings. The Taoiseach was pulling away. This man whom he'd backed, thrown everything behind, money, influence, muscle, was pulling away.

"You do realise the man wants Paudie to bring the guards in on this. Paudie's stalling, but who knows? And there's more, Ralph. You could have worse trouble. The bastard's been carrying a dictaphone around with him, he says. Our Mr Bell isn't the big dumb cunt he appears. He has Larry. And he has your man, Clarke. Well, blackmail is the word he's using. I told Larry I never authorised anything like that. I'm sure you never told this Clarke to go that far. I said it to him, Ralph. But he could have you up against a wall, Ralph. I don't know what I'm going to do about Larry if this gets out. But I suggest you terminate any plans you had regarding Derek Bell. I can do a deal if you do that. If you press, I can't be responsible."

"Shit, Frank, the bastard's screwed me to the wall and you expect me to roll over."

"I'm telling you to, Ralph. I said I won't accept his

resignation. My Government's at stake, Ralph. The press are all over me. I'll do what I have to do. All bets are off. Back off. Back off and lick your wounds and give me some time to work something out."

Martin was working overtime in his brain. Desperate thoughts. He had never believed he would ever retreat into desperation. Desperation was for others, petty nothings who fawned around him, who invited him to parties just to have him refuse. Being refused by Ralph Martin was a status symbol. Having it in writing was something you could show your friends. There were other ways of dealing with problems. There was the way of the jealous publican whose wife was having it away with a dentist. They found the dentist's car at the airport, doors open, presents for the kids in the boot. Good dinner-party talk; what happened, the big mystery. Everyone had their opinion. Ralph Martin knew what happened. He knew what happened and how it happened. The publican brought in outside talent. A barber from Clerkenwell. Clean as a whistle. The job was done with the hands. Hello, snap, broken neck, body driven off in a passenger seat, body buried deep in a part of the border country where bodies are ten a penny. And all for five grand. Publican had his satisfaction; barber had his cash. Martin found himself wandering down those paths. It had been a long time since he had used muscle. There had been no need. With the kind of money he dealt in you didn't need muscle; you could buy anything, even the odd government. But earlier, when he was starting, when he needed to leave his mark, he had used it then, reliable stuff, ex-forces. He didn't care which, the kind of men who don't talk except to say, sir, who dress well and scare shitless on sight. Nothing major. A few threats, collection of unpaid bills. But he'd done it and it had kept him afloat when others weren't up to it. You had to be up to it, to do what had to be done.

"I never told Jack Clarke to go that far," he said to Costello.

"I'm glad to hear that, Ralph."

"Jack Clarke can face up to whatever Jack Clarke did," Martin said. "I gave no instructions that any pressure was to be put on a minister of the state. I wouldn't do a thing like that, Frank, you know that."

"Of course, Ralph. Mr Clarke was ambitious. I know his form. Young, desperate, he did a desperate thing. As for Larry Tallon, well, Larry claims he was as shocked as Derek about the proposal Clarke made. Bell has him, though. Now Larry might be able to squeeze out of it. You know Larry. Anyway, Larry's dispensable. Maybe he can do something. Bell's a friend. I don't know."

"You're going to deal with Bell if he wants?"

"Certainly. With this kind of mess, an election would be suicide. I'll do what I have to, Ralph. This fellow, Clarke, may have charges to answer. I'm having Paud look into it. Difficult business. You might think of giving him some extended leave while this thing gets sorted out. With pay, of course. I believe his father has just died. Maybe he was under strain."

Ralph Martin leaned back in his chair and put his feet on the bed. They had a pot of coffee between them. Martin leaned his head on the wall. He looked out the window at the building across the way. He could see five windows from where he was looking, all curtained, and he wondered what was going on in each of them, whole worlds on their own.

"I'll sack him. Will Derek Bell see me?"

"I don't know. He's angry, Ralph. Pull off whatever dogs you have on him."

Martin exhaled through his nose.

It had been a ridiculous trip to get to that Paris hotel. Helicopter across Dublin, private jet to London, helicopter across London, private jet to Brussels, car to Paris. Two cars in fact. They had switched cars in Brussels. There was a hotel room booked at one of the more fashionable places in Brussels in his name. And that was where he would emerge from. He was back calculating. He still had cards left to play. The thing was to play them slowly, get himself time. Too many people depended on him to let him disappear like that. Even Frank Costello couldn't let that happen.

"We can rubbish this Kelly weasel," Costello said. "Paud has subversive links he's been seen with. Old school friends. Tenuous, but enough. We can get him on that alone. Maybe we can make him think his best interests lie with us. You know, let him know we could put the word around that the press and Industry people aren't the only ones he's been talking to. They're so bloody paranoid down that way now, they'd probably shoot him for the relief of it. See, we do have a way to get this muddied. Very important that, Ralph. Don't you agree? There's all kinds of ways. Committees, tribunals. The banks can sit around a table. They're interested in one thing. Money. You tell them there's a good way for them to get their money and they'd fuck their own mothers if you asked them. I may have problems in the party, Ralph. Phil Cassidy might want to go for me. This would be a good time. So I might have to call a snap election, whether I want to or not. I don't want to, not in the present climate, but we must make provision for all eventualities. What about cash? You could set some aside before things get a bit difficult. I assure you once we've won, we can see about getting MartinCorp back to where it belongs."

A wedge all right, Martin thought, but nothing too wide. The bastard still needs me. He smiled and nodded his head.

The meeting over, each man took it in turn to use the bathroom. Then they left the room, Martin five minutes after Costello. Costello was picked up by a car around the corner driven by one of Paud Henry's heavies. He was taken to an engagement at the Irish College and then the airport. Ralph Martin took a taxi to the Bois de Boulogne where his car was waiting for him. He drove to Brussels and stayed the night there. Before leaving, he talked to a journalist from a British newspaper and a hack from one of his own.

On the flight back to Dublin, Martin transferred several million pounds from one private account to another private account. He was getting himself ready for the fan.

Frank Costello held a short cabinet meeting at which he discussed unemployment. He made no mention of the difficulties of MartinCorp. He asked Phil Cassidy and Paud Henry to stay behind for an emergency meeting of an innocuous protocol sub-committee they were all on. None of the other ministers argued. Partly because of Frankie's hold on them, partly because they knew there was trouble and they wanted as little exposure to it as possible. No civil servants were present at the meeting. Frank Costello was already moving to clean up any links which might expose him to whatever Ralph Martin might have coming at him. To secure himself. That was why he decided to hold this emergency meeting. If flak was coming his way, it was going to come from Cassidy. He knew Bell and Cassidy had talked but since they got on marginally worse than Frank himself got on with either of them, he wanted to know how Cassidy was thinking. Under official cover. So he might just be off his guard. Paud Henry always put Cassidy off his guard. Cassidy considered the Justice minister a life form somewhere between amoeba and worm, and he often said it in public. But his contempt for Henry had become a weakness and Costello knew it. Everyone had contempt for Henry, anyone with a brain would, but it took a real brain not to show it. If Cassidy was feeling confident, he would show it now. If he had been seeing Bell in secret, out of Paudie's eyes—and it could happen: his lads had missed a meeting between Mossad and the South Africans in the Mont Clare a couple of weeks before. The army had covered it but Paud had come out of a security committee meeting fuming and bawling out his commissioner about chasing subversives up his own arse. Paud's language was choice when he was made look a fool.

Cassidy was tired when the meeting began. He kept rubbing his eyes. His daughter wasn't well. There was always some kind of trouble, he had said in a moment of exasperation with his wife the night before. He said he might dump the whole damn thing, give it up, go do something useful. But he just couldn't get it out of his blood, his damned addiction to the whole business, his wanting to make a difference. He had part of the picture about Martin, what he'd been given, and what he'd read in the papers. And there were funny sounds coming from Industry, rumours about more revelations, a whole conveyor belt of skulduggery. But the Industry people kept their business to themselves, guarded it jealously. He sometimes wondered if the public had any idea how jealous departments were of one another, how much they kept for each other, how much yelling and pompous pontification went on when channels were circumvented. A whole subculture devoted purely to its own perpetuation. You couldn't joke about the service. It was beyond a joke; it had a life of its own. It would quite possibly keep on functioning even if the entire country ceased to exist. Those bastards in Industry knew they had something good and were trying to make sure their own backs were covered before they went official. Then everyone else would get it in the mouth.

Cassidy's tell-it-like-it-is style clashed head on with the civil service. And he never hid his dislike of the people he had working for him, myopic tunnel-visioned smallholders, he called them in the Dáil bar, the worst kind of narrow mind imaginable, no matter what country they came from, and now they had the whole bloody European Community going round in circles, applying Alice-in-Wonderland logic to fulfil their demands. He watched Frank Costello take out a small manila folder with a couple of sheets of paper.

"I just thought I'd better let you know that what's going round is true. Derek Bell intends to withhold insurance from MartinCorp. I will wait for his department to announce it publicly, he being the appropriate minister."

Cassidy looked at Henry. The Justice minister's piglet

face was alive with schoolboy anticipation. Bell hadn't said anything to him yet. Gave it to the papers first. Typical of that lot. So that was it. All behind his back. Frank Costello had kept him out. Now he was presented with a *fait accompli* and his signature was all over it. He thought about losing his temper but there was no point. He had his immediate future to think about.

"And that's it?" he said.

"I don't see we can do anything," Costello said. "It's his prerogative. I have explained to him the seriousness of such a move but he's going ahead."

"You could bloody fire him, Frank. You could bloody tell him that this party doesn't need that kind of shite in coalition. Call an election. If you're up to it."

"Not so easy, Phil. There's other considerations."

Costello wanted to smile but the subject prevented him. Cassidy was caught out. He didn't know enough to press it. And he was closing ranks. He wasn't using it.

Maybe Bell and Cassidy might have been closer than he knew. This could all have been something to get him out. Cause a major embarrassment and see Frank Costello squirm, risk short-term loss for the Government for long-term gain for themselves. It had happened before. It would be a smart move. Maybe get Larry Tallon to turn. It wouldn't take much to get Larry to turn if he thought it was in his own best interests. And Larry had an eye for his best interests. Frank Costello's mind did acrobatics with the possibilities.

"I have presented our case to him. Forthrightly. The damage will be substantial. But I think we can ride it. Obviously our minister colleague thinks his duty to some semantic detail is greater than that to this Government, his comrades and his country. As for firing him, the damage is done. The file is prepared. I have seen a copy. It says MartinCorp was facilitating the export of embargoed products to the Gulf. Chemicals are on the list. It says they have proof. I have not seen that. Maybe Derek Bell has it with him. I have been in touch with our insurance people and they are adamant. It invalidates everything. We must deal with reality, Phil. He goes, this Government goes."

"I knew that bastard was no good, Frank, from the moment I laid eyes on him. No fucking loyalty. That's what you get with these flycrap boys. Give them a portfolio before they've proved themselves. He was a nothing, Frank. Then he gets a couple of seats and hold us to ransom. Has no experience, gets a portfolio, looks honest, speaks well, talks liberal and then shafts us up the arse. Bury him, Frank. I don't care if his ticker gives in completely. Maybe that would be a good thing. Bastard."

Costello tried to figure out Cassidy's reaction. It could have been genuine. On the surface, he and Bell hadn't been the best of mates, but Frank Costello wanted to believe his own paranoia. It made life easier for him, gave him an enemy to combat, out in the open. Cassidy could have distanced himself from Costello. It would be his chance to press for the leadership. But he was sticking fast. Maybe he was just being a good soldier. Good soldiers were expected to stand by their leader. Good for their image. Good for their prospects. It came back to the leadership and Frank Costello's position.

18

If there were arguments for and against they had ceased to be relevant. Kate Keyes had come to the conclusion they were more cosmetic than anything else. She had made up her mind well before; maybe it had always been made up. She didn't go into it any further. The bed was an old one with springs and an oak headboard. You could see faces in the headboard if you were of a mind to; you could see anything you wanted to. There was a picture of the Sacred Heart on the far wall and a small red bulb under it, a little leftover cliché in a country desperately trying to free itself from stereotype. Some people were obviously more subversive than they let on.

The B&B was a bungalow-blight shell off the main road to nowhere, down a side road to anywhere, a Mogadon place where if time didn't actually stop it was only because it was going so slow anyway it did not seem to be moving. There was the town, Crossfin (a village in any other country) back a couple of miles, a single street bottle-neck with a fast-food palace, an amusement hall where the teenagers looked like the machines, a video shop where Stallone and Schwarzenegger got the most plays and a fish and chip odour that penetrated atoms. Plastic battled neon. There was a country-and-western band playing in one of the bars when they arrived. They didn't go in. Kate bared her teeth and shrugged her shoulders. Her side had its advantages.

The fellow in the Sacred Heart picture looked as if he needed Bisodol, or maybe he was bass player in a punk band years ago, local boy trying to make good, probably playing Irish bars in Boston and New York and talking about how he could have been the new U2 with the right management. Kate knew an agent in Dublin who had a similar problem. Only he was the genuine article. He had turned down U2. She didn't know him enough to sympathise and he had other interests and managed his tan well and his skiing trips to Aspen.

There was a lived-in flavour to the room. The carpet felt old but looked new. The bedclothes—she pulled some more over her body, it was cold even with the radiator on—were imports, from Asian countries, the sort they make for a penny, sell for a pound and sell on and sell on. She allowed herself a trip against that kind of exploitation for a moment. Then she ran out of steam. She did not have much steam for anything. Angie was pregnant again. Carl didn't know yet. They were having difficulty as it was, nothing major, but their life-style was being pared, small splinters being shaved away. Another kid would only add to the strain. Angie wanted another kid but not right now. It was important to get it right, to have them when you wanted them. Kate gave her friend a shoulder to cry on and said she'd see if her brother could let them have his place in Fuengerola for two weeks in January.

Her clothes were on the floor. She could just see her slip. And her skirt was beside the radiator. She thought about getting up and moving them, making it look less obvious. There was a case perched on the dresser at the window and the curtains were caught on it. This allowed some of the scarce light outside to creep in. The netting that passed for lace at the window enhanced the light and let her see more of that bit of the room than the rest. She moved herself onto her side.

She wanted to reach out and touch Jack. He was about

six inches from her. That was different, she thought. She had been looking for differences, and that was one: they had fallen asleep apart, only six inches but it might have been six miles. She considered the distance and its significance. His hair had become tossed in a boyish way. He had a boyish face, lying there, naked, without the expensive body armour he usually wore. She could make out his smell even over the smell of the room. He had a good smell. He was breathing slowly. His hand was gripping the sheet. Tight, afraid someone would whip it off. She watched him for a while.

It had happened effortlessly. She kept saying that to herself. It had happened. As if she had been a victim of something. She had asked him to come with her. She had booked the single room. She had kissed him. Had she? She had to go over that again. They had come in—yes, she had, a long deep one, with open mouths, against the wall, and the taste was of Italian and red wine, a very delicious taste. And then it had followed a natural course, choreographed almost, except there was no one else except them. A gentle teasing with lips, a slow touching, beautiful warmth, some nervousness, reassurance then, each to the other, gentle kisses and touches, very tender, then undressing, one the other, no rush, slow, button by button, kiss and movement in harmony.

She grinned and touched his tossed hair.

On the sheets, inside her, he had said something she did not hear. Her head was back and her arms were up, holding the board. She did not need to hear. She knew what it should be and that was enough. There was never enough, she thought: you always wanted more, no matter how deep he came. She pulled her knees above his waist and told him to shove deeper. He did. He did everything she asked. He was a good lover, Jack: real. Maybe bed was the only place he could be real. For a while, when she was moaning and her breaths were coming faster and she was digging into his back with her nails, she thought the landlady would hear.

They were the only guests. She thought the landlady would hear and she thought she should stay quiet. But that was too difficult. And when he was moving faster and his face was full of want and she could feel every sinew in him, it was impossible to stay quiet, so she let go.

She touched herself between her legs. She could feel it now, it was coming back to life, but the beautiful feeling was still there, the glow that had run through her body in waves, and it made her close her eyes and think again.

He'd said her name. Over and over again while they were coming. She could not remember if it was the first or the second or—she gave up trying then. It was all one. She reached over and put her arms around him.

"Hi!" he said.

He hadn't really opened his eyes.

"I want to hold you," she said.

They fell asleep again, holding one another.

She had put the challenge down. Come and see for yourself, Jack. She didn't expect him to accept it but he did. It wasn't difficult. He needed to get away. He needed Kate more. He might be able to help, he said. He needed to feel he could help. He'd never even been down to the place before. It was just one on a list. He'd bought people off, greased them down, ordered this, directed that, but he'd never been there himself. Someone lower down in the pecking order got jobs like that. Usually Barney Small or the local head honchos. Their patch. It was just another problem on Jack's desk, among a score of problems he had to deal with at any one time, and he allocated whoever he thought would get the job done. Truth played very little part in it. Kate was too involved to understand.

The plant was a standard IDA model, the only occupied one in a standard IDA business park, a Lego-ish warehouse with offices. Fitted together by numbers, Kate said. Jack wanted to laugh but could not bring himself. A matter of residual loyalty or something. Maybe he thought it was a criticism of him. The ridiculous thing about the place was its isolation. There was nothing else near it. You had this village five miles down the road, with all its plastic, and then this business park with a computer plant and lots of tarmac; complete incongruity, a monument to prefab industrialisation, slap bang in the middle of nowhere, surrounded by bog and low hills, a kaleidoscope of brown and green and bordered on one side by the stream they called a river on local maps and on the other by a coniferous forest. And the wind was a constant companion.

Jack went to the plant sure he could sort out the whole thing in half an hour. The element of surprise, he said. High rank and surprise. Just another tick on a list. And, at first, it looked as if he just might. Roy Doherty's face took about an hour to recover from the shock of having Jack at his door, unannounced. But he was even more upended by the sight of Kate. They'd had words, as she put it. Every time she'd come to inspect the place, he'd given her fifteen minutes and told all his people to keep their mouths shut. Now she had heavier ammunition and she found herself enjoying the manager's fawning. He was a swollen man with big ears and not liked by his work force, though they'd swung in behind him when he told them they might lose their jobs if the skirt and her loonies at Crossfin House had their way. He couldn't speak Aengus Kelly's name without wanting to spit. Jack played it really cool, asking questions only someone with inside knowledge could ask. But Doherty was on to him. The manager stalled and spoofed and just plain lied. Jack kept saying he knew what had happened, as if that would swing Doherty into a confession. Doherty stuck to the MartinCorp line. Jack left the place angry and cursing and ready to sign on with Kate. It was not the whole reason for it. But it was sufficient.

If the story Doherty had spun turned Jack towards Kate's cause, meeting the people he had called weirdos at Crossfin House fixed him in place. The house was a mixture of mock-

Tudor and neo-Georgian. All grey and covered in lichen. It had belonged to a family named Cooper. The Coopers had come over with Cromwell and gone into decline almost immediately. The last of the Coopers had dabbled with Eastern philosophy and donated the house to the Hare Krishnas when he died. There were six of them living there, five of them Germans. The house was in danger of falling down when they got their hands on it. They did some restoration work, grew vegetables and kept some dairy cattle for milk and cheese. What they had in surplus, they sold. It was this small dairy herd that was wiped out when the stream that ran past the Martin plant was polluted. It was more than the dead animals for them now. No one around them could understand that. And when they gave the stream a Hindi name because they felt it should have a name and no one in the town could tell them what it was called, no one could understand that either. People laughed at them.

There had never been terrific relations between the locals and the Krishnas. They were strange. Their clothes were strange. Their gods were strange. Their life-style was monastic. The locals said they were a cult. And there was talk; there was always talk—about the house. Kids would run up and throw stones at it at night. A dare. Others did it for other reasons.

Kurt, the head of the group, said he thought it was the superficial things that really caused the problem. The rituals, the dress, the chanting, the music. People saw it as a kind of cultural subversion. They seemed convinced the Krishnas were out to wreck the place. It was an irrational fear but it was strong.

It would have been easy to leave them alone. They only wanted peace and quiet and a place to meditate and practise their way of life. They never preached in Crossfin. Some people took that as an insult. Said they should move if they didn't like the place. Maybe they might have if they could. But they couldn't sell the house because the old Cooper will had a stipulation that it was theirs only so long as they lived in it.

Bent over the stream at the bottom of a garden which sloped through some oak and hawthorn, Jack dipped his finger in the water. The bottom had a rusty colour. Jack said he could see the water had been polluted by the colour. Kurt, who was tall and very quiet, said that was merely bog colouring, that the water was now clear except there were no fish in it any more. It left no traces. The spill was long gone. Diluted. It should have been tracked at the time, except that no one would believe them.

"I'll try and get you some kind of a case," Jack said. "But it could have been someone else. It's not a hundred per cent. Other people use pesticides. They'll use that. And him."

He pointed to Aengus Kelly in another field, feeding a goat.

"He's not rock solid."

"I talked to a lawyer who said that."

Kurt wore an ear-ring and his nose was red and slightly running. He sniffled. He wore a polo-neck, dungarees and a donkey jacket. He had steel-rimmed spectacles and bloodshot eyes. The joints of his hands were very red, redder than the end of his nose. His arthritis, he said. He was having some success, trying to control it by a vegetarian diet. The electric fire he slept beside was becoming too expensive though.

He left Jack and Kate on their own. There was digging to do.

"They couldn't afford court, Jack," Kate said. "You had it all in your favour. They couldn't prove anything. All they had were a few environmental groups and us. Now we have a little more. They have to buy their food twenty miles away—twenty miles away. No one here will serve them now. You do see?"

Jack could not pin down exactly why he had come. He wanted to be exact but all the reasons were jumbled. There had been the challenge, yes, and Kate and what he knew, but there was more. And it had to do with his father's death. Something in him had been released. As if it had been held captive for so many years he'd forgotten about it and now it was released. There was a sense of urgency in his life. And proving things did not seem so important. Proving to whom? Proving what? It had struck him that one day there would be no one around to prove anything to. And there he would be, still proving things and no one there to make it worth a damn. It was clear when it came. And then she came. And they were here.

They walked in a wood, by a stone wall, on the edge of a bog, wind whistling in their ears, razor-sharp cold, blue sky blotched with bruises, ridges building at the horizon. They had walked in heavy coats, arm in arm, through a wood, on pine needles and under trees dripping from the last rain. A deer shot out and ran ahead and then disappeared and they stopped and listened to the emptiness.

"It's the right thing, Jack," Kate said. "They've lost everything. A drop in the ocean to your Mr Martin but everything to them. He doesn't say it but he cried to me. He is a brave man. The locals call him Krauty. He doesn't say anything but it hurts. He's a tough nut. Most of his family went to the gas in the war. Funny the things you find out about people."

Jack had to drive miles to find a place to have dinner. Neither of them wanted to go into town. And fast food didn't appeal. There was a rumour that someone in the area had won the Lotto. People were gathering in corners and making guesses and judgements. Whole lives were summarised in five seconds. Jack got drunk and had to take a pill in the toilet before he drove back. There was a mist down and the sheep's eyes were green in the mist and the fog lamps barely made it through an inch of the stuff. It was a lonely drive back and both of them felt lonely and did not say it to the other. They just held each other's hand and when they did get back they went to bed without saying anything.

It was better than the first night. Kate did not even think of the things she had thought of the first night. It flowed better and the ecstasy was deeper and longer and their feelings took over. She said his name this time, when they were coming, willing him into her, mouth open on his, tongue tasting the taste of him, body touching the touch of him, sensing the feel of his movements, smelling his smell.

The first time he came in long movements, and she thrust herself up to him, pushing her pelvis hard at him, staring into his eyes, holding his hands. The second, they were together, up against the oak headboard, right up close, as one as they could ever be, and she had her fingers digging into his bottom. The third time, she was sitting, watching him arch, pushing herself down on him, right to the edge and down and he reached up and pulled at her hair and she brought her mouth to his and they came like that.

In the morning, the landlady was serving breakfast, and Jack could feel the citrus burn his throat. The woman was young and girlish, and she wore Nike shoes with the laces undone. She asked them if they'd had a good night. Jack could not answer; the muscles in his throat were contracting from the orange juice. Kate nodded and put some sausage in her mouth to avoid saying more. The landlady smiled and said it was beautiful outside if they were going out, but either way they should wrap up warm.

Jack took Kate's hand and stroked it. It was a gentle movement. She had her eye on a robin at the window, big red breast pushed up to the glass.

"I once went on an anti-hare-coursing demo," Jack said.

Kate did not answer. She felt he was trying to say something. So she let him go on. Getting things out of Jack sometimes needed tweezers and even then you couldn't be sure of getting anything.

He cut a piece of bacon and dipped it in his egg.

"Angie made me go. I thought she'd told you. We had a big fight. I got drunk and spent all our bus fare home. We had to hitch in the rain. She didn't speak to me for days after that. I got a cold."

"She never said."

"Maybe she forgot. It was ages ago. Do you ever think that ages ago isn't ages ago any more? It just isn't. I mean, besides a few snapshot images you carry around in your head. I only have a few images of him in my head."

"Your father?"

"Yeah. That's all his life has become. They're good images. But the brain is selective. I wanted it all for him, Kate."

"All what? Take your time, Jack."

"I'm not used to this. It's been years. I thought if I just got money everything would be fine again. That Dad would be back where he belonged. It's just I spent so much time getting the money I forgot that he might not survive to enjoy it. I have loads of money, Kate. Sounds bovverish, doesn't it, like some little barrow-boy? I could buy those people over there hundreds of cattle. I could give it up now. For a while, anyway. I did everything for him."

"Did you?"

Jack had to ask himself that all day. It was as if he was pulling the paper off a parcel. Once he had pulled some of it off, he had to go on, no matter what, to see what was inside. The whole of him was laid out, in a neat parade-ground order. He thought of the look on Derek Bell's face, a kind of horror mixed with contempt. A concession that they had him against a wall but a promise that he wasn't giving up. Mutual assured destruction promised by someone who had nothing to lose. And he had lived up to his promise. Jack had come away from the meeting, hoping Bell would fight back, wishing he would. It was the first time. Maybe he was having a premonition.

The banks were back on Ralph Martin's back. The whole bloody media were camped outside MartinCorp. Ralph was supposed to be in Zürich, then New York, then Amsterdam. Then he was supposed to have tried to kill himself. That was a Dan Meehan special. Jack could recognise the Dan Meehan specials. The friendly papers, the ones Ralph owned, spread Dan Meehans like an infection. He did not even bother to listen beyond the headlines in the car.

"There's been a worthlessness dogging me, Kate," he said to her.

The next day they drove to the plant again. Kate had asked him not to go. There was nothing there they could use. Any evidence was gone. Surprise too. But Jack insisted he could get it out of them. He could handle a no-hoper like Doherty; he'd done it a million times. Then Kate begged him not to bring Kelly. It would only cause trouble. Jack said he needed to. It was leverage. He knew what he was doing. Actually he did not. He was trying to prove things again. A sudden reversion to type. It had not gone. And afterwards he wondered if it ever would.

Kelly did not want to be there. He'd had an argument with Jack and the two of them had ended up shouting at each other. Jack brought Kurt in. Kate came in on Kelly's side but Jack could be persuasive. Kurt said Kelly should go. Kelly obeyed. He smelled as bad as Kate said.

A security guard at the gate held them up. Jack tried to argue his way in. The security guard would not budge. They had to wait. Doherty would be down in a moment.

Kelly was fidgeting in the back of Jack's car, mumbling to himself. Jack told him he was going to get a chance to prove what he was claiming.

"How?" Kate asked. "You think they left it all lying around? There's nothing here but trouble. Leave it to the courts."

But Jack wasn't listening.

"You just sit there, mate, and do what I tell you. You've been talking a lot, now I'm giving you a chance to show me."

"Jack!" Kate said.

"Don't worry, Kate, I'm with you."

Doherty came to the gate with two men in overalls. He was moving fast on his elephantine legs. A couple of birds were singing madly in a tree somewhere around. The singing got to a kind of frantic pitch. Doherty's legs looked like they might topple at one point. There was no sense of welcome on his face. There hadn't been much the day before but now there was nothing. The two flanking him had no sense of anything on their faces. One looked as if he been burned once. Kate noticed that. The manager leaned in the window. He looked at Kelly. Then he turned to Jack.

"You keep dirty company, Mr Clarke," he said.

"We want to come in," Jack said. "I want this man to show me exactly what he says happened. You can have your say too, Doherty."

Doherty looked around.

"Mr Clarke. Can I have a word?"

"What about? We want to come in," Jack said.

"Yes, yes, if you would just bear with me for a second. I want to talk to you, alone."

Jack looked at Kate, who indicated he should do what the manager said. He got out of the car. Doherty led him a couple of steps away. He put an arm on Jack's shoulder.

"Well, you see, we've had word from Dublin," he said.

He drew Jack closer.

"What's that heap of shit doing here?" he whispered.

Jack was about to give him back as good when a fist caught him in the kidneys. He broke off his words and let out a roar and fell forward on to the tarmac.

"Alan Kennedy sends his regards," Doherty said. "Now fuck off."

He kicked Jack in the stomach. Kate came out of the car, screaming abuse at Doherty, Kelly behind her, tying his trouser belt which had become loose. The two expressionless lads in the overalls caught Kelly and pinioned him against the security hut wall. The security guard grabbed Kate and held her fast. Jack was still moaning on the ground.

"Now let me show you what we think of this bastard," Doherty said.

He leaned into the security hut and pulled out a wooden pole, about four feet long. The two overalled men had Kelly tight against the hut wall, blind side to the rest of the business park.

"This is from Ralph Martin and, of course, us."

Doherty smashed the pole into Kelly's face, breaking his nose. Blood fell out of his nostrils in large drops, down his denim shirt onto his jeans. Doherty hit him again, six times, into the ribs. Kelly lost all his breath and buckled, still held up by the two in overalls.

Kate was still screaming and trying to break the hold of the security guard.

Doherty hit Kelly again, into the shins and knees and Kelly collapsed onto the tarmac.

"See," Doherty said. "No bottle."

He put a couple of boots into Kelly. Then he walked over to Jack and grabbed him by the lapel of his coat and lifted him up.

"Take him with you, love," he said. "And you can have that shit too if you're a good girl. Don't worry, I don't hit girls. I suppose you're fucking glad with yourselves."

He hit the side of the car with the pole. Then he kicked it.

"And don't bother with the police. They're not seeing today. This is their place, too."

He opened the door and threw Jack into the driver's seat. The security guard put Kate into the passenger seat. The two in the overalls were dragging Kelly along the tarmac, scuffing his boots.

"Bastard," Kate said to Doherty.

"Orders, love. I don't mind, though. Keep your nose out of our business. Go back to wherever you came from, love. And—"

He did not finished what he as going to say. Jack had him from behind.

He rammed Doherty into the car and grabbed his hair and cracked his head off the car.

Kate jumped out and tried to pull him back, pleaded with him to get inside and drive off.

But Jack kept doing it, putting his fist into Doherty's kidneys while the manager's teeth rolled across the roof of the car and down the front window to the bonnet.

The security guard and the two dragging Kelly dropped him and came at Jack and pulled him off. Jack came back at them with his elbows, right into the security guard's mouth and one of the overalled bloke's necks. The guard retreated, holding his split lips and the overalled bloke sank to his knees, gasping. But the second overalled bloke caught Jack across the face and sent him rolling across the tarmac.

Kate could do nothing but scream at all of them. She tried to get Jack up but Doherty was already moving at him. He hit Jack just as he was rising, well-placed, into the plexus. Jack folded and fell down.

It was over and Kate was still trying to stop it.

"Get up," Doherty said to Jack. "Get up and take your lady and him and fuck off. And don't bother checking in back in Dublin because if Alan Kennedy or Ralph Martin get you, they'll make sausagemeat of you, son."

He tossed a fiver on top of Jack.

"This'll pay for the suit, I don't think. I should fucking kill you, son. If I see you here again, I'll break you into so many pieces they'll never find you. Understand?"

Kate was down on her knees lifting Jack. The two in the overalls had backed off on the orders of their boss, one of them still trying to breathe easier. And the security guard was standing holding his bleeding lips, tipping his head back. The wind picked up more than usual and some rain began to spit on all of them. In the car, Kelly was muttering something about not wanting to come, his head bowed.

Jack Clarke pulled himself up with Kate's help. He straighted himself. Then he faced Doherty down.

"I hope they plough this fucking place into the ground," he said.

"They probably will," Doherty said. "And then we're all fucked, Mr Clarke, all of us."

Out of sight, Barney Small watched from a window and grinned.

On the way back to Crossfin House, Kelly kept saying he disapproved of violence, cursed Jack and told him he wanted nothing to do with anything like that again. Jack told him to shut up. That got Kelly more incensed. He threatened to hit Jack. Kate had to calm him. She wanted to hit Jack herself, and only they had Kelly in the car, she might have jumped out.

"I couldn't let it go, Kate, I couldn't."

"You don't get it, Jack, you just don't get it."

She shook her head.

They had a vegetarian meal with the Krishnas, on cushions on a varnished floor in a big room in their grey stone Victorian house. The cardboard at the broken windows gave the whole place a Band-aid look. Jack felt uneasy throughout the meal.

Only doing it for her, he said to himself.

Kate had argued with him for two hours. What the hell had happened? Why had he done that? Fought. In broad daylight. What kind of thug was he?

He wanted to tell her he'd done worse. They could get him for worse if they wanted. It would be ironic if they got him for the one and only piece of violence he had ever used in his life. He felt excited after, and horny. He did not tell her the second emotion. She said the first was excitement and stress, and a meal and some conversation would take it away.

19

F rank Costello's head cold made his image advisers even more of a pain in the neck than they usually were. Stand like that, sit like this, maximise, minimise, think combinations, speak bites. They had a couple of hours with him every few months, to go over what had been won and lost in the meantime. His press team insisted. Frank always went through the usual cursing before agreeing. It was a practised ritual. His vanity could not admit there was anything about him that needed changing and yet he always used what came out of the sessions.

Fidelma was about thirteen stone and wore colour combinations that would scare a rabid dog. She spoke a south Dublin dialect that was a cross between Foxrock and RTE continuity announcer and she had the posture of randy wildebeest. Fergus was gay with much the same mannerisms. He was thin and sharp with a tongue that would put a rattlesnake to shame. Frank Costello hated when he came up and touched him. Frank was purebred homophobic and while he gave every indication to the different delegations that came to see him that he was willing to legalise homosexual acts, he let it be known in the right grassroots party circles and GAA clubs that he was fucking damned if he was going to allow a bunch of dungpunching perverts loose on his country. The his country bit was always emphasised.

They had been at it over an hour, complaining that Frank was tending to let his posture fall during interviews. Frank wasn't giving too many interviews right now and wasn't altogether concerned. He had different problems. Fashion sense and posture just didn't seem as important as holding on to office. The party had its back to the wall. Right where it should be with Fergus around, Paud Henry said. Henry had the hots for Fidelma and she was playing him along. She had the hots for Costello herself and Frank knew it. He used it when he needed to use it. He didn't need to use it now. And there was nothing these people could offer to get him out of the mess he was in. Fidelma was getting on his wick. She was reading out another bloody check-list to him and Costello was a thumbnail away from throwing her and her partner out and cancelling their contract. He pushed his chair back and stood up and slammed his hands down by his side.

"Enough, enough," he said. "Listen, I'm fine the way I am, Fidelma."

Then he took his glasses off and smiled at her.

"I'll have to ask you to fuckoff, love," he said.

Her mouth tensed in a cross between temper and fear. Frank smiled and touched her bottom.

"Well, really, Mr Costello," Fergus interrupted.

"Well, really what?" Costello barked.

"We're used to more courtesy. Really. I think you should apologise. We're not some slave outfit."

Frank smacked his hands together and came right up to Fergus. An inch away.

"I apologise, Fergus. Now, please, please, fuck off. And if you have any complaints, go to Alex."

He pointed to his rodent-like press officer, Alex Byrne, standing in a shadow, holding a clipboard, mouth pressed tight.

"Maybe you'd like to consider ending our contract."

You're a rude fucker, Frank Costello, a callous rude son of

a bitch, Fergus said to himself. And you know you have us by the short and curlies. He swore at himself for taking Costello and his mob on in the first place, for all the licking and crawling they'd had to do to get them on-side, the sheer pissing against the wind nature of it all, trying to make cavemen look civilised, he thought. I'll do what you say, Mr Taoiseach. I'll do what you say, because you hold the purse strings but Christ as soon as I get the chance I'll drop you in the biggest shitpile I can find.

He grinned at Costello.

"Maybe next week, Taoiseach," Fergus said.

"Yes. Ring at the end of the week. Things are a bit rushed as it is."

He held Fergus's hands in his. Tight. It could have been an attempt to imply affection or threat, Fergus did not know. But he felt scared.

"Sure, yeah."

"We'll have a grand session."

As soon as the image consultants had withdrawn, Costello gave Byrne a bollocking for bringing them in at a time like this. Byrne took it and then they went through the press plan for the day: what should be leaked, what should be put around, how they were going to deal with the Martin mess. The bankers were piling into Dublin for a meeting. Ralph Martin wanted to see Costello before he went in. To get guarantees. There was a union delegation to see before lunch and a bloody industry confederation delegation after lunch. The unions were more important. They carried more votes. And they were kicking up murder over the Martin business. Where was the next meal coming from? It depressed Frank Costello. He wanted to be able to present them with a rescue. Make it look like he was some kind of shining knight. It looked good in the papers. The morning's clippings were in a drawer in his desk. Always the first thing Costello read. Byrne was to have a complete briefing ready for him the minute he came in, and a cup of tea and some digestives.

The Martin business had taken on a momentum of its own in the couple of days since Derek Bell had officially announced he was suspending insurance cover. It was banner headline material the same day. Except in Martin's papers. Opposition leaders were screaming for the recall of the Dáil. Bell kept the reasons for his actions out of his statement. Pending further investigations, it said. But the papers were full of speculation. Ironically, the problem had become a simple one now. Survival. Costello felt he could cope with it better that way. Easier to muddy waters now it was a national crisis. Irish industry's star player was in trouble. There was no question of the business going under. That was the tack they were playing. They had shifted responsibility on to international circumstances and a growing Middle East crisis, and were acting as if the country itself was under attack. Anyone who went deeper was accused of being unpatriotic. Alex Byrne and Paud Henry were working together on it. And Derek Bell was still sick and out of circulation. That was a bonus.

Costello met Ralph Martin again two hours after Martin had met the thirty or so international bankers he owed money to. The meeting with the bankers had taken place in a castle in Mayo to avoid the media who were all waiting at a Dublin hotel. The bankers were frantic. Seven hundred and fifty millions worth of frantic. A couple of them had rung Phil Cassidy to say they were pulling out of Ireland if they didn't get their money back. There was a lot of temper talk. The Irish were sharp business practitioners. One Englishman said he'd never met such practices before. Ralph Martin told Costello that same man's bank had backed an English computer exporter who'd spread black propaganda about the quality of MartinCorp all over the Middle East. The English supplier lost the contract—Martin spread blacker propaganda about them—and the British bank shifted support. It was a tough business, Martin said.

It was a small lodge on the edge of an estate in Meath.

The lodge had one of everything in it and was surrounded by trees. Frank Costello had ensured security by taking some Branch lads armed to the teeth with him. He liked travelling with armed escorts. One of the trappings of office. Sometimes he had the Rangers from the Curragh around his house, plenty of choppers and face paint. Practising kidnap rescue, just for the publicity. It looked good. He didn't need some image consultant to tell him how to look good in front of the people, he said. He'd been doing that for twenty years before anyone heard of an image consultant or a sound bite. The party was a personality party. Leader image was a vital part of that. Frank Costello knew how to to play it. The set-pieces, the posters, the songs, the key-note speeches, videos, badges, tapes—the whole bleeding lot.

Now he was just concerned with keeping his position. Damage limitation. Without Derek Bell making more trouble, it would be easier. They had come to an arrangement. Bell wasn't anxious to go to the country. Not with his health the way it was. But he wanted his pound of flesh. Frank Costello felt he could do a deal. And when he came into the small parlour room, he felt confident.

It had a stone floor and an Aga in the corner. It was like a set from a clichéd play. Maybe people did still live like this. He didn't know who lived there. A supporter. One of many who gave up their houses at a moment's notice if asked, without question or recompense. The backbone of the organisation, where Costello had his real support.

"So where do we stand?" Martin said.

"You tell me, Ralph."

Martin tried to figure out what Costello was thinking. He watched for some hint in the Taoiseach's eyes. Costello took his glasses off and rubbed them with his handkerchief.

"Are you dumping me, Frank?"

Costello smiled without taking his eyes off the glasses.

"God, no, Ralph. But we do have a situation here. You see my problems? I have a Government to keep afloat. I've been talking to Derek again. He's had to go to London. Private clinic. Felt it was better that way. He wants assurances, Ralph. If he doesn't get them from you, I have a general election on my hands. At his say so. I don't want that. I'll have an election when I want one. And I'll get my majority. But if we went now, with all that's happening, I can't risk it. I've told him I don't accept his resignation. So that's how it is, Ralph."

"And I'm fucked. I can't pay."

"There might be a way round it. Give you time. To get things together. Maybe a rescue package. So the whole damn thing doesn't go down the drain. I can't come out and give you the cash now, Ralph. The press would eat me. But there's ways."

"What?"

"We can put someone in anyway. Through the courts. All legal. Very quickly. That'll be like giving you our backing. You know, get the company credits. Who knows what you can do then?"

"But I'll be out of the chair."

"You don't have a lot of choice, Ralph. And I won't have my Government fall over this. That's the bottom line. What can you sell off? Stuff that's not in MartinCorp. You could raise funds that way, Ralph. I'm giving you all I can. I've done a lot for you, Ralph."

"You've screwed me, Frank. Hung me out to dry."

"Oh, come on, that's not true. You knew the score. We gave you everything you needed, Ralph. I backed you one hundred per cent. You just got greedy, Ralph."

"And you were screaming, stop!"

"I'm going to cement things with Derek again, Ralph. For the moment. You're going to have to look penitent. Must look penitent, Ralph. Three-quarters of a billion is a lot of readies to owe."

Ralph Martin kept rubbing his bald head. Costello could see some veins pulsating. And the businessman had bags under his eyes. Purplish bags. The strain was telling. He never would have believed that anything could faze Martin. Now, looking at him, tapping his feet on the stone floor, he might have been a civil servant trying to excuse overspending. Costello didn't know if he liked this change in their relationship. The Ralph Martin he had latched on to years earlier wouldn't have got himself into this kind of trouble. He'd overstretched himself. Now he was just another eighties highflyer experiencing total engine failure. There was a sense of disappointment in Costello's tone when talking to Martin. He had expected things of Martin. The country had backed him to the hilt and he had failed to deliver. Costello had a deep antipathy to failure. He was intolerant of it. He felt his trust had been let down, too. It had been a mistake to put so many eggs in one basket. He could almost see the eggs smashed all over the floor.

"I'll have to distance myself from you, Ralph," Costello said. "And I will do what I have to do."

"But you'll need money, Frank. You'll need money in the kind of amounts I can get."

"Can you any more?"

It was not a genuine question. Martin's personal wealth was more than enough to finance an election. Not enough to pay his business debts, but then he kept his personal finances well clear of his business.

"Watch this space," Martin said. "You've had two elections in the last four years, Frank. And they're pricey commodities. Last I heard you lot were a million in debt. Maybe more. I can get you what you want when you need it. I told you. I'll be good for it."

Costello smiled. Maybe Martin wasn't so down after all. He cut a piece of fruit cake on the table beside them and placed it on a plate and handed it to Martin.

"Eat it, it's good. Home-baked. Like the ma used to do. We'll see, Ralph. See what your next donation looks like. But I want it all coming to us. No playing the field. And cash. So we don't have people asking why we get so much from you. A million, at least. To begin with. That'll give me a chance to organise an election I can win. Otherwise I'm playing to other people's timetables. Can't have that. Let's see how this thing runs for a while. I think it's best if we don't meet. You take care of your end and I'll take care of mine. And don't take offence if I say things about you you don't like. Politics is a difficult game at the best of times."

Martin ate his cake and considered what was being offered. There wasn't much else he could do. Britcop was marked ten per cent down on its cost price already. Nothing had happened to the company; it was trading the way it had been trading the day before the insurance news broke but it was already ten per cent down. His advisers were telling him it could fall by twenty or thirty per cent, especially if he wanted to sell it. The news was out that Martin was in trouble. And the bastards were around him like a pack of scavenging dogs. They wouldn't have dared come at him before. He'd have taken them apart. Now they had him down and they would put the boot in mercilessly.

"Right," Martin said. "Anything else?"

"Derek isn't letting go of this blackmail thing, Ralph. I've assured him it had nothing to do with me. I might have to ask Larry to stand down. Larry keeps saying he knows nothing about it. Except he's on tape. I wish he'd kept his fucking mouth shut. But if it comes to it, I'll have to let Larry go. We'll see. Things can be done with tapes. But your man could be in trouble. Derek wants to push it. I told him you knew nothing about it. But he's adamant. Got the bit between his teeth, as they say. Self-righteous bollocks."

"He's not my man any more. Clarke."

"No, so I believe. But all the same..."

"He got carried away. Exceeded his authority. He's ambitious. Maybe there were things said in the heat. Assure Derek Bell I have nothing against him. The matter will be cleared up. Promise him that."

"And your—your ex-employee?"

"Paudie's problem, I'd say."

"Fine. What kind of linkage would he have to you?"

"None."

"Fine. Difficult business. By the way, Derek's heart is worse than he's saying. Much worse. They were going to operate but his doctors say there isn't much point."

"Is there a time-scale?"

"I didn't ask. Didn't like to. But maybe we should find out."

Frank Costello found himself following the directions of his image consultants unconsciously. Hold yourself this way, talk in that tone, sound concerned, address at that pace, give it a smile at that word, use your hands when he says that, allay his fears with a movement. He wondered if Martin knew what was being played against him. He wondered how his party would react to him, how he would hold on this time if things got rough. There were ways. There were always ways.

Ralph Martin drove north and then flew back to Dublin in a helicopter. The autumn mist cloaking the countryside made it seem that large sections of the land and foliage were being stripped away, and a bare rawness would be left for everyone to see. It caused him to shiver. He had shivered at the bankers' meeting but no one knew. He had been shivering for a week now, before Bell went public on the insurance. Sanctions-buster. It was a catch-phrase now. The press made it sound so bloody dramatic. Arseholes, he thought. Jesus, they knew nothing about business and they were going to tell him how to run his. Typical, he thought. And the first sign of real trouble and they scarper like scared rats. They couldn't get off the ship quick enough.

The bastards, he kept muttering to himself. I try to make this country the best and they run away first chance they get. He felt exposed, too. For the first time since he was a teenager and that had been the problem of whether to ask a girl out or not. But this feeling ran deeper. It centred on all that he was. The vulnerability he had felt during the past few weeks was gathering in him, and his defences, what he had used before, were worn out. He felt tired in the helicopter, exposed and tired and he wanted to sleep suddenly, take a couple of hours to himself and lie down.

He came into his head office barking orders and moving fast through the corridors. Several of his staff, the two marketing guys from Carlow in particular, got a bollocking the like of which they hadn't had since they were school kids. He told them they'd better get the fucking lead out of their fucking dicks and a load of other places—the fuckings came thick and fast—and continued to bawl them out without stopping to even face them. It was designed as an example and it had the desired effect.

People turned and ran in all directions. It gave him a feeling of power he had been missing for a while, the sort of invigoration he needed. He had his secretary make sixteen phone calls immediately and tracked down all his senior executives, no matter where they were. This was a time to measure people's mettle, not time to have extra deadweight. Whoever wasn't with him was against him; it was that simple.

The meeting with Phil Cassidy had been shorter than the meeting with Costello. It took place at midnight in a tacky mansion in Monaghan with imitation Doric columns at the porch and eagles perched on the gate posts. Both men drove alone. They did not even take their coats off.

"He'll be gone by Christmas," Cassidy said.

"You sure you can swing it? He's slippery."

"Certain. People are angry at the way he's handled all this Gulf thing, Ralph. You may take some stick in the fight. I might use you. You wouldn't mind. We can feed the papers some stuff, can't we? You could help there, I'll bet. I want it systematic, Ralph. Might need some money. So we can hit him with a *fait accompli*. Can you help?"

"I want assurances, guarantees. If I put up, Phil, you'll back me."

"You have them. We'll have to do something to keep you going. These banks you're going to meet, they'll want some kind of assurances themselves. I'll leave it all with Frank at the moment. Maybe let it be known that I'm not keen on what's going on. Your papers would be good for that."

"If they stay my papers."

Cassidy nodded.

There was an inevitability about what was happening, Martin thought. It had taken on a life of its own, and shocks were coming from so many different directions now he could not keep up with all the problems. It was like watching a pipe beginning to leak. One leak you can deal with, same with two, maybe even three, but after that…It was out of his control now, he realised that, and the realisation shocked him and paralysed him. It was not the money alone—it had never been the money, and anyway, he had enough tied up in trusts—it was more than money: it was power and prestige. He was losing both and once lost they were difficult to get back. The mystique that had surrounded all those years had vanished and he was standing naked and exposed and very vulnerable. He sank his head into his hands and closed his eyes.

Dan Meehan burst into Martin's office before his knocks had reached his boss's ears. It was always the same with Meehan when things weren't going right. Martin had made up his mind he was going to fire him, no matter what happened. He was fine when things were going well and scared when things were bad. He could do without that. Meehan had been working round the clock for several days, living out of a hotel-room near the office. He looked as if he were living out of a hostel for down-and-outs. His tie was loose, his shirt was creased and stained with small spatterings of blood from his uneven shaving. Martin hated his people to come in unshaven; he hated bad shaving even worse. Meehan stood before him in a sort of military pose, with just enough shake in his right leg to let Martin know he was on the edge.

Martin paused for maybe a minute before speaking, allowing himself more time to study his press boss. The skin at his neck was developing folds, beginning to hang off his jaw, too. Meehan had a weak jaw, looking as if it was about to disappear at any moment. His chest was thin and his jacket folded right over itself when he stooped forward at all, making it seem he was wearing a size too big for him.

"Jesus, you look shite, Dan," Martin said.

He knew that would faze Meehan. He knew what Meehan liked to present, the way he wanted to be viewed. He had the pillow talk. And that hatchet of a wife of his, with her suck-up philosophy. Maisy Meehan. Alan Kennedy said it sounded like the name of a cartoon character. Always telling him to put himself forward, come up with an idea. Martin used to love waiting for Meehan to work for a week on an idea, busting his guts, giving hell to his staff, wearing out a dozen pairs of underwear. Then he'd ring down and call him up and say he had a terrific idea and promptly give Meehan back his own plan. It never occurred to Meehan that Martin had a listener on him. He was so in awe of Martin, so scared of him, it never got near his brain.

"I've been spinning all morning, Ralph. We have our papers and that's fine but I've been trying a sweetness and light campaign with the opposition. I'm having a reception tomorrow. To give our side."

"Terrific. Sounds fine. It's just there might be a problem giving our side since I'm not sure I'll be running the business much longer. We're insolvent, technically, you know. How would you put that to the assembled gentlemen and women of the press?"

Meehan tried to figure out where Martin was coming from. He stepped back for a couple of steps.

"I don't understand. I—we—what does that mean, Ralph?"

"What I said. I will try and raise the cash by flogging what can be flogged, I will fail because as soon as I try, people will screw me into the ground, and then someone will be appointed in my place. All very legal. With Frank Costello's approval. He has to. Too many votes involved. If we were anything else, he would let us sink. Lucky there, aren't we?"

"What about the press campaign?"

"What about it?"

"I've been busting my balls, Ralph."

"That's what I pay you for, Dan. Not to chase cocktail waitresses, not to swan around thinking up crass press releases, not to drive a four-litre German car. I pay you to work till you drop. I pay you to do my bidding. If I say shit, you shit, if I say piss you piss. It's the way of the world."

Meehan saw something in Martin's eyes, a sharp hostility that scared him more than anything Martin had ever said or done before. He had an inclination to turn and run. His mind was in overload and he was sure Martin could see it. He was desperately trying to work out what this meant. There was an angle to everything; you just had to determine the spin and work from there. He searched for some hidden meaning out of a possible plethora of meanings, a serious case of the frets overtaking him, pushing him back, leaning on him. And all the time, Ralph Martin sat with his feet up on the desk, staring.

"I should…" Meehan began.

"What, Dan?"

Meehan shook his head.

"I need to get hold of seven hundred—no seven hundred and fifty, yeah, seven hundred and fifty million. Got that on you, son? Because if you haven't then I'm afraid you're no good to me. What do you think?"

"I don't know what you mean, Ralph. Honest, I don't."

Martin kicked two files off his desk onto the floor. Meehan knelt down and tried to pick them up. Martin came round and grabbed Meehan by his jacket and threw him against the wall.

"I said I need seven hundred and fifty million."

Meehan was alternating between smiling and whimpering. His mouth contracted, causing his chin to lose another few millimetres. Martin had him tight against the wall.

"I'm going to lose control of my company. This, all this, all that I built up, and you don't know what I mean."

He cracked Meehan's head off the wall. Meehan's eyes let go a couple of tears.

"Ralph! Please!"

Martin slammed his head against the wall. He caught Meehan's head by the ears and slammed it again, then again, with heavy deliberate movements. Meehan was too scared to do anything. All he could do was say, please.

"I'm fucking sold out by shit, by fucking shit, and you're holding press conferences, you're fucking sucking up to the shit who are doing me, who the fuck are you, man?"

He smashed Meehan's head into the wall again and again. Blood ran down the wall. Meehan stared. The scene slowed down. Then suddenly, someone was pulling Martin off.

"Jesus, Ralph."

Alan Kennedy had his boss in his arms. Dan Meehan sank to the ground, bleeding. Sarah held her hand to her mouth.

And Ralph Martin cursed.

20

The Martin estate was on flat ground north of Dublin, a series of uniform fields laced together by neat fencing, three or four cattle in each field, the odd horse. He had stables at the back of the main house, an ivy-covered Georgian affair with steps leading up to the front door. There was a spy hole in the door and a security guard with a walkie-talkie sat in a car in the driveway opposite the house all day. There were other security guards around the tree-lined perimeter of the estate. The trees afforded just enough protection from nosey passers-by.

Jack Clarke showed his driving licence to the side of beef in uniform whose job it was to check such documents. The man had a scar on his right cheek and the beginnings of a tattoo could be seen at his wrist below his uniform sleeve. He spoke with a southern English accent and he made a kind of salute when he ushered Jack into the estate. The drive up to the house was over gravel and the sound of his wheels on the stones made Jack think of being crushed. He pulled in next to a Merc and a Porsche.

It had all been very polite. The morning after the documentary went out. Just a simple request. Maybe Martin was beaten. Jack didn't like to believe that. He had Martin fixed one way in his mind and that was how he would stay. It was easy in the end. Just sit in a seat and talk. All he gave them was skim. Embargoed technology, weapons, chemicals, smaller under the counter payments, fake shipments, fake documents. What Kelly had been yelling about. But with real clout. Inner circle stuff. The caption under his chin spelt it out. Enough to whet appetites hungry for anything on Martin. They were enemies now. If they were ever friends, it was gone. And Jack could accept that. His decision. He had gone public. Still, enemies. That was a whole new footing. And a polite summons. Something in Jack's gut told him he should be prepared. Martin would come at him with everything. He held his breath before getting out of the car.

The beef in the car next to him did not bother to get out when Jack got out of his. Jack could see him talking on his walkie-talkie. They made eye contact and held it until your man felt he couldn't hold it any longer or that he was obliged to acknowledge his employer's guest. Anyway, he nodded. Jack took it as a good omen. He would have taken anything as a good omen then. He steadied himself once more and walked across the pebbles to the steps and the front door.

He rang the bell and stood to one side of the spy hole. It was about two minutes between the time of his ringing and someone answering. Jack heard his stomach gurgling and swore a couple of times to get himself in the right mood. A maid in a kind of one-piece uniform opened the door. She might have been Scandinavian. She was blonde and good-looking and smiling, which made him feel good. She smiled and made eye contact. Second time, he thought. I'm on top of it.

"Mr Clarke for Mr Martin," Jack said.

She continued to smile and he wondered if she spoke English.

"Would you please wait in here," the girl said. "Mr Martin will be with you presently."

It had to have been practised, Jack thought. No one spoke like that. He followed her directions.

This was the first time Jack Clarke had ever been in this

place. There was a house in town Martin sometimes used for meetings but he only rarely took anyone to his sanctum. There had been talk of dinner. Alan Kennedy had been to dinner here a few times. But dinner talk faded as business took a turn for the worse. So there won't be dinner, I suppose, Jack thought to himself. He'd wanted to take an upper but Kate had kept him away from them. There was no real down, just the fear that a down might be right around the corner. He could do with a drink, he thought.

The room he was led to might have been a dining-room—a dining-room among a few—or it might have been a trophy room. It was jammed with silver, most of it bought, some of it won. And the silver was held in rosewood. Most of the furniture was rosewood. There was a big table in the middle of the floor and a Chinese rug beneath it. At the window there were French period chairs. Jack went to sit in one and felt it might break under him. He remained standing and watched what was going on two fields away.

One of Martin's daughters was putting a horse through its paces over low jumps. The grass was still wet from overnight rain and the sun was sparkling in the dew drops.

"Jackie."

Jack swung round.

Ralph Martin was standing in the doorway. He was wearing an Aran sweater and corduroys. He looked almost timid. The hardness was gone from his face. It was replaced by an expression of distance Jack had never seen in Martin before. It was a strange feeling for Jack, being there in front of his boss. He hadn't really believed he would ever see the man again. Not after what had happened in Crossfin. Not after all he had done. So he paused for a moment to make sure it was all real.

"Ralph."

Martin stood behind a chair and looked Jack over. Everything was immaculate. Even the monogrammed briefcase. Martin walked on a few steps, put out his hand

and smiled. Jack held off, then came forward and shook it.

"You've never been here before," Martin said.

As if he'd been reading Jack's mind.

"No."

Jack expected him to say he'd have to show him the place. He even imagined they'd go off on an hour's tour of the estate and everything would be fine again. Because there was a part of him that wanted things back to where they had been. That part of him that had admired Ralph Martin, that had jumped at the chance to work for him, watched and studied him in the toughest game in the world, watched him win time after time, done anything that was asked of him. He cut himself short there and allowed Kate a say and told himself that was the problem: he had done everything without question. Martin didn't suggest a tour.

"I want this over as quick as possible," he said. "Come with me."

Jack obeyed. More out of habit than anything else. Martin led him down the hall, past landscapes and antiques, into a small, very warm room. It was walled with bookshelves. There was a writing desk at the window, a Victorian piece with plenty of little drawers, covered in papers. A laptop lay on the floor by the writing desk. And two armchairs sat either side of it towards the door.

Martin locked the door behind them.

"Don't want to be disturbed," he said.

He indicated to Jack that he should sit down. Jack sat down in the nearest armchair. It was leather and he sank into it at first until it firmed behind him.

"I won't offer you anything," Martin said. "You understand."

Jack nodded.

"So, you've caused me a lot of trouble, Jackie," Martin said.

"None you didn't ask for, Ralph."

"Spare me the lecture. Doherty hurt your feelings, Jackie?

He's an ignorant thug but I thought you were bigger than spite."

"You know I am. I went there to see for myself. It was a simple issue. Our lads had poisoned their cattle. You know it; I know it, Ralph. We just fucked them, Ralph."

"All that for them. A bunch of crazies with shaved heads. You shaft me on prime-time television for them."

"There was more, Ralph. You wouldn't understand."

Martin was shaking his head.

"We didn't have a choice, Jackie. We'd have been wide open if we'd admitted liability. Anyway, there was no proof. We could have made a donation. Barney Small offered one. But they wanted liability. Then they got these green welly people—your bird for one—and they wanted court. Well, they can take us, despite what you say. We'll break them. They could have taken what Barney offered."

Jack wanted to say something about the Krishnas and injustice and a score of things that were milling around in his head, but they'd have been wasted on Martin.

"What happened to you, Jackie?" Martin asked.

"Let's say, things changed. Lots of things. Me for one."

"What's this? Some kind of road to Damascus? Jesus, Jackie, you just turn on me and casually knife me in the back. You used to be loyal. Is that loyalty?"

"I discovered right and wrong, Ralph. Remember them? And we were wrong. It was a stupid mistake. It shouldn't have happened. And having met that bastard who manages the place, I can understand why. You and Alan feel good about that?"

"About what?"

Jack opened his waistcoat and unbuttoned the bottom of his shirt. The bruising on his lower ribs was moving from purple to yellow and brown. A seasonal change, he thought. He watched Martin for some reaction. There was none.

"I hope you're not implying..."

Jack was rebuttoning himself.

"Don't worry, Ralph, it's our secret. I fell against a wall. But don't tell me that's not how you operate. Because I know."

"Our lawyers will tear their case to pieces. They'll end up having to sell that shack they live in to me. Maybe I'll have it done up and move into it. I hope she was worth it, son."

Jack did not rise to the bait.

"Don't push it, Ralph."

Martin leaned forward in his chair.

"You threatening me, Jackie?"

"What do you want?"

Martin felt he had Jack where he wanted him. He was enjoying the whole scene. Inside, he had a sense of loss he could not quite place. But he watched the younger man cross his legs and join his hands and thought, I've got you, son. I'm going to make you suffer. I'm going to make you understand what it is to screw with Ralph Martin, you bollocks.

"You've been a naughty boy, Jackie. Seems you tried to blackmail a government minister."

"Fuck off. I watched Larry Tallon go through the motions with Derek Bell. I did your bidding. You want me to own up and admit it. I'm a man who blackmails government ministers. Come on, Ralph, I did learn some things from you. There's no evidence. We were a few thousand feet up. One of Larry's flights of fancy. I hear Larry is unwell, too. Funny how illness seems to stalk the government in times of trouble. Blood pressure, is it?"

"You might have checked before you made your play, Jackie. Old Derek Bell wasn't the thick bollocks you took him for. He had a bloody recorder in his top pocket. Did you think about that? Well? I bet you thought you were dealing with a complete dipshit. Well, there were grounds, I grant you, all the posturing, that sanctimonious I-hold-the-conscience-of-the-nation-in-my-top-pocket business. What he didn't say was he was carrying some nifty Japanese technology, too, and you, lad, are on it making improper suggestions to a Government minister."

Jack knew what was happening. He had seen it before with Martin. The lean-on. There might be a tape, there might not be a tape. It didn't matter.

"All right, all right, Ralph, you want something. Get to the point."

"Do I? Paud Henry might. You might like to know you are the subject of an investigation. Maybe some of Paudie's finest will be calling round to interview you. Naturally, I've told them I know nothing about this."

He sat back and smiled. For a moment his harsher nature came back into focus. Jack Clarke got up from his seat and went to the window. Martin's daughter, who had a nice backside, Jack thought, was walking towards Jack, leading a horse. She gave him a small wave and he waved back.

"I'll deny it all."

"You can do that. But there's going to be a hell of a lot of shit flying about. You might just get buried."

"That make you feel good, Ralph?"

"Some. Of course, if you retract everything you've said about MartinCorp, we could get old Paudie to take his dogs off and let you walk. And there'd be a nice earner in it for you. Something to keep you and your greenie tart in condoms for many a winter."

Jack was tracing on the window. The flow was strong but he could swim against it, if he pushed harder. He stood to one side so he could get a good look at himself in the window. He straightened his hair and his tie and thought of Kate and felt good about what he had done.

"Small price for peace, Jackie," Martin said. "What do you say?"

"Is that the best you can come up with? Jesus, you must be in a bad way, Ralph. You think that tuppence worth I gave them on television is all I have. There's a key word here, Ralph. Insurance. You always swore by it. I took your advice. I could tell them about all the other bent stuff I've done for you. The pay-offs, the threats, the leaning. I've done it all for you, Ralph. And I could give them places, dates, times, amounts. There'd be a lot of uncomfortable faces under summer Costa tans sitting in Leinster House for one."

"You'd be squashed."

Jack came back to his armchair, leaned down and picked up his briefcase. He opened it without saying anything. In it was a single large manila envelope.

"Take a gander, Ralph," he said. "My rain-gear."

Martin's mouth dried in a moment. It was visible and Jack Clarke knew he had him. Martin opened the envelope and spilled the contents out on to his lap.

"Derek Bell wasn't the only one employing the best Far Eastern gadgets. You think I didn't pick up a thing or two working for you? I kept records, too, Ralph. And the numbers are accounts and payments. I didn't bring all the transcripts, just the juicy bits. You're in there, Frank Costello, too. I expect you'd love to hear yourself on the "Six-One." Nice big medium close-up and you telling the world who had to be taken care of and what was to be lodged where and who was an easy mark. It's all there. I'll even show you the machine. Nice little thing. I used others, too. More sophisticated, for my own protection. Seems I never really trusted you. Any time I did a job I kept records. Goes back years, Ralph. There's fucking millions in grease money, and I have the names, the amounts, the places, who got what last penny. I'm sure Frank Costello would have a great time explaining that to a packed session of the house. Even that long weasel would find it difficult to slip out of this. If you think my performance the other night was good, wait till you see what I've got lined up for an encore."

Martin read through the documents and Jack followed his eyes, a cornered menace racing though them, move along every line, registering payments, words said, a private history of the game he had played over the years. His mouth shrivelled more. And Jack saw that a small residue of oral scum had caught at the edges of his mouth, forcing it down against its will. And there was more. Jack Clarke stood back. Even when he knew he had his boss at the ropes, even when he knew he had the knockout punch, he could not bring himself to stand within reach of the great man he had once idolised. It was a victory and a defeat in the same moment and it made him numb and gave him nothing but a desire to have finished with the whole thing and leave.

"What do you want?" Martin asked without looking up.

Jack sat down in his chair. He took a deep breath.

"I think you should show me around, Ralph. Better we walk. I want some fresh air. There's a stale odour in this room. Too warm for me. Maybe I smell Paud Henry. It's a fine day out. Good metallic sky. We should walk. Alone, Ralph."

Martin led him through the house to the front door with the spy hole. He took a coat for himself from the coatstand beside the door. It was old material, not what Ralph Martin usually wore, and it hung badly on him. The combination of the old coat and the Aran and the jeans gave him the look of a pensioner who had once been something but had experienced a sudden emasculation. There were faint echoes of the menace but they were fading by the second and all that was left was a thin balding man in clothes that looked incongruous.

"I'll have to sell some of my property," Martin said at the stables.

He walked over to one of the stalls and caressed the nose of one of his horses. The horse returned the affection. Jack Clarke found himself making a note of it for future reference and then telling himself off.

"I did a lot for this place. I put it on the map. And I'm returned with this. Frank Costello thinks he can duck away from me. You're right: slippery bastard, Frank. We were at college together for a year. He was a slippery bastard there, too. UCD. You're a Trinity man, aren't you, Jackie? Good snob value, that. But the balls come from the other place."

He touched his crotch.

"Frank's going to put a nice distance between himself and me. I'm beginning to feel like a leper. Yes, Frank will drop me till it's convenient to rehabilitate me. He'll wipe that mob of his up in one swipe if they try anything. Though I have half a notion Phil Cassidy might just do him. I don't think I'd be too disappointed. But Frank keeps looking too close to himself. He's missing the young Turks. I can name five offhand who'd have him out tomorrow. Anyway, not our concern."

"No."

Martin's daughter came into the stable yard with the horse she had been leading by the bit. She was in her early twenties and if her nose had been smaller she might have been attractive. Jack had had it in his mind to bed her for years, a kind of power-play thing. It was gone now. They said hello and then Martin and Jack walked on.

"I thought you and her—well, you know, fathers think those things, Jackie. I had a liking for you, lad. I'm not just saying that. I'm sorry for what happened. All of it. You understand, it wasn't all my fault. Things happen, you know. Maybe it's better you didn't try anything. I'd have beaten the shit out of you if you'd touched her. But that's fathers again for you. Something Freudian, I expect."

He stopped and looked for a while at the fields and their fencing and he cattle and horses grazing.

"Bet you never thought I knew anything about Freud. I studied philosophy for a couple of years. I still read the stuff. Don't pay any heed to it. But I read it all the same."

"I always figured you weren't the shallow bovver boy you make out," Jack said.

"I shall take that as a compliment. So what is it you want, Jackie?"

"I want you to stop calling me that for a start. You trying to do me down?"

"Old habits."

"Well, kill it, Ralph. Are you going to sell this place? I read in a paper yesterday that you were going to sell it off."

"Don't believe everything you read in the papers or hear on television, Jack. Especially when it's some bleeding-heart, love-sick Romeo spilling the beans on his boss."

"You forced me."

"Bollocks. You did me. I brought you in from some nowhere practice job and you did me."

"I did my job well."

Martin leaned over a fence.

"Yeah, you did, Jack. You were the best bloody executive I had. You had what no one else had, son: you had balls. You even had balls enough to do me. Jesus, can you imagine anyone else doing that? I liked the power. Best feeling in the world."

"Yeah."

They bonded for a brief moment. Something that stopped all talk and held the day. Jack Clarke felt a sharp breeze on his chest. He shivered and hunched his shoulders.

"It's cold. I should have brought a coat," he said. "I want you to admit liability down there. I want you to get Paud Henry off my back. I don't care how it's done. You know what you're doing there. Derek Bell can be made shut up. You and Frankie Costello will find a way to do that. Anyway, Bell's sick, only half what he used to be. I can't say I feel good about that. But that's life. We have to live with ourselves. I hope you can, Ralph. Get whatever he has and give it to me. I want to see it myself. And I want a pay-off. A good pay-off, Ralph, commensurate with my standing in the company. Not a poxy few grand. I want enough."

"There'll be someone in there soon."

"You can get it done. You have the wherewithal, Ralph. I know, Ralph. I know everything. Maybe you should have me killed. It wouldn't help. I've left word with a solicitor that if I should run over the edge of cliff or fall under a bus then everything I've shown you gets through to whoever will do the most damage. Remember that. I gave them a teaser before, Ralph. I'll crucify you if I have to. I won't care what happens to me. If I go down, you come with me."

"I admire your style, Jack."

"And I want you to give those people enough to make up for the grief they've suffered. That's going to involve spreading the word down there that they're not to be touched again. A scratch on any of them and I'll come shouting from the rooftops."

"So where are you going, Jack?"

"Away."

"Seduced, right?"

Jack was walking back towards the house. Martin stood and spoke the words again, hoping at least to halt his progress. Jack Clarke did not look back. He was determined to get to his car, and then get out of there. A jet swung in low getting ready for a landing. Jack swung his head up to look and thought he saw someone watching him from one of the widows. A creeping paranoia had overtaken him. His body was shaking now. It could have been the cold. The jet drowned out everything around him and he could feel Ralph Martin behind him, walking fast, maybe muttering to himself. And Jack felt sad. He tried to tell himself there was no reason to feel sad but he felt sad. There was an end here and ends were always sad. It brought him back to his father's graveside. The water running down the side of the coffin into the muddied ground, the priest saying words which echoed the sound of the water, the empty silence in his own head.

He was strapped into his car when Martin caught up with him. He pressed the button at his side and his window came down. Martin smiled and put his hand into the car.

"I was going to give you a hiding, Jack," he said. "I was

going to take you down to those trees and give you the biggest hiding of your life. I could have. I have help. You've met them. I had it planned. I was going to make you regret what you were doing."

Jack shook his hand. The guard who had been sitting in the car when he came in was strolling across from behind the house with two more guards and two Dobermans, both off their leashes. Jack followed the men and their dogs for a while, not listening to Martin speak.

Then he turned his engine on.

"You know where to send the money," he said. "I want it by the end of the month. And if I so much as smell one of your hounds on my tail or if I hear something on my phone I shouldn't hear, then..."

He drew his hand across his neck.

"I'll miss you, Jackie," Martin said.

Jack had already pulled away and did not hear.

21

The cottage was about twenty yards from the sea. And the waves broke heavy on the cliffs to the left of it. The sea was milky green from the cloud blanket and where it touched the sky, the cloud blanket was torn into strips.

They had been talking about it for days. Kate had some time, just some, she could take off. But she had a full report to do. Everyone at dinner in Hennigans the night before said they should go to the Bahamas. Jenny had her new man and he had approval. People always gave approval to new men. It was the done thing; you never said you didn't like a partner. But you could talk about them behind their backs. Behind Jenny's back her new man was equally acceptable. She didn't mention his previous status to her mother. And no one else did either. There was an understanding about dirty linen and its washing. There were a lot of understandings, things unsaid, the telepathy of people who are friends not just because they like each other and get on together but because they have a deeper understanding, an attachment based on mutual experience, shared pasts. It went above friendship. Jack played jazz with Carl in the front room of Hennigan's house in Harold's Cross. The women sat and talked to Jenny's new man in the kitchen.

It had been raining when they crossed the bridge at Achill Sound. And Kate had looked at him with that what the fuck are we doing here when we could have hopped on a plane to the Equator? look. Jenny and her new man were going to the West Indies. Good reason to go to Achill, Kate said. She had agreed to go because Jack wanted to go. Jack could not explain why he wanted to go. Press pressure had something to do with it. Though he could handle that. But there was more. West in winter. It had something. There would be no one else there. That was a good reason. The edge of the world. He said it again when they reached the whitewashed cottage.

The sky was clouded over, except at the edges, and the shredded cloud at the edges gave the edge of the world a magical look. The sun was a weepy yellow-orange eye in the process of closing.

"Fabulous," Jack said.

He pointed to the mountain behind them, a long cake-like two thousand footer with a sprinkling of frost on it. The colours on the mountain fading in the vanishing evening.

Jack handed the map to her. He walked along a muddy path to the small cottage and looked in the window. It was basic inside. There was a picture of JFK on the far wall and Jack laughed. He called Kate over to have a look.

Alan Kennedy had been there when Jack had gone in to clear his office at MartinCorp. They said nothing to one another. Jack gave both Sarah and his matchstick secretary a rose and a kiss and left a package for Molly. He shredded most of his personal stuff. Anything he wanted to keep a hold of was already taken. He wiped everything from his computer and left a general message, timed to come up mid-morning, concerning Alan Kennedy's masculinity. It was a subtle form of revenge. Kennedy didn't look so hard any more. The stranger in Ralph Martin's office was asking difficult questions and Kennedy was having trouble answering them. Jack had been tempted to knock him about. He was sure he could have taken him. Kennedy was twenty-odd years older. That was a problem. Jack wouldn't have felt good knocking a middle-aged man around. So he left the animosity with the wiped computer files and the shredded documents and shook a few hands, not many, and walked out the front door with a sense of relief. When he walked through the corridors of MartinCorp for the last time, he didn't bother being friendly. There was no need. The two Carlow blokes from Marketing came up to him with their hands extended and Jack decided they weren't people he wanted to shake hands with. He passed them by.

"Mr Clarke?"

A short, almost boyish, woman with glasses and a little boy hanging on to her leg stood at the car. The boy had blond hair and mischief on his face. One of his shoelaces was undone and there was chocolate at his nose and mouth.

"I thought you were coming this morning," the woman said.

"We got delayed."

Kate tried not to laugh. They had been making love all night. They didn't get to sleep until six. They fell asleep in each other's arms. She could still feel the ripples of pleasure in her body. Jack kept saying he could feel nothing any more, that he was experiencing out-of-body-ness. It had been a good drive down.

What was she doing here? She had thought about it. About what it meant to go with him. A couple of weeks, she said. Then back to Brussels. Jack wasn't going anywhere. He had no plans. He just wanted to be away. They had visited his mother but nothing much was said. A few hugs and kisses. Hints at more. Maybe that was all there should be. Things were up in the air. A cousin of hers was taking his wife and kids to the States to start a new life. They looked happy. Fresh starts made people look happy, Kate thought. You needed fresh starts. Then she cut herself off and said something about her career.

"How long are you staying?" the woman asked.

She asked a lot of other questions too. In a friendly way. The way small island people ask about strangers. Jack told her enough to keep her satisfied for a while but not enough to hold her off for good.

"I don't know," he answered to her question about how long they were going to stay. "I just don't know."

The money he had demanded had been lodged. There was enough there to keep him going for years, maybe all his life if he lived down a scale. Kate had recommended the Mediterranean. Told him to buy a bar and wear shorts. But Jack wasn't sure if he could manage that. He still slipped the odd pill when he could. He was trying to get himself off them but the craving at times was too much. Kate didn't know. There was no need. And he felt he could beat it himself. His doctor told him to go and get treatment. But Jack being Jack said he would do it himself. He had things to do.

Angie Hennigan had pulled him aside after her dinner-party for Jenny and her new man, when everyone else was busy or maybe there was just a gap, Jack wasn't sure. But she had pulled him aside and told him she was really happy he and Kate were back together. It was an awkward conversation. Jack felt he was blushing. But her sentiments were real and despite the clumsiness of his acceptance, he felt good that she had said them and that Kate was back with him. Angie had kissed him on the cheek too.

The main thing with the cottage was getting it to any kind of warmth. Jack kept saying he'd lived in places with holes in the roofs when he was a student and that he could easily take the kind of cold of Achill in winter. Kate wasn't so sure. They filled the electricity and heating meters with fifty-pence pieces and then grabbed a bucket of turf from the haybarn behind the cottage. The turf was dry and the fire was a good fire after a couple of hours. Turf takes time to build up heat. There was a shop down the road and they bought food there and went through the same interrogation they had undergone with the landlady, only more circumspect and from several different people. Jack was convinced they were working together. He grew a beard.

The dogs were bringing the sheep in from the hillsides, staring them down, racing around their flocks. The farmers smoked on their tractors behind. Jack and Kate stopped to watch. The weather had turned again and the rain was spitting in from the Atlantic. A couple of plastic bags had lodged in a wire fence near their cottage and Kate pulled them out and said she hated that, endless fences decked out with plastic and paper. The wind had other ideas. It was picking up from the south-west and blew one of the bags from Kate's hand. It had crossed a field before she could get after it. Jack laughed.

The landlady was watching them through her lace curtains. She did not stop when they looked over. Her husband stood at the door of his home, reading the *Star*. One of his dogs lay at his feet, just inside the porch, out of the rain. He was a stoic man. He spoke in monosyllabic words, full of profundity, but spare and without frills. He had a lifetime of angles etched into his face. He was on the dole and farming and running a pub and doing anything else he could do. All legal if he worked half the week and his brother in England owned everything. His brother in England owned the cottage Jack and Kate had. Jack was going to argue the morality of it all but he felt there'd be no point. Down this way luxuries, like honesty where money was concerned, were a foreign language. You got what you got any way you could. The land was shit and the tourists came for three months if you were lucky and fishing was out half the year and damn dangerous the rest of the year. Maybe that was why he had come. The clarity was attractive. And it was quiet.

It was dead quiet when they ate. Nothing special. Rice and fish in a sauce that tasted of cheese and something Spanish. Kate cooked and Jack tried to guess what was in the sauce. They polished off a couple of bottles of wine too. Then they went to their landlord's pub.

The brother in England had come back for a while with some cash and some ideas and a notion that he was buggered if he was going to be pushed out. Two years later, he had gone back, with less cash and a fear of ever coming back. No one else came into the pub when Jack and Kate were there. There was wrestling on a satellite channel. The landlord told Jack that there was a Swedish porn channel available if he ever wanted to come down without the girl-friend. Jack laughed. He didn't tell Kate. She'd need a year's defeminisation just to keep her voice down if she knew.

Everyone between twenty and forty was gone from the island. The kids and the middle-aged played and talked, according to which group they belonged. It made living in the little cottage easier. You didn't have to speak to anyone all day if you didn't want to.

Kate went back to Brussels for a couple of weeks and then came back on six months' leave of absence. She did not explain and no explanation was sought. They had learned not to ask any more.

There was a very cold patch in late February, when temperatures dropped all the way to Antarctica and they had to make love in their clothes. It called for a lot of improvisation and imagination. The days were spectacular and Kate said it was warmer outside than in the cottage. They spent as much time as they could outside, walking and talking. It was a gentle time. A kind of getting-to-know-you period, where they could smooth out the rough edges that had developed since they'd last been together. Where they could remember the bad habits and the idiosyncrasies.

Two hundred miles away Frank Costello fought off another attempt on his leadership. From Phil Cassidy this time. MartinCorp was not mentioned as a reason. They managed to keep the business going through the winter and the creditors got paid. Ralph Martin vanished from the headlines after January; various wars took his place. Jack phoned now and then to find out what was happening.

There was talk of an inquiry, but nothing certain. Lawyers were throwing writs around. Derek Bell was back in cabinet, all smiles with Frank Costello. Dublin was awash with rumours. But Ralph Martin's papers kept things just uncertain enough to avoid having the rumours turn into facts.

"I don't know if I love you, Jack," Kate said one day.

They were sitting on the rocks at the beach. The wind was howling and their eyes were streaming water. Kate's hair had blown round in front of her face. The tide was out and the sea-birds were foraging in the wet sands at the shore. There were dog prints leading up the beach to the cliffs, a crazy trail of prints from the same animal. All around the rocks pieces of flotsam and jetsam lay covered in sand. Bits of wood and pieces of life belts and rope and the odd shoe. A body had been found a couple of weeks earlier by a man out walking his dog. They said he was probably a smuggler, that smugglers were often washed up on the beach after rough weather.

"What makes you say that? We're living together, aren't we?" Jack said.

He had to shield his eyes to look at her. Some sand blew across them and stung their faces. Jack scraped a piece from Kate's cheek.

"I don't know. I want to be here, with you, but I just don't know if I love you."

"Maybe it's a different love. Maybe you're looking at before. When it was all fireworks. That was years ago. You should look at now. We get on fine, don't we?"

"Have you really changed?"

"I don't know."

He began to arrange some small stones in the sand. Pile them one on top of the other. He genuinely did not know. Everything that had gone on before was only catching up with him and now was something of a void. He knew he needed her there with him, but he did not know how much longer he would need her there. He could not predict what he would do from hour to hour. Sometimes he went off for long walks on his own. To a graveyard or a deserted village or another beach.

"I miss him," he said.

"Who? Your dad?"

"Yeah, I suppose I miss him too. But I was talking about Ralph. Ralph Martin. I miss the old bastard. I miss everything to do with him. I don't want to go back but I miss it. Does that make sense?"

She was not as shocked as she should have been. And she was more understanding.

"Some. I've seen it in you, Jack. You think I don't notice these things. I know you, Jack."

"Do you?"

"I like to think so."

"You know someone you lived with five years ago. Don't you sometimes feel you're reaching into a darkened cupboard for an old coat? Something that makes you feel comfortable. It gets like that."

"Jenny told me about you two."

Jack raised is eyebrows and bowed his head.

"Hurt?"

"No. See, that doesn't hurt me."

"Sure?"

"No."

"I think you feel there's a way you have to be, Kate. Things you are required to do. A formula."

"Whereas you follow your guts, Jack. Or balls."

"Ouch."

"Sorry."

"Is this part of the formula? Ralph Martin—there I go again—Ralph used to turn things upside down. Always keep them guessing, he said. Keep them thinking. It's not what you do that's crucial; it's what people think you're going to do. Once you can control that, you're in business. I need the buzz."

"And I don't. I need the feeling of constructive connection. I need the threads of right. All the time. I can't exist beside your chaos, Jack. Sailing that close. There is an order. You don't seem to realise that. It's part of your charm. You don't care what people think of you. But it's dangerous. You did the right thing this time, Jack, but have you always? Where's your line? I don't think you have one. Nothing consistent."

"Probably not. What did Jenny say?"

"You were good."

"Oh!"

"She's right. You are."

"I want you to be jealous."

"I can't allow myself to be."

"I know."

He took her by the hand and they walked arm in arm along the beach.

Where do you go from here? he kept asking himself. He had all he wanted. He had her and he had money, maybe not as much as he'd wanted but then he'd wanted a hell of a lot before. And what did she have and want? She had her head on his shoulder and her hair was blowing into his face. They couldn't stay here, he thought. No matter how raw and beautiful it was. They had talked about opening a pub or a restaurant but it was impossible. They both knew it was impossible and neither of them was saying. And when they made love they made love with more urgency than before. They had to get as much of one another as possible before the whole damn thing fell apart.

It took a few weeks for Jack to realise it was down to him. That he had started it and he must finish it. There was no point in telling himself he was doing it for her or even for him because he did not know for whom he was doing it, only that it had to be done. He went off one morning to a deserted village and sat on the stones of one of the ruins and tried to imagine the place when there were people there, when it was a village and the streets were full. But it wasn't there any more. The ruins were there and the outlines and all you had to do was use your imagination and you could almost reach it, but not quite. He sat and watched the mountain and the mountain changed colour several times. Kate was on the beach. It had been coming. Neither of them had said anything. She had even helped him pack his cases. But they had talked like they were staying there for ever, still making plans they knew would never be fulfilled. The night before they had had a pizza meal, nothing special, except maybe they drank more plonk than before and made love by the fire, a terrible, frightened frenzy of physical desire. The smell of the turf fire gave it an almost drug-like intoxication. It was probably just the wine and both of them knew that but they wanted to believe it was more. When they had loved all they were going to love, each of them retreated enough to allow what had to happen happen.

Jack said goodbye to the landlady and her monosyllabic husband and had the obligatory cup of tea with them. He had expected them to ask him what was happening but they did not. Maybe they were in on it all. They talked about everything but Kate and Jack embraced the couple before he got into his car and drove off.

Before he left sight of the beach, he stopped on a small rise in the road, near a pub. He watched for a while. The sea was angry and he thought he could see a figure right up at the water, just standing, staring out to sea. It might have been her.

He was in New York when he read that Ralph Martin had been arrested in Los Angeles on drug trafficking charges.